Maggie Mason is a pseudonym of author Mary Wood. Mary began her career by self-publishing on Kindle, where many of her sagas reached number one in genre. She was spotted by Pan Macmillan and to date has written many books for them under her own name, with more to come.

Mary continues to be proud to write for Pan Macmillan, but is now equally proud and thrilled to take up a second career with Sphere under the name of Maggie Mason.

Born the thirteenth child of fifteen children, Mary describes her childhood as poor, but rich in love. She was educated at St Peter's RC School in Hinckley and at Hinckley College for Further Education, where she was taught shorthand and typing.

Mary retired from working for the National Probation Service in 2009, when she took up full-time writing, something she'd always dreamed of doing. She follows in the footsteps of her great-grandmother, Dora Langlois, who was an acclaimed author, playwright and actress in the late nineteenth–early twentieth century.

It was her work with the Probation Service that gives Mary's writing its grittiness, her need to tell it how it is, which takes her readers on an emotional journey to the heart of issues.

MAGGIE MASON

The Halfpenny Girls *at* War

SPHERE

SPHERE

First published in Great Britain in 2022 by Sphere

3 5 7 9 10 8 6 4 2

A CIP catalogue record for this book is available from the British Library.

ISBN 978-0-7515-8076-1

Typeset in Bembo by Hewer Text UK Ltd, Edinburgh
Printed and bound in Great Britain by Clays Ltd, Elcograf S.p.A.

Papers used by Sphere are from well-managed forests
and other responsible sources.

MIX
Paper from
responsible sources
FSC® C104740

Sphere
An imprint of
Little, Brown Book Group
Carmelite House
50 Victoria Embankment
London
EC4Y 0DZ

An Hachette UK Company
www.hachette.co.uk

www.littlebrown.co.uk

To my nieces and nephews from my Olley and Wood families, too many to name. All of whom I love and give me love in abundance.

ONE

Marg
October 1939

Marg sat with Edith and Alice on the doorstep of her home in Whittaker Avenue, Blackpool, the street where they'd all been born within a week of each other.

Sitting like this was something they'd always done – huddled close, drinking mugs of hot cocoa, giggling over nothing and finding comfort if they needed it, whilst around them neighbours called out to one another, chastised kids or had a blazing family row. Normal life for this street.

But now, since the declaration of war, nothing was normal. Blackout curtains stopped any light from splashing onto the pavement, and closed doors blocked out the snippets of the neighbours' lives.

There was a feeling, too, of having the rug pulled from under you; that you were no longer safe and could be torn apart from loved ones at any time.

Already, Philip, Edith's husband, a language teacher at the posh Rossall School, had been conscripted into a position

1

in the War Office and Edith didn't know from one week to the next if he would be home with her for a day, or even a few hours. And Harry, Alice's brother, had received his call-up papers – though suddenly going down with appendicitis had delayed his departure.

But despite these upsetting events and changes, daily life had gone on.

'You know, I reckon this street'll always stay the same. Nothing will change the routine of those who live here, even if the menfolk go to war. The women will carry on busybodying into each other's business and shaking their heads in disgust if anyone's doorstep hasn't been scrubbed by ten in the morning, borrowing a bowl of sugar from each other, and being ready to drag anyone's name through the mud to fuel their gossiping.'

'Aye, you're right there, Marg, and yet, they stand firmly by each other's side if the chips are down, as they have by us at times.'

'They have, Alice.' Marg sighed. 'I just feel uneasy about everything.'

No one spoke for a moment. Marg let her mind dwell on what war would be like and what it would mean for them all and for their loved ones.

Edith nudged her. 'Hey, no quiet moments, we said, remember?'

This jolted Marg out of the sadness that had threatened to engulf her at the thought of it all. She giggled and hitched closer to Edith. 'Sorry, lass.'

'I know it's difficult not to mull over things, but think of something good like it only being two weeks to your wedding day, Marg.'

'Ooh, don't remind me, I've a lot to do yet, but the worst thing is having to face meeting Clive's parents for the first time tomorrow.'

'Well, about time, I say. Eeh, you've been seeing Clive for two years now and you ain't yet seen his house or met his parents!'

'Aye, I know, Alice, but with us being just friends till recently, there never seemed the need. Besides, with Clive being a widower, he had the feelings of his kids and his mum and dad to consider.'

'For all that, it took a long time for the pair of you to wake up to what we all knew, lass. But it happened in the end and Clive's a lovely man and his kids are adorable. I just know you'll be happy, Marg, and I'm that glad.'

'Ta, Alice. I know I will, but . . . well, everything's going to be so different.'

'No talk of war . . . or of you moving across to the posh end of Blackpool once you're wed. Only meeting your new ma-in-law and your wedding day is allowed!'

'Not talking about it won't make it go away, Edith, love, you know that more than most. Every time I've seen you, you've been bright and cheerful when you don't have to be, not with us. How have you really been since Philip had to leave?'

Edith let out a huge sigh. 'Lonely, tear-filled, but I have the kids to help me through and they need me to help them to cope an' all. Poor things are missing Philip, on top of missing their own families.'

'By, Edith, you were brave to take on three evacuees, lass. Mind, Mandy, Alf and Ben stole my heart when they landed

3

on the station that day, when we were helping your ma-in-law and the WRVS. And now, it feels like we've always had them around. But it can't be easy for you, nor them. Just say if you need anything as you know we're here for you.'

'I will, Alice, lass, ta. But it ain't all doom and gloom for me, I do have some hope of good news ... Remember that I told you three weeks back that I was late with me monthlies?' Edith gave a little giggle. 'Well, I still ain't started ... Eeh, what I want most in all the world is to have Philip's babby ... Oh, Alice, I'm sorry, lass. Here's me going on about wanting a babby. I – I didn't think ...'

'No, Edith, love, don't feel sorry, I'm pleased for you. I've come to terms with how things are for me – not with losing me babby, I'll never come to terms with that, but well ... Anyway, you mustn't think you can't talk about your dreams in front of me.'

Feeling now that Edith had been right and that she shouldn't have started this conversation, Marg felt at a loss as to how to comfort Edith as she coped with three little evacuees and the possibility of being pregnant without Philip by her side. And Alice having lost her newborn son earlier in the year and then finding out that she couldn't have any more children. Poor Alice had been devastated, but she'd thrown herself into her work with the Red Cross and was taking each day as it came.

Edith put her arm around Alice. 'I wish we could change everything and go back a few months, love. All our dreams seem to be crumbling.'

'I know. Every morning I sift through the post to see if there's a call-up paper for Gerald, even though he tries to assure me that he won't be called to duty for a while. He reckons that he won't be needed unless the fighting begins in earnest and the army medics can't cope, then it's likely they will call up those doctors who have volunteered.'

'Let's hope that's a long way off or, better still, never happens.' Marg sighed. She knew what it was like to worry about being parted from your man and all the wondering about how it would feel not knowing if he was safe or not. Clive had told her that he was considering asking his dad to come out of retirement for a few days a week and leaving him and his manager to take care of the rock factory that Clive owned, so that he could take up the position offered to him of full-time coxswain on the lifeboat. This could mean him being in danger at times. 'Eeh, me lasses, I'm sorry I started this now. It's just with us living next door to each other, Edith, I felt guilty not knowing how you really are.'

'It's all right, Marg, I should have been more open with you and come to you.' Edith reached out her other arm to Marg and snuggled her into a hug, giving Marg the thought that this was her safe place. As long as she had Alice and Edith she'd cope.

'Right, me lasses, that's it. I refuse to let this evening be full of war talk. We've Marg's wedding to look forward to and it's only a week since we were all jolly and having our September Christmas Day!'

This made Marg smile as Edith sounded like the schoolteacher she was. 'Eeh, hark at you. We'd better do as she says, Alice, or we'll get to stand in the corner!'

This started them giggling, and Marg felt better for it.

'Ha, a September Christmas! Were we mad?'

'I think we were, Alice, but it were a grand day, weren't it?'

'Aye, it was, Marg . . . Anyroad, no matter what's happening when the real one comes around – I mean, if things ain't good – then we'll always have a wonderful 1939 Christmas to remember.'

'Aye, we will. Me gran hasn't stopped talking about it – when she has a good moment, that is. Though, some of the time she's mixed it up with Christmases in the past.'

'Has she mentioned living with you and Clive again, Marg?'

'Aye, she keeps saying, "Me John said it would be a good thing for me to do, and so I'm doing it, but I ain't going without me chair!"'

'Aw, it was a lovely moment when Clive's lad, Carl, asked her. Both of his lads seem to really love Gran.'

'Carl does, Alice, but George is a little wary still. Mind, he's only little and it's difficult enough for grown-ups to understand Gran's ways with her dementia, bless her, let alone kids.'

Alice looked wistful. 'You know, whenever I hear George spoken of I think of me dad. It was lovely of Clive to name him after him.'

'And deserved, Alice, as Clive wouldn't be here but for your dad's saving him.'

They were quiet for a moment. Marg sensed that each was thinking of how things used to be for them.

The sound of a telephone ringing cut into her thoughts and brought Edith to her feet. 'That'll be Philip! Excuse me, lasses, I'll be back in a bit.'

As Edith disappeared into her house, Marg looked at her watch. 'Nine o'clock! No wonder Edith was on edge. Philip usually rings in time to say goodnight to the kids.'

'Eeh, Marg, I hope he's all right. Poor Edith, it must be unbearable to be without him so soon after their wedding day.'

'I know, it's me fear of raking them feelings up for her that stops me wanting to talk about me own wedding – well, and me nerves about meeting Clive's family tomorrow.'

'It'll be fine, lass. Like you say, Clive's parents lost a daughter-in-law that they were very close to. Maybe they just weren't ready to have those feelings for another yet. Though you have to take heart in how Clive's mum made that shawl for Carl and George to give to your gran as a present on our Christmas Day. Gerald said it was like she was offering a little something to say she was ready.'

'Aye, it was a nice gesture, wasn't it? Gran hasn't taken it off since. She even wants it over her when she's in bed.'

'That's good. Your biggest worry was concerning Gran. But now with her being happy to go to live with you in Clive's home you won't have to live apart from him just to keep her in her own home. I'm so pleased it all turned out in the end, love.'

Marg felt Alice's hand clutch hold of hers and they both hitched their bums into the gap Edith had left to be closer to one another. 'But, Marg, love, don't take on all of our troubles as yours. You've been through so much, you need to concentrate on your own happiness for a while . . . Eeh, I can hear someone coming. I bet it's Jackie, she'll soon sort you out.'

Marg looked up. In the little light the moon gave, she saw her younger sister coming towards them.

The joy of her life, Jackie made her proud every day. A clever girl, she'd recently taken a job in the accounts office of the biscuit factory. Marg had worked there for seven years now, packing an endless number of biscuits as they came off the line. She couldn't wait to leave when she wed as it just hadn't been the same since Alice and Edith had left to get married. Though she wondered if Edith had truly escaped as Philip's parents owned the factory and one day Philip would inherit it.

As if she'd conjured her up, Edith popped her head back out of her door. 'By, I'm sorry, lasses, but the phone woke Mandy and she's a bit upset, so I'll not be out again.'

'Aw, I'm making cocoa in a mo, shall I bring you some and for Mandy an' all? She loves me cocoa.'

'We all do, Marg. Aye, that'd be grand, ta.'

'I'll have to go an' all, Marg, sorry, love, but with Jackie coming home that means Harry and the lads are on their own as Gerald's on night duty at the hospital. I don't like to put too much on Billy. He's really good looking after Harry, but with him starting work at Clive's factory on Monday, he's feeling a bit anxious.'

'I ain't surprised, poor lad. He loved his job with Blackpool Football Club. Such a shame they had to close, and now, with the prospect of Harry going away to war when he's better, him and Joey must feel their world's been turned upside down. You tell Billy not to worry, Clive'll look out for him at work.'

'Ta, love. It's all change for everyone at the mo. But, you know, though I didn't want Harry to be as ill as he has been, I can't help feeling glad that it stopped him taking his call-up for a while . . . Eeh, it don't seem right, lads of eighteen having to go.'

'Jackie's dreading him going. It were lovely to hear them saying they wanted to get engaged before he went but I don't know how she'll cope when he's gone.'

'She will. As we all will. But we must make something of their engagement as soon as Harry's well.'

Marg didn't have time to answer this as Jackie had reached them and Alice stood up, opened her arms out to Jackie and hugged her. 'How's me brother been behaving tonight, lass?'

'He's so much better but . . . Oh, Alice, he's talking of contacting the army if he keeps improving.'

'I know, lass. Be strong, eh? Don't forget, you're a Halfpenny Girl now, and we'll all look out for one another.'

Marg felt tears prickling her eyes. She wanted to rail against all that was happening in the world, but she put a brave smile on and joined in the hug.

They were the Halfpenny Girls – a name given to them long ago by Edith's dad, as he told them they hadn't got much, but they had the best thing ever: a loving friendship that would sustain them through life. It always had and she knew it would through anything that horrid Hitler thought to throw at them.

TWO

Edith

Wanting to be out of the house the next morning, trying to make light of how low she felt, and hoping the fresh air would calm her, Edith jollied the children along to get them ready for school, ignoring their petty little disagreements.

Mandy was the main culprit. Crotchety from lack of sleep as the poor little mite had cried for a long time, she was picking on her long-suffering twin brother, Alf. Ben, who was the same age as the twins and from the same street in the East End of London, was quiet – unusually so. But then, he wasn't feeling himself, though he said his sore throat felt better since she'd helped him to gargle with salt water – the cure-all for throat infections.

Even a few words on the phone with Philip last night hadn't lifted Mandy's mood, nor had reassuring her that she and Alf hadn't heard from their granny as the letters they had sent, and Ben had sent to his ma, giving their address and telephone number, wouldn't have arrived yet.

10

Edith hadn't broached the subject of writing to the twins' ma as even mentioning her could make things worse where Mandy was concerned.

Mandy rarely talked about her ma and if she did, it was with a kind of hatred. This was sad for Alf who obviously missed her, but Edith understood how Mandy felt after she'd told her that her ma worked the streets. She knew what it was like to have a less than perfect ma, who embarrassed you. But still, the hatred was hard to understand as she'd always loved and cared for her own ma despite her drunken ways, and she missed her every day.

As they walked to school nothing improved as Alf tried to pacify Mandy. 'Don't be sad, Mandy, our gran will come to visit, I know she will. And she might bring Mum with 'er.'

'Shurrup, you. I don't want our mum to come, she'd make a laffing stock of us.'

'She wouldn't!'

Alf cowered. Edith felt his little clammy hand come into hers and felt compelled to stand up for him. 'Mandy, don't go for your brother like that.' But then sighed as Mandy stormed ahead.

Just as peace reigned, they turned onto Newton Drive, leaving them only a few hundred yards to walk to St Kentigern's Roman Catholic school.

Edith loved her teaching job there and could feel the anticipation of another day, only to have this feeling shattered by a child's voice.

'If it ain't Cockney Mandy, teacher's pet!'

The lad stood across the road from them, mocking with his gestures. The gang with him laughed out loud.

Before Edith could react, Alf took his hand from her grasp and dashed into the road towards them.

The world as she knew it stopped at that moment and went into a loud screeching of brakes, screams from Mandy and a car horn seeming to be stuck in blasting mode leaving Edith crowded by the horror of it all and unable to react.

The gasp she took to end this second of disorientation hurt her throat and stopped the air in her lungs from releasing.

Alf lay on the floor, unmoving.

It was seeing Mandy screaming as she ran towards her brother that moved Edith from the daze that had taken her and compelled her towards what she didn't want to face.

Into her anguish came the angry words of the driver. 'What do you think you are doing? Can't you control your children? You should never be allowed to be a mother!'

Tears stung Edith's eyes. She made no retort but flung herself on the ground next to Alf. 'Alf, Alf, oh, Alf, love, are you hurt? Speak to me, Alf!'

Alf didn't respond.

'I'm going to that telephone box over there to ring for an ambulance. For goodness' sake, stop your other brat from screaming the place down!'

Edith wanted to hit out at him, but took off her coat and covered Alf with it, before cradling his head on her knee. Her other arm she extended towards Mandy. Mandy flung herself at her, but Ben stood as if turned to stone on the same spot he'd been when it happened.

'Ben, come here, love. It's all right.' But he didn't move, just stared at her. Feeling at a loss as to what to do for him, she held Mandy close, trying to soothe her while her own heart was almost frozen with fear for Alf. Unconscious and with his little body twisted out of shape, she prayed he wouldn't die.

Suddenly, she was surrounded by her fellow teachers and the headmaster, Mr Raven, who took charge, urging the teachers to get the gaping children into school. 'See that they all get a hot, sweet drink. They're all in shock ... Oh dear, Edith, how did this happen?'

The sob that had caught in Edith's throat came out as she tried to tell him.

'Now, now, hold yourself together. I heard the driver say he was going to call an ambulance; I am sure it won't be long. Alf will be all right. Children are very resilient, but what on earth made him run into the road?'

Mandy answered, her voice distraught, her face wet with tears that ran like a river and joined the snot running freely from her nose. 'It were that Ivan Baker, he called me a name and Alfie went to punch 'im one, but he didn't see the car ... he ... it knocked 'im over ... He won't die, will he? Please don't let 'im die!'

'Now, now, Mandy, calm yourself, my dear. I know this is very frightening, but we won't help matters by getting into a state.'

The sound of clanging bells in the distance brought some relief to Edith.

'I don't think he could be badly hurt.'

Edith looked up to see the driver, looking pale and shaking. His voice had a kind, gentler note to how he'd spoken to her before.

'I saw him start to dash out and braked; by the time I hit him I was almost stopped.' He looked appealingly at the headmaster. 'I only nudged him, but I think he hit his head when he fell.'

'Well, that's serious enough, but no one is blaming you. There were several witnesses that have already told me as I came out that the lad just suddenly dashed out. None told me what you have, Mandy, and I will look into that, I promise.' He shook his head. 'Mind, children will be children and though we all love them, they do have a side to them that is nasty and horrible. You yourself have had a few tantrums, Mandy.'

Mandy didn't answer. Her little body trembled in Edith's arms. Edith wanted to protest, but the clanging of the bells of the ambulance took her words.

By the time they reached Blackpool Victoria Hospital, Alf was awake and, though confused, didn't seem to be in any real pain other than saying his head hurt. His movements didn't tell of anything broken.

Relief at this flooded Edith as she was told to wait in the corridor. She'd only just sat on the bench with Mandy and Ben each side of her when a familiar voice called out, 'Edith, what are you doing here?'

Gerald came towards them, his open, thick woollen coat flapping out at the sides. 'What's happened . . . Oh . . .'

Mandy had left the circle of Edith's arms and flung herself at Gerald. 'Alf's 'urt, please make him better.'

'What? How? . . . Edith?'

Edith shook as she related what had happened.

Hugging Mandy to him, Gerald looked from her to Ben. 'Are you all right, Ben?'

Ben stared back unmoving, not answering.

'He looks in shock, Edith . . . Mandy, you go back to Edith, dear, and don't worry, I'm sure Alf will be fine. Let me take a look at Ben.'

As Gerald approached, vomit projected from Ben.

'All right, son, you'll be all right, you've had a shock. Come with me, and you too, Edith. I think you all need checking out.'

Ben didn't move.

'Ben?'

Edith went on her haunches. 'Ben, love, don't be afraid. Alf ain't hurt badly. Let's go with Gerald so that he can make you feel better an' all, eh?'

Ben's large brown eyes looked appealingly back at her. Mystified, Edith turned her head to see Gerald had moved away and was speaking to the receptionist. She guessed he was arranging for someone to come and help clean up the mess.

'Ben? Come on, lad, hold me hand. We'll go together, eh?'

As soon as she had him off the chair, and his feet touched the floor, Ben's legs gave way. 'Gerald!'

Everything became a frenzy of activity then – a nurse and a porter wheeling a bed appeared from nowhere and were whisking Ben away under Gerald's instructions.

Edith, with Mandy in tow, had a job to keep up as she ran after them. 'Gerald, what's happening?'

'We don't know, it may just be the shock, which is serious in itself, but when it has this effect, we need to treat it as an emergency and check if there's anything else going on. How has he been lately?'

'Very quiet, but he misses his mum and dad, especially his dad who joined up as soon as war broke out . . . Oh, and he complained of a sore throat this morning. I helped him to gargle with salt water, and thought it would pass.'

'Hmm, any temperature?'

'I don't know . . . Oh, Gerald, you don't think there's sommat really serious going on, do you?'

'Look, you go with the nurse. They're taking him to the same bay that Alf has been taken to, it's where we assess a patient when we first have contact. I'll be with you in a moment. I was on my way home, so I need to take my coat off and don a white coat . . . Oh, and I need to ring Alice to tell her I'll be late. No doubt she'll be around here in a shot once she hears what's going on.'

Edith had no answers when, as Gerald predicted, Alice arrived at the hospital.

She was standing next to the trolley that Alf was lying on when Alice came running towards her.

'Edith, eeh, lass, are you all right?'

'Oh, Alice, for such a thing to happen. And now Ben an' all, I don't know what's going on with Ben.'

There was a curtain around Ben's bed. Doctor after doctor seemed to come and go and nurses scurried back

16

and forth but no one had taken a moment to give Edith any information.

Alice hugged her before going to Mandy. 'Eeh, lass, poor little Alf.'

'He's all right now, Alice.' Edith looked at Alf. He was shaken and pale but happy to be the centre of his sister's adoring attention – as he always was, but not in this way. Usually, Mandy took on the role of very cross mother with Alf and he could do no right, but now she was sitting with him on his bed, her little hand holding his, her other one stroking the hair back from his forehead where he had a nasty gash. 'Apparently, he got off lightly, as so far all they've found is that gash that will need stitches and they're observing him as he'd been knocked unconscious.'

'That's a relief, love, I was frantic when I heard. And I'm sure Ben will be fine. You know what kids are like, they bounce back while you're still worrying over them.'

'I just wish someone would say something.'

'I know. But, lass, they probably don't know yet, so have nothing to tell you ... Look, you're shaking, that'll be delayed shock. I'll see about a cup of tea for you, eh? And you can take the weight off for a mo. There's a couple of chairs over by the window. Go and get them and sit down. I know everyone here from when I worked here, so I needn't bother anyone, I can make the tea meself.'

The tea was more welcome than Edith thought it would be. Hot and sweet, it seemed to settle her a little.

Alice sat next to her, but didn't talk – a comforting presence, with her hand on Edith's knee. Every now and then she would pat her as if to say everything would be fine. But would it? What would happen? *Please God, don't let them judge that I'm unfit to take care of the children! I couldn't bear that.*

Edith's thoughts went back to when she and Alice had first met the three little evacuees on the platform of North Street station. As it turned out, she'd had to take the lead to organise everything as the leader of the WRVS was ill, and the volunteers were in a state of chaos without her. In the process she and Alice had fallen in love with Mandy, Alf and Ben.

But then she had been saddened to find when she later met them again at the school where she worked that they weren't happy in their placement. Sue, her ma-in-law and a big one for charity work, had helped her and Philip to be allowed to take over their care. Neither had dreamt that Philip would have to go away so soon and had hoped that all would be sorted out with Chamberlain's peace movement, so that he never would. Now, she couldn't imagine life without the children. They had brought such a joy to her and, lately, become a salve to the pain of missing Philip.

Though Philip hadn't been posted abroad like so many, London to her could have been on the moon, it seemed so far away from Blackpool – another world even.

'Feeling better, love?'

'Yes, ta, Alice. By, you were cut out to be a nurse, lass.'

'Aye, but being a teacher, as you are now, and a nurse, as I wanted to be, weren't open to the likes of us from the poor end, was it?' Alice sighed. 'Our change of circumstances in you marrying Philip and me Gerald opened up a lot of avenues to us, though a bit too late for me as they don't accept married women in the nursing profession.'

'Does working with the Red Cross compensate?'

'It does, more than. I love it, Edith. I know I haven't been with them long, but I'm loving me training. Miss Tenby, our director, is talking of me being an ambulance driver since she learnt that I can drive. Eeh, I'm looking forward to the practical training for that. I've nearly finished me advanced first aid course now.'

Edith didn't have time to reply as a worried-looking Gerald emerged from behind the curtain.

'Edith, may I have a word? Alice, darling, can you stay with Mandy and Alf?'

Something about Gerald's tone stopped Edith's heart from beating for a second. It was as if her body did things without her as she followed him into an office.

The room was light and airy after the unnatural light of the electric lamps that hung low from the high ceiling in the receiving ward she'd just come from.

Gerald didn't speak until he'd seated himself behind a desk. 'Take a seat, Edith.' He indicated the one on the opposite side of the desk. This seemed to divide them in more ways than one and unnerved Edith even more, as now she saw him as a doctor rather than her dear friend.

His expression deepened her fear.

'I'm sorry, Edith, but Ben isn't well at all. There are several things we are looking at this being. One of them is polio.'

If Edith had thought the bottom had dropped from her world when the accident happened, that was nothing to how she felt now. The shock of Gerald's words hit her in the stomach as if she'd been kicked. She couldn't speak, only stare in disbelief.

'I know this is a blow, but bear in mind it hasn't been confirmed, and if it is, there is a lot we can do to save Ben's life and even to prevent complete paralysis ... Oh, Edith, to tell you this as a doctor is painful enough, but as a friend ...'

Gerald rose and came around the desk. Edith felt compelled to rise too. To meet him and to be enclosed in his gentle hug. She could see the tears forming in his eyes. This seemed to give her permission not to be brave, but to wail against the injustice of what she'd just heard.

'We'll do everything we can, dear Edith, but be prepared, there is a lot we must put into place just in case we are right – quarantining of yourself, of Mandy and Ben, of all of the school until everyone can be tested. We need to send Ben to a specialist unit – the only one I know of at the moment is in Leicestershire. His parents will have to be informed ... the authorities ... Oh, Edith, if I could save you from all of this, I would, and if I could make it that our suspected diagnosis is wrong, I would – anything ... I'd do anything to be wrong.'

His anguish came out on a sob. He, like them all, had given their hearts to these three children snatched away from their families to what was supposed to be safety ... *Safety! Oh my God, what if all three come down with polio! No! I couldn't bear it, I couldn't.*

THREE

Marg

On waking that morning, Marg hadn't felt any of the strength and confidence about today that she'd begun to feel last night as she'd sat on the doorstep with Edith and Alice.

Her nerves had made her clumsy as she'd prepared for her part-time job at the biscuit factory. Jackie had teased her as they'd walked to work, and that had made her giggle but hadn't helped.

Now she felt a dread at the thought of the visit to meet Clive's mother and father as she prepared for Clive to pick her up and her nerves intensified. *What if his ma doesn't like me?*

She looked at her reflection in the mirror for the umpteenth time, pleased with how the navy costume that she'd teamed with a pink blouse looked, but sighed as she tried to pat her mousy-coloured, frizzy hair down and to wish away the freckles that covered her face. *If only I was pretty and dainty, like Alice with her tamed blonde curls, or tall, dark and beautiful, like Edith.*

★　　★　　★

All these misgivings dissolved when she saw how timid Clive's mother was. His father was the one who did all the talking.

'Well, now we've finally met you, Marg. Beryl has been looking forward to this day and been on at me for a long time to push Clive along, but, well, when a man's been through what our son has, then he must be allowed to do everything when he's ready.'

At last Marg understood. She looked back at Clive as he lifted George, aged three, from his car and she wanted to run to him, tell him that it was all right to feel how he did, that him doing so told her what a wonderful, loyal husband he would be, as he'd done everything gradually, to make sure he knew his own mind, to make things easier for her and to ease himself into his new relationship. This visit, she now knew, was his last act of breaking with his old life and embracing his new one with her by his side. She turned back to face Beryl. 'Eeh, I'm pleased to meet you.'

'And me you, lass.'

Marg wanted to hug her. She took a step forward. Beryl came towards her. Marg held out her arms, afraid now, but she needn't have been as Beryl came into them and they did hug. 'Ta for the shawl, for me gran, Beryl. That were a lovely gesture. She loves it, I can't get it off her, even if it's warm outside. She tells me that I don't understand old bones like Clive's ma does.'

'Aw, I'd love to meet her.'

'Do you know, I thought you'd speak all posh, like Clive does, though he does say the odd "lass".'

'No, I'm a Blackpudlian, Arthur is too, but his family have always been in business. We met in the rock factory when his father owned it. I worked in the office.'

The afternoon went so quickly. Marg loved every minute of it as she and Beryl chatted on in a way that old friends did.

When she left, she couldn't wait for her wedding day, but there was one more visit she was excited to make today.

Ten minutes later she stood in awe of the lovely, detached house standing in its own garden on St Anne's Road, but was surprised to see that there was scaffolding up on one side.

On her tour around the house, she loved everything about it. The large kitchen with its huge cooking range, many cupboards and a dresser, its shelves empty, waiting for her to arrange her own choice of china on. And she loved the long, scrubbed table in the centre.

'Anything you want to change, darling, you can.'

'It looks like you're making changes already, Clive.'

'Yes. Come and I'll show you. It's for Gran. I – I'm having an annexe built. It won't be finished for a few weeks, though, maybe a month, but, well, I thought to give Gran her own bedsitting room and a bathroom.'

'Aw, Clive, that's lovely, ta, but where will we sleep? I'd need to be near her.'

'In the daytime, yes, but at night, a nurse can do that job. I've seen how well Gran responds to a nurse, Marg. I think it is ideal for her to have her own, one who she can relate to. I don't want you to be her nurse, I want you to enjoy being her granddaughter for the time that you have left to have her with you, or before ... well, I hate saying it, but before she can no longer recognise you.'

Marg wanted to scream out against the awful dementia that had afflicted her lovely gran, but she gritted her teeth and listened to Clive as he explained the layout of the annexe and how a nurse would have a sitting room next to Gran's. 'She will be yours to care for in the day, darling, but at night, I want you to myself and I want you and Jackie to have a good night's sleep.'

Marg didn't know what to say. For a moment, she wanted to say that she wouldn't come to live here on those terms, but Clive took hold of her hand and turned her towards him.

'I love you, Marg. And I want to take Gran and Jackie as my family. Please let me take care of you all.'

When she looked up into his loving gaze, Marg knew that in this, he was right. Caring for Gran night and day was wearing her and Jackie out. 'It'll take a bit for me to get used to, but aye, I'll give it a go. Ta, Clive.'

The rest of the house did need a bit of loving care. But Marg knew she could do that. 'This house has known a lot of love, Clive. Well, I want to bring that love back to it.'

'Oh, Marg, you are already, darling. But, yes, bring to it your special self and feel free to furnish everywhere just how you want to. I accept that you'll want to replace everything.'

'I will, but very gradually to make it easy for the boys ... and for you an' all, love.'

'Oh, Marg, thanks. For me, I am ready, but for the boys, as little disruption as possible would be best. But mind you make sure that Gran's chair has pride of place next to the fireplace, lass, or you'll be for it.'

They both giggled at this. 'I wouldn't dare do no other, she mentions it every time she talks of coming here – that, and how she thinks her John said it's right for her.'

'She must have adored your granddad, Marg, as he's constantly in her heart.'

'She did, we all did, but he could be a rum 'un – ha, I learn more about him every day and not stuff I want to know.'

They both laughed. Marg knew that Clive knew what she meant as more than once Gran had mistaken him for her late husband and asked him to take her to bed for a cuddle. Clive had always handled it in his kind way and they'd both distracted Gran so that she didn't feel hurt by rejection.

As Clive sobered, he said, 'It makes me so happy, darling, that we're all going to be together. The thought of us living apart when we were wed was breaking my heart. But I was willing to do it.'

It dawned on Marg then. 'Clive, you've been planning this, haven't you?'

'Ha, I wondered when you'd realise, but yes, as soon as you agreed to marry me, I had the builders in the next day.'

'And did you put Carl up to asking Gran to come here to live?'

'No, that wasn't me. He loves Gran and he understood that our planning to live together on a sort of part-time basis so that you could stay with her in the home she is used to wasn't right. He wants us to be a family. He knew, too, that it was all down to Gran, so took his moment at the pretend Christmas and it worked. He may only be eight years old, but he's a clever lad. He works everything out and comes up with a solution.'

'I know, I've seen his way of dealing with everything, like the time George didn't like Gran trying to make him sit on her knee and Carl took charge by saying that they like to kneel on the floor with their other granny and she strokes their hair. Gran loved it ... Eeh, it's good to hear that he and George want me gran and Jackie to live here, it could have been a big thing for them.'

'They need a fresh start, as I do, lass. And now with Gran accepting the move to here, we will all have that – a home where we can all be together.'

Marg found his hand and squeezed it. As he turned his head to look at her, the low October sunbeams coming through the window caught the glints in his sandy-coloured hair. She caught her breath at the love that surged through her. All she could manage to say was, 'We will, love.'

After a moment of looking into her eyes, Clive spoke. His voice held a grave note. 'Marg, I've something to talk to you about. Shall we sit in the garden? We can watch the lads playing, as they ran straight out there when we arrived.'

When they sat on the bench that stood on a paved area in the middle of the lawn, Clive took her hands. Instinctively, she knew what he wanted to talk about – her rotten supposed da. This was confirmed when he said, 'It's about Eric.'

A shudder went through her as she dreaded that he was going to say the date for the trial was fixed. She held her breath.

'I've been speaking to Bob, and he tells me that Eric's trial has been postponed – it's not likely to take place for another five months, if at all. You see, the police are gathering evidence, rounding up more of his gang; many are telling all to save their own hides. They are hoping to corner Eric and then offer what will look like a good deal if he comes clean ... But, well, Bob says that you're to prepare yourself and Jackie as, even so, the sentence could be ten years or more.'

Bob was their local bobby. It amused them to call him Bob the bobby, but Marg didn't feel amused at this moment, only a fear of the trial, though the fear was mixed with the relief that it might never happen and at the possible sentence. 'I'm glad. For me, they can lock him up forever. But if it happens, Jackie might be upset. She hasn't spoken about it much, so I won't tell her anything yet. I want our wedding to go ahead without any worries ... though I do have one – I haven't yet decided on someone to give me away. Do you reckon Gerald would be a good choice? He's been like a big brother to me, Jackie and Edith.'

'Yes, I do, I think he would be honoured.'

'Aye, I think he would but I'm worried that me plans could be mucked up if he had to go to war.'

'He won't go any day soon, darling. Look, what about you ask him, and we'll ask my dad to be on standby? That way you've got it covered.' His arm came around her and he squeezed her to him. 'I love you, Marg. I will do anything to make you happy.'

Marg smiled up at him. Tears of joy filled her eyes. 'I know. And I love you an' all, lad.'

A giggle made them both turn to see the boys standing watching them. Carl looked at George. 'Daddy's being all sloppy, George.'

George nodded. 'He still loves us, though, don't he, Carl?'

'I do, I love you both dearly.'

'And I do an' all, me lads. Come here.'

The boys ran at Marg and into her waiting arms. As she held them, she knew a feeling of deep love for them. She lifted her eyes to the sky. *If you're watching, Harriet, I want you to know that your lads are safe with me. I'll never let them forget you, but I'll love them as if they're me own.*

With this, Marg felt at peace with the memory of Clive's late wife and knew she could truly look forward to her wedding day.

This thought and everything about the wonderful afternoon she'd had left her when she arrived home later that evening. Jackie was standing outside waiting for them, her look of anguish as they pulled up making Marg's heart sink.

'Eeh, Marg, Marg.'

Marg pulled Jackie to her. 'What is it, lass? What's happened?'

As Jackie told them what she knew of what had happened, tears ran down her face. Marg couldn't take it all in. 'Alf, knocked over, and Ben? Little Ben ... Polio? But they were only playing out yesterday evening!'

'I knaw, and all the kids that were playing with them, and Mandy and Alf and the kids at school have to be quarantined in their homes until they've all been tested and cleared of having the virus.'

'Good God!' This came from Clive. 'Have my boys been with Ben lately, Marg?'

'Not since our Christmas Day. But I don't know if that counts or not. But, oh dear. Eeh, poor little chap. And Alf, how's Alf?'

'He's badly bruised and being kept in hospital. It would have been overnight to keep a check on him, but both he and Mandy are being put into an isolation ward till they are cleared.'

'And Ben?'

'They are waiting to be certain, but then Alice told me, if he is, he will be sent to a specialist unit in Leicestershire . . . Aw, Marg, Marg . . .'

Marg held Jackie close, unable to process all she'd heard. 'Come on, let's get inside, Jackie, love.'

As soon as they stepped through the door, Gran, who'd been nodding, lifted her head. 'Is that you, John?'

For once, Marg didn't feel like playing along. 'No, Gran, it's Clive. Are you all right, love?'

Gran looked at Marg, the usual puzzled look on her face. Her bottom lip quivered. 'Me ma said she'd be here today, but she ain't come, nor John, he was due in an' all.'

Marg's irritation left her when she saw the lost and frightened look on Gran's face. She went over to where Gran sat next to the fire and knelt in front of her. 'It's all right, Gran, they've been delayed, they'll be here soon. You close your eyes again, eh? When you do that, they come to visit you, don't they?'

Gran smiled. 'Am I your gran, lass?'

'You are, and a lovely gran you are an' all.'

29

Gran looked intently at her. 'Marg, me Marg, where have you been, lass?'

For Marg, it was a magical moment to have her gran know who she was, something that rarely happened but for now, she had suddenly zipped back to the present.

Her gaze went to Clive. 'Where's your boys, eh, Clive? I like to see them, they remind me that I had little boys, who I never saw grow up, but who would have been like them. I love your boys.'

'They've had quite a day so their granny's seeing to getting their tea and putting them to bed, Gran. They sent love to you.'

Gran smacked her lips together, smiled and then put her head back. Her eyes closed, and Marg knew she'd be away in seconds, but it was good to see she was happy now.

Turning to Jackie, Marg asked where Edith was.

'She's at Alice's. I'll be all right here if you want to go to her.'

'But will I be allowed to go to her, lass?'

'Aye, I think so. Gerald said it mostly affects kids.'

'Are you sure you want to go, Marg? I'd be a little wary.'

'I'm sure, Clive, but I understand that you mustn't. I'll phone you from Alice's phone, love, and tell you what's advised for our lads.'

'I'll drop you round there . . . and Marg, it's good to hear you refer to them as ours.'

'They are, and will always be so, Clive.'

'And mine. I love them an' all, Clive. And you knaw as Gran does.'

With this from Jackie, Clive grinned. 'Ha, I feel like I'm being given a whole new family and sharing mine as I already look on you as my sister, Jackie.'

Clive held out his arms and Jackie went into them. 'It's grand to have a big brother, ta, Clive.'

'You've nothing to worry over now, Jackie, love. I'll take care of all of you. You'll never want for anything again.'

Marg could feel the tears in her eyes, but she brushed them away and made herself smile. Though she couldn't help thinking that as one wonderful door opened for them, another closed on their happiness and gave them sorrow again.

When they pulled up outside Alice's house in Newton Drive – the house where Gerald had grown up with his doctor parents, who were at present sailing back from Africa, where they'd been on a mission of mercy – Marg wondered at how familiar it all was, when, as kids, she, Alice and Edith had looked on this street as 'the posh end of Blackpool' and as somewhere they weren't welcome.

Clive turned and kissed her cheek. 'Will you be all right, love?'

'Aye.'

'I've been thinking about Ben's mum. This is going to be a shock to her, and with her not having her man to turn to, and no doubt already missing her son, it's going to be very difficult for her.'

'I know. It don't bear thinking of, poor lass.'

'Look, more than likely Bob will have to contact her. The police usually undertake these tasks. I'll go and see

31

him and tell him to tell her that if she wants to come up to be with her son, then I will fetch her.'

'Aw, Clive, that's kind of you, love . . . Eeh, I do love you. You're heaven sent, lad.'

Clive smiled. 'Give my love to Edith and tell her I'm thinking about her.'

'I will and I'll ask Gerald's advice about whether I can pass it on to our boys and if so . . . well . . . Eeh, Clive.'

Clive took her hand. 'Don't think of the worst, love. Our wedding's so soon now, think of that . . . We will still get married, Marg, won't we? No matter what?'

'Aye, we will. And if it's only us and Gran, Jackie and your lot, well, so be it. If we can celebrate Christmas early, then we can celebrate a wedding later when all is safe to do so.'

His smile warmed Marg's heart, but as she turned to go up the path, cold fingers clutched it once more.

Edith looked full of anguish, fear and despair. All Marg could do was to hug her. Whilst she did, Alice patted Edith's back, a gesture that showed she, too, was at a loss as to what to do for the best.

'Is Gerald in, Alice?'

'He is, he's talking to Joey. Poor lad is distraught by this, as are Billy and Harry. They've all come to love the children.'

'I don't know what to do, Marg.'

'None of us do, Edith, love. There's not a lot we can do, lass, and that makes it harder as we're used to coping with all sorts, but this has kicked us in the stomach.'

'I worry about his ma. How will it be for her, not being with him? And what will she think of me? I should have protected him.'

'You couldn't do that from sommat you couldn't see, Edith. Don't blame yourself. And as for her not being with him, I've a suggestion for you.' Marg told them what Clive had said.

Gerald came in just as she did. 'That would be wonderful, Marg. Just what Ben and his mother need, though until the tests come back, we're not sure if he will go to a specialist unit or not.'

'So, there's hope he ain't got polio?'

'There is. Though I feel certain it is that. But it isn't all doom and gloom. Many children shake it off in a few days and have no effect, then there are those that suffer paralysis in one leg, or both, and . . . well, we won't even think of the worst-case scenario.'

Marg knew he meant death. She remembered when she was about seven or eight, the women in the street talking about lots of kids dying in America from polio. And then there was a lad at school who caught it and died. Her body shuddered. *Don't let that happen to Ben, please.*

FOUR

Alice

With Gerald having left to drop Marg off at home before going to work, Edith and Alice sat sipping their cocoa, made by Marg before she left. No one made cocoa like Marg, it was always a treat. But tonight, it was more of a comfort.

'I don't know if I'll be able to sleep, Alice. Are you sure you want me to stay?'

'I'm sure, lass. I doubt any of us will sleep, so we may as well be awake together. And you can get in with me if you like.'

'I'd like that, ta . . . Eeh, Alice, how could this have happened? And poor Marg – her wedding plans will be all upset. I can't see it going ahead, there's only twelve days to go!'

'Marg had a word with me in the kitchen, love, she said they would go ahead no matter what. It would break her heart to do so without you there, but she has given notice on her Whittaker Avenue house and there's new tenants already waiting to move in.'

'Oh, but we were meant to help her to pack her stuff up this week.'

'I know, but Clive's sorting everything. Marg only wants to keep a few things and at the moment that's the sum total of Gran's chair, and a stool that her ma used to sit on outside in the summer.'

'I remember that stool. I haven't seen it for ages.'

'It's been up in Marg's bedroom since her ma became bedridden. Anyway, the rest of the stuff is going to Par . . . well, a second-hand . . . dealer.'

'Aw, Alice, it's all right. I guessed it would be Parker. I don't mind you mentioning him. I've rid meself of all me demons surrounding what happened to me family, including how callous he was over the handling of what furniture I had left, and can remember the good times without clouding them with the bad.'

'That's good, lass. It ain't easy to get over these things. They come back to bite you when you least suspect it.'

'Aye, they do, but I think living opposite to where it all happened has helped me. If I'd have stayed away, it would have been a dreaded place to return to – mind, I've had me moments.'

Alice shuddered as she remembered the fire that badly damaged Edith's home, but worse than that, the events immediately before that caused the death of her ma and da, at the hands of Edith's demented brother. How she'd managed to come to terms with that, Alice didn't know, and yet her doing so had been an inspiration to herself when she'd suffered her own loss of her baby son.

'That was a big sigh, love.'

'Aye, me memories visiting me. It only takes a small thing to trigger memories of what we've been through, lass.'

'It does . . . Oh, I do wish Gerald would ring.'

'He will. He'll hardly have got to the hospital yet, let alone caught up with how everything's progressing. Let's hope the results are in and they're not as bad as we think.'

They'd hardly finished their cocoa when the telephone rang. Edith jumped up and ran out into the hall. Alice could hear the fear in her voice as she said, 'Edith speaking.'

After a pause, during which Alice held her breath, she heard, 'Oh? So, it might not be as bad as we thought? Eeh, Gerald, ta. Ta ever so much, lad.'

Alice found herself smiling, not just because the news sounded good, but because Edith had done as they all did when their guard was down – returned to her roots and spoke in her full Lancashire dialect.

Edith was crying when she came back into the living room. Joey, the youngest of Alice's brothers, was with her, clinging on to her hand. Behind them was Harry, the eldest, and looking very pale, and Billy, the middle brother. They'd been upstairs giving Alice and Edith some time together but must have heard the telephone ring. Their faces told of the same tension Alice felt.

'Aw, Alice, Gerald said he'd only just arrived, but had been met by his colleague who was just leaving and who told him that Ben was showing signs of improvement . . . but . . . it's been confirmed. It is polio.'

Alice caught her breath. She looked from one to the other of her beloved brothers, then intently at Joey, who'd been playing football with Alf and Ben on Saturday, just two days ago. The fear for him had been pounding around her head since hearing what Ben might be suffering with; now it was compounded.

'He says they are keeping him in isolation overnight and monitoring him closely.' Edith's voice shook. Her expression wasn't the one of relief that Alice had expected.

'They ... they're hoping that Ben has the strain that can disappear in a few days. But if he deteriorates, then they have a bed on standby at the specialist hospital and an ambulance to take him there ... I can't see him, Alice. He may be whisked away, and I won't be able to see him or reassure him ... It's unbearable.'

Alice had no words. She did what they always did, whether sharing a sadness or a happiness – she took Edith in her arms. Not always easy with Edith who was taller than both herself and Marg, but Edith, needing the hug, bent a little to receive it.

The most beautiful of the three of them, with her dark hair swept back into a bun and her huge hazel eyes, Edith had always seemed the strongest too. But without Philip by her side so soon after their wedding day, her strength seemed to be deserting her.

'Come and sit down, love. Let's hope that the message got to Philip to ring you here and he does that very soon.'

'But how will I tell him this dreadful news? Eeh, Alice, I wish he was here right now.'

'I know, lass. So do I. So do I.'

Harry stepped forward. Mature for his eighteen years – made that way by all he'd been through at their da's hand – showed his empathy by putting his arm around Edith's shoulder. 'We're here for you, Edith, you knaw that. You're not alone.'

Billy, just as mature as Harry, though two and half years younger, did the same. 'He'll be all right, Edith, the Cockneys are known for being tough.'

Edith turned from Alice's arms into theirs. 'I knaw, me lads. I'm lucky to have you all. And you, Joey. Come here, lad. I need a cuddle from you all.'

As the four of them swayed together, Alice's eyes filled with tears. She wanted to rail at God for sending them more trouble, but then, they had the comfort of each other as they were like one big family, her and her lot, Edith and hers, and Marg, Jackie and Gran. Depleted in numbers now, but no less strong for the bad happenings, and full of good memories to counter the bad.

The telephone ringing again made them all jump. Edith ran into the hall.

'Leave her to it, lads . . . By, I'm proud of you three. You're a credit. I don't tell you often, but I love the hearts of you, me lovely brothers.'

Joey came rushing at her, but Billy laughed. 'Aw, don't get all sloppy, our Alice.'

She laughed along with them. 'Look, let's have five minutes in the conservatory, eh? I've not had a minute to ask how you are feeling, Harry, nor how you got on on your first day at the rock factory, Billy.'

'Ha, he reckons he's learnt my job in just one day.' Harry cuffed Billy in a playful manner and both boys giggled.

'So, you did all right, then?'

'Aye ... it were strange to try to imagine Da there, though. I – I, well, for the first time, I missed him.'

Harry answered Billy: 'That happened to me when I started there. It was as if you could sense him watching you ... and, well ... sort of feel he was proud of you at last. It's what kept me there.'

Alice sighed. She knew Harry had chosen to follow their late father into the rock factory for just these reasons, when being a very clever young man, he could have gone to university with Gerald's help.

'I'm glad you settled in, and it's good an' all to have nice thoughts about Da. We always knew he couldn't help how he was after the accident and losing Mum ... So, what about you, Harry, how are you, lad?'

'I'm feeling almost back to meself. I – I, well, I'm thinking of contacting the army now and telling them I could start me training.'

Alice's heart flipped over. 'Let Gerald be the judge of when you're fit enough, love. It's no good going before. You won't pass the medical and you'll just waste the army's time.'

'The thing is, now I knaw I've got to go, I just want to do it and get on with it. Thinking about it is driving me nuts.'

'I know, lad. I can understand that. We'll talk to Gerald tomorrow afternoon when he gets up. Thank goodness tonight is his last night duty for a week.'

'Will you talk about me school an' all, Alice? I don't want to board. I want to be at home.'

Alice ruffled Joey's hair. 'We will. But Joey, grab every opportunity you can, me lad. Do it for all of us who didn't

39

get the chance you're being offered. Think where we would all have been if we'd have had the education you're going to get, and do all you can to be worthy of it, eh?'

'Do you want me to go away? Is it because you want to go with the Red Cross?'

'No! No, you dafty. I don't. I will go away for a few days at a time if needed, but there's no need to worry about that. Averill and Rod will be back then and will take care of you and Billy while I'm away, or . . . well, I've met a lady, Heather. She's lovely. She was widowed recently and has no family. I . . . well, I'm going to invite her to tea on Sunday. You'll love her . . . me and Gerald had the idea that she might come and cook meals and be here for you if we can't be. Look, you going away to school is the last thing any of us want, Joey. It was just a suggestion as you have such a good brain, and with your talent for art, the world would open up to you with good schooling.'

'I don't want it to. I want to be like Harry and Billy. Me and Billy want to be footballers.'

Seeing Joey was near to tears, Alice didn't push the conversation further. 'All right, don't worry about it. Nothing will happen that you're not happy with.'

'Why not have a tutor at home, like I did, Joey?'

'That's a good idea, Harry.' Alice smiled at Joey. 'What do you think, love?'

'Yes, I'd like that . . . not sure about this Heather, though.'

'Wait till you meet her. I haven't asked her yet. She may not want to do what I have in mind. But I just had the idea as I want to do my bit for the war effort and I'm thinking that Averill and Rod may want to go back to working in

40

the hospital and if . . . Anyway. Lots to talk about. We'll call a family meeting, eh? How would that be?'

Alice still couldn't put into words that Gerald would go if needed and still hoped he wouldn't. But she knew that if a few doctors from Blackpool Victoria Hospital went to war, then once Averill and Rod arrived home from Africa, they wouldn't be able to care for Joey as they would want to fill in at the hospital. Both were highly skilled surgeons.

'Right, a meeting it is, and I'll be in the chair and have the deciding vote.'

'Naw, that ain't fair, Harry.'

'Ha, I'm the eldest, Billy, lad. You've got to get used to your elders taking the lead.'

Billy hit Harry with a cushion. A trigger for pandemonium as though Harry was a young man, the boyhood version of him that he hadn't long left behind was never far from the surface.

For Alice, this was good to see, so soon after they'd nearly lost him.

Edith coming in and having a smile on her face stopped the hilarious antics.

'Philip's coming home. He asked for leave as soon as he got the message about what had happened. They've given him two weeks! Eeh, Alice, I can't tell you what a relief that is.'

Alice jumped up. 'That's just grand. Philip will take charge of everything – aye, and keep that smile on your face, lass. Aw, love, everything will come right. I know it will.'

But in her heart Alice wondered if anyone could ever make everything right again.

FIVE

Marg

When Edith opened the door to Marg's house and popped her head around, Marg jumped up from where she'd been sitting on the sofa. 'Eeh, Edith, lass, I'm that happy for you. I've been worried sick about you all day. Then to see Philip's car here, me heart lifted. Is there any news?'

'Aye, love, and a lot better than we ever expected.'

'Come in, lass ... Ta ever so much for coming round, I didn't want to come to yours and push meself on you.'

'You daft ha'peth. You're always welcome. But I understand. I saw you go by the window as you came home from work, so gave you five minutes to get in.'

Before Marg could answer, Gran piped up, 'How's me little lad? I don't want to lose another one.'

The distress in her voice as she said this upset Marg. She crouched down in front of Gran and took her hand and gently stroked it, loving every vein that stuck out, and all the knobbly bits on her fingers.

'You told her, Marg?'

'Aye, I did. She was having one of her good moments and she wanted to know why I was worried.'

'Aw, Gran. You're not to worry, love. Things are not so bad for Ben as they could be. It seems he may have a mild strain. And so far, there are no signs that anyone else has been infected. It's good news on Mandy and Alf an' all. Alf's bruised badly and feeling the shock of what happened, but is all right, and Mandy is bouncing back already and mothering him as usual.'

'Me John likes to bounce around, you knaw.'

Marg jumped in, not wanting to hear about her late grandfather's antics; she'd heard it a few times when Gran went off with the fairies. 'I bet you'd love a pot of tea, wouldn't you, Gran?'

'Aye, I would, ta.' As Gran looked up at Marg her expression changed. 'Ma? Ma, you came to see me ... Eeh, Ma.' Her arms reached up. Always, before the dementia struck, Gran would say how like her ma Marg was.

Going into her arms, Marg hugged her gently.

'You're a lot thinner, Ma. But you're here, that's all that matters ... Aye, we'll have a pot of tea, eh? I'll put the kettle on.'

'No, love, you sit still, I'll do it.'

'You didn't used to talk posh – what's changed you, Ma?'

Marg smiled as she thought of the lady who had taught her, Alice and Edith. She'd always corrected them and not allowed them to speak in the strong Lancashire dialect that Gran knew and loved, and the younger members of their families still used. She'd said that no one would be able to

43

understand them if ever they travelled out of Blackpool. None of them had done so far.

Edith cut into this thought. 'You stay there, Marg, I'll put the kettle on. Philip will be round in a mo, so I'll make him one an' all.'

'Ta, Edith. Eeh, it's good news about little Ben and the others. Are Mandy and Ben coming home?'

To the sound of filling the kettle and getting the cups down, Edith called back, 'Soon. But such a lot has happened, Marg. The police contacted Ben's mum and she wants to come up, so Bob accepted Clive's offer and he's going to fetch her. And it's been arranged that Mandy and Alf's gran will come with her. It appears that she got the kids' letters and then heard about Alf's accident and what's happened to Ben. She rang me all anxious, bless her, and then jumped at the chance of a lift.'

'Eeh, lass, where're you going to put them all?'

'Here we are, tea up! There you go, Gran.'

Gran's hands were surprisingly steady as she took the cup. 'Ta, lass. Me ma likes two sugars – I knaw there's a shortage, but she's a special guest.' Gran patted Marg's hand. Happiness shone from her.

Marg played along. 'Drink your tea, lass.'

'I will, Ma. Look. I'm blowing it, like you told me to. "Blow away the steam, and it'll taste like a dream." Does you remember telling me that?'

With tears brimming in her eyes, Marg nodded. She felt a mixture of happiness because Gran was happy, and deep sadness as she felt the last shreds of the gran she knew leaving, and that left her in a lonely place.

Sighing, she concentrated on Edith's plans. She could see her question of where they were all going to sleep had triggered further upset as Edith's sigh was even bigger than her own. 'I – I'm going to have to say goodbye to little Ben. You see, Gerald thought it best in the circumstances, as the fears for London have been unfounded, to have him transferred to a special hospital down there. Ben's mum will only stay a couple of nights and then travel back down to be with him. Alice is going to put her up and Mandy and Alf's granny will stay with us . . . but . . . well, eeh, Marg, it's all been happening, and in such a short space of time, it feels like a whirlwind has hit . . . You see, it seems Philip didn't give up on the idea of finding a new home for me. He's been in constant touch with Entwistle Green, the estate agent, trying to find a place and, well . . . I'm moving in a few days, Marg.'

'By, lass, that came out of the blue! But I'm pleased for you. I didn't like the idea of leaving you in this street with me and Alice gone. I know how that felt when you went to Alice's after . . . Anyroad, where to? And I'll help you all I can. By, I'm that pleased.'

'Ta, Marg. I will need a hand, but you've got your wedding in eleven days.'

'That's all sorted. More than sorted now Philip will be home for it an' all.'

The door opened. 'What's sorted now I'm home?'

'Philip!' Marg rose. 'Eeh, it's good to see you, lad.' She went into his open arms for the hug he offered. Being hugged by him and Gerald had been a new and strange experience for her, never having had a loving male figure in her life till they came into it, but now she loved it and felt as though she'd gained two big brothers. 'Me wedding. I were worried you wouldn't be home for it.'

'I wouldn't miss it for the world, Marg, and as it happened, I've just had notice that it is to be my first weekend leave.'

Edith looked surprised.

'I know, darling, I didn't tell you. I only heard about an hour before Gerald rang, and had the idea of just turning up and surprising you all ... but anyway, that's all by the by now.'

Both girls giggled at his look of consternation.

'That would have been grand, Philip, wouldn't it, Edith, lass?'

'Aye, it would have, Marg, but even better that he's here now.'

Philip crossed the room and kissed Edith's cheek. 'I just wish the circumstances were different, darling.'

'I know. I was just explaining to Marg what's happening, though I've hardly taken it all in meself.'

'You will once you see the house, I'm really pleased with it. Life will change for the better for you – for us both when I am at home ... though saying goodbye to poor little Ben will break my heart.'

'So, will Ben not come home ... I mean, back to you, Edith?'

'No ... at least it seems that way.' Her voice shook. 'His ma sent a message to say she wanted him back for good. That a lot of kids are returning as their mothers can't cope without them and there just don't seem to be any reason for them being taken away in the first place.'

What Philip said to this made Marg's blood run cold. 'I still think there is a danger. With Poland beaten to the ground by the Russians and the Germans, Hitler will turn his attention elsewhere. France is the most likely and why we are sending troops out there, but ... well, I don't want to be a scaremonger, but it is likely that we are in his sights too.'

To Marg, it was as if Philip saying this meant that it would happen. After all, he was working at the War Office, so he would know, wouldn't he?

'Look, I'm only speculating like everyone else. But we do have to be ready. And not just those of us who will have to offer our services to fight, but all of us. All will be asked to give everything they can to beating this threat to our beloved country.'

His words mesmerised Marg, and she could see they did Edith, too. He was like a statesman — more so than Chamberlain who was meant to be one, but often came across on the wireless as someone ready to give in.

'You tell 'em, lad! Eeh, these girls knaw nowt about war and what they're in for. Someone needs to educate them and get them ready — what was the first thing they did when they heard? Held a Christmas Day, that's what! By, you're in for a shock, me lasses.'

Gran's voice boomed out, making Marg want to laugh out loud. Not at what she said, but with the joy of her having returned to the present once more. Though what she'd said did temper that joy with fear.

'Sorry, Gran, I haven't greeted you yet. You were busy with your cup of tea. Can I get a hug?'

'By, John, you can do more than that, lad.'

This time Marg did laugh. More at Philip's face than at what Gran had said. Gran would mistake any man for Granddad. To the point where she made you either laugh or cringe with embarrassment.

Stepping in to save Philip, Marg told Gran, 'Philip and Edith are moving, just like us, Gran.' Gran's mouth dropped open but before she could say anything further, Marg asked where this new house was.

'That's the best bit, Marg. It's on St Anne's Road, just a few houses away from yours and Clive's!'

Astonished, but pleased beyond words, Marg clapped her hands. 'Aw, Edith!'

Gran put her mug down on the side table and mimicked her clapping, which made them all laugh.

'Yes. The estate agent knew exactly what I was looking for and found they had this one on their books. It belongs to a retired doctor, but he moved into a nursing home when his wife died. It appears that it will be for sale eventually, so if we love it and settle in well, I can put a reserve on it and then one day it will be ours.'

Edith face lit up.

'We're just going to see it now. And as I told Philip, I don't care what it looks like, I'm moving into it as it means we'll still be close together, Marg.'

A tap on the door interrupted them. It opened and Ada Arkwright stood there. 'Eeh, I didn't knaw you had company, lass.'

Marg felt Edith look at her, but didn't dare look back as she knew she'd giggle. Ada was one for turning up when you had company. She felt entitled to know everything that happened in Whittaker Avenue. But then, her being a Red Cross nurse in the first war meant that she was the saviour of many of the residents in times of ills – at a price, that was.

'You're all right, Ada, come on in.'

'Ta, lass. Eeh, I'm worried about all the kids. The women in the street are having a job to keep them in. Have you heard when the testing will start, Edith?'

'Not yet, Ada. It's all happened so quickly, but you can tell everyone that Ben's not as bad as first thought. Mandy and Alf have been tested and they haven't got it, so that might reassure everyone.'

'By, what a relief, poor mite. Mind, even a mild form can leave them with a leg in a brace and a lot of other problems an' all. I've seen it.'

Marg thought that most people had; everyone knew someone who had been crippled by polio and wore a brace. 'Let's hope none of that happens, eh, Ada?'

'Too right, Marg, poor little soul. So, has his ma been told?'

Nothing but the whole story as it was to date would satisfy Ada. 'Look, love, we've just made a pot of tea. I'll see Edith off as she and Philip have business to attend to, then I'll tell you all about it, eh?'

Edith looked grateful. Ada could be full of doom and gloom and that was the last thing she would need right now. But then she surprised Marg by saying, 'No, Marg, we hoped you would come with us and Ada coming over is just what we need. Have you got a mo, Ada? Only, well,

49

you're the first to know after Marg, but me and Philip are going to look at a house to rent.'

Ada's face went through the motions of being surprised to being pleased to be let in on such information.

'Aye, of course I have. I'll look out for Sandra.' She moved towards Gran. 'Now, then, Sandra, lass. How are you since I saw you this morning, eh?'

Gran looked blank, then came out with, 'Did you see me ma? She was here a bit ago, and me John.'

'Naw, you daft ha'peth. Your ma's been gone this many a year. Pushing up the daisies she is, lass. And your John is an' all.'

Gran looked perplexed. Marg wanted to shut Ada up, but then, she needed her for a few more days so didn't want to upset her.

Over the years she'd never have managed without Ada looking after Gran, and her ma, before she'd died, while she went to work, though at times, finding the money to pay her had been difficult.

Ada always thought the best policy was to make Gran face reality, when she couldn't. Reality for her kept changing and leaving her grasp. It had been Betty, Edith's late ma, who'd had the best idea. She told them to just go along with Gran or to cause a distraction. Gran always responded well and happily to this. She'd loved Betty as Marg had, despite her drunken ways.

'No tears, now, lass, they won't help you. I'll get you into your wheelchair and take you for a walk. It's nice now and I need a few bits from Fairfield's shop.'

'I'd like that, Ada. Will you take me to the churchyard to visit Ma and John's graves, lass?'

50

Ada looked triumphant. 'There, you see. Keep telling her the truth and she comes out of it. I've told you many a time, Marg.'

Marg was already on her way upstairs to get her cardigan, so Ada didn't see her stick her tongue out in defiance. But the gesture released the tension in her and made her giggle and so the moment of annoyance passed.

When they reached St Anne's Road, Clive's car was outside his house.

'You'd better pop in and tell him, Marg, as he may be planning to go to yours to see you. We'll carry on with the viewing and you can come and find us when you're ready.'

'Ta, Edith, I won't be long.'

Clive was taken aback by her opening the door. 'Marg, love, what brings you here? Is everything all right ... ? Gran? Is Gran all right?'

'She is, Clive ... Eeh, let me get in, lad.'

Clive had rushed at her and taken her in his arms.

'You are in, darling Marg, in my arms where you belong.'

Happiness surged through Marg. She accepted his kiss, still amazed all this was happening to her, or that she could feel such happiness and, yes, feel safe, for the first time in a long, long time.

When he released her, she told him why she was there.

'That's grand news.'

'Eeh, you sound like your da now.'

'Well, that's how it is. For you to have Edith just up the road is grand. So, have you heard all the latest about my trip to London?'

51

'I have, love. When are you going?'

'Friday. I was just getting ready to come to you, I was hoping we could arrange for you to come with me. It's your last day at work and you could leave early. We could get off by midday.'

Taken aback and yet excited about the prospect, Marg's mind was in a whirl. Could she? Would it be possible?

'Please, love, there must be a way. Only, I don't think I would cope on my own driving all those miles back with two Cockney women in the back of my car!'

'By, lad, here I was thinking you didn't want to be away from me.'

'That as well – that more than anything, darling. But it will mean you being away overnight. Could that be arranged?'

With this, the excitement died in Marg. She couldn't leave Gran all night and most of Saturday. It wouldn't be fair on Jackie.

'Look, I can see that's a problem, but, well … please, Marg, there must be a way.'

'Let's go and join Edith and Philip, and I'll think about it. I so want to come, but eeh, I don't know …'

The house stood just three doors away from where Marg would live after she and Clive married and this lifted Marg's spirits. She couldn't believe this was happening. The thought of leaving Edith in the street on her own had marred her joy a little – not that Edith would have been without friends around her. The folk in Whittaker Avenue were a community and would have looked out for her. Marg felt a pang at this thought as she knew that she was going to miss them all when she left after her marriage.

Lawned at the front as Clive's was, the house Edith and Philip would live in looked like his and was just as beautiful.

As Marg gazed up at it, she again had the feeling of everything being unreal. *Is it really true that me, Edith and Alice are having such good fortune? By, it's like a fairy tale – three ragged-arsed kids from Whittaker Avenue and look at us now.*

She didn't allow the thought that tried to dampen this feeling of wonderment and prod her into remembering what might happen soon if war really did escalate, but linked arms with Clive. 'Come on, love, I can't wait to see inside.' This helped to brush it away for now – but would it just go away? She didn't think so.

SIX

Edith

Edith looked over at Philip. His eyes were still closed as he lay beside her. To her, he was beautiful.

Her body quivered with the rebound thrills of their lovemaking through the night. She should feel exhausted, but she felt as though all her troubles had been halved with having him by her side.

She glanced over at the clock. Eight o'clock already, and there was so much to do today! Not least, a wonderful visit to see Mandy and Alf . . . Oh, how she wished it was to see Ben too, but she had to accept that wasn't possible.

Throwing the covers back, Edith swung her legs out of the bed. She wouldn't dwell on the sadness of all that surrounded Ben but would busy herself packing her clothes and knick-knacks ready for the move, which had been hastily arranged for the next day. How on earth they were going to achieve it all, she couldn't imagine.

When her feet touched the rag rug beside the bed, a dizziness came over her. Her stomach lurched. As her throat constricted, she put her hands over her mouth and ran into the kitchen. She just had time to grab the bucket from behind the curtain that draped around the pot sink before she was retching into it.

'Darling . . . Oh, my darling!'

Philip gently patted her back, but then suddenly grabbed the bucket and was sick himself! Edith could give him no attention as the next couple of minutes they almost tussled over who had possession of the bucket. Philip gave in first as he turned to the sink and ran the tap. Putting his head under the running water and then his mouth, she could hear him drinking great swallows of the cold liquid.

With the bout of sickness passing, she left him to it and took the bucket outside, shivering as she emptied it into the lav before she swilled it under the outside tap.

After rinsing out her mouth and splashing her face, she leant against the wall. A laugh welled up inside her. A bubbly, happy laugh.

Composing herself, she went indoors but seeing Philip looking all sorry for himself, the laugh released itself again.

Philip looked astonished for a moment, then put his head back and let out a roar that was a cross between a laugh and a triumphant cry. 'We're having a baby! It's true, it's really happening, Oh, my darling Edith.'

Happiness filled every part of her as he held her. 'It would seem so, lad!'

'Ha! Oh, Edith, thank you.'

'No. It's me who has to say ta. You did all the hard work.'

They fell about laughing again. And for that moment, Edith forgot all of her troubles and bathed in the wonderful feeling that took her.

By the time she arrived at the hospital, some three hours later, Edith's heart was beating with joy at being sure now that all her hopes were real, and at being allowed to see Mandy and Alf. If only she could see Ben too.

She'd been to the shops on her way and bought them a new toy each. A rag doll for Mandy and another engine for Alf's train, which had been a gift for him on their pretend Christmas Day. And crayons and paper for them both. Then she had a bag full of clothes for them for when she could bring them home, and clean pyjamas for now. She'd also bought a train set for Ben but wouldn't be able to give it to him as not only couldn't she visit him, but she couldn't take anything in for him either, as everything that went near him needed to be sterile. So, she would pack it with his things with a note expressing their love for him and send it with his mother to give to him when he finally went home to her.

As she passed the office where she knew Gerald wrote up his notes, she glanced through the window of the door. He was sitting staring out towards the lawned area behind this part of the hospital building.

Feeling she wouldn't be intruding, she knocked. As soon as he saw her peering through and waving, he rose and came to her.

'Edith! I wondered what time you would come . . . No Philip?'

As she came out of the hug he gave her, she shook her head. 'He's coming later, he's got a lot to do to move us and not much time to do it in. The owner's son is as keen as we are to get us in. He's sending a van around this afternoon to take the furniture from the house that we can't use, which is pretty much all of it, as we have most things we need. We're just keeping a couple of the big armchairs and the cane furniture in the conservatory.'

'Gosh, everything's moving at the speed of light for you.'

'It is. We have a van coming tomorrow to move us in. You see, we want to be in by Saturday when Clive returns with the twins' gran and . . . well, Ben's ma . . .'

Before she could say anything about the pain of having to say goodbye to Ben, Gerald asked, 'Do we know if Ben's father has been posted abroad yet?'

'Not for sure, but we think so from what Ben has always said.'

'Pity, as seeing him too would do Ben the world of good.'

'Will his ma be able to see him?'

'In a controlled way, yes. We're fitting a net around his bed, so she will be able to sit with him, though she will have to wear surgical garments and gloves. And we'll involve her as much as we can in his care. You could see him too, if you like. It will only be through a window, but still . . . it's up to you.'

'Eeh, that'd be grand, ta, Gerald. I'll go and see the other two first as they know I'm coming and will be waiting for me.'

'Yes. But I have good news on that front too. There have been no further reported cases in the town, so we will

57

possibly be letting Mandy and Alf out on Saturday. We still have Alf under observation, but he isn't showing any signs of anything untoward. The nurses have nicknamed him Rubber Alf as he must have bounced like a ball. It's incredible from what I have heard of the accident that he hasn't any serious injuries.'

Edith couldn't stop herself from giggling. The name tickled her. And as she always did, she snorted, making Gerald laugh out loud with her.

'I'm sorry ... Eeh, Rubber Alf. That'll stick, you know.'

'It will. I've been calling him Rubber, and I'm not sure I can go back to calling him Alf!'

They laughed again.

'No snorting. I know you can't help it, but I have work to do, I can't stand here creased with laughter, and that's what it does to me.'

Edith controlled herself and dabbed at her eyes with her gloved hand. 'I know. Me and Philip take ages to calm down with me making that noise – you're a doctor, can't you do something for it?'

'No, and I wouldn't if I could. It's part of you and we all love it. Now take yourself and your snorts away and let me get on with doctoring.'

Edith hugged him. 'See you in a bit.' But when she got a little way along the corridor she had to stop as the rubber and the doctoring remark grabbed her again. She dived into the toilet to calm herself.

As she looked into the hazy mirror, she told herself, 'For someone who's clever and a teacher, you're a bit of a daft ha'peth, Edith.' Then hurried out before the tears of laughter turned to tears of pain.

Mandy jumped at her when she entered the side ward where they were, knocking Edith's bags out of her hand. She could do nothing but hold the sobbing child to her.

Alf didn't move, just stared at her. With her free hand she beckoned him. 'Hello, Alf, lad. Ain't you coming for a cuddle then?'

Alf crawled along his bed to her, his bottom lip quivering. Edith swallowed. 'Eeh, I come to see you, and this is what I get. Cheer up, the pair of you. You're Cockneys, remember? Cockneys are tough and have a spirit that no one can dampen, ain't that right?'

This worked magic on Mandy. She straightened and rubbed her eyes.

'Yes, we are. Come on, Alf, be a man, mate.'

Edith had to swallow again, this time to suppress a laugh. Alf squared his shoulders but still didn't come to her. This worried her as he'd always been so loving to her.

'I've brought presents, and, by, we've missed you both so much.'

At this, Alf came forward. ''Ave yer missed us?'

'I have, lad. There's been an emptiness in me house without you.'

His smile lit his face, and Edith realised that without her being able to visit, they must have felt abandoned.

'Here, look at your toys, and then I've some wonderful news for you both.'

There followed a scramble, and then an 'Ooh' from Alf and an 'Ahh' from Mandy. 'Ta, Aunty, I love her. I'm calling 'er Edith.'

Not to be outdone, Alf piped up. 'And I'm calling my engine Philip.'

'Yer can't call an engine a name, stupid!'

'I can. They do 'ave names, yer know.'

Mandy sighed a sigh to make any mother envious, as that's how she behaved towards Alf, as if she was his ma. And yet, as she hugged her rag doll to her and stroked its wool hair, she showed the vulnerable child that she really was.

The picture she made tore at Edith's heart. And even more so when she asked, 'Is Ben going to die?'

Alf's head shot up; his unblinking stare held fear.

'No. He's going to get better, but it will take a long time. Look, I'll sit on your bed, Mandy, and you can sit each side of me, then I'll tell you all the news I have.'

Choosing to tell them the bad news first, she started with how Ben would have to leave them. Then went on to the new house they would return to. At this point, Alf chimed up, 'But how will Ben find us when he can come back to us?'

His eyes filled with tears.

Shying away from telling them that he wouldn't, Edith made herself smile. 'Ha, you daft ha'peth, we'll make sure he does.' She moved swiftly on to the best bit so as to avoid further questions. 'Anyroad, the reason we're moving quickly is because your gran's coming on Saturday!'

There was a silence and then a squeal of joy from Mandy. Alf had a grin on his face but a question to ask: 'And me mum too?'

Before Edith could answer, Mandy snapped, 'We don't want 'er to, she's trouble.'

'She's not!'

The hardest thing Edith had to do was to tell Alf no, but even worse to tell him that Ben's ma was.

'But I want me mum.'

'I know.' Edith drew him to her.

'You'll 'ave Granny, and she's the best. And Aunty Peggy. So that'll be good.'

To Edith, this told her that the folk of the East End weren't much different to them, as calling a special neighbour, or friend of your ma, 'Aunty' was what they'd all done, and she knew Ben's ma wasn't really related to the twins.

'I'm sure your ma will come next time, Alf . . . Anyroad, what's this about your new name? I hear you're called Rubber Alf!'

Alf grinned. 'It's a daft name.'

'I like it, and I think it will stick, love.'

Alf ignored this. 'Will me granny really come to the new 'ouse?'

'She will, Rubber Alf.'

His grin spread across his face. 'I like it when you say it.'

'Well, you can stop being snotty when I call you it, then.'

'Mandy, show a little kindness to your brother.'

Mandy pouted.

'She does when you're not around, she's been nice to me all the time.'

Typical Alf to stand up for his sister, Edith thought. But then Mandy surprised her. 'I have to be a mother to 'im,

61

me Granny told me to. And that's 'ow me mum keeps 'im from being soft, she tells him off all the time.'

Flummoxed for a moment, Edith picked her words to try to explain that there were other ways, but then Alf put a spanner in the works.

'I don't mind, Aunty, it makes a picture of me mum come into me 'ead.'

Edith felt the pity of this and for a moment wanted to slap the woman who had the privilege of being a mother to these two, but to her mind abused it – but then, her own ma came to mind, and it didn't matter to her how many times she'd been let down by her drunken ways, she'd still give the earth to have her here at this moment. With this, she hugged them both to her.

'I'll try harder to be a ma to you. Then when it's safe you can go home to your own ma. But in the meantime, I've something else for you. A drawing pad and some crayons for each of you. I want you to draw your granny, your aunty Peggy and Ben a picture each as a present. Do you think you can do that?'

'And for you, Aunty. And for Uncle Philip to take with him to his office.'

'That would be lovely, Mandy, lass. There, you can be really kind when you want to be.'

'Granny said it's better to be kind . . . Is she really coming?'

'She is, love, she truly is, and she's going to stay at our house. She can stay as long as she wants.'

This won Edith one of Mandy's rare smiles and a huge hug. Edith's eyes welled up. Her free hand went to her stomach. Soon she would have a child of her own. *I must learn to love other children in a different way to how I will love my own. If I take every child I teach or have some dealing with into my heart as if they are mine, I know I will suffer . . . How am I to say goodbye to Ben?*

Parting with Mandy and Alf was a wrench as they tearfully begged her to stay, but promising to come back with Philip at the proper visiting time settled them and by the time she left, they were already crayoning, which helped her to feel happier about leaving them.

But more heartache was to come as she stood gazing through the small window in the door of the isolation ward.

Ben looked as though he had shrunk. His face was bright red and pinched. A nurse was tenderly mopping his brow. When she spotted Edith, she smiled and spoke to Ben.

Ben turned his head. He seemed at that moment to be so near to her that she felt she could reach out and touch him and stroke his lovely ginger hair. His eyes told of a picture of appeal.

She mouthed the words, 'I love you.' His face remained expressionless. Fear gripped her. Gerald had spoken of this lightly. She'd thought that Ben wouldn't be paralysed, but him not being able to smile or mouth any words back seemed to indicate that parts of him would be.

As if she'd conjured him up, Edith heard Gerald's voice behind her. 'Well, you certainly cheered Mandy and Alf up.'

She swivelled around. 'But Ben! Eeh, Gerald, is he really all right?'

'He is. But, of course, he is a very sick boy . . . I'm sorry, I thought you realised that. Me saying he isn't as bad as he could be didn't mean he wasn't sick. Polio has many forms

– well, three that we know of, and each in themselves are very serious, but some not as others. The worst one will kill the patient. But the strain we think Ben has makes him very poorly – very high temperature, burning throat . . . and, well, it is affecting some of his limbs and reactions, but not all of that will be permanent; some may be. We cannot tell. Poor little chap has a lot to go through yet, but the best we could do for him is to reunite him with his mother.'

Edith took a deep breath. 'I didn't realise the extent of it . . . Eeh, Gerald, how did this happen? Where did he get it from? And why him? And how am going to say goodbye to him?'

Gerald took her hand. 'Edith, these are all questions that I wish I knew the answer to, but I don't . . . I do have an answer to your last one, though. I understand from Alice that you think you might be pregnant?'

'Aye, and I feel positive now as I was sick this morning.' She didn't tell him about the fiasco of them both fighting over the bucket.

'Well, that's a good sign, though it might not have felt like it. So, this wonderful news will give you something to hold on to. All children are precious, but your own . . . you cannot put a price on that.'

Gerald's voice broke. Edith knew he was thinking of his little lost son. But before she could offer comfort, he continued. 'Nor can Ben's mother. Think how hard it was for her to say goodbye – not only to her little boy but to her husband too, never knowing if she will see either of them again. And for Ben as well. We all know how much he has been pining for his mother and father. And now he has this to contend with, and so do his poor parents. Imagine letting your own child go . . .'

'Aw, Gerald, I've been so selfish . . . Thank you. You've helped me more than anyone has. I will always love Ben, Mandy and Alf, but I'll work towards reuniting them with their own families and be a good aunty to them.'

Gerald dropped her hand and hugged her instead. 'And when this war is all over, Alice and I will look at adoption and we will be parents then, too.'

She hugged him back. 'By, that's good news, lad.'

As they came out of the hug, Gerald said, 'Now, I must gown up and go in and check on Ben. I'll tell him that you love him and will hug him as soon as you're allowed to.'

'Ta, love. Does he know his ma's coming on Saturday?'

'Yes. And he has picked up a lot since then. But in the meantime, come as often as you can, Edith. I know you can only stand here, but I think it will do Ben good to see you.'

'I will. I'll make some signs and hold them up for him to read. I'll start at visitor time tonight.'

'I'll make arrangements so that you can come at any time. How long are you on leave from work?'

'The head gave me until Philip goes back. But he told me it isn't all to do with what I have on me plate, but he has to think of the parents of the children. Some have said they don't want me near their kids till they know for sure I can't give them polio.'

'I can understand that. It's a natural fear. But as no new cases have arisen and look unlikely to now, I'm sure they will feel confident in a couple of weeks. We've all had a big scare. But there are many random cases in Britain, sometimes with no other cases reported in the near vicinity of the patient, and sometimes in little clusters. Amongst the medical profession we do fear an epidemic, but though these random cases are on the increase, thank God we aren't seeing it run rife in this country yet.'

Edith sighed. 'I hope it never does.'

'Anyway, put a smile on your face for little Ben. I've to get on now. I'm off tomorrow so after I have checked Ben I need to make sure I leave all my notes up to date. I can come and lend you a hand to move if you like? I'll be on my own most of the day, though I think we have a family meeting planned for sometime – it's our way of treating the boys with respect and giving them a say in any future plans we have.'

Edith smiled. Gerald had done a grand job in taking on Alice's brothers when they'd wed. She so admired him. 'That'd be grand to have your help, ta, Gerald. The van's coming at nine in the morning.'

'Right, I'll see you after ten. If you're not at yours, I'll come to your new place . . . And, Edith, I'm so happy for you . . . new home, new baby. Does Philip know he's going to be a dad?'

'I reckon he feels as if he's carrying it.' Now she felt able to share with him what had happened. His laugh as he walked away lifted her as she felt sure she'd evoked sad memories for him and hadn't wanted to do that.

Turning, she went to wave to little Ben, but he had his eyes closed. Her heart once more plunged. *How could all of this be happening to us? On the one hand, my happiness is bubbling over, but on the other . . .*

SEVEN

Alice

Alice couldn't believe how quickly the days were flying by. It didn't seem a minute since she sat on the step with Marg and Edith on Sunday evening, and now it was Thursday, her main training day with the Red Cross.

As she stood in front of the long, elegant mirror on its carved stand and smoothed down her uniform jacket, Gerald's arms came around her. When his lips found her neck, delicious thrills zinged through her and relit the feelings he'd given her and the place he'd taken her to before she'd got out bed.

'I wish you didn't have to go, darling.'

Turning into his arms, Alice looked up into his beloved face. 'I know. We seem like ships passing in the night these days. But you've a busy day helping Edith, and I'll be home at three. Maybe we can do something nice together and then have our family meeting later.'

'Nice, like just now?'

Alice giggled as she snuggled into his arms and then looked up into his lovely blue eyes. Swallowing hard to control her tightening throat, she nodded. 'Or go for a walk, maybe.'

His laugh made her feel happy, but her mind was still troubled by the emotions stirred in her at the news that Edith was almost certainly having a baby.

Sighing, she turned back towards the mirror.

As if Gerald had read her mind, but didn't want to pursue the sadness they tried to avoid, he patted her bum and went back over to the bed.

'Well, I must get myself sorted, and dress. Have you finished in the bathroom, or shall I go and use the family one?'

This still sounded strange to Alice. How did it happen that she, the lass brought up with only an outside lav and a tin bath, now lived in a house with a bathroom off the bedroom and one down the hallway?

'I'm done, ta.'

As he disappeared, Alice busied herself making the bed and tidying around. Her thoughts turned towards the unhappiness Edith was facing – well, them all really. The three evacuee children had stolen their hearts from the moment they'd stepped off the train. She didn't want to imagine life without any one of them. It was unbearable to lose Ben, but would the twins' granny want to take them home too?

When Gerald appeared already dressed, she couldn't believe she'd taken so long, she'd been so engrossed in the path her thoughts had taken her – to her first hug with little Ben and the twins. To how she'd so wanted to take them in but had been too weighed down with her with grief.

'That was a big sigh, darling.' Gerald was back by her side. 'I know how you feel. It's like a shadow passes over us with everything connected to babies.'

'It does. But that'll get better with time.' She brushed a stray blond hair from his forehead. 'But I'd gone on to think of the sadness that's tainting Edith's happiness.' She shared her thoughts.

'Yes, I've been wondering if the twins would go too. But I hope their granny is sensible and doesn't take them. All the threatened doom hasn't happened, and please God, it doesn't, but just in case, I think they should stay up here. London is bound to be a target at some point.'

Alice shuddered. She hated thinking about it all, and yet knew that in some ways everyone was getting used to what might come as the weeks went by. Yes, it felt like a phoney war, but at the same time, she could see that folk were beginning to prepare themselves, to be strong and encouraging towards each other. The initial shock of being at war had worn off and there was an acceptance, and a feeling that everyone was ready.

Was she ready? She felt she was for most things, but still she fretted at the possibility of Gerald going.

'Hey, you're squeezing the breath from me.'

'Sorry, love, just me thoughts making me a little nervy.'

'Well, let's not give them time to. I'll go and rally Joey and give him a lift to school. Billy left about an hour ago for work and I think I heard Harry up and about with him, no doubt gone for a walk, or a run, even. He seems determined to get fit, but I worry he is overdoing it. He seems really keen to get on with—'

'Don't say it! I don't want to think about him going . . . Race you downstairs. Last one has to do the washing-up for a week.'

With this, Alice dashed for the stairs, but was pushed aside and overtaken by Gerald. Not to be outdone, she grabbed his cardigan and held on for all her might. But to no avail. He pipped her to the bottom, where they fell about laughing.

Joey's *tut tut* sobered them. 'Eeh, who's the kids in this house, eh?'

Alice grabbed him and ruffled his blond curls. 'We've something to tell you, lad. We're thinking of going along with the idea Harry had and getting you a tutor. I thought I'd tell you that to stop you worrying, but we'll still have the family meeting.'

Joey flung himself at her. 'Ta, Alice, I didn't want to go to naw posh school, but I want to learn a lot more than they teach me at me school now. It's boring as I seem to know it all before the lesson even begins.'

'That's because you have your head in a book all the time and are absorbing information as you read, son.'

Alice loved it when Gerald called the boys 'son', it was like they were a real family.

Joey left Alice's arms and turned to Gerald. 'Aye, well, I like learning, and besides, I wanna be like you, Gerald. I want to be a doctor.'

'Hey, that's wonderful, Joey. I would be so proud of you. And it can be done. You can do it . . . Look, I know there's snobbery at Arnold School where I attended – but you would hold your own, Joey, as your intelligence, kind-heartedness

70

and enthusiasm for sport will stand you in good stead . . . You should never change, but you can make a difference to others. The values of the school and the respect the masters give you will be a different experience for you. And having attended there, all doors will open for you.'

Alice sighed. It shouldn't be like this. Why were all the doors open for moneyed folk and not for the likes of kids like her, Edith and Marg used to be? Well, she knew one thing, if things did get bad in this country over the next year or so, then the value of ordinary, poor folk would be recognised for sure.

'All right. But if I give it a go, you will let me leave if I ain't happy, won't you, Gerald?'

'I will take you out of there at a minute's notice, Joey, I promise. But I don't think that will happen. If I did, I wouldn't even think of getting you a place there. I love you too much to make you unhappy.'

Joey hugged Gerald around the waist. Alice could feel the tears prickling her eyes, but she swallowed hard and made herself smile. She didn't know how Gerald had worked this magic to get Joey to change his mind so quickly but was glad that at last, he was going to take this golden opportunity. 'By, me little brother going to Arnold. I never thought I'd see the day. But I know you'll make us proud, lad.'

Joey looked a little unsure when he looked up at her, but he smiled his lovely smile. 'I'll do me best as I like you to be proud of me, Alice.'

'Right, one more hug and I must go. Get your school bag, and don't forget your slate and box of chalks.'

'That's one thing that will change, Joey. At Arnold you all have exercise books for each lesson, no more working with a slate and chalk.'

An eagerness entered Joey's voice. 'Really? You mean, I can keep me work, I won't have to rub it out to do the next bit of working out?'

'No. You won't. A lot of things will be different, but if you make your mind up to be adaptable, then it will all be a wonderful experience for you. They have military training and play cricket and rugby – not so much football, but in my day, lads did kick a ball around at playtime . . . Oh, and no girls to distract you, either. You'll be all lads together and make lifelong friends, as Phil and I are.'

As Alice kissed them both goodbye, telling Gerald to give her love to Edith, she had mixed feelings about how suddenly everything had changed. She'd seen groups of schoolboys from Arnold in the town and had found them all to be very posh. Mind, she had to admit they were very polite too. They would open the door for her or allow her to go first if they were headed in the same direction, or boarding a bus, and none of it done in a condescending way, just with a natural courtesy.

This thought settled her mind as she cranked the engine of her car but didn't stop her worrying how a lad from Joey's background would fit into their environment. She would rather he had lessons to teach him to speak properly first, but then, he wouldn't be her Joey and she didn't want that to happen either.

★   ★   ★

Janette, another trainee who Alice had made friends with, met her at the door of the Blackpool Red Cross headquarters on Whitegate Drive, which occupied part of the building that had once been Blackpool Hospital until their lovely new one was built on East Park Drive just a few years ago.

'Nearly there, love, only a couple more of these lessons and we'll be fully qualified to work anywhere we're needed.'

Alice detected the same excitement in Jan's words as she felt herself. 'Aye, it'll be grand to be able to help wherever we're needed. Have you thought what you'd like to do yet?'

'I've made me mind up, lass. If there's a chance of us being needed abroad, I'm going. I've been reading about all the good that our predecessors did in the last war. Some went to Belgium in the very beginning and were trapped behind enemy lines.'

As they took off their cloaks and hung them up, Alice listened to how Jan had read about a nurse called Edith Cavell who had saved the lives of two hundred servicemen.

'Ech, that's a brave thing to do.'

'It was, but poor soul ended up being executed – shot after being found guilty of treason.'

Alice's blood ran cold. The reality of all their brave words of what they would do in the war hit her like a kick in the stomach.

'I can see from your face, love, that's upset you. Well, I don't reckon anything like that'll happen to us. Anyroad, let's get that certificate first.'

Concentrating after that wasn't easy for Alice and she wondered if, after all, she was up to the work she'd planned to do. A glance at Jan, with her head bent over her books, told her that if Jan could, then she could.

Similar in age, Jan was as tall as Edith, but missed out on being called beautiful because of her hooked nose – 'I take after me dad, with this conk,' she'd told Alice when they'd first met. And that had sealed their path to getting along well as they had both giggled. Jan, she'd found, often made fun of herself. She had the kindest blue eyes that always seemed to be twinkling with fun so you never knew when she was being serious, and lovely golden hair. All far outshone her crooked nose and made her an altogether nice-looking young woman who was easy to love.

With study over, they had a briefing with Miss Tenby, the Red Cross director for the north-west.

'Now, then, girls. Your final exam is very near, and we are needing to know the areas you would prefer to work in. Nothing will be set in stone. If you are found to be more suited to something different to what you choose, then you will be approached and transfers can be arranged, but a starting point is what we are after.'

After Jan had said what she wanted to do, Alice felt torn. Part of her wanted to do the same, and a big part of her hoped that in doing so, if Gerald went to war, then she would be working close to him, but she was torn as always by the tug of her family on her emotions. 'Ambulance driver, locally, or wherever I am needed, for me, Miss Tenby.'

'Excellent, I will arrange for practical experience for each of you in your chosen fields ... Let's hope that Mr Chamberlain wins the day, and a peace treaty is agreed upon, then none of us will be needed for anything more than to be on standby at sporting events. Good day, girls, well done. I'm very proud of you both.'

Alice knew this wasn't the thinking of Gerald, or Philip. Both felt we had to beat Hitler to preserve our country and our freedom as we knew it.

Jan interrupted her thoughts: 'What do you think, Alice?'

'I think I need a cup of tea. And then, as we've been let out early, I need to go to see a friend I made when Harry was taken into hospital. I want to put something to her. She's lonely and I may need help, as we have to be prepared and I have young Joey to think about.'

'Me too — the tea, that is, but I meant about the peace thing. I don't want Chamberlain to succeed. Me dad says they should put Churchill in charge, he's the only one capable of getting the job done.'

Alice nodded. She didn't want to get into a discussion about politics, she knew very little about it. 'Well, whatever happens, it won't be down to us, lass. We just have to get ourselves ready for whatever we're called to do. Me visit is part of that, so I have to get going as I promised to be back home just after three. Love you and leave you. See you next week.'

Outside, Jan got onto her bike, and waved like mad as she peddled away. Alice smiled. Jan was all you would want by your side in a crisis, and she knew their friendship was deepening.

Heather was pleased to see her. 'Alice, my dear!'

The hug was a motherly one that brought a lump to Alice's throat as memories of her ma came flooding back to her. Not that her ma had ever been rounded as Heather was, always slim; the last hug they'd had together, her ma had been like a stick as cancer had ravaged her body. A lot to cope with for the thirteen-year-old she'd been at the time. But it was the kind of love that she felt from Heather that was similar, even though it was only a few weeks since their first meeting.

'How have you been, Heather? I have thought about you often.'

'Eeh, lass, it's hard without my Harold, and lonely. Come on in. How lovely of you to keep your promise to visit me.'

The little terraced house in Sharrow Grove, about a mile and half from where Alice lived, had a welcoming frontage. Its small front garden was surrounded by a two-foot-high wall and planted round the edge of the paved centre with small shrubs that still gave off a nice scent. The windows were draped with pristine white net curtains and when she stepped inside, the homely feel after her own very modern home once more gave her the feeling of being back in time.

'This is lovely, Heather.'

'Ta, lass. Everything shines like this as I polish it over and over – anything to keep me from sitting in me chair moping.'

'Have you friends nearby?'

'Aye, I have, and they've been good, but sometimes I have the urge to do something different. Eeh, I wish me and Harold had been lucky enough to have kids.'

Alice felt this was her cue and told Heather why she was here. She couldn't believe how Heather jumped at the chance of visiting her and getting to know her brothers.

'That'd be grand, love, ta for thinking about me. I have never said, but I used to teach. It was a good job for me as I was able to help children along their way in life.'

Their conversation flowed after that and the more Alice got to know Heather, the more she knew she would be perfect to call on to sit with Joey if ever the need arose. Now she needed to get her brothers on side, but she didn't think this would be too difficult. She just knew they would love Heather as she did.

Back home, Alice was met by a grinning Gerald who took her straight into a bear hug. 'I've been busy. Not only have I placed box after box in the rooms they were marked to go, but I have a place for Joey to start next term at Arnold.'

'That's a bit rushed, love.'

'Strike whilst the iron is hot, I say. This is important to Joey's future. And in any case, he won't start until January, so that gives us plenty of time to have his uniform made and buy all he needs and for him to get used to the idea.'

'Oh, I don't know.'

'No, and you don't need to. All you need to do is to support me all the way on this. In doing so, you will be paving the way for a real change in the lad's life and helping Joey to come to terms with it.'

'I will. Ta for doing this, Gerald, it means a lot to me. I'll try to put all me doubts to bed and help you to make it work . . . Where's Harry? His car isn't in the drive.'

'He went out just after I came in. He didn't say where, but no doubt he'll be back soon. How did your morning go? Are you ready to perform an operation yet?'

Alice hit him on the shoulder in a playful way as she came out of his arms. 'You daft ha'peth! No, but you are looking at a future ambulance driver.'

After she'd asked umpteen questions on what Edith's new house was like and brought him up to date with all that had happened at the Red Cross, she left him and ran upstairs to change. It seemed to her that all would work out for them if the worst were to happen. She would have something to throw herself into – she would cope.

When she and Gerald came in after a walk around Stanley Park – a carefree, happy hour of throwing bread to the swans and watching them dive for it, admiring the flowering autumn shrubs and the still flowering begonias, and sitting on a bench to just chat – Harry's car sat in the drive. Previously owned by Gerald's father, the car was given to Harry for his eighteenth birthday and was his pride and joy. 'Eeh, I'm glad as Harry's home. I need to tell him all about my visit to Heather. He's a good 'un for getting the lads on me side.'

'I've already charged him with buoying Joey up and keeping him enthused about the new schooling arrangements, so he's going to be busy plotting and planning for us.'

But as they entered, Alice felt her stomach knot with trepidation. Harry wasn't grinning in his usual way as he came down the stairs to greet them.

'Well, it's done. I go for an army medical next week.'

'What? No, lad, no, you're not ready.'

'I am, sis. At least I will be by the time I'm stationed somewhere for me training . . . I have to do this, Alice, lass.'

Alice felt Gerald take hold of her hand and squeeze it as he said, 'I'm not sure you'll pass the medical yet, Harry, but you have my admiration, son. This was courageous of you. You could have hidden behind your health problems for months, but instead you've chosen not to shirk your duty. I'm proud of you.'

'Ta, Gerald . . . Look, Alice, this had to happen sooner or later. All those called up with me are halfway through their training by now. I need to catch up with them. The sergeant I spoke to said that I was showing courage an' all. He looked up me details and said he was surprised I was still there, and that they didn't expect me to call. He said it showed I have character.'

Knowing she was defeated and hoping with all her heart that Harry failed the medical, Alice opened her arms to him. 'Eeh, me lad, I am proud of you, but afraid an' all. I didn't want you to be ill, but, well, it was like a bit of a reprieve, but now . . . Anyroad, I'll support you all I can.'

'Can you start by lending me the money to take Jackie to the flicks tonight? I thought that a good place to tell her.'

Alice laughed out loud. 'How much do you need?'

The moment had passed, but that didn't ease the ache in Alice's heart. This seemed like another giant step towards the unknown – the war they all hoped would never happen. But it was happening and she was feeling the effects of it, right here in her own home, as Harry was going, Gerald was prepared to go and she was getting herself ready to do her bit too.

At the thought of it all a hate for Hitler welled up in her and knew that if he was to walk in here right this moment, she would spit in his face.

But despite this thought, she forced a smile onto her face and put a jolly tone into her voice. 'Right, well, we've a wedding next week, but the week after that we'll have a party to send you off and to celebrate yours and Jackie's engagement.'

Harry put an arm around her shoulder. 'You're the best sis ever, Alice. I knaw I have me duty to do, and I'm willing – but it's been hard to face it, so I needed to get on with it, to put it all in place. Thinking about it was driving me mad and breaking me heart to knaw that it will mean me being apart from Jackie and all of you. But now, you're making me feel like a hero already . . . Only, well, it depends when I go, but if it's soon, I will be home after me initial training till I'm posted, so we can have a party then, eh?'

Alice nodded, then turned into his hug. 'You've always been me hero, lad.'

Of her three brothers, Harry had been the quiet, clever and yet nervous one. Billy the champion of them all, wading in to try to save or protect them whenever their da had a violent flare-up, and Joey the studious, artistic type. She loved them all dearly, and yes, they were all her heroes.

EIGHT

Marg

Marg sat close to Clive on the bench seat of his car. Most of the time he had his hand on her knee as they chatted about this and that. Her mind was at rest over Gran as Alice was looking after her until Jackie came home from work, and Jackie had assured her she'd be fine with Gran on her own overnight.

The journey had gone so well. They'd been travelling for about seven hours, stopping a couple of times to refuel and to eat. The roads had been busy at times, but Clive had said that was usual for a Friday.

Marg hadn't often seen the sleek black car Clive had picked her up in as he usually drove a small green car, but this one he seemed very proud to tell her was an Austin Cambridge, with a top speed of sixty miles per hour. Which meant nothing to her. She only knew it was comfortable and not too noisy and appeared to go very fast, which she loved on the open roads that didn't seem so busy with traffic.

'We're coming into the outskirts of London soon, darling. Once we do, I don't know how long it will take us to get across to the East End, and my maps are not good at telling me. So, I've been thinking of a plan. I think if we check into the first decent hotel we see, then in the morning we get a taxi to take us to pick the ladies up and bring them back to the hotel.'

Marg just nodded. As they drove deeper into London, she was in awe of everything around her. The streets seemed packed with vehicles, from cars to vans to buses. The noise was horrendous as hooters were going off ten to the dozen and people were shouting and everything was moving at a snail's pace.

Even the people looked different. They all looked like models to her. The ladies fashionably dressed and the men looking like they were going to a wedding in their dark suits – many wearing a flower in their buttonhole. Most swung a walking cane or had one hooked over their arm. And all looked as though they had somewhere important to go, and as if they were very rich.

'Ah, I can see one ahead, and it has a sign for a car park. I expect that is underneath it.'

When Marg looked along the tall, crowded buildings and caught sight of the hotel that he meant, she could only say, 'Eeh, Clive, that looks posh.'

'No, it's an ordinary hotel, nothing plush, don't worry – not that you have any reason to, darling, wherever I take you.'

The hotel was like walking into a film set. Everything was red and gold. The carpet, the curtains, the cushions that sat on deep red sofas. It was beautiful.

'Good evening, sir, double room for you and madam?'

Clive hesitated and looked at her. Marg felt trapped. She knew it was wrong and yet was scared to leave Clive's side. She nodded.

The gentleman coughed. To Marg, he was condemning her for being a hussy. She tucked her left hand into her pocket, glad that she had worn the lovely coat that she'd bought at the church Christmas fayre, which Edith had taken her to. Chocolate brown, it hung to her thighs and had a huge collar. The style was flared which gave the option of snuggling it around you, or, if left to hang loose, looked very sophisticated.

'This way, sir. The porter will fetch any bags you have.'

With every word he uttered, Marg felt more and more out of her depth.

As if sensing this, when they reached the top of the second flight of stairs, Clive turned and took her hand. He squeezed it in his huge one, but she didn't feel reassured.

Once in the bedroom, all she saw was the huge bed draped in a cream silk.

As soon as the door closed on the gentleman, she was in Clive's arms. He looked into her eyes. 'Don't worry, darling. I'll sleep in the armchair. I'm just glad you consented to stay with me as I didn't want you out of my sight.'

'Eeh, Clive, no, it's all right ... In one week, we'll be wed ... I – I, oh, Clive.'

His lips came down onto hers, his arms enclosed her, pulling her into his body. She could feel his desire, matched it with her own as the feeling she'd had many a time washed over her.

Clive pulled abruptly away. 'I – I'm sorry, Marg, forgive me.'

A knock on the door prevented her answering. Clive's colour drained. Marg giggled. 'Go through there, I don't know where it leads, lad, but you can't answer the door looking like that!'

He grinned as he disappeared.

The lad at the door shuffled Clive's case and her bag through to her and then stood there. Marg didn't know what to do.

A calmer, and in control, Clive reappeared with his wallet in his hand. The lad gratefully took what he was offered and left.

As soon as the door closed, they burst out laughing.

'By, I felt like a naughty girl, caught red-handed. But eeh, with this laughing, I need to pee.'

'The bathroom's through there, love.'

When she came out, Clive was sitting in the window. She crossed the room and sat in the chair next to his. They were facing the bed which loomed in Marg's eyes as the place where she would become Clive's. What was a week? She stretched out her hand. When he took it, he looked into her eyes and asked, 'Are you sure, Marg?'

'I am, lad. I've never been surer of anything in me life. I love you, Clive, more than anything in the world.'

'Oh, Marg.'

Unsure of how it happened that they had risen and were in each other's arms, Marg thrilled at Clive's kisses, at him undoing her blouse, and cried out when he gently cupped her breast.

Still naive as to how everything should happen, she let Clive take the lead. And as she was willingly guided by him, she felt all fear leave her at this being her first time and allowed herself to relax, to drink in the strange, but wonderful feelings that were zinging through her.

She loved Clive and wanted more than anything to be his wife, to be his completely. Which way around that happened no longer mattered.

'I love you, my darling, Marg. You've opened my life up again, you're so beautiful.'

Marg had never felt beautiful, but at this moment, she did. Her freckled skin seemed to take on a glow of its own as the last of her garments fell to the floor. Never did she think she would stand naked and have a man look at her proclaiming she was beautiful.

As Clive took off his clothes, his eyes never left her. When he stood naked in front of her, she thought him beautiful too. But then had no time to think, only to drown in his love of her as he scooped her up and laid her gently on the bed.

The feel of his skin against hers took away any last shred of doubt. She was ready. Ready to give herself to her man.

When it happened, she tensed, shocked at how uncomfortable it was, but Clive gently stroked her hair, his eyes deeply transfixed into hers, his lips saying her name, his movement slow, caressing, taking her to a place where there was only joy and wonderment in the love that he was giving her, and in the ecstasy of being his.

She heard her voice calling his name, heard his cries join hers and she was lost – lost to wave after wave of exquisite sensations she thought she would die from. When they subsided, she was being held in a cradle of love.

But then fear trembled through her as she heard a sob. Clive, her Clive, was crying as he released himself from her and lay down beside her.

Reaching for him, she held his hand. 'I'm sorry ... I – I ...'

Clive shot up. 'No, my darling, never be sorry. I have never experienced anything like that. It took my breath away and released the last of my pent-up emotions. I wasn't crying out of sorrow, but joy that I could be privileged to have such ... such ... I just don't know how to describe it.'

Marg thought this strange. Hadn't it happened like that for him and his first wife? But she said nothing, just went into his arms and lay peacefully with him. Clive was truly her man, and that was all that mattered.

By the time they sat in the taxi the next morning, they'd made love twice more and to Marg, it all seemed so natural – not sinful as they had always been taught. Nothing that wonderful could be a sin, could it?

These thoughts didn't stay long with her. No guilt entered her, only peace and a feeling of being safe.

'It's going to take a while as I've asked the driver to take us past Buckingham Palace, darling.'

'Eeh, Clive.' She couldn't say any more. Never in her wildest dreams did she think she would see where the King and Queen lived. But suddenly it was there and looking just like the pictures she'd seen of it, only much, much bigger.

Her heart beat strongly against her chest. 'By, lad, that'd house the whole of Blackpool. It's grand.'

She took it all in, the way the sun glinted on the windows and lit up its light grey bricks. The balcony, where she could imagine the King and Queen sitting in the evening sun. And the huge monument outside the gates, which Clive told her commemorated the reign of Queen Victoria.

'It's grand, just grand. I'll never forget this day, Clive.' She looked at him and wanted to say thank you for everything. But she knew he read that in her eyes as she saw in his how much it all meant to him too.

The streets of Poplar, where the three evacuated kids had lived, reminded Marg so much of home. 'By, this could be any street in Blackpool.'

'Mmm, though I've never seen this many women out cleaning their front steps. I think they've heard that us northerners are on our way and want to see if we look human.'

Marg laughed. As she did, she caught the eye of a young woman brushing invisible dirt into the gutter. Impulsively, she waved. The woman smiled and waved back. 'See, they're just the same as us. And that makes me feel even more pity for them having to send their kids away. In our street the kids are out playing and being a nuisance, but here, there ain't a kid in sight.'

When they pulled up outside one of the terraced houses, a woman came over to them.

'Miss, yer ain't seen me little Freda, 'ave yer? She's five and 'as long 'air. 'Ere, I've a photo of 'er.'

Marg took the photo, creased from being in the woman's pocket and looking like it had been handled many times, it showed a little girl of about seven with a lovely cheeky grin.

'No, sorry, lass. Was she evacuated to Blackpool?'

'Yes. She went with Peggy's kid, Ben. And them twins from across the road. Only I've never 'eard from 'er.'

The woman gave a small sob.

Marg wanted to take her in her arms. Small and dainty like Alice, her body trembled. 'Everyone else 'as 'eard from their kids, but not me and I can't find anything out.'

'Look, me friend works as a teacher and has a lot of the kids in her school. I'll ask her, and if she don't know, her ma-in-law might or could find out as she works for the WRVS. Give me your address and I'll write to you, I promise.'

The woman disappeared into the house she'd been sweeping the pavement in front of. Clive took Marg's arm. 'Darling, I think it's been said to you before that you can't take the world's trouble on your own shoulders ... but I love you for it. That was a very kind thing to do.'

'Are yer 'ere for us, mate?'

The voice interrupted Marg's reply. She swivelled her head to look in its direction. A woman not much younger than her gran, and similar in her shrunken height and bent shoulders, stood on the pavement, her arms folded. 'Yer ain't come in a taxi all the way from Blackpool, 'ave yer?'

Marg smiled. 'No. Only from the hotel we stayed at. Eeh, you look like me gran.'

The woman smiled a toothy grin. 'I'm Minnie. And yer talk funny, girl, but me Mandy warned me of that in her letter. Though I'm grateful to yer all, as she tells me yer all smashers and she and me little Alf love yer.'

'Aw, well, we love them an' all.'

Without warning, Minnie opened her mouth and hollered, 'Peggy! Peggy, girl, they're 'ere,' making Marg jump.

A tall, slim, strikingly beautiful woman came out of a door opposite. She had the same ginger hair that Ben had, and it frizzed as Marg's own did, making it appear like a halo. She smiled and waved to Mandy and Alf's granny, then bent down and pulled a large bag through her door. Clive got out of the taxi and dashed over to help her.

'That your 'usband, girl?'

'Not till next week, and you're invited to the wedding, Minnie.'

'Ta, mate. Well, there's a turn-up.' Her voice rose again. 'Did yer 'ear that, you lot? I'm going to a wedding. 'Old on, I'll just go and get me glad rags, as I didn't put anything such as wedding finery in me bag.'

Before Marg knew what was happening, Minnie had left and was unlocking her door. But she had no time to do anything about it as Freda's ma came back to her. ''Ere yer are, luv. Ta for this. I've 'ad me 'eart broken with me nipper being taken from me. But if I could 'ear from her, it would mean the world.'

'Aw, I'm sorry for you, lass. I'll do me best, I promise. What's her surname, eh?'

'Freda Parkin. Will yer write if yer find 'er or not, eh?'

'I will, I promise.'

Clive was back by her side and must have heard this. 'Not all of the children were brought to Blackpool. But we will try to find your child for you, Mrs Parkin.'

'Lil, call me Lil.'

Marg reached out and took Lil's hand. 'Try not to worry, lass. We'll do our best.'

A tear plopped onto Lil's cheek. 'I've been so scared that she might catch the polio.'

'No other children have gone down with it, so don't worry about that. My friend's brothers were playing with Ben just before he went down with it, and they're fine.'

Lil nodded her head. 'Ta, luv.'

Marg wanted to hold Lil and never let her go, she seemed so vulnerable – her broken heart visible in her eyes and her haggard look, which was making her appear a lot older than Marg suspected she was.

'Well! Are we going, then? Get in, Peggy, luv. We've a long journey ahead of us.'

Once they were settled in the back with Minnie and Peggy and their luggage was stored safely in the boot box, Marg told them, 'You're right there, Minnie, we have got a long way to go. It'll be gone eight tonight when we get back.'

'Well, I 'ope yer've got a comfy car as me back always aches if I sit for a long time.'

Marg just smiled at this. She looked over at Peggy, who hadn't spoken yet and had her head down. 'Are you all right, Peggy, lass?'

Peggy looked up. Her eyes, a light blue, were huge. 'Yes, ta.'

Marg didn't know what to say to her to comfort and relax her. But it was Peggy who started the conversation. ''Ave yer seen me lad?'

'No. Me friend, who's been caring for them, has.'

'What's she like? 'As she treated them good? Is she clean in 'er 'ouse?'

Marg felt affronted at this for a moment. *What do they think, that us northerners are all dirty or something?* But she just nodded. 'You could eat your dinner off her floor, lass.'

'So, 'ow did me little Ben get this polio then?'

'I don't know, but it were nothing to do with Edith.'

'Peggy, girl. Don't go and put the girl's back up before she's 'ad a chance to get to know us. We want to be welcomed, not shunned, but that's what'll 'appen if yer carry on like this, luv.'

'I'm sorry. What did yer say yer name was?'

'Marg, short for Margaret. Edith, me friend, did well to take yer kids in. Her man, Philip, was called to duty the minute war was announced and is away most of the time. He does something in the War Office. And she copes on her own. She's a teacher an' all and makes sure all the evacuees are treated right at school. She got your Ben and little Alf into the Catholic school when they'd been put into the Church of England one.'

Peggy smiled. 'It sounds like I owe Edith a debt, then, when I were thinking she were the cause of all this.'

Marg felt exasperated, but Minnie saved the day. 'I told yer you were being daft. Our Mandy wrote saying 'ow 'appy they all were, and Ben wrote the same to you. So, stop this now, and be grateful that our kids were sent to someone as caring as Edith and 'ad Marg looking out for them too.'

'And me other friend, Alice. We all love all three of your children. All of us are breaking our hearts over what's happened to little Ben and at the thought of losing him.'

'He's a lovely boy, me Ben. 'E takes after his dad ... Anyway, I'm sorry. I shouldn't 'ave come across all critical like that.'

'Eeh, lass, don't worry. If anyone had taken me sister Jackie from me, I'd never rest, and would never believe they could love her in the way that I do or take care of her.'

A sudden pain cut into Marg's heart as it hit her that with all the talk of young women being needed to do their bit, she might be separated from Jackie! The thought gave her an insight into how these women felt. She leant forward and took their hands. 'I'm sorry you've been through what you have, and about all that you had to face an' all, Peggy. It must have been bad for you. But I can promise you, you'll get a warm welcome in Blackpool and we'll all look after you. You're going to be staying with me friend Alice, Peggy. Her husband's a doctor and'll be able to answer all your questions.'

Both smiled back at her.

'And you, Minnie, will be staying with Edith and your twins. They're coming out of hospital today and you'll all be in Edith's new house.'

'New 'ouse? It ain't posh, is it?'

'It is, Minnie, but Edith ain't. Look, on the way home, I'll tell you all about me friends and me. I know you Cockneys have it hard, but what we've been through will make your hair curl.'

Minnie let out a cackling laugh. 'We'll 'ave a competition, girl, north versus south in the 'ardship stakes, eh?'

All three laughed out loud at this, and Marg thought she'd easily grow to love Minnie, as she was the London version of how her gran used to be. *Eeh, I wonder how they'll get on?*

Releasing their hands, and sitting back in her seat, Marg allowed herself a minute to think of Gran. Gran's lovely smiling face came to her, and it felt as if she was sitting beside her. *Eeh, Gran, I'm bringing someone who's more than a match for you on your good days, love.*

With this, she smiled to herself and suddenly, for all the glitz of London with its special palace, she couldn't wait to get home to lovely Blackpool.

NINE

Edith

Edith was on tenterhooks. There was still so much to do. Why did they think they could move into a new house and have it all ready and straight for guests in two days?

Thank goodness they'd decided at the last minute to keep the guest bedroom furniture as she would have had no chance to furnish it as she'd planned to do.

But as she looked around it, she was quite pleased with the effect of the few tweaks she'd made. A new candle-wick bedspread in a lovely cream complemented the purple silk eiderdown that sat on top of the double bed. And the lilac duchess set looked lovely on the highly polished dressing table. She'd picked these colours on her shopping trip yesterday to complement the square carpet, which had a cream background with purple and lilac flowers in its centre and covered almost all of the floor, leaving polished floorboards at the edge. With cream curtains, the final picture it all made was very welcoming and cosy.

A clatter from the next room had her running to see if Philip was all right.

He stood surrounded by pieces of Mandy's bed.

'It went together easily when we bought it, now nothing seems to fit. The nuts and bolts won't go through the holes in the bedstead to fix it to the frame.' His face was a picture of frustration.

Edith smiled. 'I think we need a pot of tea, love.'

'You're right. Though how are we going to get everything done in time?'

'We've at least three hours before we collect the twins and six maybe seven hours before their gran arrives. We will. I just think we're panicking. We haven't even eaten breakfast!'

'But—'

A voice calling up from downstairs interrupted whatever Philip was going to say and filled Edith with relief.

'Reinforcement has arrived!'

'Gerald!'

As they hurried out towards the stairs, Philip had the biggest smile on his face. And that widened when they got to the top of the stairs and saw five faces grinning up at them.

'Eeh, Alice! You're all here! By, we need you, lass. We're in a right pickle.'

'Well, before we start, we've brought bacon butties. I'm thinking you wouldn't have stopped to have breakfast.'

Edith laughed. 'No, I can't eat first thing in the mornings other than a biscuit. But the queasiness has gone now, and I could eat a dozen butties!'

'Ha, you're only getting one. No eating for two, or you'll get fat.'

They all laughed at Gerald, who'd put his best 'doctor' voice on to say this.

Hugs followed as Edith took Alice and then Harry, then Billy, then Joey, and finally Gerald into her arms.

'Ta for coming. I can't tell you what a pickle we're in. Most jobs need two and Philip won't let me lift a cup hardly.'

Alice was already opening the two biscuit tins she'd brought with her. Each released a delicious smell of bacon.

'I'll put the kettle on.'

'Ta, Philip, love. There speaks a man who'd been so cosseted he didn't have clue how to fill a kettle!'

This brought more laughter and Edith felt herself feeling happy again after all the anxiety.

'I'm not staying, Edith. That's if you can manage without me.'

'Aye, we can, Harry. I can guess where you're going, lad.'

'I'm worried about Jackie. She's never been left on her own all night with her gran before. She might need a hand. But I thought I'd just come and have me breakfast and see your new house.'

'Well, take yourself on a tour while we get sorted. We love it. And, well, I know you're used to space now, but I ain't, and it still feels like a mansion to me after me terraced in Whittaker Avenue.'

Harry laughed. 'Ha! I didn't think you and Marg would be outdone for long.'

'Don't get cheeky, lad, you're not too big to have a clip around the ear.'

Harry grinned at her. Edith felt a jolt in her heart as he did. The thought of him going to war frightened her. For all his eighteen years he was still a kid – she'd always looked on him, Billy and Joey as her own brothers. With this, Albert, her own tragic brother came to mind, and she raised her eyes. *Eeh, lad, I wish you weren't gone, but I'm glad that I'm not facing seeing you off to war.*

'Are you all right, Edith, lass?'

'Aye. I just had a fleeting visit from Albert. It happens when I least expect it.' They were in the kitchen on their own now as the other two lads had followed Harry, and Philip and Gerald had gone through to the sitting room. Gerald had brought two newspapers with him, and Edith thought that no doubt they were deep into reading the latest on the war front.

She sighed.

'Eeh, lass, it happens out of the blue, doesn't it? Catches you unawares, and knocks you back for a mo. I'm the same. Suddenly, me ma's there, or me da ... or, well, I remember the few fleeting moments I had cradling little Gerald.'

Edith regretted saying anything now. The pain on Alice's face cut her in two. She put her arm around her. 'Eeh, Alice, we've been through the mill, lass.' She almost said, *but our future looks better*, but it didn't, not really. It loomed like an unknown horror of things that might happen.

'Anyroad. I didn't come here to get us all gloomy, lass. The kettle's boiled now. Let's make the tea and take the butties through, they're still warm.'

The whistling of the kettle and it spurting water everywhere had Edith sighing. 'He's overfilled it again! Eeh, Philip does his best, but domesticated he ain't.'

Alice laughed as she disappeared through the door juggling a plate piled high with butties in one hand and a pile of small plates in the other.

The butties were delicious, swilled down with the hot tea. The chatter started off light, but Harry set the tone lower by asking if there was any war news in the paper.

Gerald answered. 'Yes, but not good. The British forces were manning the border while the French advanced into Germany, but they've been forced back and have retreated, they're now behind the Maginot Line.'

'Well, don't worry, Harry, when you get there, the Germans will take one look at you and run for their lives.'

This from Billy lightened the mood that had seemed to come over them all at hearing the news.

'Aye, your face'll be enough to scare them, won't it, Billy?'

Harry threw a cushion at Joey and Billy, who were a bundle of giggles now. Edith mockingly told them off. 'You're here to help, lads, not mess up the rooms me and Philip have sorted!'

Billy got up and came to her. Putting his arms around her neck, he kissed her cheek. 'Sorry, Edith, but you knaw, cushions are made to be thrown.' As he released her, he said, 'Anyroad, Harry were practising throwing hand grenades, but with his shot, he'll blow up half of our blooming army!'

Although this brought more laughter, and Edith thought that this British spirit that they all seemed to have of making a joke out of everything would stand them in good stead over the coming months, she didn't miss the shadow that passed over Alice's face.

'Right. No more talk of war. We've to talk of who is going to do what!'

They decided that whilst she and Alice emptied boxes and put things away, the two men would build the beds for the twins, and Billy and Joey would empty Philip's car of the last remaining things shoved in on the back seat just before they left Whittaker Avenue.

'Was it a wrench to leave, Edith?'

'Aye, more than I thought it would be, love. I hope Marg don't feel bad when she gets home and sees me empty house.'

'She'll be fine. She'll be on cloud nine after a night away with her man before she's wed, eeh, the hussy.'

Edith burst out laughing, but then it struck her . . . 'You don't reckon . . . ?'

'Aye, I do. I think Clive got that impatient that he dragged her away and seduced her.'

'Eeh, Alice. Don't, you'll have me blushing when I see her with thinking that. Marg wouldn't, would she?'

'Wouldn't you, with only a week to go?'

They giggled at this, but Edith tried to put it out of her mind for fear she'd say something without thinking when she saw Marg later today. The thought did come to her that if it had happened, she hoped with all her heart it was as good for Marg as it was for herself, and she guessed for Alice too, as she was so happy with her Gerald. *Eeh, I like to think how well we lasses have all done. We landed on our feet no matter what was thrown at us.*

★   ★   ★

They'd got on with all that had to be done so well that there was only one bag to be emptied by the time Edith and Philip had to get ready to go to the hospital.

'Leave that to me, Edith, lass, I can see it's only towels. I take it they'll go into the airing cupboard in the bathroom?'

'Aye, ta, Alice.'

'And then we'll set to and prepare lunch for when you get back. But we'll leave, we won't stay to eat with you. The twins will be overwhelmed as it is with so much to take in and their excitement of their gran on the way.'

'Will you come back later when Marg arrives, or has she to take Ben's mum around to yours?'

'I reckon it best we come here. It'll help Peggy if she meets us with the twins and sees how we all are together. I hope it's all right to call her Peggy, seeing as how the kids call her Aunty Peggy.'

'I should think so. I bet she ain't a lot older than us, and by all I hear, them Cockneys from the East End have it just as bad as we've had it, so I reckon she'll just be an ordinary lass with no airs and graces.'

At the hospital Edith was taken aback to enter the front door and see Mandy and Alf sitting in the foyer with a little paper carrier bag each. They both jumped up, leaving the nurse who'd been with them, and ran screaming with joy towards Edith and Philip.

With her arms wrapped around Mandy, and Alf now having his around her waist, Edith had mixed emotions. Such happiness at having them back, but sadness that there were only two, not three.

'I'll go up and peep at Ben. Edith, you wait here, then when I come down, I'll get these two into the car while you go up.'

'Ta, love. Have you got your message to him?'

Philip nodded. She could see he was near to tears. They had sat yesterday evening and written a few messages to hold up at the window of the ward where Ben was in isolation.

Philip had put encouraging words. His handling of children – a natural talent but developed through his years of teaching – gave him a way with words that they understood and related to. He'd drawn pictures, too, that he hoped would make Ben smile. Edith hadn't told him that she didn't think that he could yet.

Her own told of her love for him. While writing it the thought had come to her, what a terrible thing Ben's condition was for any parent to have to take on board. She only hoped that Peggy didn't blame her and Philip.

By the time evening came, Alice and Gerald were back, this time without the boys. They thought it would be too overwhelming for Peggy to meet them all at once. Alice was just as nervous as Edith, but this left her when Clive pulled up at seven that evening, and the lovely Peggy greeted Edith with a hug and a thank you for looking after her child and helping him to write to her. And then hugged Alice and thanked her for putting her up. But when she was introduced to Gerald, her eyes filled with tears as she thanked him for caring for Ben and for going to all the trouble to find a special unit in a hospital in London to take him. 'I can easily get to the St Bede's polio unit from where I live. I can't thank you enough.'

Gerald took the hand she offered and then you could see the surprise on her face as he hugged her.

'There yer are, Peggy, girl, yer don't get that down the East End. The doctors there like to see the colour of yer money before they even speak to yer. And only touch yer if they 'ave to. What I've seen so far of these northerners, they ain't a bad lot, girl.'

Minnie, as the twins' granny was introduced to Edith by Marg, went straight into Edith's heart with a hug and a lovely smile that creased her face with lines, saying, 'Come 'ere, girl, let me give yer a Londoner's hug. I can't thank yer enough for looking after the two apples of me eye. And like Peggy, I'm grateful for yer getting them to write. A lot 'aven't 'eard from their kids, one of them Marg will tell yer about.'

Minnie had hardly come out of the hug with Edith when Mandy dashed at her, almost knocking her over and overcome with emotion, but Alf looked at her and asked, ''Ave yer brought me mum, Granny?'

Minnie looked heavenward. 'She sends her love, me little darlin', and says she'll come on the train one day. Now, give Granny a hug and kiss. I've missed yer, big boy.'

''Ave I grown, Granny?'

'Yer 'ave, sunshine, but you're still me little darlin'.'

'And I am, aren't I, Granny?'

Minnie cuddled them both to her. Edith could see that for all her tough exterior tears glistened in her eyes. 'Come on, me little sweethearts. Let Granny get a hug from these handsome men. I don't often get the chance.'

Mandy and Alf giggled at this, and Marg, who'd at last been able to get near to Edith and Alice, said as she cuddled them, 'Eeh, me lasses, Minnie has so many ways of me gran.'

'Well, that's good. Should keep us on our toes then ... So, how did your naughty night away go?'

Edith regretted saying it, as both Marg and Clive blushed.

Minnie saved the moment as she greeted Philip. 'Well, now, I 'ear yer already doing yer bit, son. I'm very proud to stay in the home of someone like you.' She looked around her. 'And it's lovely. Ta for 'aving me. Now, what about a cap of Rosie Lee, eh?'

They all laughed as they'd been prepared for this by Mandy, and yet hadn't really expected to hear Minnie say it, nor for her to pronounce a cup like a cap as this conjured up a picture that nearly undid them all.

The moment relaxed into giggles, as they all went upstairs so that the children could show their granny her bedroom. 'You've got a double bed, Granny, so if me and Alf want to, we can come and get in with yer.'

'We'll see about that, darlin'. Granny needs her sleep.'

'In the mornings then before we go to school.'

'All right, but don't go getting it into yer 'eads that yer can run me ragged. I've got old bones, yer know ... Now, where's the blooming lav? Granny's dying for a pee.'

Edith smiled at Marg. 'I expect you all are. The children will show you where to go, you have a choice of two as we have a downstairs lav an' all. Me and Alice will make that Rosie Lee, while you sort yourselves out.'

This made them laugh again. Edith had heard of rhyming slang and heard it used occasionally by the children, and especially by one of the evacuees she taught. It was sometimes difficult to interpret what the boy was saying but she had made her mind up to learn and not to stump his heritage. Now, she thought that what she'd picked up would stand her in good stead with Minnie.

While they were having their cup of tea, Edith asked Marg about the mother Minnie had mentioned who didn't know where her child was.

'Eeh, I've never heard that name, but the twins'll know if she was brought here or dropped off at another station on the way. I'll talk to Sue an' all. She and Tom are coming tomorrow. I wouldn't let them come before everything was done. Ha, Sue would have taken over directing operations and we wouldn't have had a say in where everything went.'

Philip smiled a wry smile. He knew his parents – at least his mother – better than anyone, and still couldn't get over how Edith had won her around. His father had been easy to win over. Owner of the biscuit factory and her old boss when she worked there for six years, he never spoke a word to her in that time, but when she turned up as his son's intended, she'd found him adorable, and as broad Lancashire as the rest of them in his speech.

'One thing Mother is good at, though, darling, is knowing everything. She will track this little girl down if she's in Blackpool, that's for sure.'

Minnie saying that she was hungry broke the conversation up. Edith was already learning that Minnie was very blunt and didn't beat around the bush when she wanted something. But an idea had formed in her mind. When she was back at school, she would check with all the evacuees in her class if they had written to their family and, if not, encourage them to. She'd also ask the head about making it something each class did.

'Mandy put in 'er letter about the fish 'n' chips you eat up 'ere. That's something I'd like to do. Made me mouth water, she did.'

'They're lovely, Granny, but yer have to have them out of newspaper and sitting on the prom. Mind, yer have to watch the seagulls, bleedin' things'll pinch them soon as look at yer.'

There was a stunned silence. Edith didn't know what to do. Normally, either she or Philip would correct Mandy for swearing, but it felt now as if it wasn't their place. But would Minnie see anything wrong in it?

She needn't have worried.

'Mandy! I hope yer 'aven't been using that language, my girl.'

'Sorry, Granny, I didn't mean to.'

'See that yer don't use it again. Now, we'll forget it for now as we won't spoil us being together after a long time apart with tellings-off. But yer made yer granny laugh when yer described what happened when the seagull nicked your chips, darlin'.'

Mandy was smiling again, and Edith could see that Philip was relieved that their granny had the same values as they did where the use of such language was concerned.

All in all, she felt relaxed and happy about this visit, but one worry niggled at her – would Minnie want to take the twins home with her? The thought saddened her, and she hoped with all her heart that it didn't happen.

105

TEN

Marg

There was a frenzy of excitement as they all gathered for Marg's wedding the next Saturday morning. All were crowded into Marg's living room – Edith, who was to be the matron of honour, and Alice, who, as a married woman, still had to be called a matron of honour, but who would leave all the duties to Edith as she had done the job at Edith's wedding. Jackie and Mandy, who were to be bridesmaids, Clive's lads, George and Carl, who were her page boys and Gran, who sat by the fire, with her hair – what little she had left of it – curled around pipe clips, and in her dressing gown. Marg had thought it best to bath her early and let her rest like this, then to dress her at the last minute. The children were around her as usual and she was keeping them laughing with her tales.

Marg, Edith, Alice and Jackie were also in their dressing gowns. Everyone had their make-up on and their hair done – Marg was particularly pleased with hers as she, too, had kept it in pipe clips for most of the morning and it had undone into lovely soft curls rather than her usual frizz.

And now the time had come for them to get dressed, but Marg had one last thing she wanted to do.

She went into the kitchen where the kettle was boiling, and poured the hot water onto the prepared mugs. 'Edith, Alice, Jackie, come and get it.'

When they came through the kitchen door, Marg handed them a mug each.

'Cocoa? Eeh, Marg, what're you thinking? Have we time for this?'

'Follow me, Alice, and you'll find out.'

Outside, she plonked herself down on the step and patted the places each side of her. Alice and Edith giggled as they sat beside her. Jackie perched on the chair that had stood outside all night from when Gran had sat out for a while.

'Eeh, Marg, the Halfpenny Girls, eh?'

'Aye, Alice. We'll always be that. No matter that you and Edith have left here, and now I'll be leaving today and Jackie and Gran tomorrow. This place – our growing-up place – will be etched into our hearts forever.'

They put their mugs down in front of them and held hands. Each had a story engraved into the fabric of this street. Each had a lot to go through, as everyone did in the near future, but Marg knew that no matter what, she'd always have Alice and Edith. 'I just wanted to sit like this with you for the last time before I go to me new life.'

Edith put her head on Marg's shoulder. 'I'm going to miss doing this, Marg. The three of us sitting on the step together. But I don't regret leaving, even if it is only a few days that I've been away. I think in me heart, I've grown away from it. Just as you two have.'

Marg couldn't deny this. The only thing she was going to miss was sitting on this step with these two.

'Right, come on, lass, let's get ready — you've to get married, you know!'

As they went inside, Marg let Edith and Alice go in first. She caught hold of Jackie's hand. 'Eeh, lass, are you all right with saying goodbye to this place?'

'I am, Marg. It holds a lot of memories, but we'll never leave them behind, and I'm ready. By, how could I not be with the lovely room Clive has earmarked for me, eh? It's that big, I intend to have a lovely chair up there so I can be on me own when I want to. I've saved some money lately and can buy it meself.'

'That'll be grand, lass, though you must never feel that you're in the way. Our home is just that. Ours. Yours, mine, Clive's, Gran's and the boys.'

They hugged.

'Right, lass, let's do this, eh?'

'Aye, let's make an old married woman of you.'

They giggled together and Marg thought how blessed she was to have a sister like Jackie.

They gasped when they saw Marg's wedding dress. Marg had bought it out of the money she'd been given by her da, before she'd been attacked by him for trying to stop him storing contraband goods in the Anderson shelter.

She'd thought it kind and caring of him to install the shelter to protect her, Jackie and Gran if any bombs were dropped on Blackpool, but that hadn't been his intention at all.

Now, as she lifted her arms to help Edith and Alice slip her frock on her, she tried hard not to think of how she came about having such a lovely frock, or of Eric, as she preferred to think of the man that she'd not long ago found out had fathered her. She wanted nothing to spoil her day.

It was already marred by little Ben having left for London with his ma the day before. If the poor little lad hadn't been taken ill, it had been planned that he and Alf were to help Harry, Billy and Joey to look after all the guests and see they all had a seat.

Not that it was to be a big wedding — just her family, in which she included Alice and all of hers and Edith and all of hers, and a few friends from work and from the street. Ada, of course, was one of these and she would take care of Gran.

As the frock slipped effortlessly on, Marg was reminded of what it symbolised. She couldn't believe that tonight she would spend the night in her new home with Clive.

Stopping herself from thinking that she really shouldn't be wearing white, and in particular about what she knew was in store, she didn't quite manage to stop the thrill that zinged through her as memories of last weekend in London persisted to assail her.

'What's that smile for, lass? Eeh, it looked like you thought of something really nice.' Edith winked at Alice. Marg blushed. They'd both been hinting all week, but she hadn't told them. This was something too precious to share, even with these two who were like sisters to her. But she needn't have worried, as both forgot their teasing and gasped as they saw her in her frock.

Simply cut, with a slender line that flared out at the bottom, the frock, made of silk, felt lovely on her. Its square neckline, which she had worried about, was no longer a problem to her as Clive had made her love her freckly skin as much as he did.

With her feet slipped into white slippers and her veil attached to her hair, she felt like a princess.

'Have you got them pearls of mine, Marg, lass?'

'What pearls, Gran?'

'They're in that box under me bed.'

Marg was mystified. She didn't know of a box under Gran's bed.

Gran rose unsteadily.

'Eeh, Gran, I'll help you.' Jackie jumped forward and took Gran's arm. Carl took her other arm and, not to be outdone, George jumped up off his knees and held on to her dressing gown.

'Eeh, me little lads, I can always manage with your help.'

With them gone to look for what Marg thought was a non-existent pearl necklace, Alice did a twirl. 'Eeh, Marg. It was a good idea of yours to use these bridesmaids' frocks again.'

'And you all look lovely, lass.'

Edith wore the cream-coloured frock she'd worn for Alice's wedding, only with a purple cummerbund, and Jackie and Alice wore the rose-coloured frocks they'd worn for Edith's wedding.

'And they still look as fresh as new an' all.'

'Aye, well, I can't get out of the idea of being careful with money. I've never known what it's like to have any.'

'Well, you will now. You need never worry again, lass.'

Marg thought the idea strange to even imagine but looked forward to it. Clive had offered to help her out for a long time, but her pride would only let her accept practical gifts from him – the odd bag of spuds, or some eggs, that sort of thing. But now, as his wife, her life would change for the better in so many ways.

'Alice, love, would you mind going to see where Gran is, please? The cars Clive has ordered will be here soon.' For the first time, Marg felt her tummy fill with butterflies as she said this. Suddenly, it all became real.

When Gran came out of the bedroom, she looked lovely in a lemon frock with a matching jacket, and her little black hat. 'Here you are, lass. I wore these pearls at my wedding, and your ma at hers. Now, you must wear them, and pass them to Jackie for hers.'

Marg stood in wonderment as she gazed at the string of pearls. She'd never seen them before in her life. She looked at Jackie. Jackie had a look of bewilderment that matched her own. 'They weren't under the bed, Marg, but under the seat of that little chair in the corner. I never had an inkling that the lid lifted up. There's some lovely memories in it.'

'By, we were going to chuck it out an' all.'

'Naw, Gran wouldn't have let you. That's the chair she wouldn't go to Clive's without, not the one she sits in by the fireplace. She said so as she lifted the lid.'

'I can't believe it. Eeh, me Gran. Thank goodness the fairies hadn't taken you away with them this morning, or we would never have known.' Marg hugged her gran. 'And you look so lovely.'

A tear escaped from Gran's eye as Edith clasped the pearls around Marg's neck.

As Marg stroked them her ma came into her mind. She was smiling, and Marg knew she wasn't in pain anymore. She smiled back. Then fancied her ma saying, 'Eeh, you've got a good 'un, Marg, be happy.'

Not realising she was speaking aloud, she said, 'I have, and I will, Ma.'

Alice stepped forward. 'Come on, love. Don't dwell too much. It's time to go. I heard the car pull up.'

Marg felt a smile break her lips. The tears faded as she looked around her at Edith and Alice.

At this moment everything was all right for the Halfpenny Girls. Even though everything had changed for them.

She'd been the one who had never wanted anything to change. Now, she could step forward and embrace her new life. And she would be strong no matter what the future held. For no matter where this war took them all nothing could break the bond she, Edith, Alice and her beloved sister Jackie had. It was a bond that would sustain and help them to face all they had to.

ELEVEN

Jackie
Winter 1940

Saying goodbye to Harry when he'd set off to do his initial six weeks' training, earlier than expected, hadn't been a hardship as he was only to travel to Preston and at least they'd let him come home for Christmas – as it happened, they'd had everybody together, even Gerald's parents, Averill and Rod, who'd arrived home from Africa early in December and were now living in their house in the Lake District.

The only one missing had been little Ben, but they had been able to send him lots of presents and had received a card back from him.

The day had been wonderful, and they'd all had a good laugh about them panicking back in September and holding their pretend one, but everyone had good memories of it and especially of Marg's lovely wedding day.

For Jackie and Harry, the six weeks hadn't been like a real parting as getting to see each other had been easy as he'd only been a short train journey away, and besides Christmas, he'd been able to meet her for a blissful hour every two weeks.

Now his training was over, and he was on his way home on leave, before sailing to France to join his regiment, the 2nd Battalion, Lancashire Fusiliers, on the Belgium front.

Jackie's heart thumped in her chest as she waited on the station with Alice for the train to come in, having been given the afternoon off from work. Her thoughts were in a turmoil. How was she to bear parting again when the time came?

She looked across at the platform next to theirs and saw the heartbreak of sobbing women clinging on to their men before they boarded a train to take them to war.

Alice's hand came into hers. She didn't speak, and yet Jackie could hear her silent emotion – touch it almost – and knew it was choking her as her own was.

Next week, Alice was to say goodbye to Gerald, who'd joined the Royal Medical Corps and would leave for training, somewhere in the south of England.

Everything had happened so quickly – the news had been full of the German advance, of casualty lists, of the threat of invasion and it seemed the whole country had mobilised.

Her lovely brother-in-law, Clive, was out on the lifeboats full-time now. His father had come out of retirement and along with one of the old managers, who'd also come out of retirement, was running Clive's rock factory.

Philip was hardly home these days, but Minnie was still with Edith and was such a help to her, and now part of the family as they all loved her and dreaded the day she decided to return to London.

Ben had made great progress since being in the special unit, and Peggy wrote or telephoned often to update them.

Despite it all, Marg was the happiest Jackie had ever seen her, as was Gran, who loved her nurse and her little flat, as she called her room in her lucid moments – sadly, they were few and far between now, but it helped to see how content she was.

'Eeh, Alice, how did everything change in such a short time?'

Alice's arm came around her. Her eyes were still fixed on the heartbreak happening on the next platform. Her simple reply of, 'We'll cope, lass,' didn't hold any conviction.

'I – I have sommat to share with you, Alice. I haven't told Marg . . . I had a strange telephone call at work.'

Alice turned to look at her. 'What do you mean, strange?'

'Well, it was a woman. She didn't give a name but said she was attached to the War Office. She asked a number of questions – random things like, had I considered what contribution I could make to the war effort? Did I feel that I had a part to play? Was I willing to do whatever was asked of me? How was I at keeping information I have been entrusted with confidential? Eeh, I tell you, Alice, it made me blood run cold, as she ended the conversation abruptly and I was left staring at the telephone feeling that I'd somehow been recruited for sommat and had an interrogation.'

'Eeh, lass.'

'Don't tell anyone, Alice. Not Marg, or Edith, and not Harry, please. I was told not to tell a soul, and now I have, and I feel as though I've betrayed me country or sommat.'

'You haven't, lass, and I promise I won't tell a soul. How strange is that? It seems war is changing us. I've never in me life not shared something with Marg and Edith, and here I am, knowing that I won't share this.'

'What do you reckon it could be? Me mind's been all over the place. I've been imagining this and that, even the Secret Service! Do you reckon I should tell Philip?'

'No! Him least of all, Jackie . . . You may put him in a bad position. Look, love, you could be being tested for something very important. You're a clever girl. What if Philip has put you forward knowing you're the right person, but yet will keep you safe? If you told him, then he would know immediately that you can't be trusted. I wish you hadn't told me, really, lass.'

'I'm sorry. I'll never tell another soul.'

'And I'll pretend I don't know, so we'll never speak about it again. Anyroad, you might not hear from her again. These people, whoever they are, must be sounding out a lot of folk for different work.'

Jackie stuck her hands into the pockets of her coat. A new grey woollen one that fell to her calves, the coat was a change to her last fitted one as this one was flared and had a large fox-fur collar. She loved it. But concentrating on it didn't alleviate the guilt she felt at having done what the woman on the telephone had asked her not to. Now, she didn't feel worthy of serving her country in any capacity, when that's all she'd thought of for the last six weeks.

The train appearing in the distance took these thoughts away from her as once more her heart fluttered uncontrollably, and a sense of joy filled her at soon being with Harry.

When he stepped off the train, it seemed he'd grown rapidly in the time he'd been away. She'd noticed this before, but now, looking smart in his uniform, his beret with its red Lancashire Fuselier badge and primrose hackle – a lovely feather plume – sat jauntily on his head making him look rakish as well as handsome, he seemed to tower above her.

Another two lads alighted with him, and the three engaged in playful banter, pushing each other and laughing out loud, until an official-looking soldier, obviously an officer, alighted from the first-class carriage. Then they stood to attention and saluted.

For a moment, pride overrode any other emotion Jackie felt as she looked at her Harry. But when the officer said, 'Dismiss, and enjoy your leave, lads. I'll see you in a week's time,' and Harry looked towards her, she filled with love for him.

They both broke into a run, and yet, it felt as if they were in slow motion and that no one else in the world existed. This was compounded when she was in his arms. They'd once been ticked off by the local bobby for kissing in public, but she didn't care about that anymore as Harry's lips came down onto hers. She was lost in her own world that only contained him.

As they left the station, the three of them were giggling at Harry's tale about how he had a hangover, as for the first time in his life he'd got drunk with his mates the night before.

'I were dancing on the tables of the mess! Naw one could stop me, until it collapsed under me. Eeh, I've a big bruise on me leg an' all. Me first medal to me heroics.'

He squeezed her waist and she laughed up at him. She felt strange, as if her reactions were detached from her, as she really wanted to scream that she didn't want him to be a hero of any kind, but just to be with her.

What came out of her mouth wasn't related to any of these mixed feelings. 'You're all coming to tea at ours tonight, love. Marg is preparing the veg as we speak, and I'm going to be the cook.' Why she was telling him all of this, she didn't know.

'That'd be grand. But you don't have to start doing that till later, do you? I thought I'd get me car and we'd go for a drive.' He turned to Alice. 'Is that all right, sis, or did you have plans for me an' all?'

Alice laughed. 'No, lad. It's your leave, you do whatever you like, love.'

'Eeh, I were sorry to hear that Gerald's joined up, but can think of none better to tend to me injured mates than him.'

'Aye, it'll be a wrench, but I'm trying to be brave for him.'

'How's the lads? Jackie tells me that Joey is used to his new school and seems settled. And Billy, by, I bet he's grown. He were shooting up at a fast rate afore I left.'

'They're fine, they can't wait to see you, lad.'

'And Heather? Eeh, she's a lovely woman.'

'She is, and a godsend. She's loving being me helper. Not that I look on her like that, she's more like the gran we never knew. We all feel it, and I think you will an' all.'

'I felt it before I left. It were like she were meant to find us and us her. And what about your gran, Jackie, love? I knaw you've kept me up to date with her antics, but reading between the lines, I've a feeling that she's not as well as she used to be.'

This chatter went on till they reached Alice's car and all the way back to Alice's house. When they got there, this being a Saturday, Billy and Joey came racing out of the house and hurled themselves at Harry.

'By, you've grown, Harry! I thought I'd catch up with you as me pants have gone to half-mast with how I've grown, but you can still give me an inch.'

'Ha, you'll never catch me, Billy lad, you want some manure in your boots to do that.'

The lads fell about laughing, their joy at being together again tangible.

This turned into a tussle as they playfully wrestled.

'Eeh, you'll never grow up, you three.'

'They've time enough for that, lass.' Heather appeared at the door. 'By, it's good to see you, Harry, lad. But I hope them boots are clean. I don't want you mucking up me clean floor.'

What followed brought tears to all their eyes as Harry ran towards her and hugged her. 'It's good to see you, Heather. Have you missed me?'

Heather was red in the face. This was a new, confident and clownish Harry, that Jackie almost didn't recognise. Gone was the serious chap who hung back and did more thinking than talking.

'I have missed you, lad, we were just getting to knaw one another when you had to go.'

'Aye, well, I'm glad you lasted. It's a wonder with this lot. You must be made of tough stuff.'

'Give over. Being here has been the saving of me. Now come in and have a pot of tea, it's brewing ready for you.'

It amazed Jackie how quickly Heather had settled in and taken on the role of housekeeper come surrogate grand-mother, but she was just what Alice needed as her job with the Red Cross had escalated.

Now fully qualified, having been put on an intensive course to supplement those she'd already taken, she'd also had practical experience of a mock landing of casualties which took place at Liverpool docks. The operation was to pick up wounded soldiers to take them to hospital, giving treatment that may be needed on the way – all the 'pretend casualties' had labels on them telling what injuries they had. And then there was the real-life transfer of wounded from the south to Manchester. It seemed her job would take her everywhere. And Jackie knew that Alice wasn't just the saviour of Heather, but Heather was, and would be, the saviour of Alice.

At last, an hour later, she and Harry were on their own, driving towards the Trough of Bowland.

Harry was a lot quieter now.

'How are you really, love?'

Harry shrugged. 'Scared. Unhappy about leaving you and everyone, but that's now. When I'm with all the lads it seems like it's going to be a piece of cake.'

'Eeh, Harry. It's like someone took our simple world and turned it upside down.'

The car slowed. Jackie could see that Harry had welled up. When they came to a halt, he turned to her.

'Aw, Jackie, I don't want to go.'

The tears were streaming down his face. Jackie felt herself crumble as he slid across the bench seat to her and took her in his arms. Their tears mingled; their sobs joined. No words were spoken or needed. This last six weeks had been torture for them and now they faced months, maybe years of the same – but it wouldn't be the same. She'd never know if Harry was dead or alive, or if she would ever see him again. God knows what he was going into.

After a few moments of crying like children, they calmed.

'We can do this, me darling Jackie.'

'We can. We have to use this week to build memories to keep in our hearts while we are apart. Alice, Edith and Marg each have a photo of themselves together with their man, taken on the prom. We've never done anything like that. Let's do it, eh? Let's have a day when we eat fish and chips and ride on the tram, and paddle in the sea.'

Harry wiped his eyes and let out a laugh. 'Aw, it'll be blinking freezing! But aye, let's.'

'Tomorrow?'

'That'd be grand . . . I'll be all right now, Jackie. Crying like that was a release. I needed that, and you're the only person in the world I can do it with and not feel like a blubbering coward.'

'It's like that for me an' all. I'm me when I'm with you. Warts an' all.'

'In my eyes, you have naw warts, or flaws. You're beauti-ful, Jackie.' He held her left hand where his ring sat and twirled it around her finger – a simple gold band with a single, small stone in its centre. It was the world to her.

'When I come home on me first leave, let's get married, Jackie. I want to make you me wife.'

Jackie felt the breath catch in her lungs with the joy this gave her. 'Yes ... Eeh, lad, let's.'

His lips found hers. The kiss wasn't like any other he'd given her but held longing and passion and awoke in her feelings that weren't strange to her, and yet were far more intense than she'd ever felt before.

When his hand slid over her breast, she didn't object, but heard herself give a soft moan in her throat. It was then that Harry pulled away from her. 'By, I'm sorry, me lass. I shouldn't have.'

Jackie couldn't breathe, let alone speak. Her emotions were heightened as they'd never been. She put her head back and closed her eyes. She loved Harry with all that she was, and she wanted to express that, but knew it was wrong to do so.

She felt Harry stroking her hair. 'All that church-going has given us a barrier, but I'm glad. I would hate meself after. I want us to wait till we're wed, Jackie.'

She nodded. 'Shall we go, love?'

'Aye, I think it best.'

He drove on, turning towards Lancaster. Here, nestled in the hills, was a vantage point that allowed you to see across Morecambe Bay.

As they sat on the grass gazing out at hills that sloped away from them, fields with grazing sheep that looked as though they would tumble over and roll down, and in the distance, the sparkling sea, Jackie said, 'It's beautiful. I wish we could stay here forever. But if I don't get home, I'll never get that dinner cooked for everyone.'

As they set out on Sunday afternoon to walk to the prom, the early March sun had a little warmth in it. Blackpool weather never did what it was supposed to do. The only thing you could rely on was the strong winds once the illuminations were switched on in the autumn. Not that they were last autumn and wouldn't be until the end of the war. That in itself had left all Blackpudlians feeling deflated. The dinner she'd cooked – Lancashire hot pot served with chunks of homemade bread followed by apple pie – had gone down well the night before.

Edith, who was blooming in her fifth month of pregnancy, had managed to get some mutton from the farm near to her sister-in-law's house and apples were still plentiful.

Everyone had been in a jolly mood and the laughter had been wonderful.

It had been touching to see Gerald and Harry together as they'd donned their coats and stood in the garden having a man-to-man chat.

When Jackie had glanced out, she'd seen the two men in a hug. A lump had come to her throat. Both faced the unknown, and both needed each other to bolster themselves up.

Clive had joined them after the hug. It seemed at that moment that Clive was the lucky one being able to stay at home and only carrying out manoeuvres, though she knew he could be called into a dangerous situation at any time.

When they reached the prom, the first thing they did was to go to Bendy's stall. Always open winter and summer, he kept anyone who had ventured out amused with his acrobatic antics that had earned him his nickname.

He was that pleased to see them that he did a cartwheel, and then put his head between his knees till he was looking at them through his legs. They both giggled at him though they were in wonderment that anyone could get themselves into such a position, but it seemed easy to Bendy.

Today the prom wasn't as quiet as it could be as what seemed like hundreds of servicemen, who they knew would have been billeted here for training, had prompted the stalls and fish and chip cafés to open, bringing out a lot of locals too.

Some of the girls hanging on to the soldiers' and airmen's arms Jackie recognised from work, and more than one she knew was married and their men had left to go to war.

They were both greeted many times as Harry was wearing his uniform – to stop anyone thinking he wasn't doing his duty. A fear all young men had as some had been set on for being judged as cowards or conscientious objectors.

'Let's get on the tram to Cleveleys. It won't be so crowded there, and we've naw chance of getting anywhere near the beach here.'

'Aye, that's a good idea, Harry, but the landaus are out, let's go on one of those, eh? Though we won't get as far as Cleveleys, we can get out of these crowds.'

No sooner had she said this than a voice said, 'Where to, lass? And you, sir, I'm for taking me hat off to you. Half price for His Majesty's armed forces.'

'Eeh, ta, that's kind of you. Can you take us to the Gyn, please?'

'That's normally two bob, but one to you, sir.'

When they sat in the carriage with the horse jogging along, Blackpool seemed like a different world to what they'd known. The beach was covered in sea defences, when normally it would have been deckchairs, most occupied, but those that weren't fluttering in the breeze – a sad change. But the sea itself didn't let them down. Today with the clear, wintry sky reflected in it, it was a sapphire blue.

Nor did the sounds and the smells as the air was alive with organ music from a busker outside their magnificent tower and with calls from stallholders. All was familiar and loved.

'Why the Gyn, love?' Harry asked when they were on their way.

''Cause there's a grand fish and chip shop at the bottom of Dickson Road.'

The journey only took fifteen minutes. As soon as they alighted, Harry grabbed her hand. 'Come on, last one to put their feet in the water is a cissy!'

Amidst giggles and pushing and shoving, and ripping off her boots, Jackie had the sense that they were kids again, as they ran down the slope and onto the sand. The feel of its velvet touch softly giving to her tread and seeping between her toes felt good. All her cares left her.

The water was icy cold and only saw the tip of her toe. But the feeling was exhilarating, even if she didn't win the race down to it.

Kicking the water at Harry, she said, 'You cheated!'

'Ha, you're a sore loser.'

His splash towards her reached her face. His apologies and gently wiping her wet cheeks with his hanky brought them close together. 'Eeh, me Jackie.'

His lips covered hers, transporting her to another world as she forgot everything but the magic of this moment as the waves lapped her ankles.

The rest of the afternoon was funny, happy and poignant as they ate their fish and chips, walked hand in hand, and made it back to Blackpool prom, had a few goes on the stalls and had their photo taken.

It saddened them both when the time came to go home, not knowing when they would have such a time together again. Jackie didn't want to leave, and as Harry kissed her under the red sky of the sun setting, she wished with all her heart this day could have lasted forever.

TWELVE

Alice

The last week had sped by for Alice. And now the time was on her to say goodbye to Gerald and in only a few short weeks they would be doing the same to Harry.

This war was so real and personal to them all now with their men going. It was breaking their hearts. Not that they moped around, they made the best of things as always.

'That sigh tells me you are doing the same as me, darling. Telling yourself to be brave. But it isn't easy, is it?'

Alice shook her head, not trusting herself to speak. She carried on washing the cups they'd just used. To her, it felt as though that was the last cup of tea they would share.

Gerald's cough told her that he was as near to tears as she was. 'Well, I'll go and change into my uniform.'

Already having been given the rank of officer, Gerald had been issued with his uniform and told to report wearing it to Camberley in Surrey where he'd receive the training that he'd need to adapt his skills to a tent hospital situation.

An hour later the station felt a lonely place, even though it was packed with servicemen and those waiting with them to see them off, the hissing train puffing out smoke filling the air with noise.

Alice stood in the circle of Gerald's arms looking up at him. Her eyes brimmed with tears, but she made herself smile at him.

'You will be all right, won't you, Alice?'

'Aye, don't worry about me. I have me work – thank goodness I'm on duty tonight as that'll help and having Heather will be company. And your ma and da will be coming to stay soon.'

'Yes, they're talking of starting back at work. The hospital knows to call on them if they are needed. I expect they'll time their visit for when I come home on leave before—'

'Let's not think that far ahead. Let's just get through this day by day.'

'Yes. Well, darling, I have to go, almost everyone has boarded now.'

As soon as he was in the first-class carriage the porter slammed the door and blew his whistle. The next few moments were a whirl of others' waves, kisses blown, shouts of 'write soon' and 'take care', but Alice couldn't speak. She could only watch as the train disappeared, and she could hardly see the arms waving through the windows.

Turning, she headed for the gate feeling as if her heart had been wrenched from her. Maybe she should have let someone come with her for now she felt as if she was the only person in the world.

As she walked out of the station, she was shocked to see Edith and Marg stood there with their arms out towards her. She ran to them and sobbed as they held her.

Neither of them made an attempt to stop her. They understood.

When her tears subsided, Marg said, 'Fancy going to Stanley Park with me, love? I've brought a flask of tea for us.'

'Aye, that'd be nice, ta, Marg.'

'Edith must get back to school so can't come with us. But as you're at the Red Cross tonight, we're both going to come around tomorrow evening to have a chinwag and make sure you're all right.'

'Aye, I took the shift because I know it will keep me mind off it all.' She turned to Edith. 'Eeh, Edith, lass, how do you cope? This has been going on for months for you.'

'You do get used to it. I promise you. It never stops hurting and you never stop longing for it to end, but it becomes a way of life. And anyroad, at the moment, I do get to see Philip every couple of weeks or so, which is good to have to look forward to. How I'll cope if he ever gets posted abroad, I don't know ... Come on, let's get to your car, Marg can go with you to the park. I'll get back to work and see you tomorrow night.'

'Ta for coming, Edith. Will you have enough time to eat your lunch?'

'Aye. I'm not due back into the classroom till two.'

'Joey is almost ready to come home by then, they start a lot earlier at Arnold. But he likes to walk so if I'm not there, he'll be fine, and Heather will be at mine by now. I told her not to worry about me, that I might go for a drive or a walk.'

Marg asked, 'How's Joey getting on? I ain't seen him in a while.'

'He's loving it. He's made lots of friends and never complains about the work. He's straight into his room when he comes home to do any work that he's been set. He says he can use a room called a prep room but prefers to be at home. He asked Gerald the other day for a microscope as they are studying insects. Gerald fetched his childhood one from the attic. I didn't get a look in after that as they were engrossed in studying all sorts of things. Joey's going to miss Gerald . . . We all are.'

Alice couldn't stop the small sob that escaped her. They'd reached her car. Before she knew what was happening the three of them were in a hug again. Something they'd done so often in the past, but no matter what had happened to them to prompt it, nothing compared with how Alice felt at this moment. It was as if she'd been split into two people – the one who had to cope, who she knew would be all right, and the blubbering mess who felt her world had ended.

Although the park was barren of flowers, some of the overnight frost still clung to the branches of the trees and coated the spider webs, making this a haven – a world apart from the real world. As they sat on a bench near to the lake and watched the swans gliding up and down, a small sense of peace entered Alice.

'Ready for your cuppa, love?'

'Aye, I am, Marg.'

The tea was still hot, and this further relaxed her as she sipped it gently.

'I'm the lucky one of us all, Alice. Me Clive will only go overnight at the most if they're called upon to help other crews along the coastline, but I still worry about him, it can be dangerous work.'

'Now, don't go feeling guilty, Marg, lass. Clive's role is just as important as Gerald's. Both will be saving lives.'

'I wonder just what it is that Philip does? I reckon he's the safest, even though he has to live away.'

'I don't know. Don't say anything to Edith, but he was talking to Gerald at Christmas and—'

'No, don't tell me, I can't bear you both having to face so much. Besides, you know what the papers have been full of – "Careless talk costs lives".'

Alice felt immediately ashamed of herself, but she'd been worried since hearing of how Philip had confided in Gerald that there was talk of putting together an elite band of highly trained intelligence gatherers who would possibly work behind enemy lines. When she thought about it, she felt shocked at Philip sharing such information. Her mind went to what Jackie had told her and a shiver went through her. What did the mystery person want of Jackie and how would Marg react when she was told?

'Are you cold, lass?'

'Getting that way. We'll go when we've finished this, eh?'

'Aye. I'll tell you what. I've still got a good step, you know. One of these nights we could put our coats on and wrap blankets around us and do as we did on Whittaker Avenue.'

'We will, Marg. Eeh, I'm going to need you and Edith. There's never been a time that I haven't needed you, but now more than ever before.'

When she arrived home, Heather was there to greet her. 'Eeh, me lass, are you all right?'

'Aye. Sorry I was delayed. I went for a walk with Marg.'

'You said you might. I expect it did you the world of good and there's nowt spoiling here, lass . . . Alice, I knaw the timing ain't good, but can I talk to you about something?'

'Of course, anything. Is everything all right?'

'Well, naw . . . Eeh, it's embarrassing but . . . well, I've got to give me home up.'

A tear plopped onto Heather's cheek.

'Come and sit down, love, and tell me all about it.'

'I don't like bothering you with how everything is, but . . . I may have to move to Preston to live in one of the almshouses.'

'No! That ain't going to happen, Heather. You're comfortable when you sleep over in the guest room, ain't you? Well, you can have that as your own. We still have another one. It's smaller but all right for when Averill and Rob come to stay.'

'But won't they want to lodge here when they come to take up their work again?'

'I haven't discussed it with them, but if they do, I can have Harry's room and they can have mine. I was going to do that anyway so that they had their own bathroom and, with there being those lovely chairs in my room, they can relax in peace and quiet when they are home from the hospital. Mind, knowing Averill, she'll have it draped with African materials, and exotic plants will abound.'

Alice couldn't help but giggle at this and felt better for it.

Heather giggled with her. 'Aye, she's like a film star with how she dresses in flowing clothes and wears her hair long and loose. She's a beauty.'

'She is and adorable with it. Now, tell me what brought all this on?'

'I can't keep up me bills ... Eeh, I feel so ashamed. Me Harold left me a nice little nest egg from what he saved, and what I earn here and with having me food mostly here – not that I ever wanted you to pay me but was grateful when you offered.'

'I had no idea. That's terrible.'

'I never thought it would come to this and so quickly, but the house is in disrepair, and leaking in places. When it rains, I have to use bucket after bucket to keep it from soaking me rugs. You see, Harold used to do all of that, but when we got older, it just got left. The cost of repairs is too much for me. And the estate agent said I'd only sell it for a pittance, the state it's in and with there being a war on. He doubted it would sell for years. But he told me he'd take it off me hands for a hundred pounds.'

Alice felt infuriated by this but could see that Heather didn't need her to shout the odds against it.

'If I came here, I'd not want no wages, Alice, lass. A hundred pounds will see to me needs until I pass on, and besides, I'll have no bills to pay and ... well, I won't be lonely.'

'Aw, Heather. You coming here to live is the best thing I could think of happening, love. We'll be company for each other, and I'll have no worries if, without warning, I'm asked to stay out for a night.'

'Ta ever so much, lass. Eeh, you're like the daughter I never had, and I love you like you are an' all.'

Alice got up and went to sit next to Heather on the sofa. She put her arm around her and drew her close. 'Aye, and you're like a ma to me, Heather. I reckon we were fated to meet.'

Heather patted her hand. 'Well, they say that God moves in mysterious ways, but you think He could have found a nicer way of bringing us together, not through our suffering.'

Alice didn't answer this but held Heather for a moment, before standing up. 'Right. We'll get everything done that needs doing while we have Harry with us, eh? He's at a loss in the daytime with Jackie at work. Is there a favourite chair that you need to bring? There's plenty of room for one and then you can have a quiet hour up there if ever you need one.'

'There is. I've taken to sitting in Harold's chair as it feels like he has his arms around me.'

'I know he does, love. And that's a good idea. I reckon Gerald's chair will become mine now as I see exactly what you mean.'

'Can I stay from tonight, Alice, lass?'

'Aye, of course.' Alice felt there was more to this than she'd been told. Heather looked afraid. 'What is it, love? No one is frightening you, are they?'

After a moment, Heather nodded. 'It's ... well, there's noises at night. Not the noises that the wind makes but I think there's someone prowling around. Me bin was upset last night.'

'By, you should have said. Of course you can stay. We changed the bed at the back end of last week, so it's all fresh. You pop up and turn the radiator on, love.'

As soon as Heather left her, with a much sprightlier step than she'd had over the last few days, Alice crossed over to the telephone.

The house filled with banging noises as she dialled the local police station. The radiators all needed attention, but plumbing wasn't Gerald's forte. Clive had said he would look at them when he next called.

'Hello, is that you, Bob?'

'Aye. Who's this?'

'Alice.'

'Alice, me little lass, how are you?'

Bob was like a father figure to them all and laughed when they called him Bob the bobby. She told him her worries.

'By, Heather should have said sommat. But I'm glad she's going to be with you. I heard the doc left today. Very proud of him we are. He didn't have to go. He's a brave chap. Now, you leave this with me. I'll see that Heather's house is watched for a few days; we'll get to the bottom of this. Tell her not to worry.'

Harry popped his head around the door. 'There's nowt wrong, is there, sis? I heard the radiator banging, and then you on the phone.'

'Eeh, Harry. I need a hug.'

She was in his arms. Her sobs wracked her body. Harry's tears wet her hair. For all he was trying to be brave and to jolly them and himself through all of this, she knew that in his heart he was afraid. He was meant to be using his brilliant mind, and yet, still trying desperately to do what their da would want him to do, he'd gone into Clive's rock factory to work, just as their da had, and now here he was going to fight, when that was so against his nature.

Harry loved the Church, believed deeply in God, could have been anything he'd set his mind to. But the hold their late da had over him influenced him still.

'By, lad. Crying don't help owt.'

Harry laughed. 'Hark at you talking Lancashire! Ha, I ain't heard that for a long while.'

Alice giggled. She knew it was a kind of hysterical giggle, so she curbed it before she gave into the belly laughter it would have become, as she was afraid then that it would turn into screams that she would never be able to stop.

They both dried their eyes.

'Gerald will be all right, you knaw, sis. We were told about the field hospitals. They're near to the fighting, but they're protected. As their vehicles are when they travel about as they have a big red cross on them, which tells the enemy they are medics. We were told if we were taken to one, we might find ourselves in a bed next to a German, as if picked up injured, then they are treated just the same. But that we ain't to think of him like our enemy, just as another wounded soldier. I loved that ... I ain't for killing. It ain't right. I – I don't knaw if I can do it, sis.'

'I knew something were troubling you, lad. Look, why don't you go and see Father Malley, eh?'

'I want to, but sommat is holding me back. What will he think of me going to war to kill?'

'I reckon he'll put your mind at rest. They'll have chaplains out there with you. Well, that wouldn't happen if they thought you were all sinners, would it?'

'Naw ... I thought once about being a priest, Alice.'

'Aye, I guessed as much. I remember Jackie being upset because you were so distant when you came out of mass and she asked us if we thought that was on your mind, but we thought better to let you come to your own conclusions.'

'It was only me love for Jackie that stopped me. It were like a massive decision between me love for her and me love for God ... Am I talking daft?'

'No, Harry. You should have talked to us at the time. We knew you were troubled, and we'd never laugh at you, we'd always listen and take everything that's on your mind seriously. Do you still have those feelings?'

'Aye, I do. I'm still torn. I've often felt that if we weren't Catholic, the problem would be solved because I could have both. I could serve God and marry me Jackie.'

Although they'd both been brought up as Catholics – more so when their ma was alive, as she was a devout Catholic – they'd all lapsed after her death when all the happiness they'd known as youngsters dissolved into a hell pit of violence and was measured by the swing of their da's moods.

Harry had gone back to the church after their da died. They'd all been to mass to attend the special prayers given for their da and the experience had a profound effect on him. After that, he'd gone every week, as had Edith and Jackie who'd also seemed to get something from it. But for herself, though she believed in God, she didn't go in for all the Church stuff. Mind, she prayed. She prayed so hard, so many times, even though He rarely listened.

'Maybe you should change your religion?'

'I can't. You knaw what we're taught – the Catholic Church is the one true church started by St Peter at the bidding of Jesus. All the other English churches began after Henry the Eighth wanted to make his own rules on divorcing his wife.'

She wanted to say that didn't matter as Anglicans, Baptists, Methodists and the rest of them loved the same God and were good people, but she didn't want to get into a debate. Harry had his beliefs and she respected that. But it didn't stop her thinking it was a shame that he was still torn between serving his country and serving God, and yes, marrying the girl he loved deeply, as she could sense these conflicts in him.

'Eeh, look at us. We're like a pair of wet blankets and I must get ready as I'm on duty tonight till ten, and Joey will be in any moment . . . Harry, is Joey happy? I mean, well, I don't think he would tell me if he wasn't. How's he really fitting into that school?'

'He's fine. He loves it. He does get a bit of ragging, but that ain't bothering him. His best mate – the son of a lawyer – is teaching him to speak proper. By, he had me and Billy in tucks the other night with how the lad had said, "Joey, it isn't *ain't*, it's *isn't*." Ha, we couldn't stop . . . it were like when we were kids and . . . well, when Da were out and we had a good giggle.'

Alice burst out laughing.

'Anyroad, our Joey's getting it, and told us that while he's at school he talks like them and then reverts to his true self the minute he walks out the gates.'

'Aw. How does he cope with that, poor lad?'

'He thinks it's a joke. He don't mind at all. Anyroad, you ain't far off speaking correctly yourself. Dinner has become lunch and tea is now dinner. I don't knaw where I am with you.'

They both laughed then. Proper belly laughs, which surprised Alice.

When she'd left the station, she'd thought she would never do anything but cry ever again, but now she knew she could. She knew she had the great British spirit that everyone was talking about. She'd get through this. She only wished it was with Gerald by her side . . . *Eeh, Gerald, you're the love of me life and for all me bravado, I don't really know how I am going to live without you by me side.*

THIRTEEN

Edith

'There's another letter from Aunt Peggy, everyone.'

Edith looked at the happy faces of Mandy, Alf and Minnie as they tucked into the bowls of porridge that she'd served them.

Mornings were an easy affair now, as all she had to do was to get herself ready. Minnie got the twins up, washed and dressed them and organised anything they may need to take to school. Edith was so grateful for this as though she was now five months into her pregnancy, she still felt queasy first thing in the morning. Mrs Brown, a lady at church who had a rook of kids, had told her that she'd been the same with all the girls, but with her sons, she'd been fine after a few weeks. Now Edith thought of her bump as being a girl and had even called her Philippa. A little posh, but still, she'd always wanted her firstborn to be named after her beloved Philip.

'What does she say, Aunty? Is Ben better? Is he comin' 'ome?'

It touched her that Alf should talk of this as being his home, but she looked at Minnie concerned that she wouldn't like him to. But Minnie, always the one to say everything just how it was, just smiled, which meant she approved. 'I 'ope it's good news, girl, we could do with some.'

'It is. Ben's making such good progress that he is learning to walk again!'

Mandy clapped her hands. 'Eeh, that's grand news.'

Both Minnie and Edith looked at Mandy in astonishment, but then a cheeky grin crossed her face and they burst out laughing. 'Yer 'ad me going then, me little darlin', I thought for one moment that I'd lost me little Cockney Mandy to the Lancastrians!'

'I'm both, Granny.'

'Oh, well, yes. You can be that, but don't you be forgetting your roots. You're East End, born and bred, darlin', and that's the way you'll always be.'

'Anyroad, Peggy says that Ben is to be fitted with a calliper on his right leg and'll have to wear that for life, but in a few months' time he may be able to go home.'

'Will he come back to this 'ome?'

'To visit, aye, I'm sure he will.'

'You'll see him, son, don't yer worry about that. Granny'll be taking yer 'ome one of these days.'

Edith's face must have told what she was thinking as Minnie went on to say, 'But if Edith'll 'ave us, that ain't going to be anytime soon.'

'Eeh, Minnie, of course I will. You're me saviour.'

'Ta, girl, that makes me 'appy and I've come to love yer like yer me own now.'

Edith crossed the kitchen – a room in which she could fit her previous kitchen three times over – and she loved it with its bright yellow walls and dark oak dresser and table and chairs, complemented by the yellow gingham curtains draped prettily at its large window. An identical curtain hung around the pot sink hiding all her cleaning products that she stored on the shelves beneath. There was a row of cupboards in dark oak with a marble slab on the top of them, which was wonderful for working on as well as looking lovely displaying her biscuit tins and her tea caddy. On the opposite wall and set back in an alcove stood her pride and joy – an Aga cooking range.

'Aw, Minnie. And I love you, love.' She stood behind Minnie and put her arms around her, bending to kiss her cheek.

Alf and Mandy were beaming. Alf, not to be outdone, piped up, 'And I love you, Aunty and Granny.'

Mandy, as ever, reprimanded him. 'You should say Granny first, because you must love Granny the most!'

Alf looked nonplussed. Granny saved the day. 'Well, all this love is all very well, but it won't get you two to school, nor Edith either. I need yer all out of me way as I'm giving the place a spring clean.'

'But it ain't spring yet, Granny.'

'The sun's shining, so that's spring enough for me.'

'Granny loves cleaning, Aunty, but we're best to get out of her way as she can be a tartar when she's doing it.'

Edith laughed. 'Come on, Alf. Go and get your coat and let's get going before your tongue gets you into trouble with your granny as well as Mandy!'

*   *   *

Looking around her class an hour later, Edith reflected on the evacuees she'd taught and wondered how those who'd returned home were faring. She'd been pleased to have located Freda Parkin. The twins had said that she had been brought to Blackpool, and Sue had found her and the family she was with. They'd been thoughtless and misguided in their assumption that it would help Freda to settle with them if she had no contact with home. But on hearing the distress this was causing her mother, they changed their minds and said they would encourage Freda to write.

Her suggestion that all the children should do the same had gone down well with the head and it was now a regular weekly school activity for the evacuees. Everyone said what a success the scheme was as the children were a lot happier now that they heard from their parents. Edith imagined that the parents were too, as she shuddered to think how it was for them having to send their children away – a sacrifice that showed the greatest love.

By going-home time, the day had seemed to drag, and a feeling had taken Edith that something bad was going to happen. She brushed the feeling away and let herself look forward to the evening. She couldn't wait to see Alice and Marg. She and Marg were going to Alice's, hopefully to cheer her up, but Edith knew this wasn't possible to do, not really.

Sighing, she settled Mandy and Alf in the back of the car as they set off for home.

It was when she arrived that the something bad that she'd been dreading happened. Philip telephoned.

'Darling, it's me, are you all right?'

'Philip! Yes . . . are you? This is early for you, we've only just got in . . . Is something wrong?'

'I – I . . . well, yes, in a way. I have to go away . . . remember we talked about this, though we shouldn't have done . . . Darling, I'm going tonight.'

'No, Philip! Where? Why? Will you be back soon?'

'I can't tell you any of those things, darling . . . I'm sorry . . . Oh, my darling, I love you. Remember that. Remember that evening on the prom when we spoke about this and how we'd always be together, no matter where I was sent? We will, darling. We'll do as I told Ben to do: look at the moon every night at nine and know that the other one is doing that and tell each other that we love each other.'

Edith felt her legs go weak. She lowered herself onto the chair that stood in the hall next to the telephone. Yes, they'd talked about this, but she didn't think it would happen like this. She'd thought Philip would be on leave just before he went so they could say a proper goodbye.

'Edith? Edith, are you all right?'

'I will never be all right until I see you again, me love. How can they do this to us? Why couldn't they have let you home for a while first?'

'Darling, we talked about questions, remember? I can't answer any of them, but I do know you will have hundreds, as I have. It's natural. You just have to try not to ask them as there can be no answers given.'

An anger flared in Edith. She wanted to shout, scream even. Though Philip was being logical, there was no logic in tearing husband and wife apart.

'Edith, please . . . this is very difficult. My heart is breaking, darling.'

Drawing on all she'd practised that she would do if this happened, Edith took a deep breath. 'I'll be all right, love. It's the shock. But it's what we knew would happen. I know you told me more than you should about what might be expected of you . . . What do I tell people?'

'Just say that I've been posted to France. So many are going, it won't seem odd.'

'But it will. They are having proper goodbyes. Their men are coming home on leave before being shipped out.'

'I know. But, darling, those who know you have an idea of my work, so they'll accept that I've gone away, and should know not to question you. You only have to use that story to others.'

'And the children?'

'Darling, you're a teacher. Use the knowledge you have of how they will accept this and come to terms with it to tell them in a way they will understand . . . I wish . . . Oh, Edith, my darling, I so wish that it wasn't like this, but it is. I can only tell you that what I have to do is vitally important.'

'And . . . and dangerous? You will be safe, won't you, Philip?'

He didn't answer for a moment. Edith thought she heard a sob. The sound gave her the realisation of how difficult it was for him and increased the fear she felt. He hadn't denied that his mission would be dangerous. Her heart beat painfully against her chest, her throat tightened. His name was an almost whisper. 'Philip?'

She heard a huge intake of breath. 'Be strong, my darling Edith. Be me as well as yourself. Do all the things we would do together, have fun with the children, go for walks, go for drives and hug a pillow like you hug me and I will think of you doing so and that will make me happy.'

Edith couldn't speak. She'd filled with dread. When Philip spoke again, he was back in control once more. 'Darling, I won't be able to telephone you, but I will write, only there won't be any details in my letters, and they will all come via the War Office.'

He had prepared her for this, and they had made up a sort of code. They'd giggled when they'd come up with some of the things as they'd been about them making love and been funny – nothing that they would write in a real letter but had been fun. Now, she wondered when they would ever be in each other's arms again.

'Remember, I want to know everything. How everything really is. I want to support you in all that you do – I can't physically, but I can champion you, darling. Now, write this address down, it is where you send any letters to me: Room 47, Foreign Office.'

Edith scribbled the address on a piece of paper. To her, it was as if Philip was being divorced from her by bureaucrats. She wanted to spit at them.

'Now, my darling, you will be all right for money. The bank account that we opened for you was for this purpose. I have made your allowance much bigger so that you can cover any bigger expenses that might occur. And my solicitor will finalise the purchase of the house, I have signed everything I needed to.'

All this was practical stuff that she knew was important, but she was so full of emotion, it was all too much.

'Edith, you aren't saying anything ... Oh, my darling Edith, I love you beyond anything in my life and with my whole life. You will be my rock. I will cling on to our love for each other if I'm ever in need of a crutch. You will be that to me. My love for you. My need to get home to you ... and, Edith, when ... when our child is born, tell ... tell our baby that Daddy loves him and will one day be with him.'

'I will, my love, my Philip, I will ... I'll do all that you've asked of me. I love you, my darling. I love you with all my heart.'

Tears rained down her face.

'Goodbye, my beautiful Edith, I love you.'

The word 'goodbye' stuck in her throat. She couldn't bring herself to say it out loud. 'Ta-ta, my darling, take care. I love you.'

The last thing she heard was a sob. It joined to her own as she bowed her head, and her body shook.

The hallway of this house she'd come to love, and which would soon be theirs as Philip had put in a bid to buy it that had been accepted, now seemed a vast, lonely space. Had she ever really prepared herself for this happening? She'd tried, but now she knew that there was nothing that could prepare you for it. Philip, her beloved Philip, had been taken from her and she didn't know when she would see him again – or if. *How am I going to cope?* At this moment she wanted to open the door and run and keep running, but she dried her eyes, stood up and went towards the kitchen where she knew Minnie was giving the children their tea.

Three pairs of eyes looked at her. The children's held fear. Minnie's, pity. Alf spoke first. ''As something bad 'appened to Uncle Philip?'

Edith swallowed, then made herself smile. 'Not bad, but, well, you know how Ben's dad went to war, and that Harry will be going, and Gerald? And a lot of the kids that you play with at school, their dads have gone an' all? Well, now Uncle Philip has gone, and I am very proud of him.'

'And I am, and when I get bigger, I will go.'

'Alf! You're such a daft sod! There won't be a war when you're bigger. Anyway, I won't let you go, I'll hide you.'

Mandy's lips quivered. The sight undid Edith. She sat down heavily on the chair nearest to her and tried desperately not to cry.

'It's all right to cry, scream and rant and rave, yer know, Edith.'

'Aye, Minnie. I feel like doing that at times.' But though she was calm, she knew the tears she'd tried to suppress were trickling from her eyes.

Alf and Mandy were by her side like a flash. 'We'll look after yer, Aunty Edith.'

She put her arms around them. 'I know you will, Mandy. You do already, you make me life worth living . . . I'm so glad you want to stay, Minnie, thank you.'

Minnie smiled. Edith could see she didn't trust herself to speak.

Alf snuggled into Edith. She knew he was trying not to cry. This wasn't how she wanted it to be. She was the strong

148

one here. She'd come through so much and triumphed; she could do it again. 'Right, me lads and lasses, that's our crying for our man done. Uncle Philip will be grand. He's looking forward to sorting those Germans out. We'll write letters to him and draw pictures for him and tell him all the things we get up to, eh? And we'll have fun. Spring is just around the corner. We'll clean out that greenhouse in the garden and buy some seeds. We'll dig half of the garden up for vegetables and the other half, we'll sow some nice flowers around the shrubs that are already there.' Feeling enthused herself now, she said, 'Come on, let's go into the garden and plan where's best for everything.'

The children grabbed a hand each, eagerness shining from them. Minnie was grinning. 'That's the spirit, me darlin'.'

She followed them outside.

'I'll still be able to play footie, won't I, Aunty?'

'Aye, we'll plan for that, Alf.'

'And what about the swing Uncle said he'd put up from that tree over there?'

'We have that ready, we'll ask Clive to do it. It will be done, Mandy, lass, don't you worry.'

The garden was a really good size. All given to lawn with borders and a shady tree in one corner, Edith knew she could easily divide off the opposite end to the tree and dig that for planting vegetables. There were already a few fruit bushes in the corner – a gooseberry bush and what she thought was a blackcurrant one too.

Memories of going to the allotment with her da assailed her. Not in a sad way, but in a proud way as she could remember all the things that he'd told her — when to sow beetroot and how far apart. How you had to have canes to support the runner beans and peas. And all about compost and how necessary it was.

'We'll start a compost heap straight away.' She explained it to the children. 'So, nothing gets thrown away now. Everything goes on the compost to rot.'

'Ugh, it'll stink. Stuff that rots stinks!'

'Ha, well, we'll sort that out. We'll ask Clive for his advice on it.'

Ideas came thick and fast then. And along with it a plan. Minnie volunteered to clean the old greenhouse out. 'I'll 'ave that done by the time the week's out, Edith. Don't you worry about that. The windows will gleam and we'll 'ave the biggest plants in the world come spring.'

As they talked it became apparent that Minnie was really knowledgeable about growing vegetables. She and her late husband had had an allotment and she'd loved working in it. 'I fed all the street from it, too. All through the Great War when food was scarce. I tell yer, me darlin', what you're planning is a good idea. We'll not go short of anything with our own patch. I'd give more of the garden over to it if it were me. Alf can go to the park to play.'

Alf looked unsure.

'It'll be our war effort, Alf. Granny knows what it's like in wartime. We need to plan for it, and boys and girls need to make sacrifices so that we win through.'

'All right, Granny.'

'Besides, knowing you, Alf, you'll break the windows on the greenhouse quicker than Aunty can get them mended!'

Alf laughed at Mandy. 'That's because I've got a good strong kick. I can kick the ball further than any of the lads at school.'

'Aye, the head told me that you'll be in the football team next year, Alf, he reckons you're a football star in the making,' Edith told him.

Alf grinned.

Minnie looked puffed up with pride, but always the fair-minded granny, she said, 'And Mandy will be the best cook. She loves helping to roll out the pastry, and she makes a good job of beating the eggs for me. So, I've got the best at everything grandkids in the East End.'

They were all laughing now. Even Edith managed a chuckle.

'Well, now, we'd better go in and get our tea, Edith. I've fed the twins so they can go and play for a while and leave you in peace to 'ave yours. I minced the last of that joint of lamb Patricia got for us and made a shepherd's pie for tonight and a meat and onion pie with a thick-crust pastry topping for tomorrow night.'

'Ta. It sounds lovely. Then I'll have to get off to Alice's. We're meant to be cheering the lass up tonight, but it'll be down to Marg to cheer us both.'

'No doubt with her lovely creamy cocoa ... If there's anything I can do, I'll do it, darlin'. You only 'ave to say. I owe yer a big debt.'

'No, don't be a daft ha'peth. This is your home as long as you need – I know I'd like it to be for as long as forever takes. But I know your heart's in the East End with your own folk.'

'It is. And with me daughter. For all her faults, I love her and miss her. I wish she'd write.'

Edith felt the pity of this but didn't pass comment, only to say that if Minnie wanted to make a visit back to her home, she would help her to. This seemed to cheer her up.

As Edith left the house, she'd thought she would cope, but when she got into her car away from all those she'd had to buoy up, her defences cracked, and her eyes filled with tears. Wiping them away, she knew she had to go to Layton Cemetery. Nothing else mattered. She needed to be with her ma, da and brother Albert.

The gate to the cemetery creaked as she pushed it open. The wind whipped across the open space. Edith pulled her wool coat around her. Her legs felt as though they didn't belong to her and, in her heart, she knew this wasn't a good idea, but she felt compelled.

When she caught sight of her brother's grave, she felt again the sadness of him being buried in unconsecrated ground because he'd taken his own life, but she was glad that he was at peace. She'd done her grieving for him, and she wouldn't want to think of him being here and going off to war.

But as she neared her ma and da's grave and their names came into focus, it brought her to her knees. A cry, which was more like a pain-filled holler of anguish, came from her, then a torrent of tears and wails of distress as she knelt on the cold, unyielding, damp grass. 'Help me, Ma. Da, help me! How am I to bear it?'

FOURTEEN

Marg

Marg couldn't believe it when she stepped out of her door and Edith went roaring past in her car instead of picking her up to give her a lift to Alice's.

Her stomach muscles tightened as the sure knowledge came to her that something awful had happened. This propelled her to run to Edith's house to ask Minnie.

As she listened to Minnie, Marg felt her heart drop. How was she to help Alice, and now Edith, when she knew that both would be devastated as what they had dreaded had now happened – their beloved husbands had gone away?

Why Philip had gone and what it was he would be doing, and why in such a rush, was a mystery to her. Though she and Clive had speculated about what he really did and what he might be called to do in the future.

'I'll go after her, Minnie. I'll call you later and let you know she's all right.'

Taking a moment to put Clive in the picture, Marg ran to the sideboard and grabbed the keys to her small Austin

Seven car – her pride and joy but one she hadn't much experience in.

Clive had bought it for her as a surprise and taken her on a couple of lessons. Edith had promised to give her a few more, but that hadn't happened yet.

She hesitated when it dawned on her that she'd have to back it out of the drive; she'd only driven forward so far.

Clive came out of the front door. 'I'll back it out for you, love. Then I'll give you some lessons on how to do that when you have more time.'

Once the car was on the road, Clive said, 'Don't worry, you're a good driver. And going out on your own is the best way to learn, anyway.'

Marg shook all over for the first hundred yards, but the road was empty, and though she'd crashed the gears a few times, she soon became confident.

Her intention was to pick up Alice so they could go together to find Edith. Where they would look wasn't a mystery as there were only two places that she knew Edith would go when in distress – the church or the cemetery.

Alice had her coat on the moment she heard what had happened. 'Where shall we try first, love? I think the cemetery.'

'Aye, I do. Poor Edith. It must have been devastating to learn of Philip going and it being instant – no proper goodbye.'

When they drew up at the cemetery, they spotted Edith's car. They were both out like a shot and running through the gate.

'Where is she, Marg?'

'There, look. On the bench.'

'Edith, Edith, we're here, lass.'

Edith rose. To Marg, she looked like she'd shrunk in height for a moment. 'Eeh, Edith, Edith.'

They were in a hug without another word being spoken, their tears flowing freely. To Marg, the realisation that the war was a reality stirred her fears for them all. She patted the backs of her beloved friends; she had no way to comfort them. 'Come on, you two. Let's get to Alice's, eh? By, you're froze, Edith, lass.'

Neither protested. 'Leave your car here, Edith, and come with us. We'll come back this way later and pick it up. And I'll make you both a nice hot cocoa when we get to Alice's . . . You'll both be all right, I promise. Come on.'

Heather and Billy came out to stand on the step when they arrived. They must have seen her car lights turn into the drive. For a moment, this annoyed Marg as she didn't think Edith would want to see anyone until she'd composed herself. But she surprised her when she got out and Billy came running to her. Edith put her arms out to him, and they hugged.

Billy stood as tall as Edith now. When he came out of the hug he said, 'I were sorry to hear your news, Edith. If there's owt I can do, let me knaw.'

'Aw, ta, Billy. I'll be right. It's the shock. Anyroad, how are you? Work going down all right?'

'It's not bad. I'm learning a trade, but, well . . .'

'It's not football, is it? Aye, I know.'

'Clive's manager treats you all right, don't he, Billy?'

'Aye, he does, Marg. He's a grand bloke, as is Clive's da. Everyone misses Clive, though, and loves it when he pops in. We're rolling a new rock, you know. It has Land of Hope and Glory written through it.'

'Ha, does Clive know?'

'Naw. His da wants to surprise him.'

'He will that. Anyroad, lad, let's get Edith and Alice into the warmth.'

Heather put her arm around Alice's shoulder and guided her inside. The scene touched Marg and brought a lump to her throat. They looked like ma and daughter at that moment. She could only nod when Heather said, 'I'll put the kettle on, Marg.'

'Aye, do that, but it ain't tea we want. I'm making them both cocoa.'

'Eeh, we're in for a treat, then. Jackie and Harry won't knaw what they're missing.'

'Aye, me poor Jackie'll be the next one we're comforting.'

'She will. And me an' all. I'm sweet on Harry.'

Billy took Alice's hand as he said, 'Ha, Heather, I thought I was your sweetheart.'

'You are, lad. You all are.'

They were laughing as they went inside, and Marg was glad to see that Edith and Alice were too.

'While the kettle's boiling, can I use your phone, Alice? I'd better ring Minnie and let her know Edith's all right, and Clive an' all as he'll be worrying.'

'Aye, of course . . . Do you know what I'd like to do? I'd like us girls to sit in the summer house.'

'I'll go an' light the stove for you, Alice.'

'Ta, Billy, lad. I – I just want to be with Edith and Marg.'

The summer house was hidden behind a tall hedge at the bottom of Alice's garden. Built of wood, it had a veranda that had a thick glass roof. The sides were just windows, with French doors that opened onto a small garden shaded by a huge tree. Inside was furnished with a comfy sofa and two chairs made of cane. These had thick, soft, gaily coloured cushions on them that seemed to hug you when you sat down. The floor was highly polished light oak, but in winter, Alice covered this with a huge Indian rug.

Marg loved the summer house. It had often been a haven to them, and they had spent many a happy hour in there.

'Eeh, this compensates for not being able to sit on the step in Whittaker Avenue, don't it?'

'It does, Marg. It's comfier an' all.'

'Cheeky thing, Edith, there were nothing wrong with me step.'

'Ha, except that it made your bum hard and cold! . . . I miss it sometimes, though. And the folk and their antics.'

They were quiet for a moment, till Alice said, 'Are you ready to talk, Edith, lass?'

'Aye, Alice, love.'

They listened as Edith told them what had happened. Well, at least the gist of it, as Marg felt there was information she was holding back. She couldn't see it as the truth that Philip had been posted to France. And if he had, she wondered what he would do out there as though an officer, she didn't see him being sent to oversee a fighting regiment. He had no military training as such.

When she and Clive had spoken about Philip and his work, he'd said he thought that Philip was working in intelligence gathering and if ever sent abroad to do it, could be in extreme danger if caught. But he'd warned her about sharing this speculation with anybody, and under no circumstances must she tackle Edith with it.

'So, we're in the same boat, then, Edith, lass. Or will be after my Gerald's completed his training.'

'Aye, we are. You know, I never thought I would react how I did. I completely went to pieces.'

'I did an' all, and I still feel as though I've been torn to shreds.'

'Look, me lasses, you're both strong women, you are, I promise. It's like me gran always used to say when either me or Jackie fell over or had some mishap, "You've been knocked off your axle," and that's what's happened to you, but it's only temporary. You'll regain your strength. I think that we three have always needed a prop – someone to support us. The main folk that we relied on for years was each other. Then each of us were knocked off our axle by violent acts and bereavement, and we couldn't be the help to each other that we were before. We tried but others came along who filled that gap and propped us up. Gerald, Philip and me Clive. Now, yours has been taken from you, but eeh, me lasses, we're stronger in ourselves than we were when they came into our lives, they've made it that way. Now it's time for us to be the prop for each other again – aye, me an' all. I need you both at times. When me Clive goes out on a rescue. His work is getting more dangerous – torpedo boats and mines and untold dangers lurk under the sea, and I go to pieces when he is called out. But together, we can get through. We did it before, we can do it again.'

There was a silence. For a moment, Marg thought she'd said the wrong thing, but then Edith gave a tearful smile. 'By, lass, you're a wise old bird suddenly. But you're right. I can see the sense in what you're saying. Aye, I am a person that needs someone to prop me up and I never knew it until now.'

'Aye, I am an' all. And, Marg, I never thought of it like that, or lately of you needing us to be there for you. Sorry, love, I didn't realise. But I do now, and just knowing it has given me strength. Ta, lass. I think me and Edith both needed that pep talk.'

'Come here. I know I'm always the one saying it, but remember, we are the Halfpenny Girls. It's a daft title, but it has always meant so much to us and is what we are. If we cling on to that, then we'll be all right.'

'We will. By, I feel better already. I wish I could telephone me Philip and tell him so, but I can only write to him now, and I don't know how long that will take to reach him.'

'I would still write and tell him, and the sooner the better. Look how much that will relieve his mind and help him to concentrate on whatever he has to do.'

'You're right, Marg. I will . . . I – I shouldn't say anything but Philip . . .'

'No, don't say anything, Edith. I think me and Marg both have an idea what Philip might be called upon to do . . . well, the nature of it.'

Marg nodded. 'Aye. Clive gave me an idea. And none of us must ever speak of it. Clive's made me realise that all this about careless talk isn't a joke. We really can put folk in danger, and our country, by telling things we know to others. He says that none of us know who our enemy really is. That people can be got at for all sorts of reasons and can be in our midst and we don't know it. And that some simple information we don't think matters can be vital to our enemy.'

They were all quiet for a moment. It was Edith who broke it. 'Ta, Marg. You've helped me a lot tonight. And though it is unspoken, it helps that you both understand about Philip. Eeh, our Marg has come out champion – philosopher and cocoa maker!'

This lightened the mood as they laughed at Edith. Marg made more of it by preening herself and standing and bowing. Then doubling over in a fit of giggles as the others applauded her.

The moment had passed – this one at least. She knew there would be many more in the future – but she prayed that none of them were unrepairable. That all of them and their loved ones came through this war that now seemed so real to them all.

Alice sobered them. 'We'll need to look out for Jackie an' all ... Eeh, it's not easy thinking of me brother going, but to Jackie, Harry's more than that. Just as me and you feel as though we've had our right arm cut off, Edith, so will she ... and, well, there's stuff to prepare yourself for, Marg ... I mean, where Jackie's concerned ... I – I'm thinking, well, she's seventeen, she has a good brain, maybe she will be needed somewhere ... Oh, I don't know what I'm thinking really, it's just this need to make ourselves ready so everything doesn't come as a shock, and send us reeling again.'

Marg had a feeling that Alice knew something concerning Jackie. An inner battle raged inside her at this thought. She wanted to shout at Alice to tell what she knew, but that would go against everything she'd just said. 'I will. Ta, Alice. I've not let meself think that Jackie might be called upon, but you're right ... We've to be ready for anything happening now.'

Marg felt unnerved now. She picked her mug up. 'Eeh, me last drop's gone cold. Does anyone want another?'

'Aye, I do, Marg.'

'Me an' all. Edith ain't having nothing without me! She even had to send her man away just because mine's going.'

Edith threw a cushion at Alice. Alice squealed with laughter and threw it back. There was pandemonium for a minute as the pair of them seemed to turn into kids again.

Marg, who was trying to get to the door with three mugs in her hand, had to dodge flying cushions. When she made it, they had calmed down and were giggling. But she knew, for both, it was a tearful giggle. She slipped through the door without commenting. They needed a little time together. Only they could know how each other felt.

As she went across the lawn, shivering as the evening had chilled even further, she hoped she'd been a help to them. She did share something with them in all of this – fear. She may have her Clive to cuddle up to and to be a prop to her, but she feared for him so much.

When she woke the next morning, Marg turned and snuggled into Clive. His sleepy mutterings made her smile. She caught something about 'love' and knew he meant to tell her he loved her. These were his first words every morning.

Waking up properly, he turned towards her, her name on his lips, his desire pressing against her thigh.

'Eeh, me lad, I love you an' all.'

Her name this time came out in a thick voice that thrilled her as his veiled eyes looked into hers. She melted into his kiss . . . but a loud bang made her jump away, which was followed by something heavy landing on her — a giggling bundle of love . . . and at this moment, the biggest unwanted pest in the world. 'Carl! You menace, you. You knocked the wind out of me.'

Clive's heavy sigh told volumes, but always patient with his adored sons, he grabbed a giggling Carl in his strong arms and lifted him in the air. 'You ragamuffin! I'll launch you to the moon and back.'

'So does that mean I don't have to go to school then, Daddy?'

'It's your choice. There's a very strict school on the moon, where all the lads get caned a lot, and the teachers are monsters that eat the kids bit by bit. A toe first.' Clive took one of Carl's toes into his mouth. Carl screamed.

'Shush, you two, you'll frighten me gran!'

As Clive lowered him, Carl said, 'Is Gran just yours, Marg? I'd like her to be my gran, she's funny and I love her.'

'Aye, she's yours an' all. She's your step-gran as you already have a lovely gran in your da's ma.'

'But I love them both.'

'Aye, and I do. From now on I'll just say Gran. Not call her me gran. How will that suit you, eh?'

Carl took the chance of Clive having loosened his grip to jump off the bed. 'I'll go and wake George up. He's always a sleepyhead!'

Clive burst out laughing, 'Yes, and at this moment, I wish you were!' His look told volumes. Marg smiled at him. The moment had passed for them both.

'Come on, I suppose we'd better get up. I've to get breakfast, and you'll need to get off to the depot.'

As she crossed over to their bathroom, he told her, 'I'm actually going in to the rock factory today. There's a meeting. I wanted to talk to you about it last night, but I understood that you had to go to Alice, and then Edith too, as it turned out. Have we got a minute now? It's only seven o'clock.'

Marg hesitated. There was something in the urgency of this that she felt unsure of. 'Let's dress, and get a pot of tea first, eh?' Giggling, she added, 'If I come back to that bed, it won't be talking that's done, lad.'

Clive grinned. 'Ha, Carl saw that off! But you're right. You get dressed and I'll slip my dressing gown on and go and bring tea up here for us. I'll call in on the lads and tell them to start to get ready for school. They only need to wash their faces as I bathed them and washed their hair last night.'

'Aye, and will you ask Wendy to put the porridge on as I need a few minutes with Jackie after we've had our tea and afore she goes to work?'

Wendy, a widow with two grown-up sons — both of whom were married with families, and had careers down in London, meaning she saw little of them — had fitted well into the family. A retired registered nurse, she did a lot more than just seeing to Gran's needs in the evening, sleeping near to her to be on hand, and then getting her up in the morning; she'd also become a help to Marg, taking on anything that needed an extra pair of hands.

When they finally sat together having their cup of tea, Clive's face looked grim as he sipped his. He seemed hesitant to begin telling her what was on his mind. But after a couple of more sips, he cleared his throat. 'It's a worrying time all round, Marg ... Dad's not coping at the rock factory ... well, it's not him altogether, it's Mother. She's always suffered with her nerves, and though she puts on a brave face for us, she needs Dad with her and keeps ringing him every half an hour or so. Without him, she doesn't cope. It's the reason he gave up working and handed over to me in the first place, though he loves the factory.'

'She could come round here in the day. Gran loves her and I do an' all. I can get on with things while she sits with Gran and—'

'That's not the solution, I'm afraid ... You are, Marg.'

'Me? How?'

'I want to ask you if you'll be willing to learn the trade and to run the rock factory.'

'What? Me? Eeh, Clive, I've no brains for such a thing ... I wouldn't know where to start, and what about Gran? She still needs me during the day. No, Clive, it ain't possible, lad.'

'It is, Marg. Darling, you're panicking, and you're not giving yourself credit. You are very capable, none better.'

'But where has this all come from? Why haven't you said anything afore?'

Clive sighed a troubled sigh. 'Something happened yesterday. Mother had a relapse. She completely collapsed into a heap of crying and wailing for Dad not to leave her. I didn't know until last night when he'd finally got her settled – he did that by promising he wouldn't go to work again. You had to go out and were so troubled, I kept it from you, then when you came in it would have been so unfair to burden you as all you needed was a strong shoulder to cry on. I had to be that for you, Marg. You're my world. When you hurt, I hurt.'

Marg gazed into his beloved face and knew she was letting him down. He needed her, and she was refusing that need. His hurt was hers too, and he was hurting over his ma and da's predicament. She took his hand. 'I'll do it, me love. I ain't saying I'll be good at it, but I'll do me best. But what about your manager? I thought he could run the factory on his own?'

'He can, but as troubles come in threes, and with my mother's, and you having to support our friends, you would have thought that would be it, but no. Arthur Stubble has been diagnosed with cancer and cannot stay on as my manager.'

'No! Eeh, I don't know him, but I'm so sorry to hear that. By, Clive, troubles are piling up as you say. Let alone them coming in threes, they seem to come in dozens to us. Just tell me what you want me to do, and how, me love. I'll support you all the way and, like I say, I'll do me very best.'

Clive squeezed her hand. She could see he was near to tears, but he swallowed hard. 'I need you to come to the meeting. The firm's solicitor and accountant will be there. I am going to make you a full partner of the business.'

Marg couldn't believe this. It was all too much to take in, but she waited, letting him tell her all he had to.

'I have made a new will. You are to own the factory if anything happens to me, with the proviso that it passes to my sons, and any children you and I may have.'

'Why would you need to do that, Clive? Of course it will go to them — who else?'

'Marg, we have to be realistic. Anything could happen to me with us being at war. The job I do is dangerous ... I know you don't like me to talk about it, but this is a time in our lives that we didn't do anything to deserve but must cope with. The truth is, Marg, that I am in as much danger as any of our soldiers on the front line. I accept that and take it on board. You must do so, too, my darling. So, it is better that we have everything in place for you and the children ... To this end, I want you to formally adopt George and Carl.'

Marg was flummoxed for a moment. Accepting the boys as hers was the easiest part of it all. 'I will do everything you need of me, me darling Clive.' A sob caught in her throat. But like Clive had, she controlled it. He rose and pulled her up to stand too. Then wrapped her in his arms. Marg couldn't stop the tears from flowing as she clung on to him. He was and had been her saviour, and now she had to face the possibility of losing him. How would she bear it?

FIFTEEN

Jackie

Jackie was to face saying goodbye to Harry in a few days, and her heart was aching. But she'd gained strength from Alice and Edith, and, of course, her beloved Marg, who was surprising them all, as well as herself, with how she was coping with the rock factory. She was full of it.

Jackie smiled as she put the last figure into the ledger and blotted the ink dry. *Eeh, I reckon if I lost me job here, I'd be able to take one in an instant at the rock factory!*

It felt that way after being told every process from boiling the sugar to how different coloured strips made the lettering that read the same all the way through the sticks, to wrapping the finished product. What Marg didn't know about rock making in the few weeks she'd been there wasn't worth knowing. But what pleased Jackie the most was how happy she was.

And the biggest surprise of all was how she was all right with leaving all of Gran's care to the lovely Wendy, who doubled as a sort of nanny to George and Carl. And, on top of that, accepting that she needed a full-time cleaner-cum-cook! This was Martha, a nice, unassuming woman, the wife of one of the workers at the rock factory.

Jackie felt happy about her gran too, as she seemed content and settled, though wasn't fully aware most of the time. She sighed. She just wished everything could be dealt with so easily. She dreaded when she was to go to the station with Harry and wave him off.

A shudder of pain zinged through her, but she held on to her emotions and made herself concentrate on thinking about tomorrow. Saturday, the twenty-third of March, for that had suddenly been set as the date for a party! Hers and Harry's official engagement party. And she was determined it would be the best ever and a happy occasion.

The telephone ringing brought her out of these thoughts.

Picking up the receiver, the voice she heard made her catch her breath – the posh lady again!

'Miss Porter?'

'Yes.'

'I believe you know Mr Blake. Captain Blake?'

The name sent a repulsion trembling through her.

'Well?'

'Aye. I do.' Thoughts tumbled through her mind. What could the connection be between the rotten Blake and the mysterious lady?

'"Aye"? What kind of English is that?'

'Lancastrian. I'm a Blackpudlian.'

Jackie put a proud tone into her voice. This lady was beginning to annoy her. Who did she think she was?

'Whatever one of those is ... Oh, never mind. It's your ability that's important. You'll have to sink or swim amongst those of a much higher class than you. But no doubt, if Blake is correct about you, what you lack in social skills you will make up for in intelligence.'

Jackie was seething but held her tongue. 'What do you want with me, and what's Mr Blake got to do with it?'

'Captain Blake! Now, what I am about to tell you, you must not speak of. Do you understand?'

'Y – yes ... But who are you, and why do you want to tell me sommat I haven't to speak of?'

'Good Lord, what is Captain Blake thinking of? Anyway, I suppose you are what you are. But it isn't for you to know other than for some totally unfathomable reason Captain Blake has recommended that you are recruited. You have been selected to join a team of people who are secretly working on extremely important projects which could make a difference to the outcome of the war. Now you know why this is strictly confidential.'

Jackie couldn't believe this was happening. 'What do I have to do? What is this work?'

A huge sigh followed this, making Jackie feel as though the lady was sat next to her and would at any moment punch her. But surely it was a normal question to ask?

'I'm beginning to wonder if you are suitable at all! Though your inquisitive nature will be useful. However, you do need to learn that ours is not to reason why, ours is but to do and die!'

Frustration prickled Jackie. 'Aye, but you should tell a body what it is she's to do or die for!'

To Jackie's surprise, the lady burst out laughing.

'You have spirit, I'll give you that, young lady. We are to do or die for the cause of winning this bloody war. Your mathematical logic is required for that. That is all I am allowed to tell you. Do you want to do your bit to help England be victors over the Germans, or not?'

Jackie didn't have to think about this as she knew she'd do all in her power to help defeat those who it seemed to her were out to ruin the lives of everyone.

'Aye, just tell me what to do and I'll do it.'

But she did think about the awfulness of seeing Mr Blake, her ex-boss, again. Her body shuddered with repulsion against doing so but she had been called to do her duty and she would.

'You will receive an envelope with a rail ticket today. A messenger will call in to the office. You will report to the Foreign Office on Monday afternoon at three p.m. All instructions will be in the envelope. You can tell your sister that you have been called up for war duty. You will initially be a civilian, but once you reach your eighteenth birthday you will be called up to the Women's Royal Air Corps. You can tell your family that you will be working at Bletchley in Buckinghamshire, but that is all. You must not mention Captain Blake's name.'

'But me sister will go spare! She won't take that. She'll want to know sommat more.'

'Oh, I knew it would be like this! The girls we usually recruit do not have these problems. You had better be trustworthy. Captain Blake said you were but you're not proving to be! For goodness' sake, make something up – tell her you're joining the Land Army or something. Good day!'

The phone went dead. Jackie felt sick. Why had she agreed? Everything about the call was weird and even weirder was her agreeing to do anything for the hateful Blake!

Memories of his closeness, his groping her, his assumption that she was in love with him, increased the repulsion she'd felt earlier. 'I must be mad!'

'What was that you said, Jackie? Are you all right? That sounded like a strange phone call to me. Who was it?'

Jackie had forgotten Ken, her boss, was in the room and could have bitten her tongue for speaking out loud. 'It was a lady . . . I – I've been asked to volunteer for the Land Army.'

'What? You're too young to be summoned for war work. It must have been a hoax. Take no notice of it.'

'It wasn't a joke, Ken. I have to go to the For . . . forest near to a place called Bletchley in Buckinghamshire.'

'Bloody Hell! When?'

'Monday.'

'You mean, you're leaving? You can't . . . I mean, how will we cope here? This is ridiculous!'

'I have no choice, Ken. I'm sorry.'

Ken looked intently at her. 'You're not telling the truth, Jackie . . . I . . . Look, I can't see them calling anyone urgently to dig a few spuds. You need to think of something a bit more convincing than that. But whatever it is, I will miss you, but am proud of you. You didn't hesitate . . . well, you did, but anyone would. I guess you weren't told what you were needed for, which was why you were frustrated. I even smiled when I heard you ask what it was you had to do or die for. Whatever it is, I wish you luck. If you can, keep in touch, eh?'

'Ta, Ken. I don't want to go, but . . .'

'I know, lass. I feel the same and fear my call-up for similar reasons – family. But your Marg and gran are set up nicely now. They'll be fine. And you see your young man off next week – this, whatever it is, will be a help to you to get you through being without him.'

'I hope it does.'

'But, look. You need a better story . . . How about supplies? You could say that the warehouse where the army supplies are being processed has got into accounting difficulties, and you have been recruited – summoned – to go there to sort it out.'

'But what will I say about how they knew about me?'

'Just say that you were told they know everything about everyone.'

'They must do. They knew I worked here. There's a letter coming for me today.'

'Well—'

One of the typing-pool girls, knocking on the office door, stopped whatever Ken was going to say. When Ken told her to come in, the girl said, 'A letter just come for you, Jackie. It's to be signed for. The bloke at the post office on Talbot Road is waiting downstairs with it.'

'Ta, Annie.'

Jackie looked at Ken. His head nodded towards the door. 'Go on, you can do this, lass.'

As she ran down the rickety wooden stairs, through the factory floor, waving to all those calling out to her, Jackie

172

wasn't sure she could – though it would help if she knew what it was that she had to do!

'Here you are, miss. Sign here.'

'How did you get this so quickly?'

'It arrived by courier this morning with instructions it was to be delivered at three p.m. to you. You don't argue with brown envelopes, miss.'

Jackie laughed. 'Eeh, naw, they could open their flaps and bite you!'

'Ha, they often do with what's inside . . . So, what have you been up to then, to have to receive this at a certain time, eh? It's how they serve a writ or sommat.'

'By, you must have had one to know that! Anyroad, I shall knaw when I open it, as until then, I'm as mystified as you.'

He hesitated.

'And I ain't opening it now. So, ta for delivering it.'

With this, she stepped inside and closed the door, smiling at him as she did.

Leaning against the door, Jackie knew that his curiosity was nothing to what she would face. *What on earth can this work be that they need me for? And who are 'they'?* Well, she knew who one of them was – the hateful, lecherous Blake! He'd left last year to take up work he'd been 'trained to do in the last war' is what he'd told her. This she understood, *but how on earth can I, Jackie Porter from Blackpool, help to make a difference in changing the course of the war?* She giggled to herself as the thought came to her, *Jackie, yours is not to reason why, but yours is to do or die!*

When she reached the office, she asked Ken, 'Who said that saying about doing and dying?'

'Typical you, always inquisitive. That's why you have a brilliant mind for maths. You need things to add up and balance – to have a purpose and a reason. I'm the same. Well, it was a poet of last century called Byron. He also said, "Better not to be than not to be noble." You are noble, Jackie, and that is why you must do whatever it is they are asking of you. I'll let Mr Bradshaw know you're leaving today. Because I doubt you will be back.'

'Will you tell him me cover story that you made up?'

'I will.'

'I feel bad lying to him. He was so good giving me this job when I lost me other one.'

'Oh, yes, that was his son, Philip, who arranged that, I remember. He's married to a friend of your sister's, isn't he?'

'Aye, Edith.'

'Well, he's another who is noble. But we'll change the subject now – careless talk and all that . . . Have you finished the wages tally?'

Telling him she had, he told her to get off and he would see to it all. 'Spend some time with that boyfriend of yours . . . And Jackie, good luck.'

As she left, Jackie felt a deep sadness. The situation had carried her along, but now she felt a sense of fear, and disorientation. Her life had been mapped out for her. Now, she hadn't a clue in which direction she was going. Or how she would tell Marg!

The house seemed quieter than she was used to it being. But then she remembered she was early, and Carl and George would still be at school.

When she opened the door, shock made her step backwards as a nasty-sounding voice came to her. 'Drink it, you old cow! You're nothing but trouble. If you don't drink, you'll get dehydrated and then you'll wither and die, and I'll be out of a bloody job. I've got a good thing going here. Come on, open your bloody mouth and drink!'

Jackie rushed through the kitchen and through the open door that led to Gran's flat, just in time to hear a slap and her lovely gran crying out.

'Stop it! How dare you! Get out! Get out!' Jackie's screams assaulted her own ears. But she couldn't stop. 'Gran! Gran!' Turning on Wendy, she felt a hate well up inside her. She wanted to fly at the stupefied woman and tear her to shreds.

'Well, this is a turn-up. You employ me to look after a dribbling old idiot and then attack me like this.'

'I heard you! You were talking to me gran as if she was nowt! You slapped her!'

'Ha! Who says so, eh? A young girl who thinks she's a woman flaunting herself, off doing what she shouldn't when she ain't long out of nappies! If you think your word will stand up against mine – a respected, retired nurse – then you've another thing coming to you, lass.'

'Just get out!'

'Jackie?'

'Aye, Gran, it is. It's your Jackie. Don't cry. No one's going to hurt you ever again, Gran.'

Wendy turned towards her own sitting room and slammed the door behind her. Jackie hoped she would just pack her things and go.

Going down on her haunches, Jackie held Gran's shaking hands. 'It's all right, love. You're all right now. I'm so sorry you were left with that horrid woman.'

A timid tap on the door and Martha, the cleaning lady, looking afraid and worried, stepped inside. 'Is everything all right? I heard shouting.'

'Martha, did you knaw as Wendy were treating me gran in a rough way?'

Martha lowered her head.

'Martha?'

'Aye, I didn't think it right how she got angry with your gran sometimes, but she said it was the best way. She said when folk have dementia they go like children and to get them to do things that are essential to keeping them well and alive, you have to discipline them like you would a child. But I've cried sometimes. I've sat on the bottom step and cried, 'cause it reminded me of me ma. Me ma had a temper, and I could do nowt right for her.'

'Why didn't you say something? Of course it ain't right to treat anyone like she was treating Gran! You should have told us.'

A tear ran down Martha's cheek. 'I – I couldn't, I told her I would one day, and she said she'd get me the sack … I was afraid to lose me job. Me hubby … well, he … he beats me.'

Martha trembled all over, tears were flowing down her cheeks.

To Jackie, it wasn't right to let an old lady suffer to save your own skin, or for any reason, but she knew a little compassion for Martha. She remembered how Harry would do anyone's bidding when he was a child, for fear of getting a beating off his da. 'Look, go and make Gran a pot of tea, eh? And make one for yourself and me. I could do with one, heaven knows.'

Turning to Gran, Jackie was relieved to see a smile on her face. She reached out her hand. 'Jackie!'

'Aye, Gran. I'm here.' She wanted to say, *and I'll never leave you again*, but her heart was heavy with the knowledge that she would, and soon, and yet Gran looked so frail the thought terrified her.

'I'm tired, lass. I don't want tea.'

'All right, love. Let me help you onto your bed, eh? You can have a little rest then.'

When she helped Gran to stand, the faint whiff that she'd had of urine became stronger. Gran's skirt was soaked. 'Eeh, Gran. We'd better go to the bathroom first. Sit down a minute, I'll fetch Martha to help.'

When she came back in with Martha, Gran smiled at her. 'Hello, kind lady.'

'Me name's Martha, remember, Sandra? Martha Randville, as was. I'm married now. I used to play with your Vera when we were kids and you allus gave me sommat to take home with me – a jam tart, or a slice of bread and jam.'

'Aye. Where is Vera? Have you seen her? Is she playing out? You used to play hopscotch and one day I joined you and beat you both.'

'You did. Aye, I remember that ... I'm sorry for what happened to you. I'm sorry I didn't do owt. I were scared of losing me job ... me old man ...'

'Don't worry, Martha. You did wrong, but you'd a good reason. Help me with Gran, she needs changing.'

Jackie was near to tears with hearing about her ma. Such a lovely picture had come to her of Ma being a little girl and playing hopscotch in Whittaker Avenue, and Gran having a go too, that for a moment she'd wanted to sob and wail for her ma to be here. Not to be dead. But she'd pulled herself up. Gran needed her now and that's what was important.

By the time Gran was settled on her bed and her eyes were closing, Jackie's heartache had increased. Her hands were shaking as she picked up the telephone and dialled Marg at work. Her tears were tumbling again, as she got halfway through and then sobbed out to Marg, 'A – and her bottom's all bruised, Marg . . . there's the shape of a handprint . . . Eeh, Marg, how could we have got it so wrong? How did that woman pull the wool over all of our eyes like she did?'

'Eeh, I'll swing for her! Has she gone?'

'Aye, she left with her case, slamming every door she went through. We should get Bob on her.'

'Eeh, lass, I know, but I doubt he could do anything. Nurses and doctors and the like seem above the law. Let's just be grateful that you found out and it's over. I'm coming home, Jackie, lass. You say Gran's all right now?'

'Aye, she's asleep. Hurry, Marg . . . So much has happened that I have to tell you about.'

Jackie was in Marg's arms the moment she came through the door.

'It's all right now, love, and that beast of a woman has gone. I'll give up me job and look after Gran. Clive will just have to find someone to run the factory. Gran comes first . . . Or I could do half a day with Gran, and you go part time and do the afternoon. Is that possible, lass? . . . But come to think of it, why are you home, anyroad?'

Jackie took a deep breath. 'I'm not working at Bradshaw's any longer . . . I'm going away on Monday, Marg.'

'What? How? Why? What are you talking about, Jackie . . . ? No! You can't!'

'Let's sit down in the front room, Marg. We need some privacy.'

Marg's head shook from side to side. 'You're telling me that you're the only one in the country who can go and sort out a flipping warehouse whose accounts are in a muddle? By, there's something fishy about this, Jackie, I don't want you to go. You tell them you ain't going.'

'I can't, Marg. It's war work. We all knew we'd be called to do it.'

'Not young 'uns like you, Jackie . . . No, I ain't having it! I'll phone the bloody War Office, or whoever it is . . . they can't do this!'

They sat together on the sofa. Jackie reached out and took Marg's hand. 'I'll come home as often as I can, love.'

Marg stood, her stance telling of her temper. But then she seemed to shrivel as her shoulders slumped. Her body plonked back down on the sofa, and she turned and took Jackie in a cuddle. 'Eeh, Jackie, Jackie. How am I to go on without you by me side?'

179

Feeling like she was the older sister, Jackie patted her back. 'You will, Marg. We'll all do what we must do to beat Hitler. Eeh, he won't knaw what's hit him if he tries to land on our soil – you'll be there with your broomstick, Edith with her frying pan, and Alice will be ready with her bandages to see to his cuts and bruises.'

Marg gave a little titter, but Jackie knew she wasn't appeased, not really.

With Clive coming home not ten minutes later, Jackie felt she could leave and go to Harry. As she hugged and kissed Clive, she told him she was sorry to dash off, but Marg would explain everything, then she had a quick look in to find Gran still sleeping, and went out of the door before Clive could gather himself.

When she reached Alice's house, her heart quickened. Any moment she would be in Harry's arms.

As if he'd been watching for her, he opened the door. His slight breathlessness told her he'd run down the stairs.

'Jackie! Eeh, me little lass.'

She went into his open arms.

'I saw you from me bedroom window. What're you doing here? I thought you were at work. Is sommat up?'

'Things have happened. Let's get inside, then I can tell Alice at the same time. I see her car's here.'

'Aye, she's on the phone to Gerald. He's coming home tomorrow; he'll be here for our do . . . that's if . . .'

'Aye, we're still having our do, love, and that's grand news.'

His arms tightened around her. She looked up into his worried expression but couldn't put his mind at rest.

★   ★   ★

When they were all seated, Harry having told Alice when she came off the phone that Jackie needed to talk to them, Jackie looked from one to the other. Neither deserved to be worried about her, so she decided to make light of her going away. 'Eeh, I'm that excited, I've been chosen for war work!' Both looked astonished, but before they could speak, she told them what it was and ended with, 'but for leaving Marg, and you all, I'm just so glad of the change this offers me, and I knaw it will help with me heartbreak of waiting for you to return, Harry.'

'Well, if you're pleased, then we're pleased, aren't we, Alice?'

'Well, it's taken the wind out of me sails, but yes, except how will Marg be about it?'

'She knaws. And she ain't happy. But there's worse than this happened.'

As they listened, horror etched their faces.

'Naw. Eeh, Jackie, I can't bear to think of it. You have to call the police. Bob will make sure Gran gets justice. That woman wants locking up before she can do this to anyone else.'

'I knaw. I'm hoping Clive will sort that out, but in another way, I hope they leave it to lie. As I came out, I saw a letter on the hall table for Marg. It looked official and had a stamp on the front that suggested it had come from Her Majesty's law court. I reckon it will summon her to testify against me da.'

'Oh no! And here we were all looking forward to tomorrow, lass.'

Jackie nodded. From how she felt this morning to now, she couldn't have felt less like celebrating anything, but she

181

would. This was the most important thing to happen in her life – the final proclamation that she and Harry belonged to each other. 'We'll carry on, eh? We're well practised at that now, so we can . . . I can.' She looked from one to the other. 'We must.'

Harry jumped up. 'Aye, it'll all go ahead. Alice has had me helping her to make cakes. I've beaten eggs, sifted flour, filled tarts with jam, and greased tins till I'm blue in the face, so it has to.'

This made them both smile at him, but he didn't fool Jackie. Hearing about Gran, who he adored, had hurt him deeply, she could see that.

'Aye, and me Gerald is coming home – a bit earlier than he was supposed to, but he has his posting earlier so . . .'

'Eeh, Alice, what can I say?'

'What can anyone say? There is nothing that will make it better. Anyway, this won't get the food done for the party. Are you here to help, or what, Jackie, lass, as you can run rings around us all with your baking?'

Catching on to the spirit Alice was showing, Jackie said, 'Aye. Take me to a pinny, and we'll soon have everything done!'

Somehow with this, Jackie did feel stronger and as if she could do whatever lay ahead of her, but then the thought entered her that she wished she wasn't doing it anywhere near Mr Blake – how she would ever be able to call him Captain, she didn't know.

SIXTEEN

Alice

Half an hour later, leaving Harry, Jackie and Heather to it, Alice got into her car and drove around to Marg's. She didn't know what she'd find but was surprised to hear laughing.

Opening the back door, she called out, 'Marg, it's me, lass, can I come in?'

'Aye, I knew you wouldn't be long in coming around, love.'

'Well, I expected tears and tantrums, but glad I didn't find it.'

'I've wept a bucketful, but then you think, what's the use? We'll all be like wet blankets if we don't toughen up. There's nothing going to stop us all going through hell.'

'You're right, but it ain't that easy. We pick ourselves up and they knock us over again. How's Gran?'

'Eeh, Alice, that's the worst thing that's happened today, with Jackie going almost topping it, but me poor defenceless gran. Come through. Clive's in the front room.'

She greeted Clive and had a hug from him – Clive's hugs always made you think everything was fine as it seemed there was nothing he couldn't sort out. He was big, dependable, and just lovely.

Then as they sat, Marg told her, 'I've had three things to contend with, but one is resolved. A letter came from the court solicitor, and I thought it was going to summon me, but Eric's made a full confession – the only decent thing he's done in his life! Clive thinks he will have bargained with something – telling everything about his operations, et cetera, so others can be stopped, but all I can think of is that I won't have to testify. It's over. He'll be sentenced and that will be that.'

'That's good, Marg, but what are you going to do about that awful woman and how will you look after Gran now, on your own?'

'We can't do a lot . . . I'd like to, but we're thinking about Jackie in all of this. Martha has said she wouldn't dare testify, if it got to court, and she has good reasons. But I suppose you know about Jackie going?'

'Aye, how do you feel about that?'

'Clive's made me see that they wouldn't have chosen her unless she can really make a difference. We ain't believing what she's told us, but we ain't going to tell her that. We're just going to support her. Clive's convinced she is being called upon to do work that only a few are capable of. He says it could be anything as a lot of skills are needed, but he's sure it isn't in France. There's nothing a young girl of Jackie's age can do there but nursing and she ain't a nurse. So, though I'm going to miss her like part of me is torn from me, I'm going to send her off with pride.'

'That's grand. I'm sure she'll be safe and will be given leave and can come home on a regular basis. But nothing so far solves your problem about Gran's care.'

'We don't know yet, we've to work that one out. But there will be a way, we'll sort something. Clive's all for employing another nurse, but I don't know.'

'What about Ada? I saw her the other day and she's missing Gran, and all of us. But she was saying that no one seems to need her services anymore. She said there's no babbies being born, and all the elderly, sick and infirm have either gone, or have got better.'

'Eeh, it'd be grand if she would do it . . . By, Clive, she'd be the answer to our prayers.'

'But you used to call her everything, lass. I thought you were glad to see the back of her.'

Marg shook her head. 'I don't think you'll ever understand us from Whittaker Avenue, lad. We are a community. If one needs help, we're all there, and Ada was our call on for anything that went wrong healthwise. We couldn't do without her. She's one of ours, and that gave me a licence to get mad at her if she annoyed me, but it don't mean I wouldn't go to the end of the earth for her, or her for me . . . Eeh, I want to go and fetch her this minute.'

'Ha, I never thought I'd hear you say that! You're right, Marg, I'll never understand.'

'The main thing is that she's good with me gran, and when she hears what's happened, she'll be that angry.'

185

'Well, I rushed around here to the rescue, only you don't need rescuing, at least you won't if it works out with Ada. Now, I'd better say hello to Gran.'

Gran was in her chair. Not the one they all thought she'd wanted to bring from the old house, but a lovely comfy, blue patterned one that went beautifully with the pale blue carpet that covered the middle part of the room, leaving a surround of polished wood.

The chair Gran had referred to which held all her memories stood in a corner, gleaming as always with a deep shine. Alice never saw it without breathing a sigh of relief that it was revealed before they moved her here and had possibly destroyed it.

'How are you, Gran, love?'

'Have you come to be me nurse, lass?'

'No, not this time, Gran. But I think you'll like who might come.'

'Did you see Martha? She used to be a friend of me Vera's when they were little . . . Eeh, I wish me Vera would come home, lass, have you seen her?'

Alice thought this looking for people she loved and who she would never find must be agony for Gran.

'I've come a different road, so wouldn't have done, love. I've come to tell you that me Gerald's coming home tomorrow. Are you ready for the party, lass? It's going to be a smasher!'

Gran grinned. 'I love parties. Me John always dances with me.'

'I bet he's polishing his dancing shoes, love.'

'Aye, mind, he don't need no fancy shoes, he could dance in his bare feet.'

'So, are you all right after what happened, Gran?'

'Eeh, lass, I'm fine ... What happened, anyway? Is me Marg all right?'

Alice wished Marg was here to hear Gran remember who she was. 'She is. She's with her Clive. I'm just going back to them, then I'll come and say goodbye. Is that all right?'

'I don't know this Clive you're talking about, but, aye, I'll see you in a bit, eh?'

Alice kissed the top of Gran's head. 'See you in a mo, love.'

Happy that Gran hadn't suffered any ill effects from being bullied by the awful Wendy, Alice braced herself for the protests she knew she was about to face.

'Is Gran all right?'

'She is, Marg, but a little confused.'

'I was about to bring her through here when you came, Alice. Will you carry her through, Clive, love? I think with all the upset she needs to be with us.'

'Can it wait a minute, Marg? What I want to tell you might upset you.'

'Eeh, no, no more trouble, please, lass.'

'It ain't trouble ... I've volunteered. I've put me name down at the Red Cross to be considered for duty in France. They need ambulance drivers over there and a request has been sent to the Red Cross for anyone they can send.'

'Eeh, Alice ... I don't know what to say. Does Gerald know? And the lads ... Aw, I can't bear to think of it. First Jackie, and now you.'

'Gerald knows. I've been discussing it with him each time he rang me … I want to do this, Marg. I've been trained for it and have been commended in me handling of the mock-wounded in an exercise we did. But I've got more to give than practising.'

Marg had gone white. 'What does Gerald say? Surely he'll talk you out of it?'

'Well, naturally, he doesn't want me to do it. But he understands me need to. He said that I'd backed him in wanting to go so now it's his turn to back me.'

'Eeh, Alice, Alice …'

'I know, lass. You never could stand anything changing between us, but then, none of us made plans for a war. I've got skills that are needed. I have to use them.'

'And Joey? Billy? What about them?'

'I've thought long and hard about them. Heather will take care of them. She's like a grandmother to them. And, well, I'm hoping you and Edith will pitch in an' all. And I've spoken to Averill and Rod. They've agreed that if I go, they will live here and not find a flat when they take up their positions in Blackpool Victoria. And that's happening sooner than we thought as the hospital is getting short staffed, so they're coming tomorrow for the party and will bring some of their essential things but can go back and forth to their home in the Lakes till they have all they need.'

Marg let out a huge sigh as she wiped away a tear.

'I know, lass. It feels like the end of all we knew, but it will be for good and proper if those who can don't do something to help the war effort.'

Clive, who hadn't spoken since her revelation, asked, 'When will you tell the lads?'

'I'm not sure, Clive, that's going to be the hardest bit. I'm going to tell Harry before he leaves next week, but Billy and Joey ...'

'Won't you change your mind, lass? The work you do here is needed an' all?'

'No, Marg. I feel compelled to do this.'

'Is it because you'll be with Gerald?'

'Aye, that prompted me, but Gerald tells me we may not be together. Well, only some of the time, as whichever hospital he lands at, I'm bound to go there on the ambulance and as everything is happening in the north of France, we may not be billeted far from each other. We'll have to make do with what time we can snatch together – but if I'm not there, it could be years till I see him again.'

'Years! Eeh, Alice, I never dreamt ... And Edith and Philip, could that happen to them an' all?'

Alice could only nod. The thought was unbearable, but Gerald had made her see this as fact. This war could rage for years as the signs were that France could fall to the Germans, and then ... *Oh God, I can't think of it. Please don't let an invasion happen here.*

'Clive?' Marg had turned to Clive, shock still showing on her face.

'I've tried to make you realise, Marg, love. This isn't going to be over any time soon, and in fact, it's only just beginning. You must prepare yourself ... Are you really prepared, Alice? I mean, about Billy too. He could easily become of the age to go before this is over.'

'I've tried not to think about it and to keep hope alive, but aye, I have faced it, and it worries me more than Harry going. Harry will think first before he acts, Billy will be the hero.' She took a deep breath. 'I pray every night that he won't end up a dead hero.'

Her blood went cold as she voiced this fear for the first time, and she shivered.

'Eeh, Alice . . . Eeh, lass, we've faced some things in our time, but all of this is the worst ever.'

'It is, and that's why I want to do me bit. Not driving around Britain picking up the pieces when the lads are brought home – many don't make it, Marg. They're put on the ships alive, but when they get here . . . This is why there's a need for all medical staff on the ground where the injuries are happening. I want to do that. I have the skills. I have no kids and me Gerald will be out there doing what he can. Aye, I have me brothers, but they will be lovingly cared for and have me best friends watching out for them. I'll miss them more than I can imagine, but we all must make sacrifices. We have to do our bit.'

As she finished saying this, which she knew was part of still trying to convince and justify herself of her decision, she caught a look on Clive's face. 'I'm only talking of the need for medical staff to be over there, Clive. What you do here is vital to our country and to all sailors in distress after being torpedoed or shelled. You're saving lives on our seas; I want to do the same on the ground.'

Clive smiled. 'Don't worry, I understood, it's me. I know I'm needed here but feel guilty that I'm not putting myself forward for the front line action. But I also know in being a coxswain, my skills are best served in saving lives at sea. I am at home on the sea, and if not this, I would have chosen the Merchant Navy to volunteer my services.'

'Eeh, lad, you don't have to justify yourself to me. I've seen the lifeboats in action. They attended the practice landing of casualties at Liverpool. And even in that mock operation the crew risked their lives getting closer to the liner than is safe to do so. Their mission was to bring those marked as in dire need of emergency life-saving treatment to us quicker than the ships can get them into dock ... Mind, dummies were used for this part of it, but nothing could simulate what the lifeboat men did. That was for real and was terrifying.'

'I've been involved in such a practice session, and as you say, it is very difficult. In our case, it would be getting the injured directly off a distressed ship if it happens in our seas, as those injured in France are taken to Folkestone or Dover and wouldn't affect us.'

'Eeh, and the ship could be on fire, or still under fire ... Oh God!'

With this from Marg, Alice realised that she really hadn't taken in how much Clive's life could be in danger.

'Aw, Marg, I'm sorry to frighten you like this. But, lass, every one of us are in danger. I just need to go and to help those who are in the most.'

'I understand, Alice, love. More than at any time with what you've both just told me. I feel now that I want to do something.' She turned to Clive. 'There's folk who could run the rock factory, Clive, and the accountants can oversee the financial side. It don't really need me.'

Clive sighed. 'Not everyone can do something that's directly helping the war effort, Marg. Some can do it indirectly by keeping the economy going to pay for this war, by keeping men and women in work so that they can keep their families going. Leaving the factory to be run by just any Tom, Dick or Harry might mean we doom it to fail. The signs are that we can keep going as we are to be guaranteed a sugar supply. It is being said that everything that gives people a treat cannot be stopped, they will need them occasionally to help keep theirs and the children's morale up.'

Marg still looked unsure.

'You can do charity work, Marg. There will be plenty of that needed to help the war effort. Edith's ma-in-law is starting a lot of things to help folk. Edith was talking about it the other day and said that she is going to throw herself into it.'

'I suppose so. Aye, thinking about it, I can. And I will. I can do me bit and carry on keeping the rock factory going and keep an eye out for your lads.'

'And don't forget our sons . . . Marg has agreed to adopt George and Carl, Alice. They look on her as their mummy and she is going to be legally that.'

'Eeh, I'm a daft ha'peth. What were I thinking of? There's nothing more important than me looking after our lads.'

Alice was glad to see Marg had perked up. 'That's wonderful news, lass. When?'

It was Clive who answered. 'The papers will be presented at court on Monday of next week. It's only a family court and we don't have to attend. Our solicitor will oversee things and has told us that it's a rubber stamp affair. Papers are stamped and signed and that's it! Marg is an instant mother!'

Marg clapped her hands, making Alice grin.

'Do the boys know?'

'Aye, they do, Alice. We asked them and George said, "I thought you were our mummy, it feels like it." And Carl just looked mystified. So, Clive explained to them in simple terms and then Carl said. "I love you like a mummy, so you are. I don't need a paper to tell me who I love." George said, "me too," and that was that.'

'Only, when I put them to bed,' Clive told her, 'I did have a lovely moment with Carl, which Marg knows of and felt as happy about as I did. As I tucked him in, he asked, "Can George and I have two mummies? Only, I still want to think of the lady in the picture, holding me when me when I was a little boy, as my mummy. When I look at her, I know I love her. She didn't want to leave me and go to heaven, Grandma told me that."'

'It was a lovely moment, Clive. When you told me, I felt as though Carl was putting me and Harriet together – giving us the same love.'

Alice swallowed the tears that threatened as she listened to them, and the thought came to her that she hoped her little Gerald could love her from heaven. She didn't say this but made herself smile and said, 'That's grand. So, in the end all has worked out for you, Marg, and I'm glad . . . So, see you all tomorrow, eh? Party time! And when you think about it, we've a lot of concerns and sad things happening, but, by, we have lots to celebrate an' all.'

As she left the house, Alice concentrated on the good things – the best of which was that her Gerald was coming home. She couldn't wait to be in his arms.

But as most good thoughts were these days, this was tainted by the sadness of the knowledge that by the end of next week, she and Jackie would join Edith in not knowing when they would next be held by the men they loved.

SEVENTEEN

Edith

The atmosphere on Saturday evening was lovely, despite the undertone of everyone knowing that besides an engagement party this was a 'going away' party for so many of them.

Edith sat with Sue and Tom, her ma- and da-in-law. Sue was such a different person to the snobbish, spiteful lady Edith had first met and not been accepted by – a time when both Philip was almost, and his sister Patricia was, ostracised by Sue for them having partners well below what she'd considered their station in life.

And yet, she hadn't come from a wealthy background and Tom was from an even lower standing at the time. But having worked hard and risen to owning the Bradshaw biscuit factory, Sue had gained airs and graces that had turned her into someone who wasn't nice to know.

All that had changed now and Sue, Tom and Patricia and her husband Wilf and their two children were not just Edith's in-laws, but part of the family – her wider family who were gathered in this room tonight.

As were Averill and Rod, who were deep in conversation with their son Gerald.

'Now, my dear.' Sue had leant in to Edith. 'I must see you soon to discuss all of my plans. I'm thinking of a knitting group for one; we need to make warm clothing for our men who are freezing out in the fields in northern France and that wouldn't be too strenuous for you in your condition. But when the baby is born, and you have recovered, well, then you can take more of an active role in all my projects.'

'You said, all. What other plans have you in mind?'

'Well, I'm wondering how the poor of Blackpool are coping with their men and sons having gone to war. Oh, and the evacuees – someone ought to check on those left with us and make sure all is well with them. Some will have been left with a woman coping on her own. Ooh, I have so many plans. Besides which, you must know of where help is needed through your schoolwork, so getting our heads together over it all is the first thing to do.'

'I think you've covered everything and are going to need an army of helpers. I can help there, I can ask Marg and I've been back to Whittaker Avenue chatting to me old neighbours. I wanted to know how they all were. Some of them could do with some help, but some could help us. It will do them all good to do so. Make them feel they are doing their bit and that someone values them.'

'Good idea, I knew you would be my best ally – well, you and Patricia. She's enthusiastic too. Wilf's volunteered – he's ex-navy, as you know, and is going into the Merchant Navy – at least, he starts his training in Fleetwood in a couple of weeks. Whether he'll make the grade awaits to be seen.'

There it was, a little of the old Sue. Every now and then it surfaced – especially where Wilf was concerned. For all her reformation, she still had a dig at her son-in-law whenever she could. She'd wanted Patricia to marry some fella or other who stood to inherit a fortune, but instead she'd married a carpenter.

Edith was shocked to hear of Wilf's plans. She'd guessed he'd have to do something, and had imagined him in the Home Guard or some such, but the Merchant Navy? Everyone knew what a dangerous job that was, with the Germans out to disrupt all supplies and torpedoing those ships carrying anything to Britain. Patricia must be out of her mind with worry. 'Patricia is going to need all the support we can give her, Sue. The last thing she will need is to hear you speak in derogative terms about her husband whose life will be in constant danger.'

'Oh dear, I consider myself told off.'

'Aye, and so you should. Edith's right. The merchant ships, whether carrying goods or service personnel, are in extreme danger of attack.'

Sue nudged her husband. 'I thought you would get your penny's worth in. All right, I'm sorry. I'll try my best not to put Wilf down . . . but a carpenter is always a carpenter is all I'm saying.'

Tom sighed. Edith bristled, but decided the best thing was for her to escape. 'I'll just go and see if Mandy and Alf and their granny are all right. Be back in a mo . . . And, Sue,

I love your ideas. Eeh, you can be so thoughtful, and I love you for that, lass.'

She winked at Tom, who laughed out loud. He was always getting in trouble if he spoke in his natural Lancashire accent. Sue stiffened, but knew she'd done wrong and that was the main thing. It was a long road with her, but one with plenty of successes as she tried hard to drop her snobbish ways.

Philip would be proud of me . . . Eeh, me darling, where are you? Please, please, write soon.

She found Mandy and George giggling together in a corner. They were playing with a spider that they were letting run up their arm then passing to the other for it to do the same. She shuddered. Not fond of spiders, she decided to leave them to it. Alf and Carl were being entertained by Billy, who was showing them his football cards and going into the ins and outs of the game. She caught his eye and smiled. His lovely smile melted her heart. She loved Billy.

Happy that the children were all right and Minnie was sitting chatting with Ada and Marg's gran, who'd so picked up in the last few days since being back in Ada's care, Edith spotted Marg and went over to her. 'Ah, Marg. On your own like me then?'

'Aye, Clive and Wilf have got so much in common they always make their way to each other at these dos. Both love working with wood and both are seamen at heart.'

'That's good, lass. To find a kindred spirit like me, you and Alice are.'

'Aye, but for how long? It'll soon just be me and you.'

Edith reached for her hand. 'It will, but we'll be fine. It'll be our hearts aching that'll be the worst to cope with, but we've both got busy jobs, and kids to care for, and each other, lass.' She told Marg what Sue had been saying.

'Aye, Alice said that you'd mentioned it. So, she's still at the planning stage, then?'

'Well, she's decided a meeting would be the best thing. She said just me and her, but I'm going to suggest you and Patricia are there an' all.'

'Eeh, it sounds sad not to say you and me and Alice. By, I'm dreading her going.'

They looked over at Alice standing with Gerald – they hadn't left each other's side all evening.

'I'm glad for her. If I could just be in the same country as me Philip, wherever that is in the world, I would be.'

'Aye, if Clive ever had to go away, I'd be the same. You know, I never thought anything would ever come between us Halfpenny Girls, but our men have, haven't they?'

'In a way, yes. We'd leave each other to be with them, but we wouldn't leave them to be with each other. But that's a good thing. Each one of us may have had it rough as young 'uns, but we've found a love greater than anything and with good men, who will always care for us.'

Marg squeezed her hand. 'But we will always have each other, won't we?'

'Aye, we will, love. Always. You don't have to worry.'

Poor Marg. The feisty one amongst them, and yet the one who needed the most reassurance and wanted every-thing to stay as it was, but at the same time, embracing change in her own life. 'Anyroad, how's it all going at the factory, Marg?'

'Eeh, I love it, Edith. Why didn't we go into rock making when we were youngsters instead of biscuit packing, eh? It's much more interesting.'

'Might not have been. I bet most of the women you employ are wrappers of the rock, which is much the same as we were doing with biscuits.'

'That's true. But the processes involved and the way the lettering is done, it's all fascinating and I love it – even dealing with the buyers. I've a new one now, a shop over in Morecambe of all places, where there's factories making their own rock, but he likes the new range I'm doing. It's different shapes made from rock. Me latest is like a walking stick. But Billy being Billy put a suggestion in that we make rock with footballers' names going through it and have a football card in the wrapper!'

They both laughed, and yet Edith could see it being a popular line. 'You should do it. Make them small sticks that can be sold in any sweetshop. I reckon you'd make a bomb – well, not one of them, exactly, but you know what I mean.'

This made them giggle again and Edith felt better about Marg. She still had her ready sense of humour no matter that all seemed to be crumbling around them.

It dawned on her as she and Marg walked over to Alice and Gerald that this may be the last time they would all be together for a long time – well, she wasn't with her beloved Philip, but everyone else still had their man and they still had Alice and Jackie with them, though most were here for a small snippet of time.

'Eeh, Gerald, it's good to see you. How did the training go?'

'Very well, thanks, Edith. Took me back to my school days as apart from a few lectures about what we might expect to be different about working in the various conditions we might find ourselves in, there was a military drill – the army, you know, they can't resist marching you up and down and making you clean boots till you can see your face in them.'

He laughed at this, and they all laughed with him – how was it they could do so when everything they knew was changing? But Edith was glad that they could. This was a celebration – an evening to remember. She glanced over at the pile of gaily wrapped gifts for Jackie and Harry, no doubt all items for Jackie's bottom drawer. As she did, Clive tapped his glass.

'As the big brother of the future bride-to-be, I think I ought to propose a toast.'

Everyone hushed.

'Jackie, you were like a special bonus that came along with my lovely Marg. And I hold you dear as a young sister – an exceptionally kind and loving person whom I am so very proud of, as tonight, you not only commit yourself to sometime in the future being the wife of the most hand-some young man in the room, but you are on the precipice of a new venture that will take you away from us and all you have ever known, and yet you did not falter in your decision to do whatever is asked of you.'

The room erupted in cheers and calls of 'bravo'.

'And Harry. Apart from being the most handsome in the room . . .'

Harry blushed and Billy called out, 'Ha! You should see him in the mornings before he puts his teeth in!'

This caused everyone to laugh.

Clive had done so out loud, with his head back. But now he was sober again. 'We'll take that as brotherly love, Billy . . . Anyway, we are very proud of you too, Harry. You fought through an illness that laid you low and did all you could to get back to fitness so you could take up the call that had come to you. We as a nation are blessed to have such young people as you and Jackie willing to do your part and we wish you both well, though we are going to miss you. We hope that you'll soon be able to pick up your lives again and enjoy the happiness you so richly deserve, and that we all wish for you . . . Please raise your glasses, to Jackie and Harry.'

When the clapping died down, Gran piped up. 'That's me John, you knaw. He's good at talking and even better at acting.'

This caused uproar again, and Gran beamed at everyone around the room. Joey was sat next to Gran now, and she put her hand out to him. 'Eeh, me lad, you've grown. Have you had your feet in me John's manure?'

At this she put her head back and let out a cackling laugh. 'Here's to you, me Jackie.' Jackie ran over to her. 'Eeh, Gran, I'm so glad you came back to us at this moment as there's none I wanted to share it with more than you.'

'Back? I ain't been anywhere, it's all the others that keep going . . . Me Vera, and me John.' A tear seeped out of the corner of her eye. Jackie fell back on what they all did at such times. 'They're at the fairground, Gran, you know how your Vera's always pressing her dad to take her.'

202

'Aye, she's a one for the merry-go-round. She leads me a fair dance at times an' all.'

'She'll be back soon.'

Ada grunted, showing her disagreement with what Jackie had said. But she didn't say anything as Gran sat back looking content. 'If I were younger, I'd get up and dance with that fine young man.'

Ada didn't keep quiet at this. 'Well, you're not, so shut up, Sandra, and behave yourself.'

Gran grinned up at Ada. 'Ta for coming back to me, lass. I missed you.'

Ada put her arm around Gran and kissed her forehead. 'Aye, and I missed you – I missed telling you off, as you're a bad 'un at times, me lass.'

Gran gave another cackling laugh. All in the room joined in and Edith thought that none of them would want Gran to be any different, and a happiness settled in her that Gran had Ada back – a woman who had often busybodied into their business, and taken money from the hands of those she treated when she knew they couldn't afford it, and yet who was part of them all and, for all her faults, she was the best person in the world to care for Gran.

At the end of the evening, Edith felt lonely. Even though she had Minnie, Alf and Mandy to go home with, she was going home to an empty bed. *Eeh, Philip, me Philip, how long have we got to be separated for?*

Minnie, who sat in the front seat of the car, leant over and took her hand. 'Yer a brave, girl, luv. Keep going, eh? One foot in front of the other to the end of the road.'

With this, she burst into song:

'Every road through life is a long, long road,
Filled with joys and sorrows too.
As you journey on how your heart will yearn
For the things most dear to you.
With wealth and love 'tis so,
But onward we must go.'

Amidst giggles and with very loud voices she and the children joined in:

'Keep right on to the end of the road,
Keep right on to the end.'

It was the second verse that really resonated:

'If the way be long, let your heart be strong,
Keep right on round the bend.
If you're tired and weary, still journey on,
Till you come to your happy abode,
Where all you love that you're dreaming of
Will be there at the end of the road.'

As she sang '*keep right on . . .*' with the others, Edith thought, *All I love and am dreaming of is you, Philip, and one day you will be there waiting for me at the end of this war – but when will that be, and how much will we all have to bear before it happens?*

EIGHTEEN

Jackie

When Jackie came out of the Foreign Office, all she told Harry, who'd insisted on coming with her, was that she had to report to Bletchley on the following Monday morning. He didn't press her as to what it was that she'd been told she would be doing, except to ask, 'You haven't to go abroad, have you, lass?'

'Naw, I promise you, it ain't nowt like that. I'm going to be safe – a lot safer than you, Harry . . . Eeh, I wish this war hadn't have happened, we were all so happy. I knaw we had our problems, but they'd only brought us closer, and everything seemed sorted – settled, somehow, and now this.'

'Well, it's good that you haven't got to go abroad, and I wish that I hadn't, nor Gerald, nor . . . Eeh, why does our Alice want to go? That's tearing me up. I want her safe at home, not driving between the front line and some field hospital. I can't bear to think of the danger she could be in.'

'We've all got to do what we need to do, Harry. Someone else's sister would have to do it if Alice didn't.'

205

'You're right. Anyroad, let's see what London has to offer, shall we?'

Although they hadn't a clue where to go, they hopped on a bus that said Marble Arch as they'd both heard of that.

On the journey, Jackie thought of what she'd been told. She was to report to Captain Blake. Her heart had dropped at this. She was told little else except that her work would be to do with decoding messages and was vital. She'd had to sit a test, a crossword puzzle.

She hadn't done many of these, since she'd stopped working for Blake's accountancy.

Mr Blake – she didn't think she'd ever get used to calling him 'Captain' – used to call out clues that he couldn't solve, and she had no problem with them, though sometimes she thought it amused him to test her.

Lately, since living with Clive, she'd found that he did them too and he'd rekindled her interest. She preferred the cryptic clues. Clive was always asking her to help him with these and then was astonished at how quickly she solved them.

To his question of how she did it, she didn't know. She just did. The answer often seemed obvious to her, and she sailed through the one she'd been set just now.

The gentleman who was the main interviewer applauded her. 'You'll do, young lady, you're just what we are looking for, and you couldn't come more highly recommended.'

One of the women – Baroness something or other – had huffed. 'I would recommend that she works on her diction and grammar, though.'

Jackie had felt her face reddening.

'Madam, it's Miss Porter's brain that is of interest to us, not her speaking voice or anything else. If she can solve puzzles how she can, just think what achievements she'll have in unravelling codes!'

He'd abruptly scribbled something, then passed the paper he'd written on to her.

'Sign that.'

She had no time to read it, but when she passed it back, he'd told her, 'You have just signed the Official Secrets Act. To break it is a criminal offence. In short, you do not discuss anything we have said in here, or ever betray the nature of the work we are doing at Bletchley Park. You do not reveal names of the people you will be working with or under, and that includes keeping everything secret from those you are most close to . . . Now, my sources tell me that you are saying good-bye to your fiancé on Friday, so I want you on the next train that same day that goes to Preston. Your route and train times are mapped out for you and will take you to Bletchley . . . Here is a warrant for your travel and all the instructions for your journey. You will be picked up at the station in Bletchley and taken to Bletchley Park. Have with you all you will need. Thank you, Miss Porter, and good luck.'

Before she'd known what was happening, she was outside the office and being shown out of the building. Even now as she sat on the bus hardly seeing the sights passing by, she felt as though a whirlwind had hit her.

'You seem nervous, Jackie, are you sure you're all right?'

'Aye, it's just all so sudden and strange.'

'It's a mystery to me how they knew of you and what you're capable of. It's creepy, like we're being watched.'

Changing the subject, Jackie pointed out the park through the arch they were now passing. 'Isn't it lovely? Can we go and sit in there for a mo while I get me breath back?'

All they had done in London – visiting Buckingham Palace and Trafalgar Square, and having a bite to eat in a pub, both choosing pie and mash that Mandy and Alf were always on about and finding it delicious, and just being together – seemed like years ago as she stood on Blackpool North station with her huge case on a trolley, and holding hands with Harry.

Alice, Marg and Edith were with her, as they had all been with Alice the day before when they'd said goodbye to Gerald.

The scenes of that parting haunted her thoughts – watching Alice and Gerald holding hands and looking into each other's eyes had been heart-breaking.

Hugging Joey to her had torn her in two, as the lad had tears streaming down his face. He'd whispered to her that he was brave really, and could wave Gerald off, but he didn't know how it would be for him when he did the same for Alice.

Billy had stood against the wall with one leg propped up against the bricks, just staring. He'd made a joke when it was his turn to shake Gerald's hand. 'Go and put all our lads together again, Gerald. And tell them we're proud of them, but to keep their heads down, as you ain't got enough plasters to keep sticking them back on their necks.'

Gerald had laughed out loud and ruffled Billy's hair. 'You're a tonic, Billy. Take care of your sister and brother.'

Neither Billy nor Joey had come to the station today. Both had hugged Harry and Jackie before they left Harry's house, and both had had tears in their eyes. There'd been no jokes from Billy today.

But till now, leaving Gran, George and Carl had been the biggest wrench.

Now, she felt that she couldn't let go of Harry. She clung on to him with her arm around his waist and kept hold of his jacket even as he hugged Marg, making herself smile as he said to Edith, 'By, it's hard to get close to you, Edith, and babby will be born afore I see you again.' He'd become serious then, telling her to tell her babby he'd meet him in the future. Edith had a tearful giggle with him. After this Harry turned to Alice and clung on for an age.

Then it was time to do it – time to let him go. Her heart felt as though it was splitting in two. Harry's arms came around her, and his eyes filled with tears that wet her face and mingled with her own as he pulled her in close. His whispered 'I love you' was almost too much to bear, but she answered him. 'I love you, Harry, and allus have done. And though we're apart, we'll allus be together. We'll only be a thought away. A touch on that photo we had taken. And each thought, each touch, I will know about ... Eeh, me Harry, take care of yourself. Come back to me.'

'I will, I promise. Naw one'll keep us apart.'

With this he kissed her lips. Then grinned. 'Eeh, Bob's not about, is he?'

Jackie giggled a tearful giggle. 'He said he'd nick you the next time you kissed me in public, lad, but naw, he's not about, so shall we try it one more time?'

209

This time a cheer went up as Harry held her close and ground his lips onto hers, but she didn't care. The other soldiers would always take the rise out of each other, but this moment was hers and had to last her a long time.

As the train pulled out of the station, she ran alongside with all the other girls, women and children, but the platform wasn't a long one and soon all she could see were dozens of hands waving. She knew one of them would be her Harry and she hoped he could see her waving back.

'Well, me lass, you're next . . . Eeh, me love. I'm going to miss you. You promise you'll phone whenever you can, won't you, lass?'

To Jackie, these words of Marg's seemed alien to her emotions. She didn't want to talk about herself, she wanted to remember that last kiss. To imprint it on her mind, but Marg persisted. 'It'll be half an hour before your train comes in. Shall we go into the station café and have a cuppa together, eh?'

Jackie could only nod her head.

She felt Marg put her arm through hers. 'Come on, love, the sooner you do something the better.'

A hand came into hers. Edith smiled at her. 'The Halfpenny Girls are together for the last time in we don't know how long, so let's make the most of the last half hour, eh?'

To this, Jackie made herself smile and squeezed her arm on Marg's. 'I'll let you knaw the minute I arrive as there's bound to be a telephone box nearby. And as soon as I'm given leave, I'll be home.'

Alice, who hadn't spoken since hugging Harry, now said, 'Write an' all. Tell us all about . . . well, not your job, but the area, and all that ... though that's not really allowed either ... eeh, we're living in funny times.'

'The main thing is that you all knaw that I'm all right, though when you go, Alice, I'll be worrying about you.'

Alice just smiled. But the smile didn't touch her eyes. Jackie understood. It was the same for Edith and would be for her – the light had gone out of their lives.

When she reached Bletchley station, a tall girl with dark hair pulled back in a ponytail stood on the platform waving to her as she alighted from the train. She was what Jackie thought of as good-looking – not quite beautiful, like Edith, or pretty like Alice, but striking was more how she would term her.

'Jackie, is it?'

'Aye.'

'Good show. I'm Priscilla, but everyone calls me Prissy ... Just for short, not because I am. Ha, living with a lot of girls at boarding school and then here, you soon lose any inhibitions, darling.'

Despite her posh way of speaking, Jackie liked Prissy immediately.

'Don't worry about your bag ... Porter! Here. Jolly good. Put that valise into the boot of my car, please. The red one, over there.' Tipping the porter, Prissy linked arms with Jackie. 'What school did you go to, Jackie? I know most of the girls here. If I didn't go to school with them, Daddy played tennis or golf or something with their fathers, so we mixed socially, but I've never come across you.'

'Naw, I didn't go to a posh school. I went to St Kentigern's in Blackpool.'

211

Prissy looked taken aback for a moment but regained her composure. 'Spiffing! A real person. I'm going to like you, Jackie.'

Jackie didn't know what she meant by calling her a real person, of course she was. But she understood better when they got to what was to be her digs – a room in the attic of a building attached to what looked like a mansion to Jackie and set in huge grounds.

'That's the main building – Bletchley House. We don't use that much. Though there's a bar in there that's handy for the odd cocktail – not that they know how to bloody mix one! Ah, here's Katherine, who is called Katie, and Lucille, who is just Lucy.'

Both girls seemed to look down their nose at her before giving her a chance. The one called Katie looked her up and down. 'Where *did* you get that coat, darling?'

Lucy joined in with, 'And those boots? Have you no shoes? They look jolly uncomfortable and like workmen's boots.'

Feeling riled, Jackie blurted out, 'At a jumble sale, where *real* folk get all their clothes. And did naw one ever tell you that such comments are rude?'

Prissy clapped her hands. 'Jolly well said, Jackie. You two have no manners. You both know what it felt like when you first came here. Have some thought for others.'

They both apologised. Katie went so far as to say it didn't matter where she bought it, she looked nice in it, and that only her jealousy had made her say what she did.

Jackie decided to call a truce. If she was to live with them, then she'd do better to get on with them.

'Ta. It were a present from me sister as it happens. I've allus liked it.'

'I adore how you speak, Jackie. I could listen to you all day.'

Jackie could have hugged Prissy for this.

Though none of their clothes were fancy – Katie wore a navy cardigan with puffed-out shoulders tapering into a long straight sleeve worn over a round-necked, white blouse, and matched with a navy check skirt, and Lucy, a plain navy frock topped with a red fluffy cardigan, they spoke of quality, and seemed to give them an elegance and a natural grace.

'So, you are to share this room with me. Katie and Lucy share the room next door. We all share a bathroom, I'm afraid – us, and six more girls – but we get by. We have a rota and a set time we're allowed in there. It's just along the corridor. I'll take you to it, as after a long journey, you must jolly well want to pee like mad.'

Jackie wanted to laugh out loud. She never expected such frankness from any of these girls, but she did want to pee so followed Prissy.

Once in the corridor, Prissy told her, 'Don't mind them . . . But I'm afraid there are a lot like them here so just hold your own like you did back there, and you'll get along fine. By the way, have you a bicycle being shipped down? You'll need one.'

'Naw, I don't own a bike and don't even knaw if I can ride one or not.'

'You'll soon learn. You don't want to be relying on buses, they are few and far between and rattling old tin cans when they do come. I'll sort something. I'm sure I saw a notice on the board about one for sale. Do you have any money?'

'Aye, I've got plenty. I've savings in me post office account.'

'Jolly good, well, I'll find out about the bike then we'll catch the bus to the village post office and get some of your money out.'

'Oh, I thought you had a car.'

'No. I borrowed it from Simon. He's a smashing bloke. You'll meet him . . . There you go. I'll see you back in the room. You can unpack then before we go to the canteen – the food's not brilliant, but it fills a hole.'

Jackie hardly dared to sit on the lav long as she didn't know what the allotted time for a pee was, but it felt good to relieve herself. She couldn't believe all that had happened this week. It was like being taken into a wind storm on Blackpool Promenade and rushed along where you didn't want to go as often happened when the gusts were strong.

Blackpool – when will I see you again? Eeh, I miss you already. But more than me home town, I miss all those I love, especially . . . As she could feel the tears prickling, Jackie cut this thought short, stood, readjusted her clothing before vigorously washing her hands to remove what felt like grime from her journey.

As Gran allus says, you've to get on with things. And I will. I'll do the best job I can and hope that what I do really does contribute to ending this horrible war!

NINETEEN

Alice

A week later, even though this was no longer Whittaker Avenue and Marg had a garden now, Alice, Marg and Edith sat on Marg's step – a ritual that they all loved.

None of them spoke. They just sat watching the light fade, and the stars beginning to appear as for mid-April the evening was surprisingly mild.

Marg and Edith had sat Alice in the middle as if they were still trying to protect and support her, but to Alice, Edith was the one who needed them the most as there seemed no end to her heartache of not knowing where her Philip was, whereas she could soon be joining Gerald and Harry in the north of France.

Miss Tenby, the officer in charge of their Blackpool branch of the Red Cross, had told her that the situation was getting desperate there and that the army medics had pleaded for more help. They needed ambulance drivers, and so she should prepare herself for the likely event that having put herself forward she could well be chosen to go.

Breaking the silence, she told Marg and Edith of the latest development. 'Well, me lasses, it could all be happening for me soon. I've been summoned to the chief executive's office in Lancaster's Red Cross HQ next Tuesday.'

'Eeh, no, Alice!'

'I told you it was coming, Marg, love.'

'I know, but . . . so soon?'

Edith, usually the positive, brave one of them all, just muttered, 'Our lives are falling apart.'

Alice found her hand. Suddenly, the strong young woman she'd always thought Edith to be seemed to have crumbled.

'I have to do this, Edith, love . . . It isn't just to be with Gerald, but I have this strong urge to be out there, to be helping our lads.'

'You won't be here when me babby's born, lass. I – I thought you both would . . . With me not having Philip, I was sort of relying on you both being with me.'

Marg saved the day by making a joke. 'Eeh, Edith, I ain't sure about that. They say you let wind when you push. I'd have to wear me gas mask.'

This had them laughing out loud and the moment lightened.

As they came out of this, Marg said, 'I'm fed up with me blooming gas mask as it is. I don't know about you two, but it's cumbersome, it's like carrying two handbags.'

'Aye, you see a lot without them now.'

'I know, Edith. Folk get slapdash about these things, but they shouldn't, we never know what's going to happen or when. Mind, if Bob catches them without it, they're in trouble, but, eeh, gas masks are the last thing I want to talk about. Does this mean you'll be going soon, Alice?'

'Aye, it's likely, Marg. And I'm ready now. The lads are all prepared and Averill and Rod are finally moving in this week. They were delayed by a burst pipe in the attic and their house flooding. Apparently, it isn't easy to get plumbers in the remote area of the Lakes where they live.'

'That'll put your mind at rest, lass. And the lads seem to have accepted it, so it looks like everything's in place for you.'

'It is. Poor Billy and Joey are being very brave, but I am worried about what all this is doing to them.'

'I'll keep Billy busy at work, and make sure I have chats with him that'll let me know how he is. I find with him, if you give him responsibility, he shines.'

'I think you're right, Marg. If I was you, Alice, I'd put him in charge of Joey and just ask Heather to be there for them. Averill and Rod will hook on to that and be fine, but I worry that Heather might try to mother them too much when you're gone.'

'Aye, she can be like a mother hen, but we have a laugh about it. Billy seems to handle that better than us all with his joking way, but without me, Heather may step that up a bit, so I'll have a word. Mind, we've no complaints, we all love her and love having her fuss over us.'

'Well, cocoa time, lasses.' Marg looked at her watch. 'Eeh, Clive said he'd be back for nine. He went to the station to give some extra training to a couple of new volunteers. One ain't very old, but he's been refused call-up because he has flat feet.'

'Well, at least the lad will feel he's doing something, and aye, that cocoa sounds grand.'

'You're right, Edith. Well, I won't be a mo, I'll just look in on the lads and make sure they're still sleeping peacefully. Ada had put Gran to bed and was nodding off herself when I came out here.'

They had their cocoa in Marg's lovely cosy kitchen as the air was chilled now, but then called it a night. To Alice's relief, Clive arrived just as they were going, as Marg had begun to be on pins about him. Of them all, she thought Marg would cope the least if Clive had to go away for a long time and thanked God that it wouldn't come to that as he was now exempt from call-up.

Life was lived at a fast pace for Alice after she successfully completed her interview. She was surprised to be attached to the ATS, but had no time to think between uniform fittings, briefings, settling Averill and Rod in, then goodbyes, tears and heart-breaking moments with Billy, Joey and Marg and Edith, until now, here she was stepping off the boat in Dieppe.

The crossing had been choppy, and she'd felt cold to the bones of her, as feeling sick on board, she'd spent most of the time up on deck along with other medical staff.

'Not the best way to get to know each other, eh? Helping each other as we each emptied our stomachs into the sea!'

Alice smiled at Penny, a nursing sister from Leeds returning to duty after a couple of weeks' leave.

A young woman in her late twenties, Penny had a bubbly personality and had kept them all going with her sense of humour and her informative tales.

'I'm an old hand at this, and yet it still gets to me when it's like this.'

The boat had suddenly lurched and sent her reeling towards the deck rail. Clinging on for a moment, she deftly pushed herself off and, like someone drunk, somehow made it back to the bench, amidst everyone laughing with her but unable to help her.

'The thing to do is to drink water, keep sitting down and don't look at the horizon. When it appears then disappears from view it makes you feel worse,' she'd told them – complete opposite advice to what Alice had been given by Averill, but she did find that looking at her feet instead of where they were heading worked and she had begun to feel less queasy.

As they waited on the dock, Penny said, 'I don't suppose any of you know where you're heading?'

'No, I'm to collect me ambulance when it's unloaded and follow in convoy.'

'Well, it could be one of two hospitals. Number One G Hospital which has taken over the golf club and casino in Dieppe, or Number Two G Hospital at Offranville where I am stationed.'

'Eeh, you'll know me hubby then, Gerald. Doctor Meredith.'

'Yes, I do! We all love him. As soon as he arrived, the place seemed to become more organised, and we got more done. He even gets on well with Matron and she can be a tartar!'

Alice's heart swelled.

'Do the powers that be know your relationship?'

'No, no one asked.'

'Well, I'd keep it a secret. Look, I'll see him before you, so I'll tell him to just be professional around you. You do the same and this could work. If Matron does find out, she'll be less likely to have one of you shipped out if you've shown no emotional involvement but acted professionally.'

'By, that'll be hard. I'll just want to run into his arms, I've missed him that much.'

'I don't want to sound rude, but, well ... how did you meet him? I – I mean ...'

'I'm not what you expected – that would have been a posh girl of his own standing. I know, it's unusual to find them from a different class matching up. But class don't account for love.'

'What about his parents, were they all right with you?'

Alice felt herself bristle. She hadn't come across this way of thinking before – well, maybe with Edith's in-laws, but Gerald's parents loved her and she them. And Philip wasn't like his parents. Nor were Clive and his parents snobbish. 'Aye, they were fine, they're what you term Bohemian. His ma is anyroad. I love them and they love me.'

'Well, that's good. And you must love Gerald, to follow him out here.'

'That and me being a trained Red Cross medic and wanting to do me bit.'

'Well, you're just what we need for an ambulance driver. Ours is a tented base hospital. You'll be bringing in wounded to us from the casualty clearing stations. These move a lot according to how the front line moves as they are the first line of treatment – or you could be working directly from the front line. You're going to need a lot of gumption. And physical strength.'

'Aye, well, I may look small, but I've proved meself on exercises. As for gumption, I ain't sure about that till I'm faced with needing it, but they did try to simulate the injuries – just not . . . well, the war, the guns and shells. That'll be new to me.'

'Don't worry, you wouldn't be here if they hadn't seen you'd got the mettle for it. You'll be fine. The last thing they want is a hysterical ambulance driver.'

'So, have you an idea where I'll billet?'

'Not really. Our accommodation isn't bad. We nurses are billeted in the homes of locals, but most of the doctors prefer to stay on camp in tents. They don't have regular shifts as we do, but are on call a lot, so they find it more convenient. They have a tent with a canvas bed and wash bowl on a stand. I think you'll have something similar in one of the tents of the casualty treatment centres. You'll move around with them.'

None of it sounded very inviting, and the nerves Alice had felt since leaving home began to really kick in, but she took deep breaths and told herself that she could do it.

When Penny had to leave as her transport arrived, the ambulance drivers were still waiting. There were six in total. Alice moved closer to them, free now Penny had left to be able to get to know them.

'You're one of the girls who had to go out on deck, aren't you?'

'Aye, I were feeling queasy. I've never been that far out at sea afore. The most I've done is to have a paddle in our Blackpool sea.'

'I'm Hazel, I'm from Skegness, so a fellow seasider, but lucky enough to have a dad with a boat so I've been able to gain my sea legs. How are you now?'

Alice only had time to say she was fine before they were called to attention, instructed to join their vehicles and were ready to set off. She saw that Hazel jumped into the driving seat of one of the other ambulances. This gave her confidence to think she wasn't the only woman driver.

As she cranked the engine, a young man of around her own age, who Alice had seen on the boat, came over to her. 'Cannae manage, lass?' He put out his hand. 'Pete Farnley, I'm your mucca – a Smoggie, which means I'm from Middlesbrough.'

Alice grinned as she took his hand. 'I ain't no idea what a mucca is, but I'm Alice, a Sangronian, which means I'm from Blackpool, born and bred.'

'Ha, we'll get over the language barrier, lass. I'm meaning that I'm your mate – partner, well, I hope we get to be the other meaning of the word – friends.'

Alice knew they would, she liked him instantly.

As they followed in convoy – ambulances, trucks full of men carrying soldiers, others with nursing and medical staff aboard – she learnt a lot about Pete.

'I'm army Medical Corps – a combat medical technician, to give me me full title. We'll probably be working together in the field.'

'Pleased to meet you, Pete. Alice, I'm Red Cross, assigned as an ATS. Me training is in first aid and ambulance driving.'

'Red Cross, aya? Pleased to hear that, I've worked with a Red Cross personnel bloke before, we were good muccas. Sadly, though, he got killed. He were a brave man. He ran across no-man's-land to help a wounded lad; he just got him back to me when a stray bullet got him. We don't know which side it came from, German or one of our lot, but it would have been an accident as he had the Red Cross flag with him. No one shoots at medical staff. He were a good mucca. Had five kids. I went to see them when on leave. I took them his flag and was able to tell them stories about their dad. I think it helped them as much as it helped me.'

Alice felt her stomach tighten. The story gave her the reality of what she faced. 'Eeh, I'm sorry to hear that ... What's it like, Pete? It's me first time in a war situation.'

'Howey now, you'll be sound, lass. Dunnae be worrying. And the scran's good. Ha, the posh lot don't think so, but they ain't used to boiled beef and cabbage like us.'

Alice hadn't meant the domestic arrangements, but then, it seemed that no one liked to talk about what they went through or what it was like working amongst the background of crossfire, and shelling, and nothing in her imagination would give her an idea of it all.

'Oh, and the beds are not your regular sprung mattress type.'

'Aye, I know about them, I learnt on the boat, and how the heating's inadequate and that medicines and bandages are in short supply – most of the bad stuff, so it's good to know as there's good food. That's something, at least.'

Pete laughed, a lovely hearty laugh. 'You'll do. I don't like a moaner, and you sound as though you'll take it all in your stride. Some can do nowt but moan. It donnae do them any good, like, but you can't make them see that.'

Alice glanced at Pete. His words had surprised her as so far everyone had seemed to treat the conditions with good humour. He was grinning, so it didn't seem that morale was a problem.

A tall, strong-looking man, Pete had sandy-coloured hair, cut very short at the back and sides, but when he took his beret off, it seemed the barber had left him a nice bit on the top as it flopped forward, and he kept having to run his fingers through it to keep it off his face.

He had a nice face, rounded and dimply when he grinned.

'We've had a rook of bronchitis and pneumonia cases of late. It seems as most of the lads sent out here are poorly prepared for this harsh winter. It can get to you at times, lass, so I hope you brought your winter woollies with you.'

'Aye, I've packed me warm clothing.'

'Mind, you can get a sweat on at times, despite the cold. Our work ain't easy, and there's some heavy lifting.'

This last held a lot of meaning, so Alice reassured him. 'I may be small, but don't worry. I'm as strong as the next.'

They'd reached the first hospital and there was a delay as one or two of the trucks turned off. Once they were on the road again, it wasn't long before they were slowing at Offranville.

Alice's heart beat loudly in her ears. Her longing to just catch a glimpse of Gerald made it difficult for her to stay relaxed and act as if everything was normal, but she couldn't stop herself leaning forward and searching every bit of space she could see. *Please God, let him have received me letter telling him that it looked likely I'd be coming on the next ship.*

She'd written as soon as she'd heard her application had resulted in an invitation to an interview. But in any case, Gerald knew her plans, surely he would watch out for her?

What she saw came as a bit of a shock.

Number Two Hospital was like nothing she'd imagined. Tents stretched from just in front of her to as far as she could see. She'd been told there were twenty beds in each ward, and a thousand beds. Then there were the mess and the kitchens, the sleeping quarters, latrines and shower blocks, and stores – medical, and food as well as beds and bed linen. All had to be kept in tents.

As she gazed from one to the other, suddenly Gerald appeared, his eyes scanning the stationary vehicles.

'Won't be a mo, Pete.'

'Hey, where're you off to? We'll be pulling out in a mo.'

Alice didn't wait to answer. Nor did she falter as the rain lashed down on her, plastering her hair to her head, or at the sounds of explosions and heavy machine gun fire carried on the air to her – increased in volume now she was out of the cab and sounding as if they were coming from only yards away. Neither did she take heed of the many pairs of eyes that must be watching her, wondering. She only had one aim – to reach her beloved.

When Gerald caught sight of her, he motioned her to follow him. She ran as fast as she could to where he'd disappeared behind the small tent to their left and fell into his arms.

His lips came down on hers. The rain mingled with their tears as their kiss united them once more.

As they came out of it, Alice could only whisper, 'I'm here, my love. Wherever you make your bed, I make mine. I love you.'

Gerald's, 'Oh, Alice, my love, my darling,' was gasped out between sobs. But then the sound of the hooter on her ambulance echoed around them. 'I have to go, me love, but we'll be together again soon.'

With this she kissed his cheek and ran back to the ambulance.

'Yer sweetheart?'

'Aye ... well ... how good are you at keeping a secret, Pete?'

'Nowt passes me lips that I'm told in confidence, hen.'

'It were me husband, Gerald. He's a doctor.'

'And a good 'un – the best. Well, yer couldn't have picked better for yerself, Alice. We all love Doctor Meredith but the pair of you will have to watch yer backs. Even though there's a dire need of staff, matrons look down on such situations.'

'I know.'

But despite knowing they had to be careful and coming to realise just how much danger they were in, at this moment, all that mattered was that she'd found him. She'd found her Gerald.

* * *

By the time they reached the clearing station the world seemed as though it was on fire as houses in the distance burnt and clumps of trees were a mass of flames. The air was cloudy with smoke and the smell of sulphur stung her nostrils. The noise blasted her ears and a couple of times, as she was shown to the mess for hot tea and a briefing, made her cringe and hold her head as if trying to save herself.

'You'll get used to it, me mucca. Haway inside and get yerself a hot drink in yer belly.'

Before she retired to her quarters – a long tent with rows of canvas beds and canvas bowls on stands – Alice told herself that she must be strong and ready to face anything.

They hadn't been out on a mission but had seen ambulances coming and going and witnessed the dreadful injuries, the appalling conditions and almost got used to the putrid air as the smoke and sulphur now mingled with the stench of latrines and, worst of all, blood.

She'd caught up with Hazel again and found they were to sleep next to one another.

They chatted for a while, though both were exhausted, but as the lights went out it was none of what she experienced that kept Alice awake – it was the pictures that came to her of her lovely Billy and Joey settling down, kissed goodnight by others, not her. Of Marg and Edith, maybe sitting on Marg's step, drinking cocoa, trying to comfort each other, wondering about her, and of Jackie, being away from her beloved Marg and Gran. Then the forbidden thoughts that sent her into a deep pit of sadness and fear – Harry. Was he out there amongst the hell they could only witness from afar? Was he safe? *Please God, keep him so.*

She was in a world so very different to the one she knew, cold, tired and afraid. She pictured Gerald in a similar bed and her heart yearned to be lying with him in their own bed. To feel his naked body entwining hers.

The feeling was so real to her that she reached out to hold him close – it was then that the stark reality of her situation hit her.

Feeling like a lost and lonely child, she fought back the tears.

TWENTY

Edith
May 1940

The telephone ringing made Edith jump, she'd been so deep in thought.

When Philip's voice came down the crackling line, she could hardly say his name. All she could get out was, 'My darling,' then as excitement zinged through her, 'Philip? Is that really you . . . ? Philip, eeh, me Philip. Where are you?'

'I'm in London. I'm just going to pick up my car and drive through the night to come to you, my darling . . . my Edith.'

His voice triggered her tears, but she wiped them away as Minnie came up to her. 'It ain't bad news, is it, Edith, darlin'?'

Edith shook her head.

'Darling, was that Minnie? She's still there? She hasn't taken the twins home? Oh, that's wonderful. You're not alone and we still have our little Mandy and Alf!'

'Yes, Philip, it's all grand, everything's just grand.' As she said this she smiled through her tears at Minnie, then watched as she went back into the kitchen.

'Hurry, me love . . . but drive carefully an' all . . . eeh, I'm contradicting meself . . . but I'm in a tizzy.'

'Just tell me how you are before I go, darling . . . Hold on, the beeps are going, I'll just put another penny in . . . There, all right, now. I just need to know you're all right . . . The baby, has it—'

'No, not yet, me love, though I wish that it would. I'm like a barrel, but eeh, me Philip, I've missed you. Hurry home.'

'I will, my darling. I should be there by four in the morning. Don't stay awake, I'll slip in beside you and be there in the morning to hold you. I love you, Edith, with all that I am.'

'I love you. Aw, Philip, me and our babby love you so that's double love.'

As the phone clicked and there was nothing but the buzzing sound it made when disengaged, Edith's surge of happiness turned to a gripping pain. She bent double, crying out.

Minnie was by her side in an instant. 'Right, luvvie, this could be it. I tell yer, it takes a man to put the baby there, and the shocks he gives yer to make it come out.'

The pain had subsided enough to allow Edith to feel like laughing. She let out a giggle – a happy giggle that surged through her. *Me Philip is coming home. I can't believe it! And now me babby might make an appearance to greet him along with me!*

As another pain gripped her, Edith cried out, 'Go and get Marg, please, Minnie. I need her with me.'

When Marg came through the door, she seemed to sum everything up as she said, 'Eeh, Edith, lass. Minnie says babby's coming, but not only that, Philip is an' all. Aw, I'm that happy for you. Come on, let's get you to bed, eh?'

'I reckon I'd like to walk around a bit, Marg, I feel restless.'

'Well, at least have a bath and get into your nightie, then you'll be ready ... but, eeh, Edith, I ain't never seen a babby born, so do you reckon we should get Ada round? Gran's fast asleep, so she'll be all right, and Clive will sleep in the chair downstairs, so he'll hear if she wakes.'

'We don't need no Ada, Marg. I've delivered many a baby – we East Enders are like you, girl, we could never afford no midwife, so we 'elped each other. 'Aving a bath is a good idea, so if yer 'elp her to do that, Marg, I'll get the bed ready. I've got Edith to save all the newspapers – it's a trick we do to save the mattress getting in a mess. We spread it all in layers under a clean sheet. But there's no need to panic, first babies don't come for hours. Philip will get 'ere before it does.'

Feeling reassured that Minnie was more than capable of helping her, Edith went with Marg and sat on the chair in the bathroom while Marg filled the bath.

'By, Marg, Philip and me babby's really going to be with me at last.'

'Aw, lass, I'm that happy for you. When Minnie told us, I jumped for joy and Clive said to tell you he's so pleased for you and good luck with the birth ... Ha, I laughed at him and told him, it's easy for him to say that, then go back to his armchair. You, poor thing, have got the birth in front of you.'

'Will you stay with me, Marg?'

'Aye, I won't leave you. I'm excited. I'll help you all I can, Edith. I'll be strong for you – I'll be me and Alice, 'cause I know if she was here, she'd be by your side an' all.'

'I think about her all the time, Marg. What's it like for her? She's been there a month now and no word. The lads are out of their mind.'

'I know. I keep telling them that post takes a long time to come from over there but that Alice will be fine. No one shoots at ambulances or tries to blow them up. Mind, she must be suffering anguish with what she's dealing with. Things ain't good, are they?'

'No, the news is awful ... I – I worry that the Germans will invade us next, if France falls.'

Edith could see the fear in Marg's eyes, but her words belied this. 'Don't be worrying about what's happening in the world. Philip's coming home, and your babby wants to greet his da, so you concentrate on that, Edith, lass.'

Edith felt sorry she'd said what she did and decided to make light of everything. 'Right then, what're you betting it's a girl?'

'Ha, nothing as I think it's a boy. I'll put a couple of bob on that.'

Minnie came in just as Edith sat in the bath.

'Oh, me girls, are we betting then? Me money's on a girl. Two bob, is it? I'll wager that, Marg.'

Edith smiled. It had been not long after Minnie arrived that she'd found out that Minnie had no money. That she'd got by on the parish relief and the bit of cleaning she did for folk, and what her daughter brought in, so Edith had insisted she took a payment for helping with the housework. It wasn't much but gave Minnie a bit to spend on herself or on the kids, which she loved to do.

She often took the twins to the matinee at the flicks, or to play on the stalls on the promenade. They had a wonderful time with their granny and Edith thought of it as building memories for them. It all helped her too, as she needed her rest in the afternoon of late.

'I'm going for a girl an' all, but I'll not bet, I'll just hold yours, and pay out the winner.'

'Eeh, Edith, don't let Bob hear you're running a book. By, you'll be having this babby in a cell!'

They all laughed, but Edith's was cut short as she cried out with the intensity of the pain that clutched her and seemed to take her whole body into it. Gasping, she clung on to the side of the bath.

Three hours later, she was sitting up in bed, holding her little girl and feeling the happiest she'd felt for a long time.

'Eeh, Edith, I'm exhausted. I had her for you, you know. I pushed harder than you.'

'Ha! You didn't have the pain. You wait until it's your turn.' While saying this, she hadn't taken her eyes off her little one. 'Anyroad, meet little Elizabeth Margaret Alice Susan Bradshaw.'

'Aw, Edith. After your ma and me and Alice and your ma-in-law. I don't know what to say. She's beautiful. Look at all her hair. She's like Philip, ain't she?'

'Aye, I can see him in her. Eeh, I can't wait for him to get here. What time is it?'

'She were born at four a.m., Edith, and I'd guess she's about seven pounds in weight. It's now five, me darlin', and yer were the best mum I've ever attended. A lot go for days with their first, but you got on with it, with hardly any fuss. Yer didn't even wake the kids up. Ha, when I had mine, I screamed the place down.'

They were giggling at this when there was a noise which took their attention towards the bedroom door. They all turned and suddenly Philip stood there. Edith registered the shock on his face and then his amazement, which turned to joy as he ran towards her.

She knew her face was wet with tears and that nothing could surpass the sheer happiness that had put them there. 'Philip, eeh, Philip, lad.'

He was on the bed, holding them both. Edith heard the door click, but didn't look to see. She knew Marg and Minnie had gone out of the room. Reaching her free arm around Philip, her tears joined his.

'My darling, my Edith. I don't know what to say.'

'Don't, me love, just hold me, and little Betsy.'

'A girl! You have given me a daughter? Oh, Edith, I've never felt happier in my life as I do at this moment.' He moved from her and gently touched the baby's head. 'Hello, little one, I'm your da.'

Edith felt happiness surge through her. She didn't think

Philip would want to be called 'Da', but something posh like 'Poppa' or 'Daddy'.

'So, this is our little Betsy? Is that how you're going to shorten her name, darling?'

'Aye, me ma was known as Betty, as you know, and I didn't want to call her that, too many memories, good and bad, but Betsy still honours her and suits our little one.'

'Did you stick to what you said on her other names?'

While they chatted, he stroked Betsy's head and planted kisses on her forehead.

'Aye, I did. Me life would have been nothing without Alice and Marg. I put Marg first, though, as she was at the birth and then added your ma.'

'Thank you, darling, for honouring her too. She's made such an effort to change.'

'Aye, she has, and by adding it, Betsy has a grand name, for a grand little girl.'

'A beautiful little soul. Thank you, Edith. Thank you.'

Edith smiled up at him. The baby stirred. 'Eeh, I reckon she may need her first feed. Minnie was saying I should put her to me breast as it encourages me milk to come in. Do you want to go and get freshened up and send in Minnie and Marg to help me, me love?'

'No. I want to help you, darling.'

They giggled as Philip held his daughter for the first time, and Edith got herself ready. When Philip saw her, he let out a wow sound. She playfully hit out at him.

He dodged her, laughing as he said, 'You can't hit a man when he's holding a baby! Nor a husband for appreciating how huge his wife has grown. I'm entitled to feast my eyes!'

They giggled, and Edith felt a longing to be held by him, and for him to never let her go. 'Just another few weeks, me love, and then we'll be able to make love.'

'I can't wait. Please God, I haven't left these shores again before then.'

He'd handed her Betsy and was helping to guide her nipple into her little mouth. His touch thrilled Edith. She looked up and received his kiss. 'I love you, me darling Philip.'

'I love you, darling. If it was possible, seeing you nursing our child, I love you more than ever.'

He stood gazing down on them. Edith didn't say, but the sensation of her child suckling was twofold. She'd never known such love surge through her as she felt for her little Betsy, and yet feeding her wasn't a comfortable experience.

'Right, now my two girls are settled, I'll go and get a bath. I'll send Minnie and Marg in ... Ha, they sound like a double act!'

'They are. They've had me in stitches many a time over these last weeks. They hit it off the moment they met when Marg first fetched Minnie with Clive.'

Philip was smiling as he turned to go to the bathroom. When he got to the door, he blew two kisses. As it closed behind him, Edith felt a light dim inside her. And she knew, though he hadn't said, that this was to be a fleeting snatch at happiness, for the war was intensifying, and he would be needed more than ever.

She swallowed hard, made her mind up to enjoy the time she had with him, and then to be strong for her little Betsy, and for Mandy and Alf.

Thinking of them, she wondered what they would say when they got up in the morning. She knew they would be excited, but she also knew that she must be careful not to let them feel that their noses were pushed out.

Without realising it, the discomfort had left, and now, all she felt was a wonderful sensation of being at one with her child. Her Betsy, who she would devote her life to.

TWENTY-ONE

Jackie

Jackie had mastered riding her bike and enjoyed cycling along the country roads and around the Bletchley estate.

She peddled like mad now, trying to get to the village phone box. She needed to talk to Marg, find out how everyone was and if Edith had had her baby.

It had been a lovely hot day and was still muggy, which made the going harder as sweat ran into her eyes.

When she got to the top of the hill she could cruise and let the bike take her. She sat back, wiped her stinging eyes and thought of how miserable she'd been and how she mustn't show that to Marg.

It was Blake who was making her unhappy. He seemed to be stalking her. He sent for her a dozen times a day to work on some equation or other for him.

Then he stared at her the whole time she worked and once had whispered, 'I haven't forgotten what you did.'

She protested, saying, 'I didn't do owt,' but he dismissed her from the room.

There was no one she could talk to about it. Prissy was lovely, down to earth and included her in everything but, Jackie thought, she still didn't feel comfortable enough to confide in her like she could with Marg, Alice and Edith. *If only I could talk to them, but I can't. I could get into so much trouble for mentioning the name of anyone working at Bletchley.*

When she got through to Marg, her tears did fall. 'Eeh, Marg, it's good to hear your voice.'

'Jackie, eeh, me Jackie . . . are you all right, me little lass?'

'Aye . . . I'm just missing you all. But I'm fine really . . . honest. The work's easy and there's a few of me own age at the warehouse. I – I, eeh, Marg, I miss you all . . .' Pulling herself together, she said, 'Anyroad, I'll be fine, it's just hearing your voice. Have you any news?'

With asking this she really did find herself coping.

And then to hear that Edith's little girl had been born and that Philip was on leave for two weeks, after returning from wherever he'd been, was wonderful.

'It's strange, but none of us ask questions anymore,' Marg was now saying. 'We've learnt that lesson. Anyway, Edith is so happy. And Philip is. They went past a few minutes ago, Philip pushing the pram and Edith holding Mandy and Alf's hands. By, they looked like a beautiful family.'

Jackie swallowed hard. Picturing the scene made her so homesick. 'How's Gran?'

'She's grand. She asked after you the other day. Then did one of her hmphs when we told her you were doing war work, and you know what she said? "Well, if our Jackie's there, this lot will soon be over."'

Marg's laugh made Jackie laugh with her and she felt better.

'When will you get to come home for a bit, Jackie, lass?'

'I don't knaw. I – I hope it's soon. But there's a lot to do, it's very busy. I might get a weekend off but getting home from here takes such a long time, I'd worry that I didn't get back when I should.'

'All right, lass. Don't you worry. Just keep ringing once a week.'

'I will. But I must go now. I've got naw more pennies.'

'You should reverse the charge, lass. Eeh, me Jackie, I miss you.'

'And I miss you. Give me love to everyone and tell Edith I'm so happy for her . . . and, Marg, I love you.'

'I will, me love. And I lo—'

The operator cut in, 'If you wish to continue this call, please put a penny in and press button A.'

Jackie replaced the receiver. She stood a moment looking at herself in the mirror above the telephone. How she wished she could just ring Harry. She was so worried. And her heart bled for him.

A tap on the window made her jump. A woman glared at her. 'Others want to use the phone, you know.'

Coming out of the phone box, she apologised.

The woman gave her a black look. 'What you're all doing up there I'd like to know. How many blooming typists does this government need? It just needs someone with a bit of sense in charge to get you lot doing work that's of some use to the country!'

As she got on her bike, Jackie thought if only everyone knew the vital work they were doing.

She hadn't gone far when her heart came into her mouth as a car horn tooted. Before she knew what was happening, it came so close to her that it clipped her back wheel, sending her tumbling down into the ditch. Her bike came after her.

Screaming out as the handlebars bruised her head, she lay a moment, stunned and disorientated.

Gathering herself, Jackie pushed the bike off her and tried to get up, but an excruciating pain shot up her leg. Her own holler echoed around her at the intensity of it.

Terrified, cold and in so much pain, she screamed out again, 'Help me . . . someone . . . Help me-e-e-e!'

The only sound was a flock of angry birds who'd taken to the air in fright.

Panic gripped her. But when damp began to seep through her clothes, she knew she had to do something.

Making an extreme effort and in agony, she clutched at clumps of grass and tried to hotch herself along on her stomach, but the clumps came away in her hand. Desperate, she grabbed a thick-stemmed thistle – wincing at the prickling, but finding it strong, she managed a few inches by pulling on it, before she collapsed, moaning in pain and with huge sobs wracking her body.

Knowing she couldn't give up, she tried again. This time she grabbed onto some of the thick undergrowth and pulled for all her might. Sweat ran down her face and yet her body shivered with cold and shock.

Not giving up, she managed to get out of the ditch and lay back, sighing with relief for now, at least, she might be seen from the road.

She didn't know how long it was before a car came along. Lifting her handkerchief, she waved it as high as she could.

But then her heart sank as she recognised whose car it was and heard it slow down.

Blake was out of his car in no time and stood over her staring down at her. 'So, you need my help now, I see.'

'Please. I – I've hurt me leg. I can't stand.'

'A different story now, isn't it? Led me on, you did, young lady. And you told people, didn't you? Told them that I'd come on to you. It got back to my wife. You bitch. I'll make you pay for that – broke her heart, you did. And with me coming away just after, too. Crafty, weren't you, eh? Going to that slut of a friend of yours who snared Philip Bradshaw – married well below his station, he did. Got yourself set up nicely in Bradshaw's factory that way, didn't you? You scum!'

'Naw. It weren't like that.'

'Oh yes it was. You and she got Philip to tell his father, who stupidly believed your story and told his evil, gossiping, spiteful wife, who made it her business to make sure my wife knew.'

Jackie knew in an instant that this would be true. Sue used to be just how Blake was describing her. She'd changed now, but the truth dawned on Jackie that yes, it was possible that what Blake did got back to his wife. Fear at the realisation zinged through her.

'So, why didn't you carry out your threat – have me chucked in prison for a fraud you were going to make look as if I'd done?'

'Because I wanted a different kind of revenge, and I'd set this place up with others and knew you were the right material for the work we do – it was so easy for me to snare you back into my lair.' His voice changed. 'You see, Jackie, I still fancy you, and have a mind to have you ... Don't look like that, you know what I'm talking about, I know you've done it with that boyfriend of yours. Well, you're going to let me have the same, or I can make things very difficult for you. I could even have you shot for treason by making it look as though you have passed information on.'

The fear turned to sheer terror.

'Yes. I need a mistress, and you're going to be it.'

'Naw, naw, I'll never be that I'd rather—'

'What? Die? Well, like I said, that can be arranged. Now get into the car.'

'I – I can't. Me leg ... Please, please, I beg of you. I'm sorry. I – I'll do owt. I'll write to your wife and tell her I lied.' Thinking desperately of how to convince him of this, she thought again about what he'd said the last time she refused his advances. 'I'll tell her that I did it to cover up for stealing from the firm – that you let me off with the sack and I just made the story up as I couldn't tell me family and friends the truth as I couldn't stand the shame.'

He glared down at her. Never had she felt so alone, so desperate. The pain in her leg was excruciating now. Cold seeped into her bones from the damp grass. 'Help me, please help me. Me leg. I think I've broken me leg.'

'Ha, that'll make you an easy target then, won't it. I've a mind to have you right now, in the back of my car.'

Bending, he put his hands under her arms and began to drag her, ignoring her screams of pain and her begging him not to move her, but to get an ambulance for her.

When they reached his car and he opened the door, he dropped her. In front of her she saw a fresh-looking dent, with smears of blue – the same colour as her bicycle!

She was about to scream at him that he could have killed her when he grabbed her again and almost threw her into the back of the car.

This time the pain in her leg was too much to bear. Her head spun and a darkness descended. She did not resist but allowed the veil to clothe her and accepted the peace it offered her.

A noise and a feeling of being split in two, along with unbearable agony, woke her. Blake was on top of her, grinding himself into her! 'Naw, naw, please, naw. Don't ... stop it ... STO-O-OP!'

A deep-throated moan came from him, and he slumped down on her.

Jackie could bear no more. She slipped back into unconsciousness.

When she opened her eyes, everything seemed hazy and far away.

'Ah, you're awake.'

A face swam in front of her. She closed her eyes, thinking she was going to be sick.

'You're all right now, love.'

The voice sounded gentle and caring. Jackie opened her eyes and looked into the face of a nurse. 'H – how did I get here?'

'A gentleman brought you. He said he found you unconscious on the side of the road and that your bike was nearby. His kindness didn't do you any favours as your fracture is extremely bad and could become infected. He shouldn't have moved you. You will need to stay here for a few days while we monitor you.'

'My leg . . . It feels heavy.'

'It's encased in plaster of Paris, love. Now, don't worry, you'll be all right.'

Memory flooded back. The heavy weight of her leg made his heavy body come into focus and the feel of him inside her. And his disgusting, guttural moan. 'He . . .'

'He what, love? What are you trying to say? Did the gentleman have anything to do with you getting hurt?'

Pictures of a gun pointing at her flashed into her head. Blake had said he'd have her shot!

'Naw, I – I just wanted to say, he – he was kind to me.'

'Yes, he was very concerned. He was an officer stationed around here somewhere. He said he was out for a drive when he saw you. What happened, can you remember?'

Jackie did, vividly, but she shook her head. 'I was just riding along, that's all I can remember.'

But the reality of what really happened became unbearable and she burst into tears.

'Oh dear, ducky, don't take on. Have you family we can contact? Do you live around here?'

'Naw, I – I'm staying with a friend. Can you ring me sister, please . . . no, don't ring anyone, it's all right . . . I – I just feel so tired. I'll think about it, ta.'

When she lay back, and the nurse left her, Jackie cried silent tears.

She didn't know how much time had passed when a voice brought her out of the half sleep that she'd dropped into. A fear clutched her, making it difficult for her to breathe. She opened her eyes. Captain Blake stood at the end of her bed. 'Ah, she's awake. Hello, my dear.'

'I'll leave you a few minutes, but you mustn't stay long.' The nurse turned to Jackie after saying this to Blake. 'There, you are, ducky. The nice gentleman who brought you in has dropped by to ask how you are.'

When she turned her back, Blake smiled a sickly smile. 'I see, you couldn't have opened your mouth as no one treated me as if they knew what went on. Well, having you was all I dreamt it would be, Jackie . . . I'm sorry, I didn't know you were a virgin. I thought you and that young man of yours had been at it for a while, you seemed so close.'

Disgusted and embarrassed, Jackie spat out, 'Naw, 'cause he has respect for me.'

'I do too, my dear. A great deal. You are one of the cleverest young women I know. And the most attractive in a sexy way. I like them at your age . . . there's an innocence about you. A purity. Eager to learn from and to please an older man. I want you to be like that, my dear, whenever I want you to be.'

Jackie felt sick, her head throbbed. She was trapped. Who could she turn to? With a feeling of despair, she knew there was nobody. No one could help her.

Closing her eyes, she thought of Harry. His lovely face – what would he think of her? She was dirty, used, spoilt. 'Leave me alone!'

His head swung around; his eyes darted to every corner. Leaning forward, he had an evil look on his face as he ground out, 'Shut your mouth. I warned you.'

Jackie had had enough. 'When are you going to say that I told secrets, and who am I supposed to have told them to? And what secrets? I don't knaw any. All I see is figures – equations. I've never been present when a code has been cracked . . . You're nowt but a rapist. An evil man who preys on young girls. Everyone knaws it in Blackpool – everyone of your class does anyroad. You're vile . . . vile!' She could hear her own voice rising but couldn't stop it. 'You're filth, you raped me . . . YOU RAPED ME!'

The nurse, followed by the sister, came running. Blake stood, he moved away from the bed. Never had she seen him looking so afraid.

'He raped me! He . . . he knocked me off me bike, then raped me.'

'Oh my God! Is this true? Nurse, call the police!'

Blake pushed by the sister, almost knocking her over. He hurried towards the doors, went through them and left them swinging behind him.

'Calm down, ducky, this ain't going to help anything. Nurse is calling the police. She helped to clean you up and she told me things that she saw . . . Were you a virgin?'

'Aye.'

'Well, we took it that your hymen — that's the thin film that breaks the first time you go with a man — had broken in the accident, as can sometimes happen. There was blood in your knickers, and you have bruising on your inner thighs. Which does fit with what you say. And if . . . well, if the captain finished inside you, there will be semen on your knickers too. Nurse put them in the laundry, I'll ask her to check. She'll have a good idea . . . all things we can tell the police to back up your story — mind, they still might think you did it willingly. It's how it is. Very few believe that a girl has been raped. They'd rather believe that you changed your mind.'

'It hurt bad, Sister. And me leg . . . I were in so much pain.'

'You, poor girl . . . Well, that will prove you weren't willing if it happened after your accident. You just tell the police the truth, and we will tell them what we found. Then hopefully that beast will be stopped. By the way, did you know him?'

'Aye.' Jackie told what had happened when she worked for him.

'So, how come, if you're from Blackpool, that you're here in our neck of the woods? And is it just coincidence that he is too? That seems very strange.'

A sinking sensation left Jackie feeling that it was all hopeless. For a minute she'd thought Blake would be brought to justice, but now she realised how bad it looked to these people and how little she could say in her own defence.

The knowing look the sister gave to the nurse told volumes. They both walked away, leaving her with a pit of despair and fear in her stomach.

When the policeman arrived, she had her story ready.

'It's all a mistake – a mix-up. I didn't knaw what was real and what wasn't after I banged me head, and me leg hurt so much. I lost consciousness.'

He'd sighed and looked at the sister. 'Another time-waster, eh?'

The sister apologised for calling him. 'There were signs ... I thought, well, I'll be more careful before I call you again. Concussion can cause all sorts of hallucinations. It seems this is all that happened.'

'I understand. You did the right thing. Good day, Sister.'

Jackie heaved a sigh of relief. She hadn't broken the Official Secrets Act, and maybe when nothing happened, Blake would realise that and not do anything about it all. But in the meantime, she doubted he'd admit to any knowledge of where she was or what happened to her.

'Sister, can you get me bag, please. There's a number in there from where I am from, someone ought to be told as I'm due back.'

'A funny story you told back there – about knowing the gentleman and him having tried it on with you before. Wicked that was, whether you're concussed or not. Now, we'll do this one thing for you as it is our duty, but don't expect anything else, other than the professional care we have to give you.'

'There was a man ... I was telling the truth, but, like I said, it all became mixed up ... I – I didn't knaw the gentleman who helped me. I just wish I could say I was sorry to him. I'm not understanding it all meself.'

At this the sister softened. 'Well, this is fairly typical of someone concussed, so don't worry about it. I should think the poor bloke is long gone to wherever he came from.' She laughed. 'And I bet he's begging them now to post him abroad!'

Jackie felt so miserable. She was in pain and didn't know what would happen next. But at least she'd straightened things out without committing an offence and managed to get the sister on her side again. How she would cope with Blake after this, she didn't know.

It was a week later that she was transferred to sick bay, and then sent home by army transport on sick leave and told that they would get regular updates on her and she would then receive notification on whether to report back or not.

She prayed it would be 'not'.

TWENTY-TWO

Alice

As Alice ran across the rough terrain, following Pete who carried the stretcher, she felt exhausted.

For hours and hours now, they'd been rescuing the injured from the front line – a line that was getting nearer and nearer.

'Help me.'

The frightened voice came to them as they arrived at the trench. Pete's knee squelched in the mud as he knelt down. His voice soothed, 'It's all right, soldier, we're here for you. What's your name?'

'Harry, sir.'

Alice froze. She gazed down on the twisted body of her beloved brother. 'Harry!'

'Sis? Eeh, Alice ...'

'Harry, lad, where're you hurt?' Kneeling beside him, she put her arm around him. 'Aw, Harry. It's all right, me love, we'll get you out. You'll be all right.'

'Yer brother?'

'Aye, Pete. The one I were telling you of.'

A shell exploded nearby. Alice and Pete hit the ground. Debris showered them. Alice turned her head. Harry lay next to her. She reached out and took his hand, saw a tear fall down his cheek. 'It's all right, Harry, lad. I'm here now. Nothing will happen to you. They'll see our flag and leave us alone. We'll get you out.'

Harry didn't answer. She squeezed his hand, saw the sweat running down his face, saw a trickle of blood mingle with it, and then with his tears.

'Call on your courage, lad. You've plenty, I heard how you were the last man standing last week. I've tried and tried to contact you. You're going home now. Home, Harry.'

As she spoke, she saw the colour drain from his face.

'Let me take a look, Alice. We need to assess his injuries.'

Alice prayed as she moved aside. Her fear tightened her throat. Still holding Harry's hand, she hardly dared look as Pete cut through his jacket. 'Now, then, son, where're yer hurt?'

Harry didn't answer.

'He's losing consciousness, Pete ... Eeh, Pete, do something!'

The noise around them became deafening, more debris landed around them. Something hit Alice's back. Flashes so bright temporarily blinded her. Screams and hollers of agony hung on the thick with smoke air. A fire raged to their left.

And amidst it all, a look from Pete told her that her beloved brother was going to die. 'No, Pete, no. Do something!'

Pete shook his head. 'Hold him, Alice. Hold yer brother, pet.'

Moving a little, Alice could now cradle Harry's head. 'Harry, lad, talk to me. Eeh, Harry, please don't go. Don't leave me. Think of Jackie, love. She's waiting for you.'

Harry opened his eyes. 'Jackie ...' Her name was gasped out.

'Aye, Jackie, love, you're going home to her, lad. And to Billy, and Joey. Please, Harry, hold on.'

Harry opened his eyes again. His look held longing, and then lost their expression.

'Harry, no! No, no, no, no!'

An arm came around her. Her body sunk into itself. Harry was looking at her with unseeing eyes.

'No – o – o – o.' She held him to her. Her lips wouldn't work properly as she begged of Pete, 'Don't let this happen, Pete.'

'Pet, all I can do is help you not to leave him here. Come on, me mucca, help me to get your brother onto the ambulance. We'll say he died on the way, then he'll get a proper burial.' He turned to where a young lad lay face down in the mud. 'Not like his mate here ... I'm sorry, lad.' He patted the corpse's back. 'God bless yer, and may yer rest in peace.'

Alice wanted to gather the lad up and take him too but knew she couldn't. Knew they shouldn't be taking her beloved Harry with them and knew she should be grateful for the pitiful titbit of Harry being buried in a churchyard in France, instead of in one of its killing fields. And knew, too, that she wouldn't want him to be an unknown soldier ... She didn't want him dead, she didn't. A sob that hurt her throat shook her body.

'Hold it together, Alice, pet. We've young 'uns to save. Harry would want yer to do that. He would. He wouldn't want anyone else to die. None of them have a sister to hold them as they pass. You'll come to look on that as a privilege. I promise.'

As they picked Harry up and put him on the stretcher, Alice knew her heart to break. It was real. Her Harry, who she'd cared for since being a lad, was gone. How was she to carry on?

The sounds of the war came back into focus as they set off. They hadn't gone far when they were flagged down.

'Over there, a group of gunners caught a grenade. Don't know if there's any casualties, or if none of them got lucky.'

'Right, we're on to it, man. Come on, Alice, pet.'

'You all right, miss?'

'She's fine. It gets to us all at times, but Alice won't let these lads down, don't yer worry, Major, sir.'

How she got through the next hour of hell, Alice didn't know, but they tended wounded, collected as many as they could and were now on their way to Number Two Hospital.

'Pete, I don't care what's said, or who sees me, I've got to find Gerald when we've handed over ... I've got to.'

'You do that, pet. I'll cover for yer as much as I can.'

'Ta, lad.'

Feeling drained when they arrived, Alice remained professional, handing over to the medics, following the rule of laying the casualties out, tying the different colours of ribbon onto the toes in accordance with the priority of needing attention, and helping Pete to take the dead – her beloved brother – to the morgue.

She was coming from there when she spotted Gerald going into his quarters. Without thinking, she yelled his name.

Running towards him, she found herself saying, 'Harry . . . Harry . . . Harry!'

Gerald was white when she reached him. 'Where, darling, where is Harry? Is he badly hurt? Take me to him.'

'He's . . .' She shook her head. 'No . . . no, I can't, I can't.'

'Oh my God . . . No, don't say it, Alice. Don't.'

'Help me. Gerald, help me.'

'Doctor! What on earth is going on? Now, look, I've heard the rumours, and as long as you both behaved with decorum, I let it go, but this behaviour, no! I will not stand for it. Alice, get back to your station. Doctor . . . you come with me!'

'Matron, please. Alice has just brought in her brother. She hasn't been able to say, but . . .'

'Dead?'

Alice heard the wail that came from her mouth. The protest. The begging. But she didn't seem in control of it.

'Oh, Alice, I'm so sorry. Help her into your quarters, Doctor. Look after her, I haven't seen a thing.'

With this, Matron turned away.

Gerald's strong arms came around her. How often she'd longed for this feeling, when snatched moments in some secret corner was all they'd managed, but this wasn't how she'd longed for it. This wasn't what she wanted him to hold her for. And yet, it was all she wanted . . . needed.

Inside his tent, they both let go. They sobbed together, showed their denial of the truth in whispers of, 'It hasn't happened, has it?'

But in the end, they came to an acceptance of the awful reality, that they would never see their beautiful Harry again.

'How will we tell Jackie, and Billy and little Joey?'

'We can't . . . Oh God, they will get a telegram . . . though, wait a minute, Harry would have put you as next of kin. I can speak to someone – the pastor, he'll help. I'll tell him what has happened and that you know. And say that there's no need for anyone to be informed at home. We will do that in due course. He'll make sure the correct person is told. They may need you to sign for Harry's things.'

'Things? Eeh, Gerald, how can me lovely Harry have come down to just being a few things?'

Gerald didn't answer. He just held her close again – wet her hair with his tears. And kissed her face.

'We'll go together to the service. They do have a lovely service for all the lads who have fallen. I've been to a few – those I tried to save and couldn't. Some of them got into my heart. They've given me messages to deliver, and I have. I have written everything told to me and put in a few words of my own. The pastor has seen that my notes get into the belongings that are sent home to the family. I went to the services to represent the family of each young chap.'

'Eeh, Gerald, I love you. I wish it would all end.'

'Alice, why don't you ask for compassionate leave? You could go home, darling.'

'No. While you're here, I am, me love.'

'Oh, Alice, I long to be with you properly, to hold your body next to mine, to love you with all that I am.'

Alice clung to him, shocked at how she so wanted the same at this very minute, when her heart was torn into shreds with the agony of her loss. And yet, she knew that Gerald had the power to mend it, for just a little while if they could lie together.

Their need brought them together to kiss, deep passionate kisses. Their hands caressed. Their longing vocal in every sigh, every whispered 'I love you' and in every touch. Both cried out as their loving movements brought them release. Then they held each other as if they would never part.

As they came to a calm place a few minutes later, Alice said, 'My darling, I will have to go. Send messages as you hear what is happening. I will put in a request when I get back to camp to be allowed to go to the fu – funeral.'

'I think it will be tomorrow, darling. There are funerals every day of those brought in the previous day. Be strong, my darling. Your pain is matched by mine as I loved Harry like a brother.'

His hug steadied her. Taking a deep breath, she went to join Pete once more. Passing the tents from which cries of agony came and the morgue where her darling Harry lay. Tears flowed down her face, but a small part of her had been strengthened by the loving of her beloved Gerald and she knew that she could carry on – for Harry. For him, she would save as many of his fellow soldiers as she could. For him, she would get back home one day and for him, she would live her life in the best way that she could, by helping others, by seeing that Joey succeeded in all that he did, and by supporting Billy in all that he wanted to do. Thinking of Billy, she hoped that the war would end before he was called to fight. And yet, in her heart she knew it wouldn't. Things were going badly. Already they had moved the casualty clearing station back a mile and she knew there were plans to move it further soon as the front line advanced ever nearer with German gains.

Having always found it difficult to hate, she now found it so easy to hate Hitler and all he stood for, and she did so with all her heart and soul.

Even though it was three weeks into May and the sun was shining, the next day Alice felt cold to her bones as the breeze off the sea chilled her body, making her shiver. But her heart shivered too with the weight of the grief she felt as she kept her eyes on the wrapped shape of Harry's body.

The priest's prayers soared to the skies, to the backdrop of the sound of heavy fighting that seemed to be getting nearer and nearer. The crowd of mourners was made up of hospital staff and locals; the latter, Gerald told her, attended every day, bringing flowers and offering their prayers, love and thanks for the sacrifice made on their behalf.

Alice stood between Gerald and Pete. Both held one of her hands, though her body leant into Gerald's, as she tried to glean some of his strength.

Her thoughts were with Joey and Billy. She so longed to be with them, to hold them. But then a laughing, happy Jackie came to her mind – she'd never been far from it, but never so vividly as now and she cried out with the pain she had to inflict on her.

Gerald's arm came around her. As it did, she thought of the lovely engagement party and how happy Jackie and Harry had been, and how they clung to one another at the station when they were both going in different directions to do their duty for their country. How would Jackie take this? And to think she would be away somewhere and on her own when she heard.

As they lowered Harry, everything in Alice broke. Her knees gave way. She heard herself crying out, 'Not me Harry . . . no, no.'

She was in Gerald's arms, he was holding her tightly, and yet she felt adrift – alone.

Two weeks later, Alice woke with a start. Pete was bending over her. 'Come on, we've got to get everyone evacuated and then go ourselves. The Germans are only just up the road, France has fallen. Hurry, pet, hurry, just grab a few things, dress and let's go.'

For the last week they'd been shipping out many more patients from the Number One and Two Hospitals than usual. Hundreds, who were on short stays and would normally have stayed until completely recovered, had been sent back to the failing front line. It had been heart-breaking to see them, and to be part of it, but everything possible was being done to stop the escalating advance. Other patients had been taken to hospital ships and trains, only a few were left, and now Pete was telling her that they, too, had to get out.

'Where are we going?'

'There's a hospital train coming in that will take the last ones from Number Two. I don't know about Number One.

Once we've done that, we'll pick up any medics that haven't left and head for Caen as Dunkirk is still under siege. It's a long way but seems the only way we'll get a ferry home. Just hurry, pet. I'll answer your questions later.'

Pete roused everyone as he went towards the door. When he reached it, he shouted, 'I'll meet you outside, Alice.'

What followed was a mad dash and yet no one panicked. Some made for the latrines, but most, like herself, had a pee outside, and swilled toothpaste around their mouths with their fingers, before ducking their heads under a water tap.

As she made for the ambulance with Pete, nurses and doctors were running with patients on stretchers and loading the other ambulances.

Alice's thoughts were with Gerald. She wasn't going anywhere without him.

Pete had cranked the engine, and as they prepared to drive away, he told her, 'I've topped up with fuel and water. The side lockers are full. But after that, we'll just have to take our chances, see what we can beg or barter for. There'll be very few watches or jewellery going all the way with us.'

'Once we have the patients on the train and we go back to Number Two, I'm picking up Gerald, no matter what, and if he's not designated to go with us, then I'm staying with him.'

Pete didn't argue. 'All right, but haway. We have to hurry, pet.'

When they reached Number Two, Gerald came running over to her. They were in each other's arms oblivious for a moment as stretchers were brought out and loaded on theirs and other ambulances and trucks that had turned up.

'We'll be back to pick you up, me love.'

'But I can't leave yet. There are patients still.'

Matron came by. 'Yes you can and will. I am staying till the last patient is shipped out, that should be by later today, then one of the nurses and I have commandeered a jeep, so we won't be that far behind you.'

'But—'

'No buts. Go! A good doctor like you must survive, none of us know when we will be called upon again. You will be needed, this isn't the end of the road. Britain will continue the fight.'

As Gerald said he would, Alice couldn't stop herself from breaking every rule in the book. She flung herself at Matron and hugged her.

Matron was taken aback at first, but then softened and hugged her back. As Matron's hand patted her, she said, 'My dear, you are leaving a piece of yourself back here, but you will have your husband by your side as you do, that is my vow to you.'

'Ta, Matron. I hope we meet again, good luck for your journey home.'

'And to you, dear, now hurry. Get these patients to the train and get yourself back here.'

When they reached the train, the patients were transferred in minutes in what seemed like an air raid from hell. As they drove away, bombs dropped all around them, and a fighter plane came in low, shooting indiscriminately.

Through her mirror, Alice saw nurses running along the platform, many dropping before they reached safety.

Tears streamed down her face. 'How could they? They can see they are medics!'

'Don't stop, pet. Haway as fast as yer can. Some of us have to make it, we can do nowt to help. Just get out of here and pray none of them bombs have our name on them.'

There was something different about Pete's voice. She glanced at him. Pete was crying.

This increased her fear. Thanking God the track ahead was clear and treelined, her foot went down hard on the accelerator.

Not ten minutes later, there was a massive explosion.

'The train! Oh my God, they've hit the train!'

'Them's bastards, the lot of them!'

A bomb dropped nearby, its blast sending them onto two wheels. Alice screamed, but before her scream died down, the vehicle righted itself, bumping them about on their wooden seats.

'Christ!'

There was panic in Pete's voice now. Suddenly, he crossed himself. 'Our Father, who art in heaven . . .'

Alice, driving like a maniac, found comfort in the words, as if God had joined them and would see them through. She joined in. 'Hallowed be thy name . . .'

Together they prayed all the way back.

Chaos reigned everywhere as they pulled up. The hospital was under fire. Pete got out and opened the back doors. Nurses rushed forward. How he got so many in, she didn't know, but her attention was taken with Gerald climbing in beside her. She heard the back door slam and the sound of knocking, the signal Pete was to give her to get going.

As she drove out, she looked back, but all was a blur of smoke, explosions and other vehicles following her.

There was no time to think, no time to talk. A quick squeeze of her hand from Gerald sustained her as she drove off.

Once more as the hell continued, she knew she was crying, and once more she began to pray out loud. Gerald joined her desperate prayers. Then, behind her, one or two of the nurses joined in. They were crammed in, some sitting on the beds, others on the floor. All sounded fearful.

Suddenly, Alice knew she had to change that. So, she stopped praying and burst into song!

'*Run rabbit, run rabbit, run, run, run . . .*'

Shock silenced them all, and then laughter rang out and they all joined in. The mood lifted and the British spirit was back.

Gerald sang out louder than any of them and as he did, Pete joined him, and the two men's voices took over. Pete changed the lyrics to '*Run, Hitler, run, Hitler, run, run, run!*'

As the men sang this comic version, the sky became clearer, and the bombing receded. They were going to make it.

She turned to Gerald. 'We're going home.'

Gerald dabbed his eyes and mouthed back, 'I love you.'

Alice's heart soared. She never knew it could do again. She wiped away her own tears. Harry would want them to get home, and that's what she would concentrate on.

TWENTY-THREE

Marg

As happy as Marg was about having Jackie home and loved taking care of her, she worried that all wasn't right with her.

They sat in the garden. Jackie had her leg propped on a stool and her head back, her eyes closed, her face tear-stained.

'Please talk to me, lass. I know it's more than worry over Harry that's bothering you. So, what is it, eh?'

Jackie just shook her head. Never had Marg seen her so miserable.

'I understand, lass. I'm worried meself. The news from France is terrifying and me Clive's talking of going over in his own boat. He reckons he could follow the lifeboat and that way they can bring more of our soldiers home. But, lass, we have to believe they'll get back safely.' Still no response. Marg sighed. 'Are you in pain, lass?'

As if she caught on to this, Jackie nodded. 'A lot of pain, Marg. And, aye, I'm worried about Harry and Alice and Gerald.'

The click of the latch on the gate made Marg turn. She was surprised to see Averill and Rod come through.

'We heard about Jackie.' Averill floated to Jackie's side, her beautiful face full of concern, her yellow polka-dot frock flowing behind her. 'Billy told us you were home on sick leave, Jackie, and how you've had a nasty accident. He said you were in a lot of pain.' She stroked Jackie's hair.

Jackie, who'd been so near to tears since coming home a few days ago, looked up at her. 'I can't get no peace with it.'

Rod stepped forward and went on his haunches. 'Where is the pain, Jackie?'

'It's from me ankle to me thigh. It's intense and almost as bad as when the accident happened. A – a bloke moved me and took me to the hospital and that hurt so bad it made me faint.'

'You were moved without being strapped up?'

'Aye.'

Marg frowned; Jackie had shuddered. Yes, this would be a bad memory for her, but she knew there was something more troubling her sister.

'When Billy told us, I thought it would be wise to have your leg looked at. I can arrange that at the hospital with one of my colleagues. Can you get into our car, do you think?'

Jackie looked towards Marg. Marg knew she was pleading for her to come too. 'She could manage that, couldn't you, Jackie? And I'll follow on behind so I can be with her. I'll just go and tell Ada . . . And ta, Rod, it's a relief to have something done for her.'

'No need to hurry, we're popping to Edith's to make sure she and the baby are all right now that Philip has gone back, though we understand he may be back again at the weekend.'

'Aye, I think so. Sue's there with her. She comes alternate days with Patricia, Philip's sister.'

Rod stood up. 'Righto, we won't be a moment. Get some things together for Jackie as I think she will have to stay in for a few days. I'm not an orthopaedic specialist, Jackie, but neurologists often are involved if there is a back injury, so I work closely with Doctor Rainyard, who I will take you to. He is an excellent physician. He will sort out what's wrong with your leg, my dear.'

Averill bent down and kissed Jackie. 'And if you need anyone to talk to, I'm a good listener, Jackie dear. We've all missed you. The boys especially.'

'Ta, Averill. I don't knaw why I'm so tearful – fear, mostly, but disappointed an' all. I was doing well and doing me bit for the war. Now, I'm stuck at home under Marg's feet.'

'You're never that, me lass. I didn't want you to hurt yourself, but I jumped for joy when I knew you were coming home. Gran thought I'd gone mad. She made me laugh, she said, "According to how folk react to everything I say, I'm supposed to be the mad one around here, not you, Nurse" – aye, she calls me Nurse now and again, bless her.'

'I'm worried about Gran as well, Marg. I couldn't believe how thin she is, and she seems to have shrunk.'

'I'll pop in and say hello. Is that all right, Marg?'

'Aye, she'd love that, Averill. Mind, she's more confused than ever today, so don't mind anything she says.'

As Averill went inside, Clive pulled up in his car. One glance at him told Marg he had something to tell her. She stiffened, knowing instinctively that she wouldn't like what he had to say.

She watched as he stopped to have a word with Rod, his voice too low for her to hear what was said, but then Rod looked deeply worried, his head shaking from side to side. The action deepened Marg's concern.

'Is everything all right, Clive?'

'Well, not good, I'm afraid, Marg. Where are the boys?'

'Not in from school yet. It's only just gone three.'

'Oh? I lost all sense of time. But I haven't got long, so I'll go and fetch them out of class. I need time with them.'

'Clive? Clive, what's going on?'

'I'll tell you when I get home, Marg. I won't be long.'

Marg ran after him. 'Clive, stop! Don't run off. Tell me first. Jackie's going into hospital, she's going in a moment. Rod's taking her ... If you're going away, sit with her a mo ... and me, Clive, please. I can't believe you're being like this.'

Clive looked down at her. His expression changed from grim determination to concern. 'I'm sorry, my darling. What am I thinking? I will stay. He took her in his arms. I just felt for a moment that there was so little time ... so little, and I wanted us all together for what time I had. But with Jackie going, that changes my decision.'

They walked back down the path with their arms around each other. Marg felt sick with fear.

Rod took his leave, telling them he'd nip around to Edith's to tell her they'd come another time. 'Looking at

Jackie, I don't think we should hang around too long, I didn't want to panic anyone, but I am worried about the colour of her foot.'

Marg thought her world had suddenly turned upside down. Her eyes went to Jackie's foot. For the first time she noticed just how blueish and swollen it was. She'd thought it just cold, but Rod seemed to be very concerned about it.

When Rod left, Clive took Marg's hand. 'Sit down a moment, darling.'

She did his bidding, feeling the moment was on her when she would hear that he was going away. Once she was seated Clive went down on his haunches in front of her.

'We're sailing in an hour, Marg. The tide will be right then. It will take us a couple of days to get to France, but we're joining the flotilla of boats going across to rescue our boys. We're going to bring them home, Marg.'

'Oh, me love, I'm so proud of you . . . but won't there be a lot of fighting going on? Is it safe?'

'There will, love, but I think we'll be safe enough as the fighting is on the land. They've driven our men back to Dunkirk beach and have them surrounded. There's boats that must be nearly there now from down south. As they head home, we'll be arriving. We'll take the men to Dover and then go back for more between us. We can get twenty to twenty-five men in our lifeboat and my boat. There're hundreds of boats going and thousands of men to rescue, so we're all needed. We have to do this, Marg, we can't leave our men stranded.'

'What of Alice and Gerald?'

'They will be coming home, but don't worry about them, they're protected as all medics are. They'll have hospital ships to bring them home.'

'Could Harry be one of those stranded, Clive?'

'He could, Jackie. We'll get him if he is, or one of the boatmen will. They're all brave men and will keep going back till every last man of our army is safe. And the RAF are sure to give air cover to help us, so we'll be safe too.'

Averill came out then. She greeted Clive with her usual flamboyance, kissing both of his cheeks. Oblivious to their worries, she piled on more. 'I should get Gran seen by her doctor, Marg. From what Ada tells me she could have a water infection. We have noted that the elderly can get confused when they are suffering from this. In the meantime, make sure she drinks plenty of water. Ah, here's Rod. Has he been to Edith's?'

They caught Averill up with their news. Then before Marg knew what was happening, Clive lifted Jackie and took her to the car. It was pitiful to hear her cries. But worse was the fear that gripped Marg as he swung Jackie around and she smelt a disgusting smell of rotting flesh!

Rod must have smelt it too as he hurried everything along, not letting Clive linger to say goodbye to Jackie.

Marg just had time to call out, 'I'll be in to see you in a bit, lass. You'll be all right, Jackie, me love.' She didn't know if Jackie heard her or not as the car sped away taking her from them.

'Eeh, Clive, what's happening to us?'

Clive sighed. 'Let's go and get the lads, Marg, as I must hurry. I'll drop you at Doctor Jones's surgery and then come back for you when I have George and Carl.'

His anxiety registered with her. She ran with him to the car and sat in the middle of the bench seat to be close to him. He held her hand as often as he could as they drove along.

'I could be away for a couple of weeks, Marg. You'll be all right, won't you? Be strong for me, my darling. If . . . well, carry on for me. Stay with our boys. Help them.'

'Clive . . . I – I . . . eeh, Clive.' She swallowed hard, wanted to beg him not to go, but knew that she must not. 'Don't worry about anything at home, Clive. The lads will be all right. I love them, I'm their ma. And I'll always see they're all right.'

This wasn't what she wanted to say. She wanted to say that if he didn't come home, her life was over. 'I love you, me Clive. I – I'm proud of you and support you.'

Where that came from, she didn't know, but she was glad she'd said it as Clive visibly relaxed.

She lay her head on his shoulder and they drove like that in silence.

When they arrived home, Clive had only a few minutes with his boys. He explained that he was going away and that they were to be good for their ma – Marg loved it whenever he referred to her as that. It was still new to her that George and Carl were legally hers.

'Now, give me a hug, my sons.'

Marg had to look away as she saw tears run down Clive's face.

'Right, off you go outside to play, while I say goodbye to your ma.'

Marg knew she would never forget his kiss. His loving lips told her his goodbye was as painful to him as it was to her. She clung on to him. When he released her, he looked deep into her eyes.

She followed him to the car, surprised to see he already had his rucksack in there. She hadn't noticed him pack, but guessed he'd done it very early in the morning, not disturbing her.

'I won't say goodbye to Gran, it will only upset her. Well, my darling, I'll see you in a couple of weeks. If I get a chance to ring you, I will.'

They clung together for a brief moment, telling each other of their love, and then he was in the car and was gone.

Marg stood on the pavement for a full minute staring after her beloved Clive. Her heart felt like lead, the light of her life had dimmed. She felt so alone and frightened.

The hospital loomed in front of her like a place of doom as Marg pulled up outside. She'd taken the boys to be with Edith, and they'd run happily into the garden and joined in a game with Mandy and Alf.

Edith had been feeding little Betsy. Marg had hoped against hope that she would be free to come with her. But she hadn't even been able to hug her.

The loneliness Marg felt seemed to echo in every click of her heels on the tiled floor of the hospital's long, empty corridor. *If only Clive were by me side and Gerald was here to meet me – and me Alice and Edith were with me an' all.* But it felt to her as if the rocks of her life had crumbled.

★ ★ ★

The sister on the ward took Jackie's night things and toiletries. 'You're her sister?'

'Aye, and next of kin. Mrs Barnes – Marg. Can I see Jackie?'

'I'm afraid she's in the operating theatre. She could be an hour or more, but if you can stay, I think it would be good if you were here when she wakes. That's her bed over there. Put these in the locker for her and then sit in the chair and I'll get one of my orderlies to bring you a cup of tea. Do you take saccharine? I'm afraid we have very little sugar.'

'No, ta. I've learnt to drink me tea without it. I can't take to the taste of them sweeteners.'

'Me neither. I think the whole nation will be losing weight without their ten to twelve teaspoons of sugar a day. Good thing too, I say.'

The tea made Marg feel sick. She sat back, her mind awash with worries. Would Jackie be all right? How long before Alice was home? Oh, how she missed her. Was Harry all right? Would he get back safely? How long before Philip had to go to France again? At least his return and coming home regularly was a bright light in an otherwise dark tunnel – a tunnel that had now taken her love, her Clive, from her side.

Two hours later – two long hours of not being able to find out anything – Marg was staring out of the window when a cough brought her attention to the sister who stood in front of her. The grave look on her face deepened the fear Marg held inside her.

'Your sister is being taken to intensive care, Marg.

They have been battling to save her leg. But are warning that the next two days are crucial. It may mean that she will have another operation to remove her leg. I'm sorry, but they will do all they can.'

'No! No, not me Jackie . . . Her leg? No!'

'I'm sorry, my dear, I know it's a shock. But they will only take that drastic step to save her life. They are hoping they have managed to save the leg, but she did have gangrene and it's very difficult to stop that spreading. As it is, if she recovers without having the amputation, she will have a deformed leg and that will affect her gait. She is going to need your support, Marg. Try to be strong for her.'

Marg stared at the sister. The enormity of what she'd been told wouldn't sink in.

Nothing about this day seemed real as she asked herself, *How did it happen that in just a few hours my world has been torn apart?*

Her voice croaked as she asked, 'Can I see her?'

'You can. The theatre staff told me that she was just coming round as they took her up, but she will be in and out of sleep.'

'Ta, Sister. And ta for being kind to me. I – I've had a bad day of it.' For some reason Marg blurted out all that had happened.

'Oh, my dear, that is a lot for you to cope with. Let's hope all is resolved and your loved ones come home. I shall pray for you and for Jackie. Are you sure you'll be all right? Jackie will need you to be strong for her.'

'Aye, I feel better for having spoken to you. I'll cope and show me lovely Jackie that I'm here for her.'

The sister smiled and patted her arm. Marg felt like hugging her. Her kindness had partly filled the void she felt at not having her Clive and her friends by her side.

Jackie didn't look like Jackie, but some tiny creature. Her leg was suspended from a bar above her bed, an oxygen mask covered her face, and blood dripped into her arm.

'Eeh, me little lass, I'm here, me love.'

Jackie opened her eyes but only for a moment.

'You're going to be all right, Jackie. But you must fight, lass. Don't give up. You need to get well for when Harry gets home. Didn't you tell me he said he was going to marry you when he next had leave? By, that'll be a day and a half, love. Alice and Gerald'll be home, and we Halfpenny Girls will all be together again ... Aye, and remember, you're a Halfpenny Girl an' all now, and we're strong, Jackie, love. You can beat this and get well.'

Jackie's eyes opened again. She stared at Marg. And there it was again, for Marg. Something deep in Jackie's eyes.

'Jackie, love, whatever it is that's troubling you, don't worry, we can sort it. There's nothing that's too much for us to get over. I promise ... Look, love, just don't think about it. Concentrate on getting well, eh? Let's get you up and about for when your Harry gets here ... Eeh, I think I'll get one of them wheelchairs so Harry can take you for a walk along the prom. That'd be grand wouldn't it, eh?'

Jackie nodded.

After a while Jackie fell off to sleep and the nurse suggested that Marg go home and come back later.

'Will you ring me if she worsens?'

'We will. Give your phone number to Sister as you leave.'

At home Marg found that Gran was fine and asleep. Ada told her the doctor had been and had left some medicine for her. 'It's naw better than I could have made for her, Marg. I've treated many a bladder problem with me cranberry juice. You could have saved your money, lass.'

'I know, Ada, love, but Averill thought Gran needed a doctor. And when one doctor tells you that – a brain specialist, no less – then you do as they tell you.' Marg went on to tell Ada how Jackie was and received a surprise hug, and comfort as she cried on Ada's shoulder. In all the years she'd known Ada, she'd never known her to show her love like this. Straightening and drying her eyes, she thanked Ada. But seeing how emotional this woman who'd always been the stalwart was, Marg felt very touched.

'Ta, Ada, love, I needed that hug. And ta for everything you do for me gran.'

Ada blushed. 'Go on with yer. You pay me, don't you?' Then winked and gave a little laugh.

This made Marg laugh too, but she thought to herself that maybe she'd never really got to know Ada as she'd never known her to have a laugh at her own expense – or to even laugh much at all.

'I'll see you in a while, love, I'm going to see Edith for a bit.'

'That's a good idea, love. Edith'll soon cheer you up.'

The hug that Edith gave her as soon as she saw her meant the world to Marg.

'Eeh, Marg, I can't believe all that's happened.'

Minnie stood just behind Edith. 'And I'm sorry for your troubles, too, luv. I thought we East Enders had life hard, but you lot, well, I take me 'at off to you. And I'll do what we Londoners do when anything bad happens, I'll put the kettle on. We swear by a cup of Rosie Lee in times of trouble.'

'Ta, Minnie. That'd be grand ... Shall we sit outside, Edith?'

'Aye. The lads are playing out there. They were all squabbling a minute ago and George had me in stitches. He stood with his arms folded and stamped his foot and in an authoritative voice yelled, "Play nicely, or not at all!" And the others did as he said! I tell you, that one's destined to be a teacher!'

Marg tried to smile but couldn't. She covered up by saying, 'I know, he's getting to be a little bossy boots.'

Edith pushed her playfully. 'Hey, cheeky, is that what I am, then?'

'No, Edith, but you always have solutions – you can sort things out.' Marg sighed.

'Eeh, Marg, what's happening is beyond me to sort out, love. It's in God's hands. But you have to think that everything will come out fine. And if it don't, we lasses have always found a way to cope with it. Alice will be home soon and then we'll be strong again.'

'It's not just what we know that's troubling me, Edith. There's something deeply wrong with Jackie ... I mean, something troubling her mind.'

'Oh? Well, aye, I did notice she was subdued, but just thought it was being injured and not being able to carry on as she has, and all the uncertainty about Harry. Every day she must wonder if he's all right. I feel so much for her.'

'Aye, there's those things, and they're the things she is talking about, but . . . Eeh, I don't know.'

'Sisterly instinct? You and Jackie have such a strong bond, love, that if you're worried about Jackie then I'd say there is something she isn't saying. I tell you what. I'll try to come with you when you go back later. Betsy's due another feed in an hour, and after that she settles well. But what about the boys?'

'I'll nip round and see Billy, see if he'll come for a while and sit with them. When I've had me tea, I'll take them home and bath them and get them ready for bed, then let them stay up late with Billy.'

'All right, lass. And I'll see if there's anything I can do for Jackie. She's always told me what she can't tell you, in the past.'

This was true. And Marg knew it happened because she would fly off the handle and make things worse, but then, she couldn't help herself – if anything was wrong with Jackie, she couldn't stand it and would go for anyone who caused her grief. She felt like wringing the neck of the car driver who'd made her fall of her bike as it was.

But now she had Edith to sort it all out, and she knew everything would come right – but still she prayed, *please, God, make me Jackie well – don't let anything bad have happened to her or happen to her now. Save her leg, and bring me Clive, Alice, Gerald and Harry home, then all will be well for us again.*

TWENTY-FOUR

Edith

Edith loved the sensation of Betsy suckling her breast. Love seemed to flow between them as her child looked trustingly up at her and found her finger to hold.

It was a picture she knew her Philip loved and wanted to capture on his camera, but she wouldn't let him. Laughing at him, she told him that if ever that was found in his wallet, she'd say he wasn't her husband.

At the moment she couldn't be happier for herself. Her own little world was wonderful. She just wished she could make everything right for everyone else and make it so that Philip never had to go away again. But already he was talking of having to go to Scotland in a few weeks for training. She didn't ask what the training was for. She'd learnt to accept.

'I think her belly's full and she's 'aving yer on now, Edith, luv. Shall I take her and change her while you get ready to go with Marg?'

'Aye, ta, Minnie. She might play up a bit, though.'

'Ha, I can 'andle her. And if I can't, Mandy can. She's a dab hand with her.'

Edith smiled, but that turned to a laugh as Mandy and Alf came in muddied up. 'We've made pie and mash, Edith.'

Edith sometimes thought that dish brought home nearer to them more than anything else could.

'Well, I've made it for real for yer tea, me little darlins'. But Granny'll be out in a minute to see if yours look better than mine – I ain't tasting them, though.'

All four of them laughed at this and Edith knew her happiness to swell despite everything.

At the hospital, she was shocked to see how Jackie looked. She no longer had the oxygen on that Marg had mentioned, nor the drip, which Edith thought was some progress, but she looked pale and weak.

She bent over and kissed her forehead, wanting her to wake. 'Jackie, love, it's Edith . . . Hello, lass. How're you feeling, eh?'

Tears trickled from Jackie's eyes.

'Eeh, love. Are you in pain?'

'Naw.'

Her voice was low and hoarse. But Edith remembered that Alice's was like that after her operation and Gerald had said it's because they pass something down your throat while they are operating, so she didn't worry about it.

'But you seem so sad. Is it because you're worried over Harry?'

'Aye.'

Edith, like Marg, felt there was something more.

She looked over at Marg stood on the other side of the bed and nodded. Marg took Jackie's hand in hers. 'I'll leave you with Edith a while, lass, and go and have a word with the sister to see if everything's still all right with your leg, Jackie, love.'

But Jackie was on to their little ruse. As soon as Marg left, she turned her head towards Edith. 'I — I can't tell you owt, Edith. I've got to deal with it meself.'

'Why, love? You know I'm always here for you.'

'Please help me on this, Edith. Just believe me when I say I can't speak of it . . . Look, I'll tell you one thing, as I knaw you'll never breathe a word, and you mustn't, not even to Philip — Philip especially.'

This shocked Edith. She glanced over to where Marg was talking to the sister and knew then it was safe for Jackie to say whatever it was.

'I promise you on me Betsy's life, Jackie, love.'

'Well . . . I shouldn't even tell you this, but me job weren't what you thought it was. I — I had to sign the Official Secrets Act.'

'What? God, Jackie . . .'

'Shush, Edith.'

Edith took a deep breath. Never had she been so surprised at being told anything. What on earth had the powers that be got Jackie to do? 'So, what's troubling you? Is it something you can't speak of for fear of exposing something you shouldn't . . . or someone?'

'Eeh, Edith, don't ask me any more, please. I've allus told you everything and want to confide in you now. I need your comfort, I want you to make it all right, but I knaw you can't.'

'I don't have to know everything to be a comfort to you, me love. I'll always be that for you. Just know that if what happened to make you so miserable haunts you, you can come to me for a hug and I won't ask questions, not about that anyroad. But can you say if you'll have to go back there when you're well?'

'I don't knaw. I don't want to, but it ain't nowt that I can say naw to. I'm needed. I'm just praying that I'm not asked to. I wouldn't be able to stand it.'

Edith knew then that whatever had upset Jackie to this degree would carry on if she went back. She had an idea that this had something to do with a man ... *My God, Blake! Didn't he go away to do secret war work?* Suddenly, Edith felt certain this was to do with him. How would the War Office know about Jackie, if someone hadn't told them? She hadn't been to university to study accountancy, which was their usual pool for recruiting the young into special jobs – that much Philip had told her and was borne out in how he was chosen for his language skills. Jackie's skills were only known by a few – and one of those was the hateful Blake. Edith now felt convinced he was behind this. *What has the evil, heartless rotter done to our lovely Jackie?*

She reached out to touch Jackie's cheek. Like a little girl, Jackie leant her head on Edith's hand.

'Me love. Me poor love. I hope with all me heart that you don't have to go back but if you do, is there anyone there that you could talk to? A welfare officer perhaps?'

'They would close ranks, I knaw that ... Have ... you guessed, Edith?'

'Aye, I think so.'

Jackie looked fearful.

'Don't worry, love. I'll keep me promise. Eeh, Jackie. Me poor love.'

Jackie's whisper shocked Edith to the core. 'I could be shot as a traitor, Edith, if ever you tell.'

Edith bent over her and took her in her arms as best as she could. 'I don't think you can, lass. Don't be afraid. You told me nothing. And they don't shoot you for that anyway. Who told you that? . . . That rotten . . . I mean, look. Aye, I reckon if you passed secrets to the Germans, then you could be shot, but for seeking help from a friend and telling her nothing, then no.'

'But . . . there are ways of making things look worse.'

'Like was threatened last time?' Edith felt incensed. She'd never felt so angry in her entire life as she did at this moment. Blake was evil. And that evil had terrified the lovely Jackie. What had he said he would do if she told of him?

'Nothing will happen, I promise. I will never break your confidence, so it will be like you never told me a thing – not that you did, other than that you weren't doing what we thought and had to sign the Secrets Act. That's nothing. It tells me nothing about anything. I have deduced a few things, that's all. I could be wrong. Anyroad, if you have to go back, then promise me that you'll seek help from some-one you can talk to. Please, Jackie.'

'Aye, I will. Ta, Edith. I knaw it's been difficult, but you have helped me, and I trust you. I knaw I'm safe with you. I love you, Edith.'

'Aw, and I love you an' all. Try to smile for Marg, love, she's going out of her mind with worry. Don't let her start to deduce things. She's already mystified as to how they came to choose you to carry out war work. Settle her mind about there being something wrong. You know what she's like. She's like a dog with a bone if she thinks you're hurt, and she'll eventually make things add up.'

'I will ... And I'm helped by the hope I have that me Harry is on his way home. I won't let meself think otherwise ... about anything bad. As, like you say, Marg will knaw and won't give up.'

'That's the spirit, love, as God knows what she would do if she sussed it out as I have ... Anyroad, time to start acting, she's on her way over.'

When Marg came up to them, Jackie gave her a lovely smile.

'Eeh, me lass. Me ray of sunshine. Are you all right, love?'

'Aye, I am. I'm sorry I put you through so much, Marg. I was in such pain and worried about everyone. Edith's made me see that it's better to share things than bottle them up.'

Edith watched Marg cuddle Jackie and saw the relief on her face. Her sigh spoke volumes. 'Ta, Edith, you've always been the one to help us all, we all lean on you.'

'And you always can, lass. I love you all and am always ready to do me best for you ... Now, what did the sister say?'

'So far, they're very pleased with your leg, Jackie, and you haven't shown any sign of having a fever as you would if ... well ... Did they tell you what was wrong with your leg, lass?'

'Aye, they did. And they said that I might have a limp – well, it was more than likely that I would ... By, I didn't want that, but I'll get on with it. I'll allus think of it as being better than losing me leg.'

'Aw, me Jackie. I'm so relieved.' Marg burst into tears.

Edith held her close. Jackie soothed her with words. 'It'll all work out, Marg, you'll see. I'm sorry I worried you like I did. Eeh, I'll soon be hobbling under your feet, and Clive will come back bringing me Harry, and we'll be as happy as we were afore.'

Marg giggled. 'Ha, you won't get under me feet, lass. I've missed you so much. I'll get through this much better with having you by me side.'

As Edith looked on while the two sisters held hands, she prayed harder than she'd ever done before that Jackie was right and Harry and Clive would come home.

After looking in and finding that everything was peaceful at home, Minnie was listening to Tommy Handley in *It's That Man Again* on the radio and laughing out loud.

Betsy was fast asleep, and she knew she would be until around two in the morning when she would want her night feed. A time Edith loved, when all was quiet, and it was just the two of them – mostly, that was. Sometimes Betsy's crying woke Mandy, and she would come in and slip between the sheets of Edith's bed and watch, quietly sucking her thumb. Then she would fall asleep and spend the rest of the night snuggled up to her. To Edith, these were special moments.

'Are you all right if I go and spend an hour with Marg, Minnie? I feel bad as I've been out for a couple of hours, but she needs me tonight. It's her first without Clive, bless her.'

'That's fine, but do it quietly, you're disturbing me programme.'

Edith chuckled and bent down to kiss Minnie's forehead. 'You're a good 'un. Just ring if you need me.'

At Marg's home, as the evening was still warm, they sat on the step. Edith knew this was the greatest comfort for Marg – better if it was the three of them, but still, it was something for them both to be together.

'So, what was really bothering me Jackie, Edith?'

Edith mentally crossed herself. 'I only know what she told you – both of us, love. I'd told her how worried you were and how with Clive going it was too much for you to have on your shoulders. She was sorry and said she'd make it right. The pain had consumed her as everything else had. And that's it, Marg. Once she knew it was making you sick with fear for her, then she just wanted that to stop and knew she could do that now.'

'Well, I was still thinking that was all a ploy, but I know you wouldn't lie to me, Edith. Eeh, I'm that relieved ... well, on that score, anyroad.'

'Aye, there's plenty more for us to worry over, lass, and there will be for a long time. What's important is that we can all help each other. You've been a massive help to me. Now, it's my turn to help you. But I ain't doing that, or anything else, till I get me cocoa.'

They both laughed as Marg got up.

'I'll come in with you and look in on Gran. Will she still be awake?'

'Aye, she was a few minutes ago. Ada's washed her and they were both just sitting reminiscing. Gran can do that, you know. Even now that she has only rare moments of being with us in today's world, she never forgets the past.'

'Aye, that fits with how Gerald explained her dementia. He said it was like when you're reading a book, but some of the pages are missing. Do you remember?'

'I do. I began to understand Gran a lot after that. It really helped. Well, the pages that seem to go missing for Gran are the ones that let her know who we are, and what happened yesterday. Oh, and whether she's had her dinner. Getting her to eat is difficult at times as she says she's only just had her breakfast when it's teatime!'

Gran was ready for bed but seemed as perky as if it was the middle of the day. She greeted Edith, asking which one she was. 'I knaw that you're one of Betty's kids, lass.'

'Well then, you daft ha'peth, you knaw as Betty only had two kids, Albert and Edith, and Edith ain't a lad, is she?'

'Shut up, Ada, you've allus got an opinion.'

Edith giggled as Ada looked put out. 'Don't worry about it, Ada. Me ma always used to say that it was better to go along with it, not to argue something that Gran has no knowledge of.'

'She may have done, but I think we should help Sandra to see what's right, not what she thinks is.'

Edith sighed. She knew there was no use in arguing with Ada. In Ada's mind, she'd elevated herself to knowing all there was to know about nursing folk back to health. And Edith had to admit, she did know most things and had been a lifesaver to the folk in Whittaker Avenue.

'Anyroad, Gran, I've come to ask how you are.'

'I'm fine, love. I went to Stanley Park with me da this morning. We had a lovely time.'

Ada gave a massive sigh, got up and walked out of the room.

Edith didn't correct Gran. Even though this wouldn't have been possible, not only because of the obvious, but Stanley Park wasn't built when Gran was a youngster.

'I took me babby there this morning. I didn't see you.'

'You're babby? Is Betty a grandma then?'

This cut Edith in two for a moment, but she recovered. 'Aye, she is.'

'Eeh, she never told me. What did you have, a girl or boy?'

For a few moments, Edith told Gran all about Betsy. Gran listened contentedly, smiling a knowing kind of smile and nodding her head.

'Eeh, that's lovely. Will you bring her round to see me, lass? I love to hold babbies. I like to kiss their squidgy necks and I love how they have such a nice smell. Eeh, I had a few babbies, you knaw. But they're all in heaven with me John . . . I'll go soon, you knaw.'

'Not yet, Gran. We need you here. And aye, I'll bring me babby around to see you. Now, you look tired, and I have to get back to have me cocoa with Marg.'

'Tell her to make me some, lass . . . Where is she? I ain't seen her in an age.' A tear plopped onto Gran's cheek, and

Edith felt the pity of this. Gran really believed she hadn't seen her granddaughter for a long time, and yet Marg devoted herself to her. How sad must that make Gran feel as to her it was real that Marg hadn't been to see her?

Edith didn't have to go and ask as Marg came in with Ada and two mugs of cocoa for them.

'Here she is, Gran.'

'That ain't Marg, silly. That's me nurse. Me Marg's only a little girl. She's lovely. Kind and thoughtful. I do miss her.' Another tear ran down Gran's face. 'I wish she'd come and see me . . . D'yer think she knaws where I live now?'

Edith swallowed hard. Her heart felt heavy with sadness. What a cruel illness dementia was.

Marg took it in her stride, which was a relief. 'Eeh, have your cocoa, lass. Marg'll come and see you, don't you worry.'

But Ada took on the challenge again. 'You get dafter, Sandra. Marg's grown up now. This is Marg, and this is her home. She's married to Clive, and you were at the wedding!'

Gran looked at Marg. 'Was I, dear? Well, you do look like me Vera. You're very beautiful and I knaw one thing, I knaw I love you, lass.'

Marg put the cup down and hugged her gran. The loveliest thing for Edith was that Gran hugged her back and was smiling.

Outside again, Edith sipped her cocoa tentatively, blowing away the steam first. Her mind was troubled. How she wished Philip was home tonight and she could snuggle up to him and share her worries with him.

In the silence that had fallen, she allowed Marg her own thoughts while she pondered on breaking her promise and talking to Philip about all she believed was happening with Jackie. If anyone could do anything, he could or, if not him personally, then he may be able to influence someone who could. Was it her duty to tell him? If she didn't, what would the future be like for Jackie if recalled to wherever she'd been?

But then, feeling certain she was right, it occurred to her to wonder just how far Blake had gone? Had he raped Jackie? Her mind screamed against this but thinking about the enormity of the possibility determined her decision. She would definitely speak to Philip.

Philip was delayed in coming home. Waiting another couple of weeks nearly drove Edith crazy, but what it meant to them both more than made up for the delay in being together.

Their child was now over six weeks old – they could express their love fully. Thinking about this and on tenterhooks about his arrival, Edith busied herself dusting ornaments that didn't need it.

'Well, Philip will come home to the cleanest 'ouse in the street. I did those yesterday, Edith!'

'Eeh, I'm sorry, Minnie. I just feel restless. The time is dragging and even Betsy has decided to have a lazy day and hasn't kept me busy.'

'Look, girl, lift Betsy and feed her. She's gone a good four hours, otherwise she'll wake just as Philip arrives. I can then take the twins and Betsy for a walk soon after they've said hello. I'd say you will need an hour on your own, luv.'

The wink that went with this made Edith blush. But she grinned to cover that and hugged Minnie. 'Ta, lass, and you're right.'

Minnie giggled. 'I love it when you call me "lass".'

Minnie hadn't even reached the gate with the children before Philip grabbed Edith's hand and ran with her to their bedroom. Her giggles were halted by his kiss, a passionate, desperate kiss that accompanied their wriggling movements to rid themselves of their clothes.

And then came the blissful moment when Philip entered her – she cried out with the thrill and joy of at last having him make love to her.

It was a frenzied giving and taking that took her to a place she'd forgotten the intensity of. Her cries joined his as together they reached their climax.

When Philip rolled off her, he took her with him in the circle of his arms.

It was a moment before either of them spoke. The closeness of their naked bodies said all they needed to.

It was Philip who broke their silence. 'I'm here for a whole week, darling, so you'd better prepare yourself.'

Edith burst out laughing. 'I don't mind if we lie here all week, me love. You're home, we're back to being husband and wife, and that's all that matters.'

She looked into his face. The thought came to her how lucky she was to have such a handsome man to love her. At this moment he looked rakish as his dark hair, usually sleeked back with Brylcreem, had flopped over his fore-head and his dark eyes held amusement.

Suddenly, Jackie's plight came to her and marred her joy.

'What is it, darling? Your face clouded then.'

'I – I don't know how to tell you . . . I promised with all my heart I wouldn't . . . I – I . . .'

'What? Darling, has something happened?'

'Well, yes, but can I ask you something first . . . If some-one has signed the Official Secrets Act and tells someone that they have, have they committed a crime?'

Philip turned towards her. 'Of course not. They only commit a crime if they tell a secret they shouldn't. Why?'

'Eeh, Philip, this is about Jackie. She's told me nothing other than she didn't go to work where we all thought but, as she'd signed the act, she couldn't tell me any more.'

'Why would you ask her to, darling? You know we mustn't ask questions like that.'

Edith explained Jackie's extreme unhappiness and her own deduction. 'I know I'm right, Philip, but eeh, in telling you this much I've broken me solemn promise.'

'My God! That evil . . . I wish at this moment that I swore, I really do, as swear words are the only ones that fit Blake . . . Now, I'm assuming that you are right, because I had wondered myself how they knew about Jackie being a likely candidate for the work that I know she is doing.'

This surprised Edith and made her wonder just what Philip's job really was, but she didn't interrupt him.

'I can't say any more, darling, only that Jackie is so well suited to the work and would be a loss if she didn't return to it. Her injury – I mean, being left with a limp – wouldn't preclude her either. So, I would say she will be recalled . . . Are you thinking Blake might do it again – I mean, if you're right in your thinking?'

'All I know is that Jackie is afraid. She said she wouldn't be able to stand it if they sent her back. That must mean that he has told her this isn't the end of whatever he did. He'd terrified her as it was with threatening what he could make happen to her . . . I mean, eeh, Philip, she thinks she can be shot as a traitor – he has somehow convinced her of that. She's so miserable, and . . . well, I think worried an all. She could have been made pregnant!'

'Oh, Edith, the more you tell me, the more incensed I feel . . . Look, we know he is lecherous, always has been, but why this obsession with Jackie?' Philip sighed. 'Let's not say another word about this, darling. Leave it with me. I'll have to be very careful how I approach this, but I will find a way, and I know who to go to with it. Blake made a lot of enemies in the last war . . . All I can do is my best, and I would do that for Jackie. Now, we must be so careful not to let her suspect you have told me, or that will add to her worry, poor girl.'

Edith nodded, but her heart was rejoicing. She just knew Philip would sort everything out – Jackie was going to be all right. She was justified in breaking her promise. All it needed now was for Harry to come home for Jackie . . . and Alice and Gerald. Oh, how she longed for that to happen.

TWENTY-FIVE

Alice

Alice shivered. They'd been on the road for three weeks now. The last two of these had been mostly by foot over rough terrain, seeking the cover of the trees and in barns of friendly farmers as they'd had to ditch the ambulance.

Getting fuel had proved too difficult, and besides, the vehicle was an easy target from the air. Now that Germany was advancing further and further into France, they knew that such vehicles were being used by the British trying to escape.

It was just herself, Gerald and Pete now, as the group had decided a week ago to separate, thinking a large party was easily spotted.

Getting food had proved a problem. Most farmers had given them something, but not all had enough to share.

Now as they waited on the station at Le Mans to take a train for the last leg of their journey, another air raid attack was in progress.

Alice could never get used to the noise – the screaming planes coming in low to shoot at them, and the sounds of explosions still affected her badly and set her body trembling with fear.

They huddled together on the floor, herself and Gerald under a bench, Pete somewhere behind the ticket office.

A woman running towards them holding a child by the hand fell just as she got to them. Her face had gone, blood seeped towards them. The child didn't cry. A boy of two or three years old, his face drained of colour, his eyes like saucers, stood and stared down at the horrific sight.

'Come . . . come here, you'll be safe. Come on, little one.'

The boy looked at them but didn't move. Another plane came in, bullets ricocheted off the concrete platform, and the boy did a hideous dance before falling over his mother's body. His lovely eyes, still staring but now unseeing.

Alice hollered out her pain. Gerald held her tighter, his tears mingling with hers.

'Why? Why? A ch – child! Th – they could see he was just a child. They're animals – beasts!'

'Shush, darling. He's with his mother in heaven now.'

But Alice couldn't shush. For her, the boy's eyes held the horror of it all. For her, he'd become the symbol of the evil they were fighting. They'd broken her heart, now they'd broken the heart of the mother and child's family and millions of others around the world and for what? World supremacy. And at this moment, as she sobbed and wailed, it felt to her that they would succeed, and life would never be the same again.

When a train going their way finally came in, Gerald asked, 'Shall we take the chance? They may bomb the train, darling, but the alternative is more days and nights sleeping rough and all the ferries may have been stopped by the time we get there.'

'We've no . . . choice.'

She rolled out from under the bench. For a moment, she touched the boy's face, then closed his eyes. Gerald took her hand and helped her up.

'We have to hurry, darling, the guard's already waving his flag.'

'Where's Pete?'

They looked around. Alice screamed out his name, but nothing. Suddenly, Gerald pulled her along. He jumped on the moving train, then yanked her arm so that she too was inside. 'Pete? Oh God, we've lost Pete.'

The train chugged out of the station. The carriage they'd jumped into was empty. Once they sat down, Gerald pulled her to him, his kiss on her hair somehow restoring her courage. And as the night-time was drawing in and darkness was almost upon them, she prayed that the planes would head for home, or wherever they were based.

Her wish was granted. As the train drew slowly out of the station, the pilots did not turn around and attack again. Their drone receded.

Alice looked up at Gerald as he told her, 'It's likely they have used their fuel or ammunition. They're heading away from us.'

Alice found that she could smile. 'We're going home.' She didn't say it, but she thought, *If only me Harry and Pete were with us. I dread going into our house without Harry. And I pray that Pete makes it.*

★   ★   ★

They must have both fallen asleep, as the train stopping, doors banging and whistles blowing startled them. Gerald rushed to the carriage door and opened it. Another long whistle stopped the train pulling off.

'*Vite! Vite! Rapidement!*'

They both jumped off the train and stood there looking at one another in a daze before Gerald gathered himself and took her hand. 'Almost there, darling. There's no fighting here. The Germans haven't yet reached this far. I've just enough money left to get a ticket on the ferry as I'm not sure they will take our travel passes. Let's hurry. I won't rest until we're on the sea going home.'

'Well, me mucca, you made it!'

'Pete! Where did you come from?'

'I couldn't find you, so I jumped into the guard's van, just as the train was leaving the station. The guard gave me a hitch up, like, or I would've lost me footing. Anyway, he spoke English and told me the port is about three quarters of an hour if we're lucky enough to get a cab, and the night ferry goes at eleven. I reckon by morning we'll be treading the soil of old Blighty.'

Alice felt like cheering. Her relief at seeing Pete and the thought of being home filled her with a joy she never thought to feel again.

That joy was tempered by the sadness of Harry never coming home and her dread of breaking that news to Billy, Joey and the lovely Jackie.

She knew she would have to be strong for them all, but could she be? She didn't know, but she did know she would try.

The news from the crew of the ferry was of the chaos at Dunkirk and how a flotilla of small British boats was valiantly carrying out a rescue of British, Dutch and French soldiers.

'It's going well, but the casualties are huge,' the man who was telling them this said.

Alice thought it was like living in hell; all she saw and heard was death and destruction. The mood of all those on the ferry was a mixture of relief and fear. With the Germans so near, they would surely invade Britain.

It took three days to get home. When they landed in Portsmouth the normality of everywhere came as a shock. Life here didn't seem, on the face of it, to be affected by all that was happening in France.

All three needed a rest before they could tackle their onward journeys.

Alice hadn't thought herself hungry, but the delicious aroma of bacon frying coming from a dockside café compelled them to make that their first call.

The huge fry-up went down well with a mug of sweet tea.

'Well, we made it, and now my dearest wish is for a bath and a bed.'

Alice agreed with Gerald, but Pete said he would take his leave of them and begin the next leg of his journey. 'No doubt our paths will cross again.' With this, he shook Gerald's hand and hugged Alice. Knowing he wouldn't want a long goodbye, Alice waved him off.

'Eeh, Gerald, I wish that I had the energy to just carry on to our home, but me legs will hardly cart me around as it is. Mind, they'll have to, as I need to buy meself some clothes before I go anywhere! These are stinking.'

'Ha, they do. And mine. So, let's book into The George Hotel first – the captain recommended it to me and told me that it's only a minute's walk from here. That way we'll be sure of a room. Then we'll go to the bank and the shops. Do you think you can manage that, darling?'

They found all they needed in the high street. For the journey home the next day, Alice bought a navy costume with a pleated skirt and a box-shaped jacket that came to her waist. The satin edge to the jacket gave it an elegant feel. She matched this with a white blouse, navy kitten-heeled shoes and navy gloves and handbag. For her immediate needs, besides some new underwear, she bought a housecoat and a summery frock to wear to dinner. Patterned with large navy flowers and small pale blue daisies on a white background, she thought to team it with the jacket from her costume to give it a more evening-wear look. Next came a few underwear garments and some soap, a toothpaste and a brush. Finally, she spent a little on the luxury of rouge and lipstick.

Gerald was much more easily settled – two pullovers, a shirt, a pair of trousers, brogues, a shaving kit and some personal items and he was done.

As soon as they got into their room – a welcoming sight furnished in reds and golds, with a huge four-poster bed – Gerald set about filling the large bath, which the landlord had proudly told them the room had been furnished with during Victorian times. 'It be the first in Portsmouth and is still a lovely addition, sir.'

And he was right. Ornate with shining brass taps, the bath was big enough for them both.

Once in, Alice sitting between Gerald's legs, he gently covered her in the lovely, soft, sweet-smelling soap. His massaging was sensual, his kisses on her skin lighting a flame in Alice that had been suppressed for so long.

Soon they were on the bed, still damp from the hasty way they'd dried each other, and were joining their bodies in the way they had both yearned to do for such a long time.

Their lovemaking was a frenzy of desperation that took them both to a place where they abandoned the silence they'd tried not to disturb and cried out with the joy of fulfilment. But then, both cried in despair, as their grief surfaced, and they felt the intense pain of the loss of their beautiful Harry.

Neither tried to stop the other. They allowed their tears, holding on tightly to each other, letting their souls be cleansed of all they had been through, all they had witnessed – the horrific injuries, the deaths, and the sense of despair.

Alice felt stronger for it as she lay calmly now in Gerald's arms and knew she could face what she had to. She would have Marg and Edith by her side when she arrived home. The three of them had been to hell and back before. They would get through this too.

This resolve weakened as they reached North Street station and Alice caught sight of her lovely mother-in-law, Averill. 'I don't want to do this, Gerald. I – I don't want to say it. I don't want it to be real.'

Gerald held her. He didn't try to comfort her with words. There were no words. She was back in her much-loved hometown, and Harry would never come back to her, never run on the sands, or mess about with his brothers. She would never see his lovely smile again.

When they stepped onto the platform, she was encased in Averill's delicate arms. Everything about Averill was delicate and beautiful.

Over Averill's shoulder she saw Gerald being held by his dad. Saw his body heave, and his dad pat his back.

'What is it, my dearest Alice?'

Alice shook her head. 'Don't make me say it . . .'

'Oh God, Harry?'

Alice nodded. 'How . . . how am I to tell Billy and Joey? How?'

'Let's go and sit in the car. You can tell me there, my dear, or we can drive to the beach, or Stanley Park. Just to help you compose yourself. They are both home and waiting for you, as are Marg and Edith.'

Of course, it was Saturday, Marg wouldn't be at work. Suddenly, she couldn't wait to see them all.

'I'm all right to go home.' Somehow, knowing Marg and Edith would be with her, she felt stronger.

In the car, Gerald clung on to her hand as he told Averill and Rod what had happened. Hearing it brought it all back to Alice. She stared out of the car window.

When their house came into sight, her throat tightened. She couldn't do this, she couldn't . . .

Gerald looked at her through tear-swelled eyes. 'I'll tell them, darling, you just be there to hold them. Be strong for them, darling. We must be strong.'

Billy and Joey flew at her as soon as she alighted from

the car. She held them close. Over their shoulder she saw the shocked faces of Edith and Marg. No one had to tell them. As always, they knew what was in her heart.

Her eyes went to Marg, searching to see if she was all right. On the way here, Averill had told them about Clive going to Dunkirk. And then about poor Jackie ... Until this moment the enormity of all that didn't register with Alice. But now she had to pile more agony onto Marg's shoulders.

It seemed that time stood still for a moment as all just stared at each other. Even Joey and Billy had taken a step back and she knew that they knew that all wasn't well.

Rod took charge. He gathered the lads together, with an arm around each. 'Come on, let me take you two inside. Gerald has something to tell you.'

They both went, but as they got to the door, Billy looked back. In his face Alice read a plea. 'I – I'll be there in a moment, lad.'

As they went inside, Alice moved towards Marg and Edith. They did the same towards her, then she was in their hug – one of their three-way hugs that had sustained her for many years. *Would this one do so now? Would anything?*

TWENTY-SIX

Marg

Marg walked with Edith to the hospital. It wasn't far from Alice's. Both were shivering, though the weather was warm.

'How am I to tell her, Edith, how?'

Edith shook her head, as she had done each time Marg had asked.

When they opened the door to the ward and Jackie spotted them, she beamed at them. 'I can come home! Eeh, Marg, at last ... Marg?' Her head swivelled. 'Edith? What's happened? Why are you here? It ain't visiting hour ... Naw ... Naw, not me Harry!'

Edith ran forward and took Jackie's hand. Jackie's head shook from side to side. Her mouth opened. The wail that came out propelled Marg to move towards her, taking the feeling of being a statue from her and filling her with sisterly love and an urge to protect Jackie.

'Me love, me lovely lass ... I'm sorry. Eeh, Jackie. I – I don't know what to say.'

'How ... When? Naw ... It ain't happened, it ain't.'

Edith sat on the bed while Marg held Jackie to her.

Edith cleared her throat. 'I'm so very sorry, me little lass, but Harry ... He – he didn't die alone, Jackie.' Tears were streaming down Edith's face. 'He died in Alice's arms. She held him to her, and she and her colleague on the ambulance took him back to Gerald's hospital, where he was tended to. Alice and Gerald were able to be at his burial – a proper church service. Eeh, me love, I know that none of this is a consolation, but it will be a better memory than thinking of him being left to die in a cold muddy field all on his own.'

To Marg, Edith's words made the truth of what had happened really take root – Harry was dead, and they could do nothing ... nothing about it. How were they to help Jackie and Alice and the lads?

'But I didn't want him to die! I didn't. I want him – need him ... Oh, me Harry, me Harry ...'

Marg and Edith joined in hugging Jackie together. Marg's heart felt like lead. It was as if a piece of her had died too. Always she felt Jackie's pain so acutely.

'Take me home, Marg.'

Marg couldn't answer for weeping.

Edith got up off the bed. 'I'll go and have a word with Sister. She knows the situation, we told her when we arrived.'

When she came back, Edith told them that Jackie could be taken home. 'At first, Sister said we would have to wait for an ambulance, but I asked her to lend me a wheelchair and we will push you home, love. I told her that we were friends of Doctor Meredith and if she wanted to, she could ring him to confirm that we're trustworthy enough to take care of you and to return the wheelchair to the hospital. She agreed in the circumstances. She said it would be unbearable for you to stay here without us and yet, she couldn't let us stay as it would disrupt the smooth running of the ward. She also said that follow-up appointments would be sent out to you.'

Jackie just nodded.

'Can you stand up, Jackie?'

'Aye, I can, Edith. And I can manage short distances on crutches. That's why they're letting me home. And because I told them we had a downstairs bathroom and a live-in nurse.'

To Marg, Jackie had seemed to put a veil over her hurt as she gave her attention to getting home. Marg didn't know if this was a good thing or not but didn't question it.

Once outside the hospital, Jackie took hold of Marg's hand. 'Take me to Alice and the lads first. I want to be with them all as well as with you and Edith.'

'I can't stay long, lass. Me Betsy will need her feed. But I can see you when you get home.'

Jackie just nodded at Edith. 'I understand. It's all right.'

Marg looked over Jackie's head at Edith asking a silent question with her expression. Edith shrugged, showing she was just as mystified as to how Jackie had suddenly shut off her emotions.

When they arrived at Alice's, the pain of it all came at them as sobs reverberated around them.

As soon as they were inside, Jackie shouted, 'Billy, Joey, come down to me, please!'

Alice, who had been on her way towards Jackie, stopped in her tracks as Jackie kept her eyes focused on the stairs. Marg was at a loss. It felt as though Alice was being rejected but Alice shook her head at Marg and mouthed, 'It's all right. Don't worry.'

Billy and Joey came hurtling down the stairs. Both ran towards Jackie, and she held out her arms to them.

They slowed when they reached her, and Billy gently put his arm around her and leant his head on her shoulder. Joey sat on the floor and put his head in her lap. Jackie stroked Joey's hair and held Billy's hand. 'Remember when me and Harry had a fun day on the prom before he left? Well, we talked about . . . well, Harry left a message for each one of you. He said to tell you that you've been the best of brothers. That if he didn't come home, I was to tell you that he loved you with all his heart. And . . . and he said, that in his memory, he wanted you to live the life that he can't. He knew he should have striven to reach his dreams, not continue to do as your da asked of each of you – to follow in his footsteps. Billy, Harry said that he's never known a better footballer than you, and that you should play for a team and get yourself noticed. He thinks you can be another Stanley Matthews.'

Billy managed a tearful grin. 'I'll do me best for him.'

'He said he'd always be on the stand cheering for you.'

Billy's little giggle was stopped by his sob. Jackie continued. 'He said to tell you, Billy, that he wants you to be brave, he knaws you'll miss him, but he wants you to look after Joey and Alice for him and . . . me an' all. You're to be strong like you allus were for him and all of them in the past.'

Billy straightened. To Marg, it was as if, though tall already, he grew another inch or so in front of their eyes. He leant forward and lifted Joey to a standing position then held him to him. 'I'm here for you, lad.'

Joey clung to him, before asking, 'And did Harry say anything to me, Jackie?'

'He did, lad, he said he was so proud of you, and that you shouldn't be like him and throw away your chances. He loved it at the rock factory, but he could have done better. He said, tell Joey how much I love him and want him to succeed. If he still wants to be a doctor when he's older, then tell him to become the best there is. But if he changes his mind, that's all right, only tell him to do sommat that he has to strive for, not give up on all his learning to do sommat mundane. He said he would be with you allus.'

Joey sobbed in Billy's arms. Jackie reached out to them both again, and when they joined her, she cried with them, and yet soothed them too. 'We'll get through this, lads. We'll never forget our lovely Harry, but we'll allus be proud of him, and we'll do as he asks. Eh?'

Marg thought her heart would break as the lads nodded and Billy seemed to become the strong one once more. He took hold of Joey. 'Do yer want to go to the park for a bit, Joey? I want us to be where Harry loved to be.'

'Aye. I'd like that, Billy. Do you think we could take some bread to feed the ducks? Harry loved to feed the ducks.'

'I'll get you some, you go and get ready,' Alice told them.

The lads then hugged her. When they came out of the hug, Marg felt compelled to hold them too. They came willingly to her. 'We're all here for you both, me lads.'

Edith joined in. As Billy clung to her he spotted Gerald looking on, and Marg saw his face crease up again as he went to him and asked, 'Would you come to the park with us, Gerald?'

To Marg, it seemed the big lad she'd looked on as a young man suddenly became a boy again – a boy needing a father figure, something he'd found in Gerald. Gerald hugged him. 'I'd love to, son. Out there amongst the trees and the greenery and the lake, I always find peace. Come on, let's get going, eh?'

Marg sighed as they went out of the door, Joey clutching half a loaf of bread. There were some things no one could mend. And this left her feeling despair. She should be able to make things right for Jackie, she always had done, but now she could do nothing.

She looked from Alice to Jackie. Two grieving women, with a void between them – their fear of the other's sorrow being too much to handle. 'Alice, love, Edith's got to get back to Betsy. Will you be all right, or do you want me and Jackie to stay?'

There was a silence, and then Jackie said, 'I need to be with Alice if she'll have me.'

Alice ran towards her. Their combined grief was terrible to witness, and yet Marg felt glad that they were no longer apart and were sharing their love and their loss.

It was a huge wrench to leave Jackie on Monday morning and it was with a heavy and fearful heart that Marg went in to the rock factory.

She wished she hadn't to go. Not only because Jackie

needed her, but because her loyal workers would all be asking if she'd heard from Clive, and she hadn't.

She'd tried not to worry too much about this as he'd told her that if he didn't phone, it would only be because he was at sea and to think on how no news was good news.

With everything that had happened she hadn't really thought of the length of time since his last call on Thursday evening, saying he and the lifeboat crew had brought in one lot of men and were going out on another trip the next day, so it would be Sunday at the earliest before he could ring her again. But now, she had a niggly worry over whether he was all right.

Her mind had tortured her as she'd tried to sleep, with images of all that had been described on the wireless of what was happening to the little boats carrying out valiant rescues – they reported rough seas, air attacks by the Germans. Capsized boats and ships sunk.

With these worries and holding a broken Jackie as they snuggled in the same bed, Marg was exhausted and fearful.

But she was to meet with a Mr Manning, a potential new client who she couldn't let down – a gentleman from London, a man who owned several large stores in and around Britain, who was interested in her latest project.

Her idea had been to make small rock sweets as she needed something with wider appeal. Most traditional rock only sold at seaside resorts, and they were receiving fewer and fewer visitors as beaches were laid with rolls of wire, lookout boxes, and other defences against possible invasion.

This effectively took away what most went to the coast for – to walk on the beach, let their kids build sandcastles, and to laze in deckchairs.

She'd discussed her project with Clive before he'd left and he'd been enthusiastic about it, telling her he knew for sure that the rock-rollers would be able to cope with cutting the rock, and to give them a day's practice and they would turn out perfectly formed and uniform sweets for her.

Marg had thrown herself into the scheme and had sourced large sweet jars to pack them in.

They'd been so well received when presented to retail outlets by Benjamin, her salesman – a portly man, with a lovely way about him.

When first meeting Benjamin, Marg thought that she would buy anything he tried to sell her and considered him an amazing find that Clive had made as he greatly increased their business, even at such hard times as these.

Marg had been afraid that she wouldn't be up to meeting Mr Manning and that he might look down on her but then had laughed as Benjamin had told her, 'He can't wait to meet you. I told him you were a real Lancashire lass, with enough grit to take over her husband's business while he went to war. And that what you didn't know about rock wasn't worth knowing, and that you were trying new ideas to keep the business going.'

None of this seemed to Marg to be enough to impress such a man, but Benjamin had gone on to say, 'Do you know what he said? He said he had to meet this wonderful lady for himself. That he truly admired innovation, and that you were a great example of what is needed during a war – a woman with true grit.'

She'd had to ask Edith what innovation meant, but it had all served to help her to face meeting the gentleman and she prayed that he would give them a big order. It wasn't the profit she had in mind, but the workers. Clive had said it was up to her to keep them in work so they could look after their families, and with a new deal, she could do that.

As she waited for Mr Manning to arrive, Marg sat in Clive's office. She still thought of it as his and hadn't changed a thing. A photo of their wedding day sat on his desk and as she looked at it the happiness of that day increased the heartache and worry that she felt. *Come back to me, me lovely Clive.*

A tap on the door had Marg swallowing hard. She glanced again into the mirror of her compact, which she'd taken from her handbag as soon as she'd arrived. To her, she looked puffy-eyed and a mess.

Snapping the compact shut, she called for them to come in.

Mr Manning was the spitting image of David Niven, the film star. Average height and with sleek black hair and a neat moustache, he was what she would term debonair and charming.

He wanted to see everything – how the factory worked – and to speak to the workers. 'I like to have knowledge of every product I sell, my dear, even down to whether the workers making the products I sell are happy or not.'

Marg liked him. His presence and his interest provided a distraction for her as she showed him how the sugar boilers mixed sugar and glucose and brought it up to three hundred degrees before lifting it out onto the flat surface for it to be rolled.

What most fascinated him was the skill of the sugar boilers, how they layered the colours and formed the letters. And the deft movements of the rock-rollers. She told him how they must keep the rock moving until it cools so as not to let it go flat on one side whilst bringing the next length down. 'Next, they will cut the roll to precise lengths. And the wrappers will swiftly wrap each stick and pack it into boxes.'

'It's all amazing, my dear. And the atmosphere is one of jolliness. I am very impressed. May I taste some?'

He made her giggle then as he tried to bite a piece off a stick. Forgetting herself, she said, 'No . . . Eeh, you'll break your teeth, lad. You have to smash a small piece off.' She picked up another unwrapped stick and showed him by smashing it onto the table. He jumped, which further made her giggle. To her relief, he joined her and laughed out loud. 'Well, I like what I see. So, let's see how it tastes. I've never had any of your famous Blackpool rock!'

Encouraged now to be herself, Marg said, 'By, you've not lived, man.'

'And never have I met a Blackpool lass before – I think that's what you're called, isn't it?'

'Aye. A Blackpudlian through and through.'

'I like you, Mrs Barnes. And I love this rock, makes me feel like a child again. I will place an order. I want all my stores to stock your sweets, but I don't see why they can't stock sticks of rock too.' He turned to Benjamin. 'Bring me a sample with the name of each town I have my stores in, and I will make my mind up from that. But, young man, you can get your order book out right now.'

All had gone quiet in the factory as Mr Manning had been chewing his piece of rock, but now, as one they cheered.

Mr Manning beamed. 'Thank you, all. You have your lovely boss and your own skills to thank for this order. Good day to you.'

They all clapped and waved.

'What a lovely bunch of staff you have. I've enjoyed my visit, thank you . . . Now then, Benjamin, where shall we go to place my order?'

As they went towards Clive's office, Marg went around thanking all the staff. Everyone expressed their wish that Clive would soon be home, plummeting her spirits once more as she told them about Harry.

'I ain't been able to tell you afore as I had to keep meself together for this visit, but you've noticed that Billy isn't in. Well, we have lost his lovely brother, Harry.'

There was a massive intake of breath. A woman's voice said, 'Naw, naw, not our young Harry?'

Marg felt her eyes fill with tears. 'I can't tell you details yet, but you will read about it in the *Gazette* tonight. And, well, me sister were Harry's fiancée, and she needs me, so I'll be going in about an hour.'

Fred, the chief rock-roller, said, 'Eeh, lass, you've had your troubles. We all thought after you met Clive that all would be right for you both. We're so sorry, ain't we, everyone?'

'We are, Fred. And you've done a marvellous job here, Marg. Ain't she?' This was from Amy Cooper, one of the packers.

Everyone agreed, nodding their heads and saying 'Aye'.

Marg smiled. She had to leave as one or two of the women had tears flowing down their cheeks and she knew she couldn't face that. 'Have an early and longer dinner break, everyone. Ted's coming in shortly to look after everything, I'll be taking a couple of days off . . . and, well, I ain't one for praying much, but since this war started, I seem to spend me life doing so, so if you are one who prays, then pray for Clive's safe return. Ta. Take care of yourselves.'

As she walked out there was a silence. She wanted everything to be different. She loved her job here – felt like she was somebody and that she had achieved something worthwhile at last. She wondered every day at Clive having the faith in her to do it and hoped that with this order, she had done him proud and justified his confidence in her. He'd changed her life in so many ways, she couldn't bear to lose him.

When she arrived home, she was given the devastating news that Clive was lost at sea.

TWENTY-SEVEN

Jackie

Three months had passed – months of terrible low times, when Jackie hadn't known what to do with herself or with, and for, Marg.

Edith and Alice had helped as always, as Ada and even Gran had. She'd had many lucid moments when she understood what had happened to her granddaughters and had asked them to sit with her. Always she wanted them on the mat at her feet and she stroked their hair as they rested their heads on her knee.

These moments Jackie had treasured as the ones that gave her the most comfort – though she still remembered the feeling of extreme relief when she woke two weeks after she'd had the terrible shock of Harry having gone and found she'd started her period. That had eased her mind in a huge way. For her fear had given her nightmares and forced her to think that if she was pregnant, letting everyone think that it was Harry's was her only choice, and that would have felt so disloyal to him, when he'd been nothing but a perfect gentleman – though she knew he'd so wanted to make love to her.

There'd been times during these last few weeks when she wished she'd made that happen.

For Marg, Jackie knew that life had been very difficult too, as she'd tried to keep the rock factory going and to care for George and Carl – George seemed lost, but Carl didn't really understand, and had asked a lot of questions. Now, as children do, he seemed to have accepted it.

But George hardly spoke. He spent long minutes in front of Marg and Clive's wedding photo that hung on the wall and gazing at the photo of Harriet, his own mum, which Marg had insisted stayed hung up over the fireplace. The one he loved the most was of Harriet holding him as a baby, and this he kept in his bedroom.

Clive's parents were inconsolable. His father wanted a memorial service, but Marg had refused. 'If we hold one of them, we're making me Clive dead, and he might not be. He were only lost at sea, his body has never been found.'

Jackie, Alice and Edith didn't know how to cope with this, but they didn't deny the possibility. They couldn't.

For Jackie, her heart was broken. She'd loved Harry from when they were little children, and Clive since meeting him. It seemed as if a huge chasm had sliced through the middle of her life, leaving her teetering with no direction. She just functioned, as she knew Marg did.

But now, she faced going back to Bletchley. Her fear of this made her shudder – how was she to cope with Captain Blake? She couldn't bear to think of it.

'Well, are you ready, lass?'

Jackie looked up from the task of packing her case. 'I don't want to go, Marg.'

'I know, lass, but ... well, you've no choice. You are a WRAC now and have been passed as fit for work ... Eeh, lass, come here. We ain't hugged a lot for fear of upsetting each other, but I need a hug to think about when you're gone ... though what the WRAC think is so blooming important about a flipping accounts office, I don't know. And why do you have to be joined up anyroad? You weren't before.'

Jackie forced a laugh as she went into Marg's arms. 'It's vital supplies, Marg, they have to be accounted for. And all work of this nature has now been taken into the responsibility of the forces. I like me uniform, and the work; I just don't like being away from home ... especially now.'

'I know, lass. But you'll telephone, won't you? Eeh, I'll miss you. I – I, well, I haven't been there for you, lass. I couldn't handle your grief and me own.'

'I knaw, it's been the same for me. Don't fret about it, Marg. We've done our best under terrible circumstances. And I've allus felt your love, wrapping me in comfort. We just daren't express it for fear of unleashing sommat we couldn't control.'

'When did you get to be so grown-up, eh? Eighteen already, but with a head of a thirty-something ... Eeh, lass, it ain't been an easy life, has it?'

'Naw. Will you be all right, Marg?'

'Aye. At least I have hope that me lovely Clive ain't dead.'

Jackie sighed inwardly. The word 'dead' hurt as it did apply without doubt to her darling Harry, and yet, she wondered which was worse, knowing and having to accept, or not knowing for sure, like Marg, and not being able to accept. Jackie feared Marg never would have peace as there was no possibility of Clive's body ever being found. And legally things were complicated, because without the proof of death – having a body – everything had to wait for seven years before it could be settled. That left Marg in limbo, though she was well paid as a director of the business so wasn't struggling for money.

To her own mind, Clive had drowned and was now, sadly, in a watery grave. The thought hurt so much. She loved Clive like a brother. A wonderful, kind, gentle brother, and she didn't want to accept that she would never see him again.

Coming out of the hug, Jackie said, 'I'll just pop and say me ta-ra's to Edith, Betsy, Minnie and the twins, and Philip an' all, if he's there. Edith's expecting him home, ain't she?'

'Aye, but he did warn that at any time he could be sent away again. Poor Edith, she lives on tenterhooks.'

'I knaw, Alice does as well, as she says there's talk of her being sent to London on ambulance duty.'

'London! I didn't know!'

'Aye, she told Edith and Edith told me ... I'm sorry, Marg, I shouldn't have said. She'll want to tell you herself.'

'No, it's me own fault. I haven't wanted to be included, though both Alice and Edith have done their best. I'll change that, love. I'll be more open to them both. I – I shut them out, but I couldn't help it.'

'I'm glad, Marg. Eeh, love, I'll feel better going away knowing you'll lean on them again.'

Marg smiled but didn't say any more on this. Instead she asked, 'Why London?'

'By, Marg, I know you've shut yourself off, but don't you knaw that London is likely to be bombed?'

'I did, lass, of course I did, but I didn't think me Alice would have to go.'

'She's Red Cross and ATS, she's bound to go somewhere. She was given extended leave after France and ... well, it was bereavement as well, but that's over now. Gerald's time in the military hospital in Liverpool is likely to end as he thinks he may have to go abroad again – Africa. Eeh, Marg, I wish it would all end.'

'I know ... Well, go and see Edith and then hurry back to say your goodbyes here. The time's getting on and I need to get you to the station, or you'll miss your train.'

'By, you sound as though you can't wait to get rid of me!'

'Ha! I do, don't I, when nothing can be further from the truth. Eeh, me lovely Jackie.'

Marg said this on a sob that almost undid Jackie. She hugged her again but didn't hang around. Kissing her cheek, she told Marg, 'I'll see you in a mo.'

'All right, love, tell Edith to come round later for an hour, that's unless Philip does come home. She won't want to then.'

As she walked three doors away to where Edith lived, the enormity of going back to Bletchley hit Jackie. Her fear tightened her throat.

Edith took her into a hug. Then said something that surprised Jackie. 'Look, love, don't you worry, nothing's going to happen to you, I promise.'

Jackie didn't know what to say, Edith sounded so sure – had she told Philip? *Oh God, what could that mean if she has? But, no, she wouldn't have.*

As if trying to change what she'd said, Edith said, 'I – I mean, well, if anything does happen, get on the phone to me.'

Jackie nodded, afraid to pursue this any further. What if Philip did know and he said something . . . ? She daren't even think of the consequences, as someone like Blake never gave up. He'd proved that, hadn't he?'

'So, you're off, then? Eeh, you look lovely in your uniform. What does Marg say about it all?'

'She ain't mentioned me uniform – well, only to say she don't knaw why I should have to be a WRAC – but she did say that she'd like you to go around for an hour, so that's sommat.'

'Aw, that'd be grand, as me Philip ain't coming home. He ain't sure when he will be back.'

'Naw. Eeh, Edith, I'm sorry.'

'Don't be sad, lass. I've lived with this day coming for all this while. Philip's always warned me. And I know he's been preparing for something, though I don't know what . . . Mind, that's easier for me. If I thought he was going to the front line . . . Eeh, I'm the one to be sorry now, lass.'

Jackie felt the tears prickling her eyes. Their world and that of everyone was falling apart. 'Well, I'd better say goodbye to Minnie, and the twins. Where are they?'

'They're in the garden. Minnie's at sixes and sevens with fear for her daughter and her East End . . . Mind, I don't know which one she loves the most, but I think she does fear for her daughter.'

'Bless her.'

As they went outside, Mandy and Alf came running to her. 'You look the bee's knees, Jackie.'

'Well, ta for that, Mandy. I've come to say goodbye, but I'll be home in a couple of months when I could get some leave.'

'D'yer think that'll be in time for Christmas, girl? It ain't going to be much, I shouldn't think, but would be good if everyone was 'ere.'

'I ain't thought about it yet, it's only September, Minnie! Mind, we did have a September Christmas last year, the daft ha'peths that we are.'

Minnie laughed. 'I 'eard about that. A good idea, I think. Gawd knows when we'll get a decent Christmas again.'

'Can Santa still come when there's a war on, Aunty? Didn't you say as he was Greek? Aren't they in the war?'

'We'll talk about it later, Alf. Say your goodbyes to Jackie now, she's a train to catch.'

It was more moving than Jackie had thought to be hugged goodbye. She hadn't thought anything could touch her emotions after they had been torn to shreds, but she loved these young 'uns. 'Be good, now, eh? I'll try to bring you sommat when I'm next home, but only if you're good and help your granny and aunty.'

'I'm always good, it's 'im, but you know what boys are like!'

Jackie burst out laughing. 'Aye, I do. I didn't have brothers, but I've had experience of lads in Whittaker Avenue.'

She ruffled Alf's hair. 'And you, try not to annoy Mandy, lad.'

Alf grinned. 'That's asking the impossible.'

They all laughed now, even Mandy, and Jackie felt her own mood lighten.

'So, just me lovely little Betsy now.' She walked over to the pram. 'Ta-ra, little one. By, I bet you'll be twice as big when I next see you. You're getting bigger every day . . . and you're beautiful.'

A lump came into her throat. Edith seemed to know as she shooed the twins away.

Minnie stood from where she sat on a low garden wall, 'Well, luv, yer make sure yer careful. I'm proud of yer and yer look a smasher in yer uniform. Go and do whatever yer do and that Hitler won't stand a chance. Not now the women are getting into the forces, he won't.'

When Jackie left having been hugged till she couldn't breathe by Edith, she felt stronger and knew she could do this. She'd handle Blake somehow.

Saying goodbye to Gran was the worst thing she had to do. Gran looked at her with unknowing eyes, but then said, 'Eeh, you look like me Vera.' She'd never said that to her, only to Marg. 'Are you . . . me Jackie? Where you going, dressed like that, lass?'

'To do me bit for the war, Gran. I'll be home soon. It ain't dangerous work, just bookkeeping as always, but for more important things than biscuits.'

'There's nowt more important than biscuits, lass – them and rock keep this town going when there's naw visitors.'

'That's true, Gran. Anyroad, give me a hug, love.'

The hug gave Jackie the knowledge of how thin Gran was. She'd always been what she termed wiry but never so much as now.

When she arrived in Bletchley after a tearful goodbye on the station to Marg, and a tiring journey, Prissy met her with a hug. This surprised her as they hadn't had much time to get to know one another.

'Oh, it's good to have you back. They wanted to billet another girl with me, but I refused. I like sharing with you, and I knew you would be back. How's your leg? Oh, poor you. We couldn't believe what happened.'

'Well, it's left me with a slight limp, but that's getting better, but eeh, I'm back, so they must still think me useful.'

'Of course you are! You're the cleverest amongst us and if you'd had the chances we've had, goodness knows where you would be now – probably running the country!'

Jackie giggled. 'At eighteen years old!'

'Well, not that, yet! Haha, but one day. Our first woman prime minister.' Prissy sighed. 'Not that that will ever happen.'

'Naw. Women are just lackeys, until the men need us, like here. It feels good in a way as at least here we are given a bit of a better standing – they can't do without our brains, lass, that's what it is.'

'That's true. Mind, there's been changes here. Captain Blake has been transferred. None of us know where to, or why, but he was gone about a month after you had to go home.'

Jackie's mind shot to what Edith had said. *Eeh, Edith, did you tell Philip about me and Blake? Has this all been arranged by him?* Fear gripped her. If it was and Blake put two and two together, he'd one day get his revenge.

'Oh, that's upset you, sorry. I know change is difficult and you knew Captain Blake from your home town – you worked for him, didn't you?'

'Aye, but how did you know?'

'Daddy know's everything. He told me ... well, don't take this the wrong way, but he said you weren't our usual recruit, and asked me would I take you under my wing as it will all be strange to you, and you won't know anyone. Then he added, except Blake, of course, as he recruited her, she used to work with him in his accountants' office in Blackpool ... But that isn't why I'm friends with you – well, initially it was. But then I found I like you very much, Jackie. You're honest and open and have no side to you that tries to be what you're not ... Oh, I'm digging a hole for myself here. Tell me you're not cross with me.'

'Ha, I'm not, you daft ha'peth. I'm just glad to have you as not many have accepted me – and I like you an' all. I've missed you.'

'Thank you. It's good to have you back ... Only, there's something else that I know ... Oh dear. These things are supposed to be unmentionable, but I can't not mention it as I want to tell you how sorry I am about your fiancé.'

Jackie froze for a moment. She hadn't thought anyone would know about Harry here and had thought that best as she could just get on with things without everyone feeling sorry for her.

'No one else knows – Daddy again. He told me that your fiancé was a very brave young man. He said he would like to meet you to tell you about him.'

Jackie sat on the end of her bed. She couldn't take this in. No one had told her anything. Did Alice know more about what happened to Harry? Surely she would have told her?

'I'm sorry if I upset you, Jackie.'

'Naw, it's all right. It's still raw – me feelings. Me Harry were me life. Aye, I knaw we were young, but we'd known each other all our lives and . . . anyroad, why didn't your da tell Harry's sister about his bravery?'

'He will. But he wants to meet you. I've been home on a weekend's leave and Daddy told me you were coming back. It was then he said that a lot had come to light about how your fiancé died, and he told me to tell you that he will be contacting your sister, but that the story of how you educated yourself and have risen has really touched him. He found it tragic that this should happen to you.'

'How could he know all of that?'

'Daddy has his sources. They all do – the men in charge, and Daddy is one of those. Something or other in the War Office. He doesn't tell me what, but most of his colleagues went to the same university as him and most went to Sandhurst. They are an old boys' clique. But having said that, they don't do things for power. They all genuinely love their country and their king and want only the best – even for the poorest. Though they don't help directly, they see themselves as helping the poor by making the country a better place for them to live – more opportunities for

324

them to help themselves – and that is why he so admires you.'

Jackie didn't know what to say. She could only think that all this was instigated by Philip, though he couldn't be one of these 'old boys' as he wouldn't be old enough to have gone to university with Prissy's father ... But if Blake was ... God, if he was one of these 'old boys', then he would know that she had broken the Official Secrets Act by talking to somebody about him.

Her mind raced. What would happen if these men Prissy was talking about deduced that! But then, it was a deduction that got her into this mess. Not her having spoken out. All she'd said was that she wasn't doing what they all thought. Edith had made the deduction – maybe Philip was able to put this over?

With this thought, she began to relax a little. As surely, if they thought she'd done wrong, then she wouldn't be back here ... *But what of Blake? He won't let this lie. Oh God ...*

'Jackie. Oh, Jackie, I'm sorry. I – I shouldn't have hit you with all of this. Forgive me.'

'It's all right, Prissy, it just came as a shock, that's all. I thought I'd be able to come back here and get on with things – somewhere where naw one knew so they wouldn't treat me differently.'

'No one does know, I promise. But Daddy wanted you to have someone you could talk to and find comfort with. I want to do that for you, Jackie.'

Jackie felt the tears prickle her eyes. She hadn't really let Prissy in. She'd had this feeling that she wasn't good enough to be a friend of someone of Prissy's standing. And yet here she was offering her friendship and comfort. Shame washed over Jackie. She was the one who'd been prejudiced, not Prissy. Prissy was just a lovely accepting young woman who genuinely wanted to be friends.

'I'm sorry for how I've been, Prissy. I – I didn't think meself good enough for you. That must have come across like I were unfriendly. I didn't mean to.'

'Ah, poor you. I understand. A lot here are snobbish and do look down on those less fortunate, but I don't. My mama and Daddy have always brought me and my brother up to care for those who are poorer than us. And to not look on them as lesser beings, but the same as us, but who haven't been dealt such a good hand of cards. I would love you to meet my family. And Daddy really wants to meet you, and your fiancé's sister and her husband . . . He knows Gerald, as I do . . . we . . . I had an older brother. He was at school with Gerald. He was killed in a horse-riding accident.'

'Eeh, I'm sorry, lass. That's so sad.'

Suddenly, it all clicked into place. If Gerald went to school with Prissy's brother, then Philip did too! So, that was the connection.

'Thanks, it still does hurt very much, though it happened a long time ago. Francis was an amazing brother and person . . . Anyway, as I was saying, Daddy will see Gerald and his wife separately. If he has you all together, that may give away what you do. They will deduce it is something important. So, he is going to see them on official business to tell them about Harry, rather than as guests, which is what you will be. Our guest . . . Is it all right to call your fiancé Harry? I mean, I know I didn't know him, or of him, but it sounds so uppity to keep saying "your fiancé".'

'Aye, it is. Harry would have liked you, Prissy, as I do, and though I ain't used to your way of life, I'd like to come with you to your home, ta.'

'Thank you, Jackie, you saying you like me is a great compliment. I think we will use this as a fresh start and be the friends I'd like us to be.'

Jackie shyly held out her hand to Prissy. 'We will be. I shouldn't have been how I was, but I was wary.'

Prissy took her hand and smiled. 'I understand.' She patted Jackie's hand, then released it. 'It's so good that you have agreed to come home with me. Daddy will arrange leave for us next weekend. Ooh, I'm so pleased. And you'll love my twin brother. He . . . well, he has some deformities – only slight. A clubbed foot. But he is adorable and has a brilliant mind. He's studying to become a scientist. Daddy wants him to finish university, which he does in spring, and then to do war work that involves his mental ability.'

'Eeh, we'll be a pair together then, as I'm left with a limp.'

'Ha! You will and thank you for taking it like that. Bernard is often shunned.'

'Aw, why? A gammy leg don't change a person.'

'No, but, well, in our world, perfect seems to be the only acceptable. But Daddy has always taught us differently. He says it is who we are that matters, not what has afflicted us, whether that be a deformity or poverty, people are what matter.'

'I like your da. He sounds a nice bloke.'

'He'll love that you call him my "da" as that's another thing, Daddy isn't a snob ... Oh, look at the time. I'd better go. I'm rehearsing for the musical the dramatic society are putting on – I told you before, you should join, or at least join one of the activities. Give people a chance to get to know you. I know they will like you when they do. I never asked you before, but can you sing?'

'Aye, I can hold a note, as they say.'

'Well then, join us – come to next rehearsal, there's always so much to do. You can help in some way. Then you might even get a part in the next production ... Oh, do say you will.'

'Aye, I will.'

As Prissy went out waving happily, Jackie relaxed. Things were going to be different, and she was ready to take on this new life. She hadn't been before. She realised now that she'd been part of the problem herself. Well, she could change.

TWENTY-EIGHT

Alice

If Alice had thought that France was hell on earth, she now knew that it wasn't.

What was happening all around her here in London was far worse for this was mass murder of civilians – ordinary folk going about their lives.

Women, children, the elderly and infirm, none were spared. And the destruction. The burning and crumbling buildings. And the screeching of the bombs as they made their way to earth, and then the boom of them hitting a target . . . all of it made her want to cry out for it to stop. But she carried out her duty. She lugged stretchers over rubble and dead bodies. She administered to the wounded and comforted the dying and relatives. She held little children close to her, hoping her love would help them.

But it all seemed so futile as night after night, more whining, droning planes appeared in the moonlit sky and more bombs fell.

Tonight was one of the worst. The Isle of Dogs dockland was ablaze, the warehouses crumbling to the ground. The fires lit up the night sky. In their quest to help the wounded, they made many trips back and forth over the blue bridge.

As the Home Guard and fire officers cleared the rubble of houses nearby, bodies by the dozen were being pulled out, but some they could help. Alice was tending to a woman who was too badly injured to help, but she didn't abandon her.

'You're all right, lass. I've got you.'

'Help me ... me son ... he ...'

'Is he still inside, love?'

'Help him ...'

The woman's eyes closed, never to open again. She was only Alice's age. Her clothes showed her poverty. Alice called out, 'There's a boy in there! Please get him out – someone, get the kid out!'

'We're doing our best, miss. The heat's 'olding us back. Joe, get the hose on this house 'ere, will yer. There's a kid trapped!'

Alice's tears blurred her vision as she looked at the woman. 'We'll get him out, love. You rest in peace.' She smoothed the hair from the woman's face and bent down and kissed her forehead. 'Rest in peace, lass.'

'We've got him. He's hurt badly, he was trapped under a beam.'

Alice rose and ran towards the voice. 'Bring him here. Over here!'

The heat felt like a furnace and scorched her hair and her face.

'Get back! It's coming down, get back!'

Alice couldn't move – fear held her as if in an iron grip. Burning debris fell around her. A hand grabbed her arm and dragged her away. After the crashing had stopped, she stood and stared at the dead fireman with a piece of jagged beam sticking out of his chest. Next to him lay the child.

Dust stung Alice's eyes and clogged her nose, but she didn't care. Propelled forward, she knelt beside the boy and looked down into the blackened face of what looked like an angel. His blond curly hair spread out as if forming a halo. Taking him gently into her arms, she stood. The child moaned. 'It's all right, little lad, I've got you.'

As she picked her way through the rubble as fast as she could, hardly seeing through her smarting eyes, Reg, her partner, came to help her. He held her arm and guided her. 'Is he . . . ?'

'No, but – but I don't know if we can save him. The fireman said he were trapped under a beam, but I don't know if it crushed him or not. Eeh, Reg, there's so many bodies – too many dead for us to ferry.'

'Any more injured? I've three on board at the mo, but room for three more if you hold the boy on your lap, mate.'

'I didn't see any life.'

'All right. Get yerself into the ambulance, luv. I'll go and check.'

Inside the vehicle, the sound of cries and moans filled the space around Alice. She lay the boy on the bottom bunk. The bunk beds were three high and those on the right-hand side were all full, but before Alice could assess any of their injuries, Reg called out for the stretcher.

Grabbing the rolled canvas, Alice ran out to him. 'What have you got, Reg?'

'Another kid, a girl, hurry, Alice.'

The going wasn't easy over bricks, rubble and beams that still smouldered and burnt her legs, but she got to Reg as quickly as she could. 'I reckon this is the only one, mate. There's nothing but devastation and the fire's too intense.' Alice looked up to see those fighting the fire were losing the battle.

She lay the stretcher out and Reg placed a little girl on it. Her naked body, badly burnt, looked almost raw.

'Poor little mite, I think her clothes burnt off her back.'

Alice's heart bled at the sight of the child. Her hair was singed almost to its roots. Despair filled Alice. She knew the child couldn't survive.

Helping her all she could, Alice turned her attention to one of the women whose blood was dripping to the floor of the ambulance. Her pallid skin tone and laboured breathing gave Alice the fear of losing her. Ripping the clothes from her, Alice flinched at the sight of the jagged, open wound in her thigh. Blood spurted from it. *A main artery! God, how did I miss seeing that?*

'All right, me lass. Hold on. I'll just try to stem this bleeding and you'll feel a lot better.'

The woman caught hold of her arm. 'Me mum ... and me kids ...'

'Are they still in the building, lass?' Despair entered Alice.

'I want me kids ...'

'Don't try to talk, love. Everything's being done that can be. They'll find them.'

'Tell them ... Tell them I love them and ...'

'You're going to get better, lass, and then you can tell them yourself, eh?'

Alice worked quickly making a tourniquet and applying pressure on the wound, but she knew she was losing the battle. 'What's your name, love?' The woman tried to speak but couldn't. Alice felt despair rise in her as she realised that she couldn't save her.

The woman's eyes closed, and her last sigh of breath released peacefully.

As Alice wiped her tears away, she hoped that she found her mum and her kids, because if they were in the building, then it was sure now that they too were gone. *Please God, let it be that all are reunited in death.*

By the time they reached the hospital, the little girl and one of the other two adults had died from their injuries. But one, though she was in agony, Alice was sure would make it. How she would recover from her grief as she cried out for her six children who she was saying didn't get out of the tenement block, Alice didn't know. All she could do was to hold her hand and try to give her comfort.

'Don't give up hope, lass. Kids are resilient. They may yet find them. We've seen some miracles, especially involving children. Four were found three days after a building was declared unsafe with no sign of life. They just emerged having cleared the rubble that trapped them, so you never know, love.'

The woman was inconsolable, but then Alice knew the heartbreak of losing one child and couldn't imagine multiplying that by six.

The little boy was still alive, but very weak. Alice carried him through into the hospital. The team of doctors and nurses awaiting the latest intake looked worn out as, like her, they'd been on duty for six hours and in that time had dealt with trauma after trauma.

She handed her two patients over to Paul, telling him of the woman's plight.

The youngest of the doctors, Paul, looked despairingly at her. He nodded towards the child in her arms. 'Put the little boy over in cubicle four, Alice. It's been chaos. The injuries are horrendous. Our theatres are full, we've got no beds available. You'll have to stop bringing us any more for a while.'

Alice sighed. 'Have you any that we can take to the evacuation train?'

Paul told her to talk to the admissions and discharge sister.

For the rest of the night, she and Reg transported thirty patients to the waiting ambulance train in Bethnal that would take them to outlying hospitals.

By morning, Alice didn't know how to put one foot in front of the other. Her weary legs would hardly carry her up the stairs to her room. She'd only just washed and got into her nightdress when Mrs Hardman, the landlady of the boarding house in Bethnal where Alice was billeted, knocked on her door. ''Ere yer go, luv. I've brought yer a pot of tea and some toast . . . What a night, eh? Old Cecil's son copped it. 'E's a firefighter, d'yer know him?'

'No, but I'm sorry to hear that.'

Alice hadn't a clue who Cecil was either, but she didn't say as she just wanted to get her head down, but the thought did occur as to whether the firefighter she'd seen killed was his son.

The tea was delicious and more welcome than Alice had thought, and having had a few sips, she tackled the toast, realising that she hadn't eaten since four o'clock yesterday afternoon.

The images of what she'd witnessed haunted her as she tried to get to sleep. But the one most in her mind was of the little boy. *Please God, let him live.*

A banging on the door woke her long before she was ready to be woken. 'Yer've a visitor, luv – 'e says he's yer 'ubby.'

Alice shot up. *Gerald! Eeh, me Gerald!*

'Send him up, please, Mrs Hardman.'

'I don't allow gentlemen in the rooms, Alice. Get yerself dressed and greet 'im downstairs.'

'What? But he's me husband!'

'So 'e says. Sorry, luv, but it's me 'ouse policy.'

It took only minutes for Alice to swill her face in the now cold water in the china bowl on the washstand and to dress. She hadn't many clothes with her as she spent most of her time in uniform or nightclothes, but she quickly donned a pink twinset and wriggled into a straight, calf-length, grey skirt, brushed her teeth and then her hair and applied a dab of lipstick on each cheek, smoothing it out with her fingertip – it doubled as rouge and gave her a glow. Applying the lipstick to its proper place, she rolled her lips to distribute it evenly and then wet her long eyelashes.

Running down the stairs, she jumped the last one and landed in Gerald's arms. 'Eeh, me love, me love, where did you come from? And how? I thought you were in Liverpool ... You're not ... ? You're going away! Eeh, no, Gerald, tell me you've not been posted!'

'Slow down. No, I haven't. I've been moved to St Albans, to help with evacuated wounded from the central London hospitals. I'll only be just under an hour away, darling. I start there tomorrow. I arrived yesterday and have settled into a room in a house near to the hospital with other doctors and male medical staff.'

'Eeh, me Gerald, that's grand ... So, you ain't going to Africa after all?'

'No, I was told that the need here was greater and seeing what I have seen on my journey here, I can believe it. It's terrible ... Oh, my darling, how have you coped? Are you safe? What's it like?'

'It's a living hell. Eeh, Gerald, it's carnage. I feel sick to the stomach. Some awful things are happening ... children ... And ...'

Gerald held her, resting his head on hers. After a moment, he said, 'Shall we go for a walk? I passed a café that had a notice in the window. It said, "*Open*", then beneath that it read, "*No bloody Hitler's stopping me kettle boiling or me bread from toasting — breakfast special: no egg, no bacon, no sausage, no butter on yer toast and all for just one penny!*"'

They both laughed and Alice felt the stress of her job leaving her. 'That's the East Enders for you. Full of back-bone and spirit. They'll never be broken, never.'

'I've heard about them and how bravely they're coping, and I'm glad to be given the chance to help them — those that are sent to me, that is.'

'Well, sadly, there'll be plenty, love. Me and me partner, Reg, spent the last half of the night ferrying the wounded that could travel from the hospital to the train to evacuate them.'

As they walked down the street holding hands, Gerald told her about being contacted by the War Office. 'We are to meet with General Grayson, darling. He wants to give us some news on Harry. When are you off duty?'

'Harry? What news? What news can there be?'

'I don't know. I do know General Grayson, though. His son attended Arnold School with me and Philip. Sadly, he was thrown from a horse and was killed.'

'Eeh, no.'

'It was a long time ago. Anyway, the only message I got was that we were to be told something important that might help us to cope with losing Harry.'

They'd reached the café and went inside. The woman behind the counter looked up from the newspaper spread out in front of her. 'Mornin', or is it afternoon?' The smoke from the cigarette she held between her lips caused her to squint. Her hair was caught up in a scarf which she'd tied at the front. 'What can I get yer, luv?'

Gerald ordered for them, 'We'll have your breakfast special, please.'

'Yer a bit posh for around 'ere. Where yer come from and why ain't yer fighting this bleedin' war like the rest of them, eh?'

The woman's aggressive attitude frightened Alice. She gripped Gerald's hand.

'Madam, we are medics and not long back from the front line in France. My wife has been driving an ambulance all night through the Blitz, and I am a doctor attached to a receiving hospital in St Albans. I think that makes us worthy of your respect!'

'All right, keep yer 'at on. Yer never know these days with conchies about. Bleedin' cowards.'

Gerald went to protest, but Alice shook his hand and indicated with her head that they sit down. 'Eeh, love, you can't fight every war. There's a lot who are bitter about them who choose not to fight. We can't change that.'

'You're right, darling, but it incenses me.'

Alice thought to change the subject. 'Anyroad, I won't want much toast, I've not long had some, so I hope you're hungry as you'll have to eat most of mine an' all.'

When they were served, they sorted out when they thought they could make an appointment to see the general. Alice knew she had a free day on the following Monday, and Gerald said he would try to get that day too.

As she watched him tuck into his toast, spread with dripping, which he said was delicious, Alice couldn't believe this was really happening – her Gerald . . . her Gerald was sitting opposite her! She could feel happiness seeping in and taking away the desolation, because when with him, all was well in her world.

When Monday dawned, Alice set out for Westminster. Her curiosity gave her a million questions, but the love in her heart won over all other emotions as she travelled towards being with Gerald once more.

She hadn't to be back on duty until Tuesday night, so hoped that this was the same for Gerald, but communication was difficult between them as her boarding house didn't have a telephone, and she relied on him ringing when she was at the station. So far, she'd only been able to speak to him once in the last four days.

Her heart flipped over when she caught sight of him waiting on the station, his fair hair flopping over his forehead – a little bit of defiance from having to have the back and sides cut short. And he looked so handsome in his officer's uniform. A relief to see after their encounter with the café proprietor.

She, too, had chosen to wear her uniform and had been given some wonderful praise from her fellow passengers. This was shown for them both when they hugged as a cheer went up and calls of 'Bravo!' rang out.

'Well, that's a bit of a better reception than we had in that café, darling.'

His kiss seemed to put everything right for her once more, as the days since she'd last seen him had been full of trauma, horrendous sights and, the worst thing of all, hearing the little boy she'd taken to the hospital had died. She'd comforted herself with imagining him in the arms of his mother.

As they came out of the kiss, Gerald asked, 'Are you all right, darling? You're not worried about today, are you?'

'No, I'm fine. Aw, Gerald, what can it be that he wants to tell us?'

'We'll soon know, but darling, I have a surprise for you. I've booked us into the Park Hotel for the night.'

His look sent a thrill zinging through Alice and despite their mission, her face broke into a happy grin.

'I can't wait to snuggle up to you, my darling.' His voice lowered. 'Not that you'll get much sleep.'

Alice found it hard to breathe. Her heart was in a turmoil of longing. She clung to Gerald's arm, trying to calm herself, but lost the battle. She just couldn't wait for night-time.

General Grayson was a man in his early fifties, balding, upright and with a kindly face. He greeted Gerald like an old friend. 'Good to see you, Gerald. The last time was under very sad circumstances, and this one is only made less sad by what I have to tell you.'

'Good to see you, too, sir. This is my wife, Alice.'

'Ah, yes, one of our heroines of the Blitz. Pleased to meet you, my dear. Shall we sit down?' He indicated two chairs facing his own, which was behind a huge oak desk.

The office was manly and military. It smelt of polish and of the leather that covered both his chair and the two they were directed to sit on. Dark green, they blended in with three oak-panelled walls, and the one book-lined one.

'Now, first of all, my condolences on the loss of your brother. A hero, but a sad loss. I know that you tended to your brother, Alice, dear, and that he died in your arms. That must have been very traumatic, but you have shown true grit and carried on serving your country. Thank you. Now, what you don't know is what a courageous young soldier your brother was. And that he is to be awarded a medal posthumously – the George Cross, the highest honour of all.'

Alice gasped. But had no time to comment as the general continued: 'The reason for this is that three soldiers were holed up. Their mission had been to take out a German gunner who was killing our men at random as they tried to push forward. Each time a line put their head over the bunker, they were shot. Your brother managed to get over the top of the bunker. He ran whilst shooting for all he was worth. He made it to the men and urged them to run back to the bunker while he covered them. One of them was shot, and the others have told us they were afraid to go, but also wanted to stay to help Harry. But Harry made them go. They said that he told them, "It's your duty to get back, then you can cover me from there." As they went, your brother was seen from the bunker to stand up and throw a hand grenade. The men made it back, the gunner was blown to pieces. But sadly, another shot rang out and took Harry down. But because of his actions the division was able to move forward and eventually were victorious . . . At first it was thought to mention him in despatches, but then it was calculated that because of the advance and what intelligence was discovered, a massive raid on Dieppe was foiled. The plan had been to flatten both hospitals as well as the town and take the port. The failure of that mission we owe to one Private Harry Brett's actions.'

Alice knew that tears were falling down her cheeks.

The general stood. She and Gerald stood. The general saluted and clicked his heels. 'I salute Private Brett.'

Both Alice and Gerald saluted.

After a moment's silence, the general said, 'I'm sorry I conjured up painful memories for you, but I hope that I also gave you a pride to take forward and to help you with your grief.'

'You have, sir. Eeh, I'm bursting with pride in me brother.'

'That's good. It has been nice meeting you, Alice, and seeing you again, Gerald. We will have to catch up when all of this is over. Maybe at the ceremony for distribution of the medals as this cannot happen soon due to the circumstances that prevail, but I will give you plenty of notice and will call on you, Alice, to accept the medal on your brother's behalf.'

Alice knew that Gerald was choked up as he tried to keep his voice straight in his reply of, 'Thank you, sir. Hearing this today means a lot to us both and will to his brothers and his fiancé and all those who loved Harry. We look forward to seeing you again, and maybe then I can tell you some memories that I have of your son. Some will make you laugh. As Francis was hilarious at times and kept all the boys' spirits up.'

The general patted Gerald's back. 'Thank you, I would like that. If it is possible to be grateful for anything in having lost him, it is that I am not now facing having him out there fighting in this war. He is at peace.'

As they lay together that night, Alice curled her legs around her man. She was full of pride, in Harry and in Gerald, and not least in her own achievements too. But most of all she was full of love and now was the time to express that love. She allowed herself to be gently rolled onto her back and she accepted her Gerald entering her as she cried out her pain, but most of all her joy and her love.

TWENTY-NINE

Edith

Edith sipped her tea. The house was quiet. The sun had barely made it through the clouds as she was enjoying a moment's respite before the usual pandemonium of the morning began.

But this peace didn't last long as the shrill bell of the telephone ringing shattered it.

Lifting the receiver, a distraught almost incomprehensible voice came to her. 'It's Peggy . . . Oh God!'

'Peggy, Peggy, what is it, love . . . ? Is it Ben? What's happened?'

'The street . . . gone! Minnie's . . . Oh, Edith, Minnie's 'ouse took a direct hit . . . her daughter . . . she's dead! Two kids next door . . . gone! Their mum had them back now she's lost them forever . . . There's fire's burning . . . Me other neighbour's dead! Me 'ouse is gone!'

'Eeh, no, Peggy. No!'

Shock held Edith rigid as Peggy's terrible sobs came down the phone. With tears running down her face, Edith could barely ask, 'Ben . . . is Ben?'

'He's safe and . . . doing well. The 'ospital was hit, but no one was hurt. It was the outer buildings that copped it.'

'Oh, thank God! But what are you going to do? If you've nowhere to go, you can come here, Ben can be transferred.'

'Ta, luv, but I'll go to me mum's. She's on Sheppey and ain't 'aving it as bad as us, and I can still get to see Ben.'

'Oh, Peggy, lass, I'm so sorry. Is there anything you need? Look, give me your mum's address. I'll send you anything . . . anything.'

'I've no clothes or anything, Edith . . . I – I'm staying on the floor of the parish hall till they can organise parish relief money, then I can go to me mum.'

Peggy's almost hollow sobs cut through Edith. Her heart wept for this poor woman and for all the folk in London.

'We'll get a parcel to you, lass. I promise. Alice is down in London. We'll get it to her, and she'll get it to you . . . Eeh, Peggy, how am I going to tell Mandy and Alf and Minnie? Eeh, poor Minnie.'

'Give 'em me love, girl. Tell 'em to keep up the East End spirit.'

After saying her goodbyes, Edith sat down at the table. Her body quivered with the shock of what she'd just received. Once again, she asked herself, *How can I tell Minnie and the twins this dreadful news?*

Before she had time to think the telephone rang again. Alice's excited voice came to her. 'Edith, it's me! Eeh, Edith, I've just spent the night with me Gerald!'

Edith couldn't answer. She had the feeling of being disorientated – catapulted from extreme sadness to joy with nothing in between.

Alice didn't seem to notice as she went on to tell her how this had come about. To Edith it all jumbled up – Gerald near to Alice – Harry, a hero, but then sobs. 'Eeh, Edith, it's bad here, lass . . . death, destruction, grief, terrible injuries . . . and the noise, the awful noise.' Alice was sobbing now. 'And . . . kids . . . so many kids.'

Her sobs died. 'Edith? Edith, lass, are you all right?'

Dabbing her eyes, Edith told Alice what had happened, keeping her voice as low as she could. 'They . . . they've lost their mum . . . everything . . . and Peggy . . . destitute.'

When they came to a calm place, Alice promised to go to see Peggy today. 'I'll take her some stuff, and give her some money, don't worry, lass. And let me know when that parcel's on its way. Put it on a train for me, tell me which one and I'll go along and collect it and make sure that it gets to Peggy . . . And Edith, lass, I'm so sorry. Me heart goes out to Minnie, Alf and Mandy. Tell them me and Gerald love them.'

They said their goodbyes, exchanging love and hopes of seeing each other soon, then the phone went dead.

Picking up her mug, Edith took a sip, not caring that it was cold. As she drank, she decided she would have to tell Minnie first, but she dreaded doing so.

Her mind went to Philip. How she missed him, but even more so when difficult times like these were on her. *Eeh, me Philip. If only I knew where you were or could speak to you – just once!*

The sound of someone moving about upstairs helped Edith to get control of her emotions. Drying her eyes, she took a deep breath and went to the sink. Running the cold water, she swilled her face.

When the door opened and Mandy walked through, Edith's heart sank. But she opened her arms to a smiling Mandy who was making a dash for her. Cuddling her close, she wished with all her heart that she didn't have to shatter the little mite's happiness.

'You didn't wake me, Aunty. I was going to 'elp yer with Betsy. 'As she slept all night?'

'She has, love. That's the second time now. By, it's been good to get a good night's sleep.'

'Is something wrong, Aunty? You look sort of sad and puffy-faced.'

Edith changed the subject. 'Eeh, look at the time. Where's your granny, eh? She's a sleepy head.'

'And Alf, but then, 'e's always liked 'is bed. 'E takes after our mum. She can sleep the clock round! Mind, she needs her sleep.'

Edith caught her breath. If you spoke to Mandy directly about her mother, she'd show no love for her, just deride her way of life and call her a prossie, but in moments like this you could hear the love she had for her, and Edith knew that the news she had to give would tear the child's little heart to shreds.

'I'll go up and see your granny for a mo. Will you watch over Betsy for me, love?'

'Yes, but don't wake Granny if she's asleep, she's getting on in years, you know.'

At any other time, Edith would have laughed at Mandy showing the old head she had on her shoulders, but now, she could only find release in crying. Standing against the wall of the hall, she took a moment to compose herself, before, with legs feeling like lead, she went up the stairs.

'No! No, not me Nancy. I want to see her, I want to see me Nancy.'

Edith held Minnie close.

'Minnie, lass, I know how you must feel, but eeh, I don't think it a good idea to go. The twins are going to need you, love. And it's so dangerous down in London. Peggy said it's carnage. Please, Minnie.'

Minnie's sob as she gave in, in gesture if not in words, undid Edith. She lay her head on Minnie's and cried with her.

After a few minutes she dried her eyes. 'Me Nancy weren't a good girl, but she weren't a bad 'un either. She did what she did to feed us all ... Could she still go to heaven?'

'Aye, I'm sure she will. How about we go to see Father Malley, eh? You get on well with him and he's the best one to help you – us all. He'll maybe arrange a mass for her – that'd be a comfort, wouldn't it?'

'Some. Yes, we'll do that ... Will yer get me little kids in to me now, Edith?'

'Aye, do you want me to stay?'

'Yes. I'll need yer. I couldn't 'andle it on me own.'

Mandy took the news in a way true to her nature. 'Why weren't she out doing her stuff? She's always out at night bringing shame on us.' She folded her arms as if to ward off any pain.

347

Alf just sat in the circle of Minnie's arms. 'Does dead mean we never see Mum again?'

Minnie brushed his hair off his face with her hand. 'Not never, luv. When we go to heaven, we'll meet up again.'

To this, Mandy seemed angrier than ever. 'Prossies don't go to heaven.'

Edith longed to go to her but knew Mandy wasn't ready. 'Everyone who says they are sorry goes to heaven, Mandy, lass, and I'm sure your ma was sorry. And God forgives, so, if He can, then we should forgive each other.'

Mandy's frown didn't ease.

'And Mum did love us, Mandy.'

Edith held her breath, thinking that Mandy would now vent her anger on Alf. But the opposite happened. Mandy ran to Minnie, shouting, 'I want me mum! Take me to me mum, Granny. I . . . I want to tell 'er I love 'er . . . I never told 'er . . . I always said I hated 'er.' She buried her head in Minnie's lap.

Edith felt at a loss, but Alf surprised her then. He put his arm over Mandy and said, 'Don't worry, Mand.' A name he called her when she was hurt. 'Mum used to tell me that it didn't 'urt her when yer said yer hated her, 'cause she knew yer didn't mean it. She said yer loved her really, but was just mad at 'er for 'ow she made a living. She said she had to do it or we'd starve.'

Mandy looked up. She stared at Alf then turned to Minnie. 'But yer were always telling 'er we didn't need the money, Granny.'

Minnie sighed. 'I would rather we starved, that's why, girl, but at the end of the day, though I didn't condone it, we did need the money.'

'But why didn't Mum work in the biscuit factory, or the jam-making factory like the other women?'

Minnie didn't answer. But as Mandy kept asking, 'Why, why?' she seemed to make her mind up to say whatever it was she found difficult to say.

'She tried, but she was sacked from both for 'aving a go at one of the other workers. She had good reason too. They called her a slag for 'aving kids when she weren't married, but she weren't a slag. She couldn't help what 'appened to her to make her 'ave yer, but she wouldn't give yer away, she loved yer. Anyway, there was nothing else for women around us then, and we were rejected by the parish relief because they said me Nancy could work as she 'ad me to look after you nippers. It was then that she met this bloke and 'e set her off on the wrong path. I know I played up with her, but truth is that we would 'ave starved but for what she did. She did it for you two and me.'

'But yer brought money in with the things yer made, Granny.'

'I did, luv, but there was the rent and the electric to pay, clothes for you both as you kept outgrowing what yer had. I couldn't cope, even though I used to tell her I could.'

'I – I want to tell 'er I don't care what she did, Granny, I want to!'

Edith stepped forward as Mandy was getting hysterical. 'She knows, Mandy. She knows everything now. That's how it happens when we die, we understand all the things we didn't afore. Now all your mum wants is for you to put her to rest and to be happy, but never to forget her.'

''Ow can I put 'er to rest, Aunty, 'ow?'

Edith told her then about the mass she and her granny were thinking of. 'And we can make a special place in the garden for her. You and Alf can make it. Maybe the corner by the tree. You can put anything you like there that reminds you of your mum. And we can light a candle and stick it in the ground at night and all pray together for her and send messages up to her, until we are sure her soul is resting, then we'll just keep it as a nice place in memory of her.'

Minnie chimed in then with, 'I can get that picture that I have of 'er framed and it can be in 'ere, so that when we go to bed, we can all say goodnight to 'er.'

Mandy stood and turned into the cuddle that Edith was offering. 'Granny's hurting an' all, Mandy, lass. She don't need you to be cross with her.'

Becoming the loveable little girl that she really was, Mandy dropped the facade of being tough and went back to her granny. 'Me and Alf will 'elp yer, Granny, won't we, Alf?'

As Alf nodded a tear fell onto the bed. Edith wanted to make everything right for them, but she knew she couldn't.

Slipping out of the door, she went downstairs. Her heart was breaking at the sound of all three of them sobbing, but she knew there was no healing grief, it had to be worked through. Some chose to cry it out; others, like herself, fought it and put a brave face on. Who was to say which was the right way? She was just glad that they were grieving together and not miles apart as she'd thought Mandy's initial reaction would cause.

*   *   *

350

Marg came to the mass, and Ada brought Gran. Billy and Joey were there too, and Sue and Tom, Averill and Rod and Heather.

Both Billy and Joey were wonderful with the twins. And Heather helped Minnie as the two of them were good friends.

As Edith looked along the pews, she thought of how it had been so different back in Whittaker Avenue. But though they all had real family around them then, and the majority here weren't truly that, it felt as though they were. Like real family, they'd all given up what they were meant to be doing this Sunday to be a support, and Edith loved them all the more for it.

Father Malley was amazing. He was like a friend to his flock and Mandy, Alf and Minnie had been part of what he called 'his own' since they'd arrived to live with Edith. And even though Marg, Ada and Gran didn't come to mass often, he still looked on them as his parishioners and visited Gran from time to time. Sue and Tom and Averill and Rod were regular churchgoers and had always made large donations to the church, but that didn't make them any different in the lovely Father Malley's eyes.

After the service they held a wake at Edith's as Mandy had said that no matter what they had or hadn't got in the East End, they always gave everyone a good send-off.

Edith never failed to find her amusing. She was a tonic without knowing it.

Thank goodness it was a dry day and not too chilly as this meant anyone could wander into the garden if they wanted to.

At last, she was sitting on the bench under the tree with Marg. They held hands.

'Eeh, Edith, lass.' Marg shook her head from side to side.

'I know, love. It ain't a good time for us all, is it?'

'Will it ever be again?'

'Aye, it will, Marg. Anyroad, any day I have with you is a good 'un.'

'Do you look back on the fun we had, Edith?'

'I do, love. We made the best of things and helped each other through the bad times and that's what we can still do.'

'Aw, lass. I know as I've not been the same with you. I just can't function properly. It's work and home worries that occupy me most of the time.'

'I understand, but we should always make time for friendships an' all, lass.'

Marg turned to her. 'You're right. It ain't just for the big events we need each other, is it?'

'No, love. I need you and Alice in me life every day. I can't have Alice, but you, Marg . . . we should get back to how we were.'

Sue came over at that moment. 'Now then, you two. I know you've had your troubles, but I haven't yet seen you in my knitting group or helping to take food round to those who need it. There's one or two in your old street that you told me about, Edith, that now have regular parcels from us.'

'I'm sorry, Sue, I know I promised, but you know how things are for us.'

'To me, they look pretty good. Nearly every woman in this town is missing her man. Many know for sure he isn't

352

coming back. You two need to share what you have with them.'

This shocked Edith, and at the heart of her, she knew Sue was right, though she wanted to tell her to go away and leave them alone.

'Maybe it would do us good, Edith. But I don't reckon we could go to give handouts in Whittaker Avenue. I think they'd look on us as shoving our good fortune down their throats. But I did promise to do some knitting. I can do that, Sue.'

'Good. We're knitting for the East End folk now. None of our lads are fighting in cold countries so don't need socks and things. Though we do raise money for the Red Cross who send them parcels. It's the poor folk of the East End that are suffering, though. We send canned food, knitted garments and biscuits, of course. Some of your rock wouldn't go amiss, Marg.'

'How do you get it to them, Sue?'

'We beg, borrow or steal the biscuit factory van and one of our ladies takes it to the Red Cross depot and they make sure it's shipped to London for us.'

'Eeh, it sounds good. I'll make sure you get some rock when you next take a load. And though I can't attend any knitting circle, I'll knit whatever you ask of me.'

'And I will help distribute food parcels to our poor of Blackpool. I'm not so handy at knitting, though I can do a bit, but I can give canned food as well as take parcels out.' She told Sue about the parcel she was going to do for Peggy and how she was going to get it to her.

'That's so nice, and thank you, Edith. Philip will be very proud of you. Now, don't let me down again, either of you!'

As if she realised how she'd spoken to them, she suddenly bent forward and kissed each of them. 'I know you've had it tough, and I'm only trying to help you both as much as anything.'

Edith laughed. 'I thought the old Sue had returned then!'

'No, she's gone for good. Though she does occasionally pop up and even surprises me.'

They all laughed then. But Edith stopped suddenly as she remembered the children. She needn't have worried. As she glanced around looking for them, she heard Mandy's laughter, and then Alf's. Relaxing, she thought that wakes served two purposes: they helped you to grieve, and they gave you comfort. She was glad Mandy and Alf were getting that from it.

As Sue walked away, Edith looked up at the sky. *I'll always look after your children for you, Nancy. Even if they go back to London when the war is over, they'll always have a home with me.*

And she fancied that though they'd never met, she and Nancy would have been friends.

THIRTY

Jackie

Prissy's house looked magnificent as they came to the end of a long drive lined with trees coated in frost.

Simon was driving. Jackie loved him and it was clear to her that Prissy was *in* love with him. He was tall, blond and good-looking, which even his longish nose and deep-set eyes didn't deter from as these features sat well in his oval-shaped face. But it was his sense of fun and kind ways that endeared him to everyone. Especially to Jackie, as she often worked with him. He had a brilliant mind and complimented her on having the same attribute as together they solved clues to decode much that others had failed to do, and all done in a light-hearted, jovial atmosphere.

On the other hand, if he saw that she was a bit down, he didn't avoid the issues that were making her feel that way, but was more likely to say, 'Tell me some more about Harry. The more I hear, the more I like the chap. He and I would have got on well. I can be deep-thinking at times.'

Being this free to talk, to relate stories – many that ended up with them laughing – had been a salve to Jackie. It had helped her to remember, rather than to suppress, and to live with, rather than try to forget. And yes, helped her to accept, as all she told was in the past. There was no future to dream of – only to regret.

When the car stopped from a greater speed than it should have done, the wheels skidded in the gravel and all three giggled.

'Stop it! Look how cross Bramble looks!'

Coming towards them was a portly man – obviously the butler, dressed in black and white as if he was going to a wedding and with an expression of resigned indignation on his face, which had them laughing even more.

To Jackie, it was still a revelation that only a few months after Harry's death she could enjoy life's lighter moments, and this told her that some healing was taking place.

When they stepped inside the house, the stunning beauty of the cream and duck-egg blue hall mesmerised her. Her shoes squeaked on the highly polished wooden floor, but after a few steps she was walking on a blue and cream runner that matched the carpet that covered the stairs of the sweeping staircase.

'Come on, I'll show you to our room. I expect you're dying for the bathroom like me. Once we're sorted, you must then meet Mama and Bernard . . . Bramble, have our bags taken up for us, will you? Thanks, you're a darling.'

A sigh came from Bramble. But he quickly covered up with a fond smile. 'Of course, Miss Priscilla, and may I say, it is very nice to have you home.'

'Thanks, Bramble. I've missed you. Is Mrs Bramble well?'

'She is, and she has been busy baking your favourite cakes. She's hoping to serve them to you at tea. Will you and your guests take tea in the garden room?'

'That would be lovely.'

Every room proved to be as beautiful as the hall and each was decorated and furnished in soft colours – pale greens, silver-greys and delicate lemon. None were stuffy and old-fashioned. To Jackie's remark on this Prissy said, 'Oh, that's Mama's influence. She's an artist and paints the world in these colours on her canvasses – the paintings you see on the walls are all hers. She holds wonderful exhibitions and is quite famous.'

Rosalind, as Prissy's mama was introduced, reminded Jackie so much of Averill. She was dressed in the same kind of flowing frock that Averill would wear. And, like Averill, her movements when she walked gave the impression that she was almost floating. She wore her long dark hair loose and it hung in ringlets to her waist. She looked years younger than her forty-something age.

'How lovely to meet you, dear. And how beautiful you are. I must base an image in my next painting on you. You have the look of a ballet dancer! You should let your hair grow long – it would form ringlets like mine – and your freckles are divine.'

Jackie felt herself blushing, but managed to smile, and to say her thanks.

'Where's Bernard, Mama? I cannot wait for him to meet Jackie. I just know they will get on.'

357

'Simon collared him. They went off talking about boring things like the theory of something or other. They said they would wait in the garden room for you, but darling, do you mind terribly if I don't join you? I need to rest before dinner, and before your daddy arrives home – he always wants to talk so much, when I would prefer to make love.'

If Jackie blushed at the compliments, it was nothing to how she did now and she was glad that Rosalind turned away and went towards the stairs.

Prissy burst out laughing. 'Don't mind Mama, she spent much of her young life in Paris and thinks like the Parisians now. We all adore her and find her open way much easier than the stuffiness of our friends' parents. We can talk to her about anything.'

With this, Jackie relaxed. 'She would get on so well with my friend's mother-in-law; she's artistic and a flowy kind of person, and yet she's an eminent surgeon.'

'Ha, "flowy", but I know exactly what you mean. You never know, their paths may have crossed – same school or something. Most of Mama's "set" are like her. Anyway, let's go and have tea, I so want you to meet Bernard.'

The garden room was a conservatory on the side of the house. It reminded Jackie of Averill again, and so of Alice and Gerald, as it was like the one in their home which Averill had decorated. These memories gave her a pang of homesickness and now she was wishing she could have gone home rather than come here, but Prissy's father particularly wanted her to come so he could tell her whatever it was he knew about Harry – a meeting she was dreading.

As soon as she met Bernard's eyes, Jackie felt her heart flutter, but then knew an immediate remorse and feeling of disloyalty to her adored Harry.

The feeling made her nervous. She could only stammer her 'hello'. But then caught a sort of knowing smile that passed between Prissy and Simon and quickly covered up by saying, 'Eeh, it's nice to meet you. Prissy's allus telling me stuff about you.'

Bernard stood and came towards her. Her heart went out to him as his gait was very much a pronounced hobble. She put out her hand. He didn't speak for a second or two but seemed to look into her soul with his very dark eyes. He was the image of his mother – even to having dark curly hair. She smiled to lighten the moment as he took her hand.

'This is very formal for someone I have been dying to meet. I thought you would at least bend forward and give me a peck on the cheek!'

His grin told her he was only joking with her, but she called his bluff and did just that. Never had she known herself to be so forward with a stranger.

Everyone giggling at her made the moment seem normal, but Jackie didn't feel normal at all. She felt as though she'd met someone very important to her, but she didn't want to feel like that.

Once they were all seated and chatting, the feeling passed, and she brushed it off as the whole experience being a salve to her hurt as it was all so new to her. To her surprise, she was really loving it and felt at home and accepted.

The cake was delicious. Jackie had never seen a cake like it before – square and in blocks of pink and yellow wrapped in marzipan, it tasted delicious. When she remarked on it, Prissy told her, 'It's my favourite, I love it. It's called Battenberg. Cook said that it was first baked in the eighteen hundreds, to celebrate Prince Louis of Battenberg marrying Princess Victoria, Queen Victoria's granddaughter, but I don't know if that is true or how Cook knows that. She and Bramble, her husband, seem to know so many little snippets of things. But then, they did work in a much larger establishment than this humble abode, but they had to leave when they wanted to marry. We were jolly lucky to find them just as our own cook and butler were retiring.'

'It seems to be the thing to do, as Robson, our old butler, married Pringle, our old cook, once they retired.'

'That's right, Bernard, they did, and Mama was most cross that they had waited that long, thinking they would lose their jobs if they did it sooner. So now, she tells any new staff that if they fall in love with one another, she is perfectly happy if they wed. We've had a couple of lovely weddings since then on the lawn, and all of the couples are still working for us.'

Not understanding the ins and outs of household staff, Jackie just remarked how nice that was.

They'd finished their cake and were just chatting about this and that. The whole time Jackie felt Bernard's eyes on her. It was a relief when Prissy suggested a walk in the garden, until Bernard said, 'Not for me, sorry. My old leg is playing me up and my foot feels as heavy as lead. I'll sit here till you come back.'

'I'll stay with you, if you like,' Prissy offered.

'No, Prissy, thanks, but well, I – I mean, well, Jackie will stay, won't you, Jackie?'

Prissy gave one of her smiles that Jackie had seen before. It held a sort of plea, and she realised that Prissy really wanted to be in the garden with Simon on her own.

'Aye, I'd love to.' She turned to Bernard. 'Prissy tells me you're studying science. It's sommat as always fascinated me . . . not that I knaw much, just what me and Harry read in books and what me tutor told me about the stars and the outer hemisphere.'

'Well, astrology does come into the class of science, but for me, I like the science of discovery . . .'

Jackie sat engrossed in what Bernard went on to tell her about scientific discoveries and what the scientists today were working on.

Before she knew it, Prissy was back and saying, 'Come on, old thing, we need to change for dinner. Daddy should arrive any minute and as soon as he has washed, brushed up and downed his first whisky he needs to see you in his study.'

As they went upstairs Jackie said, 'Eeh, I'm not looking forward to what your da may tell me, Prissy.'

'Don't be worried at all, darling, Daddy said it is something to help you, not to upset you. Would you like me to come in with you? Daddy did say I could if you thought it would help you.'

'Aye, I'd like that . . . And, Prissy, what do you mean, dress for dinner? I ain't got much else to put on. I've only clean essentials and me uniform for tomorrow when we return to base.'

'Oh, don't worry about that. I knew that and I had a frock put out for you and all the accessories. I cannot wait to see you in it. Come on, we haven't loads of time.'

The frock was beautiful – Jackie thought it more of a gown really. The only thing she'd ever worn that was a little like it was her bridesmaid's frocks.

Plum-coloured, the satin the frock was made of had a lovely shine to it. And, although plain, the line of it – fitting under her bust and then falling out into a sweep of material – really suited her and enhanced her slender figure. She was surprised how it made her bust look a lot bigger than she thought, but she liked it so much.

'Here, these gloves will look perfect with it. They fit to your elbows and have a triangular piece that goes along the back of your hand with a loop on it to put your middle finger through. You have such pretty, dainty hands, Jackie . . . Oh, you still wear your ring!'

'Aye, I don't want to take it off.'

Prissy patted her hand but didn't say anything else except to stand back and gasp, 'You look divine, darling. Now for me. I want to look extra special tonight.'

She picked up the red satin frock that had been laid out for her. It was very similar in style to the one Jackie wore, only the skirt was more fitted to the body. Jackie helped her into it. When she pulled out the band holding her ponytail and let her long glossy hair tumble down her back, Jackie told her, 'You look a picture, Prissy, beautiful. Simon'll be knocked off his pins at the sight of you.'

'Oh dear, I've made it that obvious, have I?'

'Not obvious, naw, but I guessed. And I reckon he feels the same an' all.'

'Do you? He never shows it. I gave him every hint when we went for our walk, but nothing!'

'Give him time. You knaw we all have a lot on our minds, and with a war on, it don't seem the right time to start up relationships.'

Prissy sighed. 'This is the very time to me. We're safe where we are ... Oh, I know there are rules and things, but just to know someone returns your love is enough. Besides, we're away from there now.'

Jackie didn't know what to say; she didn't even want to think about it. She wanted to enjoy feeling how she did.

Prissy's father was very kind to her but hearing how Harry died upset her more than she thought it would. Thanking him, she excused herself. Once outside of the office, she glanced towards the door. 'How long is it till dinner, Prissy?'

'Oh, we've an hour yet. We usually all congregate and have a pre-dinner drink, then the conversation starts to flow and keeps us going for the evening – though Mama does entertain us by playing the piano and singing, if she's up to it.'

'Will it look rude if I miss that? I'd like to go out in the garden on me own for a bit.'

'Well ... it might help you to relax a little ... but, well, okay, I'll get Bramble to fetch your coat. Are you sure you want to be alone?'

'Aye, I do.'

When she reached the clump of trees at the bottom of the garden, Jackie leant against the trunk of a large oak. The tears were already streaming down her face. 'Eeh, Harry, lad, I'm proud of you, I am, but why did you take such a risk?'

Her tears were uncontrollable now. Her sobs were loud, her body shook, but with her grief gave a kind of release – an almost cleansing of her pain. Now she understood, and after the initial shock and anger, felt relief at knowing and allowed the true pride she felt of Harry take root.

Gradually, she calmed. When her sobs had ceased, she wiped her face. Life seemed to stretch out in front of her – endless years without Harry. How could she bear it?

Taking deep breaths, Jackie stood up and tried to prepare herself for going back to the house, when a voice said, 'Want some company?'

'Bernard . . . you made me jump . . . Eeh, how long have you been there?'

'I didn't want you to be alone, but I won't intrude if—'

'Naw, I'm glad you came, ta. It'll be easier walking back to the house with you by me side. I'm all right now, it was all a bit much. Do you knaw the story?'

'I do. What an amazing young man Harry was. And very lucky to have you to love him.'

'Ta. We grew up together, we were everything to each other.'

'Oh? I didn't know that. I did wonder about why you were engaged so young, but then, war has made everyone make their decisions early. Shall we get back?'

As she walked beside Bernard, she felt the pity of him having to have two crutches and wished she could help him. As if reading her thoughts, he said, 'I can manage on one crutch, you know, if someone holds my hand to steady me.'

'Aw, I'll do that for you.'

Throwing one crutch down, he put out his hand. Taking it, Jackie felt the most comfort she'd felt from anyone. He smiled at her. He really did have a lovely face.

'Right, let's see how good a crutch you prove to be.'

She giggled. 'I haven't had much practice.'

'Something tells me you won't need it. Just holding my hand makes me feel safe.'

This warmed Jackie's heart, for she felt that she'd like to do that for Bernard. She'd hate him to ever feel afraid. She smiled back. 'By, you're keeping me from that drink, and I've never had a sherry in me life!'

'Well, you'd better only have a tiny sip, then have Cook's lovely lemonade. We don't want you drunk.'

A picture of Edith's late ma came to her – swaying and swearing and kicking up her legs. She shuddered. 'Eeh, I think I'll change me mind and stick to the lemonade.'

'Very wise.'

As they walked back to the house, Jackie somehow felt lighter, as if a huge weight had been taken off her shoulders. She liked Bernard, she liked him very much.

THIRTY-ONE

Marg

Marg tried to make herself think of Christmas. It was just five weeks away and she hadn't even made the pudding, or the cake. She had the ingredients in stock from last year – dried fruit and nuts didn't deteriorate. Flour had been hard to come by but between them, she and Edith had scraped enough together, and she'd stashed away some sugar in a sealed tin, making herself drink her tea without it. But it was hard to even begin to motivate herself for what looked like being a Christmas of tears.

Two things had cheered her. Jackie had phoned and told her she'd been given a few days off to come home and Alice had arrived home out of the blue yesterday. Sadly, her partner had been killed when a building collapsed, and she'd been given two months off to recuperate.

She and Edith would be around in about an hour as the three of them were to make the cake and mix the Christmas pudding together. She knew they were trying to make it easier for her and that Alice would need this evening too.

She'd said in her letters that she and Gerald had been able to meet up regularly but now she didn't know when she could see him.

Marg sighed. She knew that feeling a million times over as for her it also held an 'if' as well as a 'when'. Not that she ever let the 'if' intrude. To her, her Clive would be found one day. And she'd believe that until someone showed her his body. She shuddered as she looked at the clock for the umpteenth time. Its ticking filled what felt like an empty space as the boys were spending the night with their Granny Barnes. She couldn't wait for her lovely friends to arrive – Alice was in for the hug of her life!

This thought made her smile as she went in to Gran to have a few minutes with her. Gran had her eyes closed and Ada motioned with her finger over her lips that Marg wasn't to disturb her. But as Marg went to leave, a feeling of disappointment took her as she'd miss out on what she did every evening – her time with her lovely gran before she went to bed.

Today Gran had been lively, and they'd spent most of the afternoon together. Marg had wrapped her up well to take her for a walk, but Gran had surprised her and asked to be taken to Whittaker Avenue. So, she'd put her in the car as that was a bit too far to walk.

When they'd arrived, Gran had told her, 'That's where I used to live with me Vera and me lovely Marg and Jackie.' She'd sighed. 'Happy days – well, they were when that rotter Eric left us alone. What happened to him?'

'He's in prison, where he belongs.'

'Good. He fathered our Vera's young un's, you knaw. Right under the nose of her husband, his brother.'

These were painful memories for Marg. Finding this out a few years back had hurt her badly. She didn't want to be reminded of it all, or of Eric Porter – to her, he'd never be her da. She hated him for all he'd done.

'Do you remember who lived next door, Gran?'

'Aye, Ethel. She was an old sourpuss, but nice really. You had to get to knaw her.'

This was a memory that had made Marg smile as she thought of the times Ethel had threatened her, Edith and Alice with the piddle pot contents all over them if they didn't shut their racket. Evenings of sitting on the step of the house they were gazing at, drinking cocoa with Alice and Edith and having a giggle had come to her, and she'd sighed.

'And that house is Ada's. She's a good 'un, but a mean old cuss. She took the last pennies from folk's purse before she'd treat them. I'd like to see her now, but I bet she ain't in and if she is, she'll be counting her money.'

It seemed Gran had forgotten for the moment that Ada now cared full-time for her and had given up her house and lived with them.

'And opposite me house, Betty used to live. She liked the drink, did Betty, but she were the nicest woman you could meet. Not good at dominoes or cards, though – I used to beat her hands down.' Gran gave a cackle of a laugh, but then became serious and shook her head. 'Killed by her own son, she were, and her hubby was an' all. He were a lovely bloke. Then the son took his own life and good riddance. I don't knaw what happened to Edith, the daughter, though.'

Marg hadn't tried to tell her that she still knew Edith.

'And Ida lived there. She were a good 'un, but one for herself and if owt weren't to her liking, she could be nasty.'

On cue, Ida had opened her door. She'd come over to them looking inquisitively through the car windows. 'Marg, lass, I thought that was you … and Sandra! Eeh, it's good to see you lasses. Have you time for a brew?'

'Hello, Ida. No, ta, I can't get Gran in and out of the car easily, but lovely to see you.' Marg had thought that Ida must have forgotten the time that she'd gone for her over her nasty remarks to Edith.

Gran just waved.

Ida pulled her cardi around her. 'Well, I can't stand out here, it's freezing, but nice to see you. Come around again in the summer, eh? We'll all sit outside and have a chinwag.' With this she'd scurried back inside.

Marg had been glad that she hadn't mentioned Clive. She couldn't have taken the condolences that surely would have come.

Gran had brought her attention away from Ida then. 'That house down there, that were where a lovely girl called Alice lived. Poor soul …'

This had gone on, rekindling memories for Marg. Bringing her back to her happier days. Yes, they were hard, and she wouldn't want to go through some of the things that had happened again, but they had all been a community and that's something she missed.

★   ★   ★

She'd just got to the bedroom door when Gran's voice, full of joy, called out, 'Marg, me Marg, where've you been? I've been looking for you for a long time. Late home from school again! I don't knaw what you get up to, lass. Come here and give your gran a cuddle.'

Marg wanted to laugh out loud. Gran seeing her as a young girl was a lovely compliment these days. 'I've been held back again, Gran, you know how feisty I am.'

She ignored the loud tut from Ada.

'Eeh, me Marg, I knaw, but though you should try not to lose your temper, I've a mind that that and your courage and strength will stand you in good stead in the future. Look how you're devoted to our Jackie. Is she in bed?'

'Aye, love, she's doing all right an' all.'

After kissing her gran and leaving the room, Marg paused. Jackie was doing all right and she was proud of her. This wasn't the future she'd planned for her, with all the sacrifices to get her educated, but she was doing her bit and her knowledge was the reason she was somewhere safe, so that was a good result.

With this settling her mind a little, Marg went through to the sitting room. She opened her work basket and lifted her knitting out. Heavy, as it was a thick, Aran pullover intended for one of the firefighters in London, she looked at what she'd achieved. This was the back. The front and sleeves were done, so when this was finished, Martha, her cleaner, would sew all the sections of it together. She sighed as she thought of Martha's bruised arms. One day she'd swing for that hubby of hers.

Her mind turned to the terrible news of London endur-
ing night after night of air raids.

It warmed her heart to think of how Edith had taught
Mandy to knit, even though she wasn't good at it herself.
Mandy was making some really nice squares, as Minnie
was, and then they were enjoying stitching them together
to make blankets. This, she knew, was helping Mandy to
cope with the loss of her mum, but Alf, bless him, was
having a hard time of it and Edith often found him sitting
somewhere in a dark corner crying for his mum. Always he
asked her not to tell his granny or Mandy as he didn't want
to upset them. It was hard to find a more kind-hearted
little lad than he was.

As her needles clicked away, she thought of how well
Billy and Joey had coped in the loving environment
provided by Averill, Rod and Heather, but she bet they
were well pleased to have Alice back.

They'd visited her last week. Billy was full of the football team he'd got together and how Joey was his star
player. He'd called the team Harry's Lads. They'd told
her that they were both so proud of Harry on hearing
about his medal from Alice, but then Joey had cried in
her arms and Billy had gone outside for a while. She'd
allowed their grief and had just been there for them. The
moment passed, and they'd soon been back on top form,
with Billy talking about his Annie, the girl he was in
love with.

Marg smiled. The pair had been friends from when he
worked at Blackpool Football Club and Annie had helped
Billy with various tasks.

'So, you ain't in love with Edith anymore, then, lad?' she'd teased him. He'd blushed but giggled and then ended up in a friendly tussle on the rug with Joey as Joey had laughed out loud at him.

Eeh, I love them lads like they were me brothers. A tear seeped out of Marg's eye. *You would have been me brother for real, Harry, lad. One day you would have married me Jackie. By, lad, that were a sad day when you were taken. Why did you have to be there, eh? Just like me lovely Clive . . .*

Her name being called took her out of this thought. *They're here!*

Before she could pack her knitting away and get up, the door was opened and there they stood, Edith and Alice, both grinning like Cheshire cats.

Marg ran towards them. The hug they hadn't had for a long time – a three-way hug – happened then amidst laughter, tears and the sheer joy of being together.

The laughter seemed to Marg to hold something more than the happiness of being together. Alice's words confirmed this. 'Sit down, Marg, I've got news.'

'Eeh, lass, what is it? Please let it be good.'

'It's the best in the world, but I ain't telling you till you're sat on the settee between me and Edith, lass.'

Marg didn't know what to expect. Her mind wouldn't give her anything that would make them this happy. They each took her hand. It was then that she knew it was to do with her. She held her breath.

'Clive's alive, Marg. He's alive!'

Marg didn't know how it happened, but she was standing, and screams were coming from her – screams of relief and of sheer ecstasy. They turned to a laugh, and then to tears. 'Me Clive, me Clive ... Where is he? Is he hurt? ... Eeh, me lovely Clive.'

'Sit down again, love, and I'll tell you what I know.'

'Clive's in Gerald's hospital and Gerald is looking after him. He has been with a French family, and they looked after him and then got him home to England. And coincidence of coincidence, he landed in Gerald's care!'

'Down in London?'

'Aye.'

'Take me to him, Alice. Take me right now!'

'Marg, lass, I can't. You're going to have to be patient. There's more to tell you.'

'What? He's all right, ain't he? Tell me that me Clive's going to be all right?'

Marg felt torn between the happiness she felt and the worry seeping into her.

'He is.'

She listened as Alice told her of Clive's injuries and how he was nursed to health by the French woman, but then she felt a wave of shock zing through her as Alice said, 'He also suffered loss of memory, Marg ...'

'No! No, no, no!'

'Marg, it isn't that bad. He knows who he is, now. He didn't but when he saw Gerald and Gerald said his name, it seemed to trigger something and now, after being told about his life, he knows who you are and his lads.'

Marg couldn't take this in. Had all they were to each other been wiped from Clive's memory? Would they never be the same again?

373

Marg, listen, lass, there is every hope of everything returning to normal. Rod and Averill said to tell you that they knew what brain injury Clive has most likely sustained and they said that if triggers can bring back this much of his memory, then gradually everything will come back to him. The only long-term effect will be that his ability to retain any new things he learns in his life will be impaired. But that may well heal with time. He wants to see you, Marg. But there will be no need to go to London. Clive will be brought home by ambulance in a few days. Gerald just needs to be sure all his injuries are healing. He told me that the French woman did a marvellous job.'

'Eeh, Alice, me Clive is coming home.'

'He is, me lass, he is.'

Marg wanted to go out into the street and holler it out loud and would have done if this had been Whittaker Avenue. But suddenly, life seemed worth living and she wanted more than anything to prepare for Christmas. 'Come on, me lasses, we've work to do. Let's make Christmas a good one, even though we'll still be sad as we won't all be together, but those who can be here deserve that of us, don't they?'

It was Edith who answered. 'They do, love. I shall have half of me missing, but I won't spoil it. I want to give Mandy and Alf a good time, bless them, and it'll be me Betsy's first Christmas an' all. And Minnie needs this – the first Christmas without her daughter – to be a good one.'

'Aye, we can't put everything right. I wish we could, but we'll do our best. Now, whose house shall we have this Christmas at, eh? 'Cause we've all got houses that'll take everyone this year ... Eeh, who'd have thought, eh? We've turned into the Two Bob Girls.'

They all laughed, and Marg thought the name they'd always given to those posh bods who'd had everything they wanted all their lives wasn't really fitting for them – they would always be the Halfpenny Girls and she liked it that way.

A week later, Marg stood outside looking up and down the street. The lads were with their Granny Barnes, whose health had so improved since hearing the news. The plan was that Marg would greet Clive and make sure he wasn't overwhelmed, then ring them and they would all come to see him. Then tomorrow, if Clive felt up to it, the others would come to see him.

Her heart beat wildly in her chest as she peered this way and that. And then she saw it – a shining white ambulance with blackened side windows – and without meaning to, she did a little hopping dance as love flooded through her.

When it came to a halt she stared at the darkened windows.

'We've a cargo for you, lass. One of our own back from the dead and eeh, it's grand to be part of transporting him home. We met the London lot along the A5 and were glad to do so.'

When he opened the back doors, Marg ran around to the back of vehicle. 'Clive! Me Clive!'

And there he was – a little thinner, and with his usual ruddy complexion looking pale, but his smile was like a thousand dreams had come true as it lit her world.

When he stepped down the last step, she could see he had a limp, but mostly she saw the tears in his eyes making his love for her glisten in his wonderful smile.

Then she was in his arms and her world became whole again.

The sound of people clapping filtered through to her as she snuggled into him. He took her hand and they both looked around. All the neighbours were out, and all were cheering. She looked towards Edith's and there she was holding little Betsy, with Mandy and Alf and Minnie. The ambulance men joined in the clapping. Marg grinned up at Clive. 'Welcome home, me lovely hero.'

His lips quivered, but he grinned back at her.

They both waved to everyone as they went inside.

Five weeks later as they gathered in Marg's house, having put all three names in a hat to see which house they should hold Christmas at, the atmosphere was just wonderful, made even better by Gerald managing to get a couple of days off.

They were all there, that could be. Alice and Gerald and their family, Billy and Joey, Averill, Rod and Heather. Edith and hers – little Betsy, Mandy and Alf, and Minnie. And, of course, Marg and Clive's lot, George and Carl, Clive's parents, and Jackie, Gran and Ada.

Edith's wider family – her parents-in-law and Philip's sister, her husband and two daughters – would be coming later, when they had a buffet tea arranged so everyone didn't have to sit around a table. Even though they had a huge table, bigger than Marg had ever seen, it wouldn't be big enough for them as well.

The table, made up of Marg's and Edith's dining tables put together to make one long one and then her smaller kitchen table across one end and Edith's bigger kitchen table along the other, filled the sitting room from which all the furniture had been removed and arranged in her best room, making lots of space for people to sit in there.

They'd just managed to get all the chairs around it.

There was a moment just before they all sat down when they toasted absent friends and a few expected tears were shed, but then Jackie had said, 'By, this ain't what Harry nor Philip would want . . .'

The door opening stopped her from carrying on. 'So, what would Philip want, then?'

A scream filled the room of otherwise stunned folk. 'Philip!' Edith's chair went flying as she ran into his arms.

When all calmed down and Philip had hugged Mandy, Alf and Minnie, had shaken the hands of the menfolk and kissed the women and children, Philip stood with his arm around Edith and Betsy snuggled into his other arm. Clive being Clive, always ready with his camera, took photo after photo of them and everyone as Philip told them, 'Please don't ask me a lot of questions. All I can tell you is that I was working abroad, but became compromised and had to be got out. I won't be going back, for reasons I cannot explain, but will be working in London for the rest of the war.'

With this last he looked down at Edith and squeezed her to him. 'So, my darling, you will have me home again on a regular basis.'

Edith was sobbing. Marg took Betsy from Philip and Philip gathered Edith into his arms. For Marg, it was the best Christmas sight ever as her Clive came to her side and held her, and she saw Gerald and Alice cuddling too.

Prayers are sometimes answered.

After a wonderful day, Marg was all ready for bed when Jackie asked if she could chat a few moments. Clive picked up his cocoa. 'I'll take this to bed, darling, I'll see you when you come up.'

Marg detected that all wasn't right with Jackie and braced herself for tears over Harry. They did come, but after a guilt-ridden confession that Jackie found herself drawn towards a young man named Bernard.

Marg listened, not offering an opinion – which she found hard to form anyway, as it was all such a shock.

When Jackie had finished, she'd learnt of Bernard's disability, and of his brilliant mind, his sense of fun, and how he seemed to have a great understanding of the world, and of Jackie, and how he respected her love for Harry and accepted that it would always be there – not between them, but with them.

It was this last bit that gave Marg the biggest surprise. As from it she gleaned that Jackie and this Bernard had already spoken of a possible future together. How could this be? Jackie had been devoted to Harry all her young life ... Maybe that was it. Maybe it was a love they both might have grown out of given the chance, for hadn't the war sent them out to different worlds? Who knows who Harry might have met and perhaps he might even have experienced what Jackie was feeling for someone else? If it hadn't happened that there'd been a war, would they have gradually found that they were no more than a loving sister and brother to each other? They would never know the answers, but Jackie was still here. She'd been through so much in her young life, she didn't deserve to suffer forever.

Suddenly, Marg felt happy for her. Not mystified, or condemning, or judgemental. She understood. In a way, it lifted a weight off her shoulders where Jackie's future happiness was concerned. 'By, lass, I'd like to meet this young man. He's put a light back into your eyes.'

'You don't think me a bad 'un, then? Eeh, Marg, what will Alice think and Billy and Joey?'

'They don't have to know while this feeling in you is so young, lass. Let yourself see where it goes first, eh? We'll keep it between us for a while. Remember how it took me a long time to see that Clive was the right man for me? Let that be the way for you, Jackie, love. Let's get this war behind us, then we can look to the future.'

Jackie clung to her. 'Ta, Marg. And aye, I will do as you say. I think we both know how we feel, but we can be friends for a while, we are already. And ta for not being mad at me. It were sommat that I couldn't help and didn't want to happen. I loved Harry with all me heart and that's still breaking for his loss, but it's as if Bernard has lit a candle and is holding it steady for me at the end of a very dark tunnel.'

'Well, you go towards that candle, but slowly. Give yourself and Bernard time to see that what you have ain't just rebound feelings – you, clutching at anything that promises better than the misery you feel over losing Harry.'

'I will, Marg. Ta. Now up those stairs you go to your Clive, you must be exhausted. Today was just wonderful.'

They kissed and as she went, Marg thought to herself, *Aye, and I reckon that both of us have plenty of wonderful days in front of us an' all. But, please God, no more heartache, not for a long time. Keep me gran safe and bring this war to an end.*

EPILOGUE

Alice
1946

Alice stood outside the magnificent Buckingham Palace gates waiting for them to open. Her anxiety was high. For her, the war didn't end until today.

Yes, she'd taken part, and in a joyous way, in all the VE parties, but Billy wasn't yet home.

He'd been amongst the victors that had marched into Germany and today, at last, he was coming in by train and was to get a taxi here to be with them.

Now, they were waiting and hoping that he would come any minute as they were unsure as to what to do if he didn't make it.

He and Joey, now a tall, handsome young man and soon to be going to university, were to be presented with Harry's medal. When Alice looked over at him, Joey was giggling with Annie, who Alice noticed kept looking back down the Mall with an anxious look equal to her own. Now engaged to Billy, they were hoping to get married in the autumn of this year.

A dainty, pretty girl, Annie looked lovely in a flowery frock and straw bonnet. The picture of innocence with her long flowing blonde hair. Alice hoped with all her heart that she would always remain like that and that nothing like the troubles that she, Marg and Edith had suffered ever befell her and Billy.

'He'll be here, dear.'

Alice smiled at Averill as she said this. Averill looked beautiful in pale lemon with a lovely floppy hat in navy. Alice thought she would rival Queen Elizabeth, who she hoped would be by the side of her husband, King George, today and who often appeared in magazines wearing lemon.

Everyone else sought to reassure her too. Clive and Marg, Marg looking radiant at five months pregnant with her second child. They had Carl and George with them, now big boys of fourteen and eleven years old. Clive's parents were looking after their little Sandra, named after lovely Gran, who passed away in 1942.

Philip and Edith were here too. They now had three children of their own and had adopted Mandy and Alf, now fifteen, after Minnie had passed away in 1943. How smart and grown-up the twins both looked. As she watched them for a moment she had to smile as Mandy brushed something off Alf's suit and looked cross with him. Nothing had changed, she still bossed him about and he took it in his stride. Betsy, who was also with them today, was now six and an adorable child, but Peter and Thomas, who were two and four years old and just as adorable, had been left at home with Philip's parents.

Lastly, lovely Jackie came over with Bernard in a wheel-chair. An eminent scientist, Bernard was adored by them all and had fitted in with the family as if he'd always been part of them. They had married just after the war ended and now lived down south, near to the general and his wife and daughter, Prissy, who they'd all met at Jackie's wedding, with Simon, her newlywed husband.

Alice always referred to the man who had first told them all those years ago about Harry's bravery and his medal as the general, even though he was retired now.

Suddenly, a familiar red head appeared – Ben! Edith spotted him getting out of the taxi at the same moment and squealed his name before running towards him. Within seconds Edith and Ben were in a hug, and surrounded by a joyful Mandy, Alf and all the young ones . . . Did she imagine it, or had Ben's eyes lingered on Mandy?

Marg sidled over to her. 'That's a sight for sore eyes, ain't it? Eeh, don't Ben look a smasher?'

'I think Mandy would agree, lass.'

'Ha! I think you're right. Edith said they were writing to each other.'

'Aw, that would be a lovely ending to their story, wouldn't it?'

Ben came over to them then, his walk a little slow, but his calliper hardly noticeable. His smile was wide. 'Hello, Aunties.' After they had greeted him, he said, 'I – I was sorry to hear about Harry. He was so good to us.'

'Ta, love. And he'll be chuffed that you could make it today. Ta for coming. It's good to see you. How's your ma?'

'Well, you know me dad didn't make it home, so she's always sad about that, but she keeps cheerful ... and busy with looking after me granny who runs her a merry dance.'

Marg laughed. 'Aye, well, you make the most of your granny, lad, you miss them when they've gone.'

Alice was glad she hadn't made anything of Ben losing his da. There was time later. For now, Alice didn't want anything to make her want to cry.

There was still fifteen minutes to go before the initial gathering inside the gate, then she, Gerald, Billy and Joey would be taken inside while the others waited outside.

After the ceremony, they were all returning to the lovely Prince of Wales Hotel, where they'd stayed last night. There they were to have a cream tea. Then it was each to his own as Jackie and Bernard were going to the theatre, as were Averill and Rod, albeit to see different shows. Annie hoped that she and Billy could go off to have a look around London while the rest of them just wanted to relax in the hotel lounge, have a couple of drinks and then dinner in the restaurant.

In two days' time they'd arranged a huge family party at Alice's when everyone of everyone's families would come together – well, they were one big family really. And that included Pete and his family – her lovely friend and one-time partner in the ambulance in France – her mucca, as he would say, being from the north-east. He was bringing his family too, and she was so looking forward to seeing him – and secretly, to Marg and Edith's reaction to him and his way of expressing himself. They'd kept in touch. Doing so had helped her to heal after losing her second ambulance partner, Reg, during the blitz.

At last, one of the many taxis pulling up and spewing people out stopped near to them and out stepped Billy.

Alice drew in her breath to contain her emotions. Billy looked at least a foot taller and so like Harry. His uniform proudly worn, he opened his arms to Annie and held her close for a moment. Alice swallowed down her tears brought on by the lovely sight, and of seeing Harry reincarnated – how could Billy have changed so much in two years?

When he came out of Annie's embrace, he looked around for her. Tears glistened in his eyes. His arms opened, and she was in his hug. Joey joined them.

As they came out of the hug, Alice saw that most of their beloved family were wiping their eyes. But what followed was a flurry of greetings, till Billy reached Edith who said, 'Now then, lad, what did you say all those years ago about asking me to marry you? Well, you could try asking again, if you like.'

This caused everyone to laugh, and Alice felt better. Her family were home – yes, even Harry, as she knew he was here by her side. *Let's do this, lad. Help me while I get through this next hour. An hour I am so proud to live for you. Let's get the medal you richly deserve, eh? My beautiful, kind, brave brother.*

Gerald found her hand as the gates to the palace opened. 'You look beautiful, my darling. I love you in that blue ... I have something to ask you. This may not be the place, but Harry just told me to.'

Alice looked quizzically up at Gerald. 'Harry said, "Come on, Gerald, lad. Now that all the lads are settled, isn't it time you got on with that adoption?"'

Alice giggled and nudged him. 'You daft ha'peth. Mind, I can hear Harry saying it. And nothing would make me happier.'

Gerald squeezed her. 'Right, you'll be at the appointment I made at the St Mary Magdalene convent in Manchester with me next week, then?'

Despite the sadness of today, happiness surged through Alice. 'Aye, I will.'

Gerald's wink told her that he'd planned to tell her this at this very moment to help her to take the last steps she could for her brother. And she knew her love for him to swell for his thoughtfulness.

It opened her heart to all the happiness now surrounding her. She, Marg and Edith had made it through.

They'd suffered poverty, pain, good times and bad times together. Always there for each other, always strong for each other.

As she stepped on the last step before turning into the building, she wondered if the lovely wife of the king, Queen Elizabeth, liked cocoa, and if she'd ever sat on these steps with her mates.

'Eeh, if you haven't, lass, you haven't lived.'

'Sorry, darling, what did you say?'

'Oh, nothing.'

Alice looked around. Both Marg and Edith waved to her. She waved back at them. She may be going through this door without them as the invite stated immediate family only, but she knew they would walk every step of the way with her.

That's what the Halfpenny Girls did.

A LETTER FROM MAGGIE

Dear Reader,

I hope you enjoyed reading *The Halfpenny Girls at War* as much as I enjoyed writing it.

Thank you from the bottom of my heart for choosing my work to curl up with.

This book concludes the Halfpenny Girls trilogy. What a journey for Alice, Edith and Marg.

When we first met them, they were young single girls living in Whittaker Ave, Blackpool, and working as packers in Bradshaw's Biscuit Factory, for which I took the location of where Burton's Factory stands today. But they have come through poverty, war, loss, and found happiness so this is a good place to say goodbye, even though I shed tears as I do so.

I am always sad when the time comes to write 'The End' to my journey with my characters as during the time I have had with them, they have become real to me, and they have nestled in my heart. Their hurts have made me cry, their triumphs have made me proud, and their eventual happiness brings me joy.

If you have enjoyed this last in the series, I would so appreciate you rating the book and leaving me a review on Amazon, Goodreads, or any online bookstore or book group, please. Reviews are like being hugged by the reader and they help to encourage me to write the next book – they further my career as they advise other readers about the book, and hopefully whet their appetite to also buy the book.

Don't worry if you missed the first two in the series; I always try to write each book as a standalone, but if you would like to step back a little in the timeline of the lives of Marg, Alice and Edith, *The Halfpenny Girls* and *The Halfpenny Girls at Christmas* are always available from many outlets.

As are all my backlist books which are listed in the front of the book if you would like to try those too. There are two trilogies/series available, as there are two standalone books also for you to choose from.

I am always available to contact personally too, if you have any queries, just want to say hello, or maybe book me for a talk to a group you belong to. I love to interact with readers and would welcome your comments, your emails, and messages through:

My Facebook Page: https://www.facebook.com/ MaggieMasonAuthor

My Twitter: @Authormary

My Website: www.authormarywood.com/contact

I will always reply. And if you subscribe to my newsletter on my website, you will be entered in a draw to win my latest book personally signed to you and will receive a three-monthly newsletter giving all the updates on my books and author life, and many chances of winning lovely prizes.

Love to hear from you, take care of yourself and others,

Much love
Maggie xxx

ACKNOWLEDGEMENTS

Many people were involved in getting my book to the shelves and presenting it in the very best way to my readers: my commissioning editor, Rebecca Roy, who works tirelessly, advising on the structure of the story and editing my work, besides overseeing umpteen other processes my book goes through. My agent, Judith Murdoch, always in my corner as she deals with so many things too numerous to mention but all vital to giving me support through the minefield of the publishing world. My editorial team headed by Thalia Proctor, whose work brings out the very best of my story to make it shine. My publicist, Francesca Banks and her team, who seek out many opportunities for me to showcase my work. My cover designers who do an amazing job in bringing my story alive in picture form, producing covers that stand out from the crowd. The sales team who find outlets across the country for my books. My son, James Wood, who reads so many versions of my work, to help and advise me, and works alongside me on the edits that come in. And last, but not least, my readers, who encourage me on as they await another book, support me

391

by buying my books and warm my heart with praise in their reviews. My heartfelt thanks to you all.

But no one person stands alone. My family are amazing. They give me an abundance of love and support and when one of them says they are proud of me, then my world is complete. My special thanks to my darling Roy, my husband and very best friend. My children, grandchildren and great-grandchildren who light up my life, and my Olley and Wood families. You are all my rock and help me to climb my mountain. Thank you. I love you with all my heart.

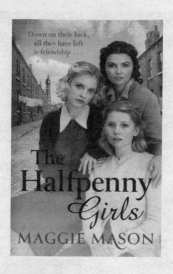

Down on their luck, all they have left is friendship . . .

It is 1937 and Alice, Edith and Marg continue to face hardships every day, growing up on one of the poorest streets in Blackpool. Penniless, their friendship has helped them survive this far, but it'll take more than that to see them through the dark days that lie ahead . . .

Alice is coping with a violent father and the weight of the duty she carries to support her family, Marg is left reeling after a dark secret about her birth comes to light and threatens to destroy the life she knows, and Edith is fighting to protect her alcoholic mother from the shame of their neighbours and keep her brother on the straight and narrow.

A chance encounter at the Blackpool Tower Ballroom promises to set their lives on a new path, one filled with love and safety and hope for a brighter future. Will The Halfpenny Girls, who have never known anything but poverty, finally find happiness? And if they do, will it come at a price?

'Sweeping drama and tear-jerking heartache' Jean Fullerton

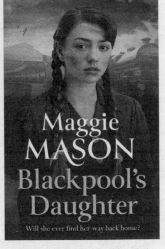

Readers LOVE Maggie Mason's Blackpool sagas:

'**Five stars – I wish I could give it more.** Wonderful read'

'What a brilliant book. **I couldn't put it down!**'

'I was hooked from the first page ... **this author is a must read**'

'**A totally absorbing read**'